# BUSINESS OF LOVE

## OTHER SIDE OF LOVE

EMMELINE WATERS

Cover created by: Xyra Brittney (@xylavie) / **www.be.net/xylavie**

**TO MY MOM. ALL MY LIFE, YOU HAVE SUPPORTED WHATEVER HOBBY OR INTEREST I HAVE HAD, NO MATTER HOW WEIRD YOU THOUGHT IT WAS.**

## MAY 13TH

### MINA

I'd been able to book the last seat on the flight back to Milwaukee, but that meant I was stuck in the middle in the rear of the plane. The two seats on either side of me were empty, and a small curl of hope twisted through me that one or both would miss the flight or rebook.

I set my purse between my feet and tucked an auburn lock of hair that had slipped out of its bun behind my ear. I smoothed out my navy suit pants and white blouse. Leaning back, I let my eyes close and took in a breath.

"Excuse me," a deep voice barked to my right.

Dang it. I cracked an eye open and took in a man in ragged clothes, tie askew, hair disheveled, likely from constantly running a nervous hand through it. Streaks of oil, from a long day, held it in odd places. His wrinkled, nondescript brown jacket was draped over his arm at his side, while he braced his other arm on the overhead bin. He raked his predatory blue eyes over my body, and I blanched, not bothering to hide my disgust.

"Are you going to move?" he asked, his lip curling into a smirk.

Normally, I'd scurry out of the way and apologize for blocking his seat. Instead, my hackles rose at the leer he gave me, and I held my apology back.

"Did you ask?" I drawled.

"I don't mind climbing on you," he said and chuckled at his perverted joke.

I bit my cheek to stop the next retort. I didn't want him to think I was taking part in the gross flirting. I shifted up, bending slightly to the right so my head didn't hit the frame.

He stood in place, not backing away.

"Please step back so I can let you pass," I said, measuring my words carefully.

He winked at me. "I don't mind squeezing past. We're going to be seatmates for the next three hours. Helps to get to know each other better."

I grimaced but stopped myself from rolling my eyes. He seemed to enjoy any reaction I gave him.

He took a step back, and I used my elbow to push past him into the aisle.

He grunted but moved and took his seat by the window.

"Maybe we start our drinks now and grab more after the flight," he said, settling into his seat.

"I'm engaged," I choked out.

Dread heated in my veins at the thought of sitting next to him for the next three hours.

His eyes scoured my hands, locking in on the rock on my left hand. The diamond glinted on my white finger.

Engaged? I was practically married.

The meeting I'd just left had gone well, and I had the signed papers in my briefcase, but it'd been a last-minute appointment, one Ethan, my fiancé, had been livid I took. Our wedding was in two days, and I was supposed to be completing final preparations for our happily ever after—even though everything was done and in the capable hands of the wedding planner—and not securing a last-minute contract that would add hours to my already full load. But the contract was taking me in the right direction to be a junior partner, and then one day partner. My career, a partnership in my firm, was part of the future I wanted too.

Both my and Ethan's careers were racing forward.

"Hm," he said, his mouth pinched into a thin line. He brought his eyes back to my face. Darkness danced in them. "What he doesn't know, huh?"

I just stared at him as I white knuckled the industrial velour seat cover, the navy blue fibers embedding underneath my nails.

He twisted so he could stare at my full frame. "So, gorgeous, what's your name?"

"Mina," a new voice called out.

I flinched in surprise at having my name outed and the nearness of the source. He stood next to me, his arm almost brushing mine.

"Sorry I'm late," he continued, stepping closer to me and dipping his head to catch my gaze.

My eyes bugged out as they took in the sight in front of me. My mouth dried out, and all I could do was gulp like a fish. Of course, he had to be here. One of the few people who could set my panties on fire with a smile or accidental touch. Like he did to Maggie, Tiffany, or anyone attracted to men. His hair was still dark brown, almost black, styled back in thick waves. His Nordic-blue eyes were intense and bright against his suntanned skin. He'd grown half a foot since high school and gained more muscle in his chest and arms.

Before me stood Jack.

A one-time crush. Long, long ago, back in high school crush. Before Ethan and I started dating. Be it the late hour or the unexpectedness of seeing him, something warm flittered in my stomach—and lower.

Jack and Ethan had been best friends in high school. We all attended middle school together, but I wasn't close to them. They were like brothers up until freshman year, when Ethan and I started dating and Jack started dating Tiffany the same week—and then changed girlfriends every few weeks. Still, Jack was part of our life every day. He'd been a good friend to me. Someone I could talk to about anything. Which was probably one reason I'd had a misplaced crush on him. Hell, he'd driven me home more often than Ethan did. Then everything changed.

Junior year, they'd had a huge fight, but Ethan said it was over something stupid that guys argue about. We went to a bonfire and had too much to drink. Nothing happened, but then afterward, Jack never spoke more than a few words to me over the years. Other than a hard glare, Jack acted as if we didn't exist. Like we'd never been friends.

With that thought, the warmth in my belly extinguished. As it should.

Now, he and Ethan worked for rival companies, each clawing their way to their respective tops. Despite hating each other, they both went into corporate land development and stayed in the Chicagoland-Milwaukee area. Granted, Jack focused on sustainable building and repurposing, while Ethan's main practice was redeveloping farmland and undeveloped land. I always wondered if they went into similar work so they could have a more even score system to outdo the other.

"Mina?" Jack said, forcing me to focus on his lips moving to form the syllables of my name.

He brushed my shoulder with his hand, and his warm touch raced through my skin and curled in my stomach. His cologne wafted around me. All my senses were on overload.

"What?" I snapped.

"Sorry I'm late," he said and nodded toward our seats.

"Late?" I parroted.

I blinked to clear my mind and realized we were the only two still standing. The flight attendant stood behind him in her black pencil skirt, white blouse, and maroon sweater vest with a terse expression, her eyes narrowed at me.

We were holding up departure.

"I know you're mad, but I'm sorry," he said.

"Sorry?" I cringed as I parroted him again like a damn fool. I covered with "For what?"

"We should take our seats and then discuss it," he said and moved to take the middle seat.

"But that's . . ." I started but didn't want to finish.

"A mis-booking. I meant to take the middle and give you the aisle. I know it's your favorite." He gave me a half grin, his blue eyes focused on me.

We had one flight together in high school for our debate team. He took my middle seat then so I could have the aisle after I said I liked it better. Something tightened in me knowing he still remembered that random moment.

"Wait, you're her fiancé?" our seatmate asked, flicking a finger between the two of us.

Jack dropped his gaze to my hand, and for once, my instinct was to curl my fingers together. It passed as quickly as it had come. I had nothing to hide or be ashamed of. I was getting married in two days. He knew it too. Ethan had proposed at an event Jack had been at. He'd left with a gorgeous brunette wearing a red sheath dress with a black tulle overlay. Her hair had been pulled up into a cascade of curls, and her lips were painted the same shade of red as the dress. Alicia . . . his last serious girlfriend. The epitome of perfection. The one he'd proposed to.

My stomach turned. I didn't know why I remembered Alicia so well.

"No" danced on my tongue as I settled back in my seat, but I didn't offer an answer. Or a glance at either of them.

"Mina, hon, I'm sorry I was late," he said, placing his hand on mine before yanking it away as if I had burned him.

Phantom tingles danced on my fingers.

"Don't hon me," I said, seething.

It was part of a nickname he'd called me in school before Ethan and I started dating. My eye color reminded him of honey, something he loved. Something I'd hoped meant he liked me. But it hadn't.

Window Man leaned forward, his hawkish gaze bouncing between the two of us.

Jack righted his shoulders and tilted his head to stare him down.

It finally clicked what Jack was doing.

I scowled. The jackass hadn't so much as said more than a curt hello at all the events we'd mutually attended. His gaze was always averted from us when I'd sneak a glance his way. Now he was trying to protect me from the buffoon by the window?

"Look, Jack," I said, my tone harsher than I meant.

His gaze shot back to me. The fucking heat twisted briefly in my stomach. I sucked in a breath at the intensity and closeness but squelched it. I wasn't a freshman anymore. He was Ethan's enemy. He stood between Ethan and his business and happiness. It made him my enemy too by default. He couldn't just decide now we were friends and be all protective. Bullshit.

"I appreciate you taking the middle seat." I shot a dark look at Window Man.

"You're welcome," he said and smiled, the full toothy smile that stalled my brain for a moment.

"Stop it." I pointed a finger at his face.

His eyes shot up quizzically, and he asked, "Stop what?"

But the stupid grin dancing on his lips showed he knew what I was talking about.

"Issues?" Window Man asked.

I leaned closer to Jack, probably a mistake as it brought me closer to his orbit. Sandalwood flooded my senses. I took a steadying breath and rolled my ring so the diamond was against my palm. I rubbed my thumb over it, grounding myself back to reality and Ethan.

More out of annoyance to shut the man up, I slid my hand over Jack's. He jolted from my touch. Or I did as shock raced through me. His fingers were quick to intertwine with mine. I lifted our hands. For a moment I only stared at them. His large fingers cradling mine. The feeling natural and right. The plane's lights flickering pulled me back into the moment.

I shook our hands at Window Man. He grumbled but settled back in his seat.

Jack's heated gaze snagged mine.

Heat curled across my cheeks. A voice in my head screamed, "Take your hand back," while another one, louder and stronger, shouted, "Keep pretending so the perv leaves you alone." The louder voice won while we taxied off the runway.

"We are nothing," I mouthed.

Window Man leaned closer to hear.

Jack's smile didn't dim, but his eyes no longer carried the merriment. Instead, they tracked over my face, assessing the seriousness and truth of my words.

"You haven't talked to Ethan," I continued.

He flinched at Ethan's name.

"Or his fiancée in over ten years."

He cocked his head to the side, and his mouth twitched up in disagreement.

"What?" I snapped.

"I talked to her at every event," he countered, giving me a mock disappointed glare.

"Hello and my— her name are not talking to m— her," I said, my voice hitching slightly higher. My anger at letting him get to me heated my cheeks.

"What is it, then? I don't grunt them or write them or relay them through someone else. I always greet her at the events."

I opened my mouth to protest his statement but closed it as my eyes searched around, unseeing. Every event, he did say hello to me. Never to Ethan. Oh, the sneak. I shook my head and leaned back, matching his disappointed stare. This caused his lips to jump in amusement.

"Mmm, nope, you doing something to annoy Ethan doesn't count. You purposely ignore him and say hello to his fiancée to piss him off."

A dark look crossed his face before he regained his composure. His jaw ticked, and he swallowed before carefully saying, "I don't say hello to . . . him . . . because I don't want to."

"But you say hello to her to piss him off and show him you're ignoring him."

"No, I say hello to her because I want to."

I blinked, the words unsettling my anger. Then it twisted raw in my veins. I slid my hand back from him.

He stared for a moment. Emotion flicked faster across his face than I could catch before he erected a granite fortress of nothingness. Images of him in high school flashed in my mind. Ones after the bonfire. The cool detachment. Everything sliding into a blasé, if even objectively handsome, expression.

Sure, he wanted to say hello to me. Because he wanted to annoy Ethan.

We settled back into tense silence. Window Man had earbuds in as he scrolled on his phone. Jack flicked a gaze his way. With a satisfied sigh, he eased out his phone. The jackass's help had worked. It was something I should acknowledge, but if he could remain silent, so could I.

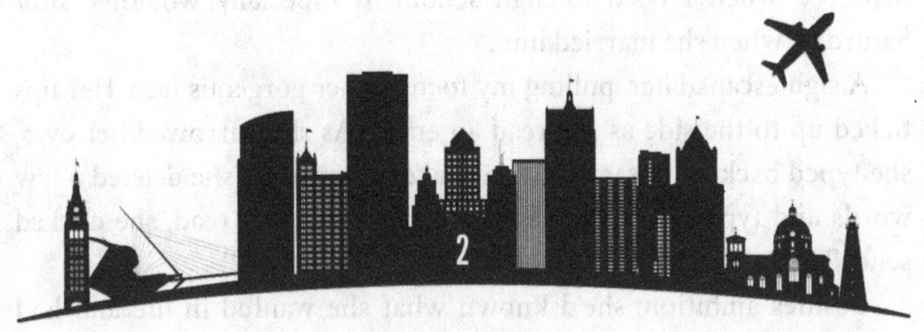


## MAY 13TH

## JACK

Silence. The plane ride continued in silence after I told her I said "hi" to her because I wanted to. Disgust twisted her face before she pulled out her phone. Her gaze fixed on the scrolling text of emails.

Of all the people I expected to run into on my way back from a conference on a new sustainable building method, Mina Henley was the last one. She was supposed to get married Saturday at noon. I'd purposely scheduled a meeting during the wedding as a distraction. Like it would help. It would be with a local client, and we'd likely go to a game afterward. Nothing like beer and baseball to distract me from . . .

I pushed that thought from my mind.

I still couldn't believe she was sitting beside me. If I shifted to the left at all, I'd brush against her. And yet, she may as well be miles away. Like every day. The one woman who could unsettle everything in my life was stuck next to me for the next few hours. I could tell her everything I'd ever wanted to, but it wouldn't matter. It hadn't mattered when I tried in high school. It especially wouldn't after Saturday, when she married him.

A sigh escaped her, pulling my focus to her gorgeous face. Her lips ticked up to the side as she read an email. As she narrowed her eyes, she typed back a message. With a shake of her head, she deleted a few words and typed new ones. Finally nodding as she read, she clicked send. Then on to the next email waiting for her.

Besides ambition, she'd known what she wanted in life and had gone after it. She had been one of the few people who could make me laugh regardless of what was going on. Her sense of justice was absolute. Despite her father, or because of him, she was truthful to a fault. My favorite part of high school—until the end of our junior year—was driving her home from Ethan's. We'd listen to music, talk about anything: school, college, world events, or the best Jell-O flavor. She was wrong though; lime is not the best. Raspberry all the way.

Then she stopped talking to me.

Familiar heaviness weighed on my chest, and I looked to my phone.

After a while, she leaned back and closed her eyes.

"Trouble in paradise?" the jackass cackled to my side.

My jaw ticked, but I continued to read my emails on my phone.

Paradise didn't exist. Well, it did, for Ethan.

Ethan had been my best friend through elementary school, middle school, and high school up through most of junior year. Even when he'd asked out Mina, knowing I wanted to, I let it slide because she said yes to him. If she wanted to date him, I didn't want to stand in the way. But Ethan, being the cocky prick he was, never liked being reined in. He never told me about other girls, even when I confronted him after seeing him at the local frozen custard place with a girl from a different school at the end of junior year. Words were said. Lots of name-calling. After I tried to tell Mina one night at a bonfire, she accused me of misplacing my unhappy penis issues on Ethan. Not able to stand by and watch him betray her, and her not listen when I tried to warn her, I stopped talking to them. The only words I had at the time were ones she didn't want to hear.

Stupidity, masochism, or hope brought me back to Milwaukee after college to set up business. My business partner, Sam, and I hadn't been friends in high school, because he was wicked smart and moved up a grade when we were in elementary, back when they still did that, so we never really interacted. We met up in college, somehow making it to USC together. As roommates, we dreamed big and naturally wanted to come home.

But then there was Mina.

She and Ethan had stayed in the area too. He naturally went to work at his dad's company, nepotism finding him a VP position without doing work. Mina went on to financial planning. Despite having Ethan at her side, her client list was growing rapidly. Based on her attire, beaming face despite the asshole sitting next to her, and her briefcase, she'd just signed another contract less than forty-eight hours before she was supposed to get married. To Ethan.

The familiar pinch in my heart twisted, and with a blink, I forced my mind from thoughts of her. She'd made her choice. If she was happy, that was all that mattered. My opinions hadn't meant anything to her in the past, and they clearly didn't mean anything to her now.

"Big bachelor party planned?" Pickle Dick, the asshat sitting by the window, said.

"No."

"Ah, come on." He nudged my shoulder with his and leaned over to look at Mina.

I turned with him, facing him so all he saw was my shoulder.

"One last hurrah."

"No, not my style."

A sneer danced on his lips. "Pus—"

"He's not a sleaze," Mina chimed in.

The kindest words she'd spoken about me since high school.

As if to emphasize it, she patted my hand. On instinct, I curled my fingers around hers. For a moment, she stiffened at the contact. A twinge of remorse skittered through me as I expected her to pull her hand back. Instead, she relaxed into my touch. I rubbed small circles over her hand with my thumb.

For the rest of the flight, she kept her hand in mine. Somehow, it stopped the man from prying further into our relationship. Into us. Even if we didn't appear to be more than a house of cards, something obviously not right, he backed off. When she finally retracted her hand during landing, my fingers curled together, chasing the feeling of her perfect hand in mine.

Mina, ever herself, slid into the aisle and waited for those in the other seats to exit. After the other side began to exit, I inclined my chin for Mina to move forward and away from the window guy. For a moment, I considered reaching a hand out to her. To take hers, keep the ploy up for even a few more seconds. But that wasn't fair to her.

She flicked her gaze to me and then him. With a thin smile, she moved up the next set of seats. My dumb heart thought maybe she was waiting for me. To say something, but once I moved to the aisle, she moved without looking back. She was keeping the ruse up. Not adding suspicion.

Once we made it out of the gate, she disappeared into a restroom. I moved to the stone wall to act like I was waiting. When Pickle Dick moved past, I took a last look at the concourse. With a sigh, I pushed off the wall and away from Mina.

Following the familiar path to baggage claim and then the exit, I skirted around the perimeter to avoid the bottleneck forming by the baggage chute. Like a fool, I let my eyes canvass the sparsely populated area. The whirl of a baggage carousel caught my attention as it came to life. Her auburn hair was like a beacon on stormy seas, and my gaze snapped to it. She frowned at her phone. She furiously tapped out a message. That's when I looked around and realized Ethan wasn't in the building, but cars couldn't be left unattended. With a quick glance outside the vestibule, I didn't see his car either. Where the fuck was the asshole?

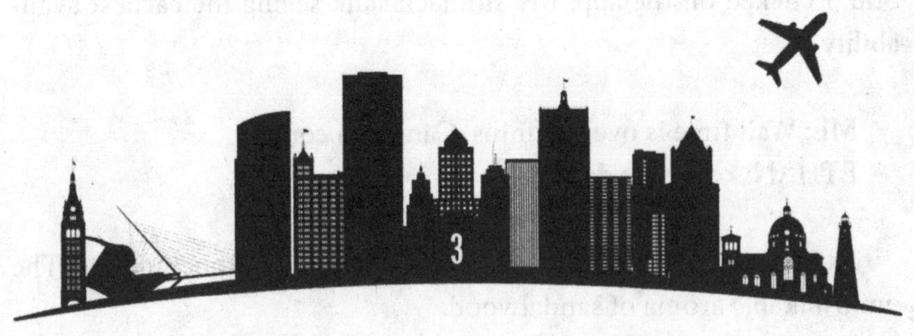


**MAY 13TH - MAY 14TH**

**MINA**

My fingers flexed, chasing the feeling of Jack's hand with mine. What the fuck was I doing? Sleep deprivation and emotions from the wedding were clouding my judgment. It had nothing to do with Jack, his touch, the memories of our youth, or the twinge of the once-there crush that could sometimes flutter my stomach.

Again, I scanned the area. Only the people from our flight mingled around our carousel. Another flight stood off to the next one over. Ethan said he'd pick me up when I first scheduled the flights, but I'd had to grab a later flight.

ME: I'm at the baggage claim
ETHAN: Grab an Uber. Your flight ran late and I fell asleep.

My eyes flicked to the wall. 11:58 p.m. I growled and rolled my eyes. Ubers would be harder to find at this time by the airport and not the bars, especially paging one now instead of setting it up earlier. Still, I clicked on the app. My stomach sank seeing the earliest availability.

ME: Wait time is over 45 mins. Can't you come?
ETHAN: <dancing dots>

As I scrolled through the app, I felt a presence shift behind me. The unmistakable aroma of sandalwood.

"No ride?" Jack asked as he grabbed his rolling suitcase from the conveyor belt.

I blinked to stop the eye roll and scrolled on the app with more urgency.

"I'm fine," I breathed. A familiar unease burned at the back of my throat.

ETHAN: It's late. Grab a ride.

"Fuck you," I muttered to the phone and then flinched.

I was working hard on cutting my swearing down. I was trying for a more professional approach per Ethan's never-ending advice but found that many clients hadn't received his memo and swore too.

"Phone arguing with you?" Jack asked and nodded to my purple hardtop descending the belt. "Yours?"

I gritted my teeth. He knew me well. I went to yank my suitcase from the carousel and dropped my phone.

He bent down and retrieved it, handing it back without glancing at the screen. Despite the hour, he still looked fresh in his black sport coat. His snug pants showed off his toned—

Shit. I needed a ride and sleep. At this point, I didn't care which came first.

"Thanks," I mumbled and blew back the stupid lock of hair that kept falling out of place.

A thought to cut it off flittered through my mind. If it hadn't taken three visits and about twenty hours for Ethan's mom and my mom to agree on a hairstyle for the wedding, I'd be tempted.

Without another word, I extended the scope on my case and strolled out to the loading zone, hoping to flag down a nonexistent cab. Just like at events we both attended, I kept my back ramrod straight and didn't turn back to give him the satisfaction of unsettling me.

Our flight had been late and had landed during the airport's downtime. A few cabbies often circled to catch the late fares, but we were so few, and at this hour, most had rides already set up, so it didn't warrant the waste of gas.

I came to a stop at the vestibule and sidled my luggage next to me. For a few minutes, I stared at the empty loading zone, waiting as the Uber times ticked down and my stupid hope for a cab dwindled.

"Need a drink and a ride?" someone sneered behind me.

My body tightened, and I felt for my keys to lock them between my fingers. My pepper spray was at home since the airlines didn't allow it. No one from security was visible. My keys and an uppercut would have to protect me if he made a move.

An expensive-looking, shiny black Audi rolled to a stop in front of me.

I narrowed my eyes and was going to give the roll-on gesture when the window rolled down and Jack leaned over the passenger seat. His blue eyes locked on me.

"Ready, hon— Mina?"

I swallowed. Nothing about this was a good choice. Not after the plane ride. But all we'd done was touch hands.

"If I promise to say more than hello and your name, will you accept a ride?" he said, his gaze not flicking to Window Man standing next to me.

Window Man narrowed his eyes at us. Although confusion still scrunched his face, I didn't want to be there when he realized we weren't engaged.

There wasn't much of a choice.

A twenty-minute ride with him was safer and more desirable than standing another minute by Window Man or waiting for a cab. I sighed in defeat but yanked the back seat door open to toss in my luggage. I slammed it shut and jumped back, seeing Jack standing next to me with my door open. Either lack of sleep was taking me off my game, or he had catlike stealth. I slipped into the seat.

"What should we talk about?" he offered as he got back in his seat and shifted the car into gear.

"Nothing, let's ride in silence." I stared out the window, watching the slants of neon white light shimmer off the exterior and float away like ghosts on the wind.

"No, I promised I'd say more." He shot me a grin that I caught from the corner of my eye.

"At events." I rubbed my head.

He wasn't to blame for Ethan not showing up. Nor my tiredness. He provided two outs from dealing with grossness, and he hadn't yet once been rude. But I had. Damn him.

"I'm sorry," I mumbled.

He stilled and looked at me. His smile faltered, and his brows furrowed as he tried to study my face but kept turning to look at the road.

"Thank you for taking the middle seat, and thank you for the ride." I gave him a tired smile.

He smiled back, his panty-dropping one. I rolled my eyes but chuckled. Still Jack.

A familiar calm settled over us. Before their fight in high school, Jack had taken me home when Ethan had been too tired. Just like tonight. I blew out a breath. Nerves between the wedding and fighting with Ethan had gotten the better of me. The walk down memory lane wasn't helping either.

"Did you meet with an existing or new client tonight?" he asked, interrupting my thoughts.

I shot him a suspicious glare.

"You're in a suit with a briefcase. It's not a hard leap."

"Yes, I signed a new client."

"Congratulations." He nodded at me.

I tried to find deceit in his excitement, but his eyes matched his smile.

"Thanks."

"You're a financial specialist, right?"

"Yes," I said.

I was sure he must have overheard it at an event.

"Working on partner?"

"Junior partner," I said and swallowed.

"This client big enough to push you over?"

"He's a ten-million investment. It's midsize for my company, but one of my largest."

"That's awesome. That's a large one for a junior partner there, isn't it?"

"How would you know that?" I asked, narrowing my eyes.

"I work with people in your field. I have a financial specialist too."

"Oh," I muttered like an idiot. Of course he did. So did Ethan.

"Is Ethan your client?" Jack asked, the words casual but with a dark undertone.

"Not yet. Ethan uses his father's financial specialist. Once I make full partner, he'll switch to me. His business would put me on the partner path, and even though I want to be partner, I don't want it to be because I'm marrying Ethan. I want it to be because I deserve it."

I swallowed. Although it was the truth, I wasn't sure why I'd shared it with Jack. Too easily we'd slipped into discussion like the nights he drove me home in high school. Like he and Ethan weren't enemies and I hadn't taken Ethan's side.

"You deserve it. You'll make it with or without him," he said with finality. His words were spoken in truth.

I stared at him. With Ethan it would be easier, but easier wasn't always better. But I agreed, I would keep pushing until I made it.

"Isn't your wedding soon?" Jack asked, catching me off guard, his voice scratchy.

"Yeah, Saturday." I rubbed my arms, suddenly chilled.

"Saturday, as in this Saturday. That, as of twenty minutes ago, is tomorrow?"

"That's the one," I said with a smile that felt brittle.

"Hm," he said, his eyes focusing back on the road.

His gaze shuttered and his face slackened. This was the Jack I was used to. The one who had faced me every day in the final year of high school. Shuttered. Stoic. Judgmental. The granite fortress of nothingness. The opposite of my once friend.

The reminder of the years prickled my nerves.

"What?" I demanded.

"Nothing."

"Bullshit," I said and flinched. "Dammit."

"What?" His searching gaze jumped back to me.

"UGH! That's another one. I owe the fu— the freaking swear jar more money."

He chuckled and licked his lips before saying, "Haven't you been working on the swearing thing since junior year?"

I stared at him, heat clawing at my cheeks. How did he remember such stuff?

"So?" I blew out a breath.

"Maybe it's just who you are, and you should embrace it."

"It's bad for business," I said.

"According to?"

I folded my arms and stared out the window.

"Ah . . ." he said and then let heavy silence descend on us.

"You think you know so much." I turned to him with a scowl.

He shrugged, and his jaw ticked before he locked up his face again in his granite fortress of nothingness.

"Whatever."

I settled back in the dark silence until we rolled in front of Ethan's apartment complex. The luxury apartment was in the Lower East Side and had a breathtaking view of the lake and vista.

As I hopped out of the car, Jack was on his feet, pulling my suitcase out.

"Thanks," I said without looking at him.

"You're welcome," he murmured and turned to leave.

"Why?" I asked before I could help myself.

"Pardon?" He cast a glance over his shoulder, the dark shadows masking his unfairly handsome face.

"Why did you switch seats and why did you drive me here?"

For some reason, my nerves tightened, waiting for his response.

"You like the aisle, and don't you live here?" he said over his shoulder.

Something curdled in my stomach. I had stuff here, but I didn't live here fully yet. Another argument Ethan and I had about my clients. I hadn't had the time to move all my stuff over or organize a mover to do it.

"How did you know Ethan lived here, then?"

A mirthless laugh growled from him. "It's a small industry, and he talks loudly."

Both were true.

"Goodbye . . . Jack."

His name felt dangerous on my tongue. Something I hadn't said out loud in years beyond "Hi, Jack," with Ethan at my side. But more concerning was the twist of something that skittered in my stomach.

He stiffened for a moment. Without looking back, he gave a nod and "Good night, Mina."

A weird hollowness settled in my stomach. Maybe hunger. Maybe fatigue. Maybe both.

I walked up to the door and nodded at the doorman, Jesse, a younger guy with a wife and child at home and second on the way. He smiled and greeted me.

"You okay?" he asked as he got a look at me under the lights.

I'd guessed my makeup was probably smeared and my hair coming undone.

"I'm fine," I said with a watery smile. "Just a long flight."

"You look sad, ma'am." He took my suitcase for me to the elevator. "Your wedding is . . . tomorrow, isn't it?"

I nodded. "I'm just tired, but I appreciate your concern." I met his eyes and forced a smile. "You've always been kind, thank you."

He smiled in return, unsure, and nodded his goodbye as the elevator arrived.

The elevator opened with a special keycard into Ethan's—our—penthouse. The spacious entrance led into a grand living room with an open-concept kitchen and dining. Only the lights of the city filtered through the window. The rest of the place was cloaked in darkness.

He must have been too tired to wait up for me. I kicked my shoes off by the door and left my luggage. I draped my suit jacket on top of it and made my way to the bedroom. The door was ajar, and soft snores escaped the confines of the room.

I thought about turning the lights on and demanding why he couldn't pick me up like I always did for him regardless of the hour, but the numbers on the clock danced close to one a.m. He normally went to bed around midnight and got up at five every morning. He took a quick nap before evening appointments. He was probably exhausted, especially from his own late meetings today, and it was a last-minute client meeting that had gone past my original flight back, and I took the last one out to make our wedding appointments.

After tossing my blouse and pants toward the closet, I trudged to the bathroom. I didn't turn the light on until I closed the door. My reflection wasn't as haggard as I expected. My hair had come loose but wasn't snarled or doing odd drooping things. My light makeup had faded but hadn't smeared too much. I touched my face too much when I was nervous, so I typically didn't wear much makeup, or I'd turn myself into a finger-painted clown.

I jumped in the shower but didn't wash my hair. I didn't want to blow dry it or go to bed with wet hair. Besides, soon a professional would be taming it.

Finally, I crawled under the covers, the soft silk cool against my skin. Sleep usually came fast, but my mind replayed the evening, focusing on the last few hours.

I licked my lips and squirmed in the bed. Forgotten thoughts danced around in my head. My youthful daydreams of kissing Jack had matured with age and still left me frustrated and embarrassed to have him show up now. I reminded myself I was marrying Ethan, my high school sweetheart and my ever after. His hand found mine in his sleep, wrapping around it and pulling it toward him. He squeezed my hand, and I flexed my fingers for space.

A phantom memory traced over my skin. The plane ride and the soft but firm touch of Jack's grip when he'd held my hand. The natural feeling.

"Mina," Ethan whispered, rubbing my knuckles.

"Yes." I tightened my fingers around his, searching for warmth in his cool touch.

"Settle down, your tossing woke me up," he said. "We have a long day before you're finally Mrs. Ethan Settlers."

## MAY 14TH

### MINA

When his alarm sounded in the morning, I startled awake and remained there. The hum of the day buzzed in my head. Although quiet, the music in his earbuds escaped in a drone of electronic noise. He moved to the bathroom, a blast of light smacking my face before he shut the door. After finishing, he moved to the living room, where I could hear his voice rise as he talked on the phone. Sounded like an issue with one of his deals. I wondered if Jack had swooped in again.

I'd managed an hour or so of sleep. My face drooped, heavy with fatigue. Pushing myself up, I trudged to the kitchen in a rumpled T-shirt that matched my mood. Not bothering with my hair, I pulled it back in a bun. I was really rocking the "perfect" fiancée and almost-wife look that would reflect poorly on him and his family.

His disapproving gaze skimmed over my haggard attire, but smartly, he said nothing this time. Likely avoiding the fight that we both felt brewing. Any other day, he'd remind me that how we started our day set up our daily success. Even eating breakfast, in the solitude and comfort of his—our—apartment deserved a polished look.

Once I officially moved in, I'd have to dump my T-shirts and cotton shorts or face this argument every day. Most days I didn't care too much. I had to go to work anyway. But the polished fiancée, almost-wife look shouldn't matter when it was just us. I blew out a breath. The wedding jitters were starting to erode at my indifference to his quirks. I had my own share. The toilet seat and lid needed to be down after every use.

We ate breakfast in silence. He didn't ask how I got home, and I didn't volunteer it.

"Greg Cremski may come to the wedding." A smile curved his lips.

Greg was a prospective client who could make Ethan's career. His business was not only extensive, but others followed him.

"If he signs, I bet we'll be invited to Mercer's Lake Geneva Fourth of July party."

"That would be great," I agreed.

The exclusive party was something Ethan had hoped to get invited to each year. With his father retiring in likely the next few years, if Ethan didn't get the invite, it'd be a mark against him. It was a spot we were both coveting to help each other's careers. Only one partner at my firm, Yang, got an invite. Deals were brainstormed and signed, while others were harpooned there.

"We'll talk with Greg at the reception," I said.

Ethan nodded in agreement. "We've got this."

He stuck his fist out for a bump.

Even in my sour mood, I reciprocated.

"Are the ladies coming over today?" Ethan asked around a spoonful of muesli.

I shook my head. "No, we're all going to Trina's."

Trina was my sister and maid of honor. Her hair was a few shades lighter, her eyes a few shades darker amber, she had two inches on me in height, and more issues with swearing. Despite being two years younger, we graduated from college a year apart thanks to all her advanced math classes in high school and dual enrollment in the university system when the high school couldn't meet her math needs.

Ethan nodded but didn't look up.

I stared at his head, watching his freshly styled hair remain immobile on his head. He'd already showered, donned a fresh slim-cut suit, and slicked his light brown hair back to highlight his fauxhawk and long-locked top. He was set up for the success he wanted today. At barely six a.m.

Finally sensing something was off, he lifted his cobalt-blue eyes to me.

"What?" he asked, searching my face.

"Are you going to ask me about my meeting?" I asked, staring back and sitting taller.

He sighed and rolled his eyes. "The meeting that was more important than our wedding?"

"It did nothing to interfere with our wedding," I shot back, nostrils flaring.

"You don't think the bags will interfere," he said, nodding toward my eyes.

Shit, not my intention. I wanted to touch my face and see if they were swollen, but I didn't want to give him the extra ammo that I was concerned about it.

"The client will help me move up," I said for the umpteenth time.

"So?" he shot back.

"So? So? You, of all people, should understand. You've worked to move up in your daddy's company," I snarled.

His face darkened at "daddy's company." He was a hard worker, but some of his mobility could be attributed to his last name and biology.

"I earned my place!" he yelled, slamming his fist on the table.

"So AM I!" I yelled back.

"Your career is cute, but what happens when we have a family?" he asked.

"What?" I sputtered, dots dancing in front of my eyes. He'd pulled this from left field. "We've talked about this."

"You still want a career when we have kids?"

"Don't you?" I retorted.

"Well yeah, but it's different . . ." he said, and his eyes bulged before he looked down at the table. He held up a hand and started, "Wait."

"Are you fucking serious?" I bellowed.

He flinched.

Fuck, another swear-jar dollar. Two if I counted thoughts, but those were free, dammit. Just like with my shorts and T-shirt, right now I didn't care about the image he wanted.

"It came out wrong," he said, leaning over to grab my hand.

A glint of deceit flashed in his eyes. The patronizing move he did to calm me.

I pulled my hands out of his reach.

"Came out wrong? Or you just finally spoke the silent part out loud?"

"Mina," he started.

"What?"

"You're right, the plan is to build our careers and then have one or two children raised by nannies."

I narrowed my eyes at him. It was similar to what we talked about, but not all of it. And we'd never agreed to nannies.

"Sweetie," he cooed, moving to crouch beside me.

I glared at him, imagining a tiny red laser on his forehead.

"Sweetie, don't imagine the sharpshooter," he said, grabbing my hand before I realized it. "We're both tired and stressed. I'm sorry."

I blew out a breath. A familiar heaviness pressed on my chest. The wedding was driving both of us wild. Soon, it'd be over, and we'd get back to being us. Or who we'd been before this nonsense. My brow furrowed as I tried to bring the old us to mind and drew a blank.

"You're my girl," he said, kissing my hand and refocusing me. "Tomorrow, you'll be my wife. Like we've talked about for years."

I nodded, staring at our joined hands, his covering mine.

He stood up and brushed a kiss against my lips. His lips were cold from the cereal.

"I'll see you at the end of the aisle. I'll be the one in a tux," he said and winked at me as he went to the elevator to meet his dad, brother, and groomsmen.

"See you at the rehearsal dinner first," I mumbled.

He waved and nodded, his earbuds already back in.

Sighing, I dragged myself up to start my day. I'd try to grab a nap at Trina's before everyone arrived. It was highly unlikely I'd get one, and there was no way we'd sleep much tonight. Hopefully my makeup artist would be a genius who could mask bags and cure bloodshot eyes.

I found my suitcase where I'd left it the night before and lugged it back to the bedroom to transport the overnight items I'd removed last night back into it. I grabbed my suit jacket to put it in the wash pile, and a whiff of sandalwood lingered in the air. I realized I hadn't mentioned running into Jack or him driving me home. I didn't want to start our marriage on a lie, or lie by omission, but what did it matter? Other than a "Hello, Mina" and now maybe a "Goodbye, Mina," we wouldn't see Jack again.

Trina rolled her eyes as she placed a mug of tea down for our mom. With a few hours before the ladies showed up, we were having lunch, just the three of us. Trina wore her typical jeans and loose T-shirt. Her long hair hung in loose waves. Mom had lost weight leading up to the wedding. I doubted it had been intentional, more likely stress. She had to get her mother-of-the-bride and rehearsal dinner dresses resized this week, and the one she wore now was baggy on her frame.

Mom's long hair, once dark auburn like mine, now sported more silvery white than red. Otherwise, Trina looked more like our mom with similar pouty lips and expressive dark eyes. We both had her oval face, high cheekbones, curvy form, and sloped nose.

"I saw that." Mom scolded her, rolling her eyes back at Trina. She blew on her steaming tea before taking a sip.

"You've always put Ethan on a pedestal." Trina sat opposite Mom, meeting her hard stare with one of her own.

"He's kind, well-mannered, loves your sister, and comes from a great family. They've been together . . ." Mom's eyes shifted up as she did the math in her head. "Fourteen years."

"Thirteen years, since they were fourteen, Mom," Trina offered. "It'll be fourteen years in the fall. Mina just already turned twenty-eight."

"Whatever." Mom rolled her hands. "My point is still valid. They've put in the work."

Trina snorted.

"What does that mean?" Mom demanded.

Trina's eyes bounced to me. Annoyance and stubbornness burned in them.

"Seriously, I want to know. What does that snort mean? Have they not put in the work?"

"Mom, they dated in high school, then went to different colleges."

"But they didn't break up. They managed long-distance."

"Bullshit," Trina said, lifting her eyebrows and putting her hands on her hips. "And I can swear all I want because I don't have a stupid no-swearing policy put in place by my idi— stu— significant other," she finally managed to finish. "Ethan replying to a text every day or answering a call is not working on a relationship."

"He's going to be your brother-in-law. The father to her children," Mom started.

My stomach curled and flipped.

Trina blanched and swallowed to right her face when she saw my glare.

Mom continued, "Just because you were blind enough to let Clay go—"

"Argh!" Trina threw her hands in the air. "Mom, I didn't want to marry him. He was a high school boyfriend. I knew that the moment we started going out. He was sweet, kind, and boring as hell."

"Boring? He rode dirt bikes!"

Trina looked to me for help.

I shrugged. She was running Ethan through the wringer and wanted my input? If I really wanted to get her worked up, I could mention Sam, but that was something Mom wasn't privy to, and my and Ethan's conversation from this morning still sat uneasily in my mind.

"If Ethan is so great, why isn't Mina the one defending him now?"

Mom turned in her chair to scrutinize me, her lips pursed as she contemplated.

"I'm tired," I offered flatly and took a sip of coffee, not caring that it scorched my tongue.

"Did you two fight again?" Trina asked, her voice soft with concern.

I blinked at the emotion welling in the corners of my eyes.

"About what?" She rested her soft hand on mine.

A sigh lifted my shoulders. With a frown, I shrugged.

"You should apologize," Mom said.

"What?" Trina and I roared at the same time.

"You don't even know what happened!" Trina screeched. "Why do you always take his side!"

"You're both stressed. If you apologize first, he'll follow suit. You both have wedding jitters, work stuff, and you had such a late flight that it put stress on a tight schedule."

"Do not apologize to him." Trina turned her gaze to me, shaking her head. "I'm guessing it's still about the client. He'd gone on the trip, too, if he had a client to sign. Hell, he'd be with a client now if it helped him."

"Trina, you don't know what happened either!" Mom retorted.

Trina snorted. She wasn't far from the truth.

The heaviness from earlier returned, pressing into my chest and choking my breath.

"He did apologize," I finally said.

"He did?" Trina quirked an eyebrow. "That's . . . something."

"What was it about?" Mom asked.

"He made a comment about me still having a career after we have kids."

"What does that mean?" Mom sputtered.

"Out of nowhere, he acted surprised that I still want to work on the partnership."

Mom narrowed her eyes, and her lips pulled back as if she smelled something bad. "What is he talking about? That's always been your plan. Jeez, since your preteens, you wanted to work with money and be a CEO or partner."

Trina folded her arms triumphantly over her chest. "I want this marked down."

"What?" Mom asked.

"Mom disagreed with something Ethan did."

Mom rolled her eyes. "Mina, how did your meeting go last night?"

"Client signed."

"That's great, sweetie." Mom patted my hand and offered me a large smile.

"I bet Ethan was thrilled with picking you up at midnight. I'm glad you were able to catch that flight back," Trina said.

My eyes bulged. My mouth opened, but no words came out.

Trina furrowed her brow. Then her eyes widened, and she tapped her lip.

Fuck. She thought I was hiding something.

"Mom, do you think I could borrow your pink sapphire earrings? I think they're the same color as my dress."

Double ass fuck. Those earrings were in her room.

"They're fakes, dear."

"So?" Trina shrugged. "They're really pretty. It's a little warm, so I thought about wearing my hair up or letting the stylist at it."

Those magic words had my mom up from her seat and darting toward her bedroom. Now Trina had the privacy she wanted.

Triple ass fuck.

Trina leaned to the side to make sure Mom was out of earshot. "Did he pick you up last night?" The words were like a threat.

"What?" I choked out as an image of Jack flashed in my mind. I shook my head. "It was too late. He was already asleep."

"Whoa, why are you blushing?" She stuck a finger in my face.

I shoved her hand away, but she just drew closer, pointing and making a wooing noise. "What is going on? What happened?"

"Nothing," I hissed.

I darted my eyes to the doorway, hoping for my mom's return.

"Liar!" she sang. "Just tell me."

"He didn't pick me up," I said, trying to keep my face neutral and not lie. If I lied, I'd bite my lip, and she'd pounce like a tiger.

"Then what happened?"

"I grabbed a ride," I said, trying to force my voice to remain calm.

She stared at me a beat and fell deathly calm.

"From whom?" she whispered. Something more than curiosity burned in her eyes.

"What do you mean?"

"If it was an Uber, you'd have just said that. 'I grabbed an Uber.' Or a cab. You said 'ride.' Ride implies someone you know. Who drove you?"

Shit. She was right. I fucked it up. She'd make a big deal about it.

"Trina, I also have a matching necklace," Mom called, her steps growing louder.

"This isn't over," Trina whispered.

Mom came back holding the necklace like her trophy—and my shield from Trina.

## MAY 15TH

## MINA

"You ready?" Trina asked me as she squeezed my hands and forced a smile.

The prongs of my tiara tugged against my hair as I fidgeted in her grasp. The sleek billow of my dress pooled around my feet, covering my rhinestone-encased heels. Our mother's antique blue sapphire necklace swooped across my collarbone, nabbing the old, borrowed, and blue spots of the rhyme.

"Why wouldn't I be? I've dreamed about this day since I was fifteen."

She rolled her eyes and muttered, "Pah-lease."

"What? I have!" I ran my fingers over the ostentatious rhinestone belt that started the intricate beaded lace of the bodice. "Trina, we've been together for thirteen years."

"So? It's not a life sentence. You can cut it off now. End the agony."

"It's not agony," I said and swatted at her.

Ethan had been my high school sweetheart. The only boy and man I dated multiple times, kissed, or slept with. He was it for me. Still, the last year or so had been consumed with wedding jitters.

I swallowed. "We're just stressing about the wedding, and both our businesses are taking off."

"Trying to convince me or yourself?"

I glared at her.

Which was met with another eye roll. "Did you at least fuck last night when you made a quick exit from the rehearsal dinner to loosen some of the tension?"

A sigh escaped my lips. Our rehearsal was a blur of being told where to stand and look. The dinner, planned by his mother, was delicious and proper, but my stomach hadn't been able to stand much. I crashed early, the girls coming in hours later. Ethan hadn't followed me. I didn't know he left when I did, but then we were in different rooms, as is tradition.

"How long has it been?"

I rubbed my forehead.

"So long you forgot, or even longer and you're embarrassed to tell me?"

"We decided to wait . . ." It'd been at least six months. Maybe eight. If not longer.

"Uh-huh . . ."

"It's to make tonight more special . . ."

She stared at me, lips pursed. She didn't believe me any more than I did. "Has nothing to do with the lack of chemistry?"

"Oh, shut up!"

She snorted a laugh. "He's all you've ever known, and it sounds like a life of blah."

"I like my life, let me live it."

She rolled her eyes and then narrowed them on me. A smirk turned up the corner of her mouth. "You should be aching to tear his clothes from him."

I lolled my head to the side and shot her a hard glare. She knew we never had that.

She pivoted on her heels, closing the distance between us. A devilish smile twisted her lips. "So, who gave you a ride?"

"What? We stayed at the hotel last night," I replied.

"From the airport, smart-ass."

My thoughts jumped to Jack, and images of the night raced through my mind. Nothing had happened or even been close to happening, yet heat clawed at my cheeks.

"See, there's that blush again. That's how you should respond when thinking of Ethan."

I smoothed out my dress. I wondered what Jack was up to today. Was he golfing? A meeting? A flight? A date? A pang twisted through me. What the fuck? I was less than two hours from marrying the love of my life. I swallowed down the burning acid bubbling up my throat. Stress. Stress had to be getting to me.

"Where'd you just go?" Trina demanded.

"Huh?" My gaze shot to her.

"You just had a stampede of emotions march across your face."

I waved her off.

"It has to be great if you won't tell me."

I rolled my eyes, trying to force my face neutral.

"Does Ethan know?" She stepped closer, twisting her body as she examined my body language.

"Of course, he knows I got home."

"That's a side step. So, I'd say no . . . So it's someone Ethan doesn't like. That list is long but not as long as people who don't like him."

I sighed. "Trina."

"Hm." She tapped her chin. "Are we thinking this year, decade, or longer than that?"

I swallowed. She'd narrow it down in seconds based on any reaction I gave her.

"Mina, Trina!" Dani called, saving me from the assault.

She ran in and hugged us, ignoring the scowl from Trina. Her ebony hair was curled and swooped back in ringlets. Her piercing hazel eyes shone brightly on her ivory skin.

My other bridesmaids, Corrine, Maggie, and Victoria, followed her, all four in matching rose dresses slightly darker than Trina's. Corrine's curly black hair was pulled back. Maggie's blond hair hung in long, loose waves. Victoria's sleek dark hair cascaded over her shoulders.

"Are we going to get you married after our pictures?" Victoria asked, her dark eyes assessing my red face and Trina's pinched expression.

"Yes," I said, forcing a smile.

The church was decked out with flower arches, streamers, and flickering battery-operated candles.

I paced the floor, counting my breaths. The plan was for the bridal party to take pictures together before the ceremony. We'd take a few candid shots afterward, and then Ethan and I would take private pictures as the guests moved on to the reception hall and happy hour. I insisted on the thirty minutes of silence to not lose my nerve. Not to hear gushing or warnings or sage but tired advice. To just breathe. The solo agony was my own doing.

The quiet hall echoed the clicking of my heels. Each beat ricocheting off the walls in a replication of my increasing heart rate. I'd expected and planned this date for years. When we made it through college still together and then started discussions on the future, I knew we were forever. He'd met all my needs, checked every box. He was intelligent, generous, confident, didn't have any major habits that were flaws. He had similar religious and political beliefs. Sex was adequate, and before the overdrive wedding prep and my increased client meetings, we'd made sure to have sex at least once a week, usually Sundays after church with his family, brunch with my family, and before we settled into the evening with our work.

Until recently, we'd agreed on children and our career paths. His curveball about my career had to be just nerves. Right? Maybe? Hopefully? We didn't have time for a major change.

I stopped myself from running a hand through my hair and turned down a different empty hall. The wedding decor ended abruptly at the archway, and a podium with wedding programs and pictures of us through the years blocked most of the path. Moving it aside, I slipped into the shadowed hall where the slants of the stained-glass windows provided dim lighting. The patterns reflected off my gown, turning it into a kaleidoscope of images. Around the next corner, the interior hall didn't have windows, and dim wall sconces lit the path. The sharp smell of disinfectant stung my nose. I turned to head back.

A soft giggle joined the clicking of my heels. Coming to a stop, I waited. The giggle sounded again, followed by a low moan and thudding. Curiosity got the best of me. I slipped my heels off and wrapped my skirt around my arm. Following the sounds, I came to a closet door, set up higher and smaller than a room door. The dark stain gleamed in the dim light.

The moans had grown to growls and yells. Thudding knocked against the door, increasing in tempo.

It couldn't be my wedding party; they were all out getting their pictures taken. They should be back any minute but didn't have time to be here yet. Not many guests had arrived yet.

Before embarrassment caught up with me, I cocked my head.

"Sh," a deep voice whispered. "Wait."

The other person tittered in response.

Shit, they were going to exit the closet and see me gawking. I gathered my skirts and, as quietly as possible, beelined for the hallway.

"Fuck, Tiffany," he growled.

The voice.

I knew that voice.

"Oh, Ethan," she moaned as her hand turned the knob and opened the door.

The two clung to each other with rumpled clothes.

"Oh, fuck yeah," he responded as he thrust into her, oblivious to the open door and my presence.

My world tilted.

The arriving wedding party heard my scream and came running, either thinking I was being murdered, had stubbed my toe, or had spilled something on my twenty-grand dress.

Trina was the first to reach me, followed by four of Ethan's best buddies, his brother, and my four other bridesmaids. Behind them were my mom and stepfather Gerald and the Settlers, Nathanial and Roberta.

"What the fuck is going on?" Mr. Settlers roared.

"I'd say they *are* fucking," Trina yelled.

Everyone turned to where she pointed.

My breath stuck in my chest and I swayed.

To the astonishment of the Settlers, my soon-to-be in-laws, Ethan was pulling his pants up with summer rose–red lipstick smeared across his cheek and his collar askew. Tiffany, Jack's old ex from high school, the bitch, had her legs wrapped around him, her dress around her waist, and was braced against the wall. Sweat beads trickled down her flushed face as she bucked a few more times against him, chasing her finale. Her groans, hot and sultry, mixed with his grunts, were the only sounds I heard.

They were fucking. On our wedding day.

My brain looped on those thoughts. Spiraling and colliding. Everything blurred together into a chaotic cacophony.

What the fuck was I going to do?

My bridesmaids, all in their rose satin gowns, flocked around me. Each one trying to offer comfort as paralysis rooted me to the floor and stalled my mind.

Dani swore and made a fist. Her hazel eyes shone murderously as she snarled. Trina moved to hold Dani back, whispering under her breath to wait until there weren't witnesses before siding up next to me. She held my arm, whispering promises to make him pay. Corrine clutched my other arm, cooing sweet words of something I didn't care to hear. Victoria, her brown eyes dark and assessing while she smirked, took her phone out and started recording. Maggie punched Ethan's brother Aiden for being related.

They were all doing something. But what was I doing?

Nothing.

But I needed to do something.

My eyes moved to Ethan. The desire to ram my fist in his face grew.

Mr. Settlers had regained his speech quicker than the others and blustered over to me, smoothing his shirt down with one hand and running the other through his thinning peppered hair. No longer toned like in his semiprofessional football days, his body still carried his bulk lithely, and he towered above me.

"Now, Mina, it's all out of his system. It's all good from here," he said.

He narrowed his large, red-rimmed blue eyes at me like I was the one in trouble for overacting. His thin mouth tightened into a scowl as he pointed a finger at me. "There is no reason for dramatics."

My thoughts shattered.

"Dramatics?" I stuttered, my vision reddening.

For some reason, the air seemed thin. I backed up, trying to catch my breath. Lights popped in my vision, and I bent over, grasping my knees with my hands to stop the spinning.

Ethan was with Tiffany? Fucking her? On our wedding day?

Fuck.

What was I going to do? Run? Fight? Cry? Get more dramatic?

Then everyone was talking. Most of it was directed at me.

Nothing made sense.

We were supposed to get married. Today . . . What the fuck was I going to do?

"Mina," Ethan started.

My attention swung back to Ethan as he fought to zip his pants, shimmying around and jostling Tiffany. Her face was flushed, and when her eyes caught mine, a Cheshire smile grew on her face. She pushed into his groin and made an O face at me.

Heat clawed at my cheeks. For starters, I was going to smack that expression off her face.

Ethan wrestled to get her off him as he tried to right himself. Despite his attempts, his shirt bunched around his pants. Disarrayed pockets bulged out with glimpses of his toned stomach.

"Mina, sweetie," Ethan panted.

Breathless from fucking another woman.

That motherfucking asshole was fucking another woman on *OUR* wedding day.

No.

It wasn't our wedding day anymore.

"You fucking moron," Aiden spat at Ethan, his face red.

Ethan flinched, his face screwed up in confusion at his brother's reprimand.

"I'll make a diversion, run," Trina whispered into my ear as she placed keys into my hand and shoved her slim purse—made for a lipstick, phone, and an ID or license—my way. "My car is up front. Don't look back."

She stepped in front of me, her head down but eyes up, feet braced, and fingers hooked into claws. A low rumble escaped her throat before she kicked her foot, ready to charge. Her copper waves swished across her shoulders as she ran toward Ethan. He froze, his blue eyes fixed on the force descending on him.

I slipped out while the others went to pry Trina off Ethan as he screamed about his face.

MAY 15[TH]

MINA

I sat at the bar, a fresh blue bomb cocktail, mostly vodka, in my left hand and my veil in my right hand. I shifted on the small stool, and the tulle and silk rustled around in a cacophony of protest.

In front of me was a two-way wooden curio cabinet filled with liquor. Thin strips of light ran along the shelves' edges. My distorted image mirrored back on the glass, a white blob with red hair and smeared mascara. I'd gone for the waterproof, believing my happy tears would wreak havoc. Instead, my miserable, broken-hearted tears had bled out, and I'd rubbed the mascara around. I had the worst smoky eye as black circled my eyes like a raccoon mask. My lipstick was long gone, left on a couple of the glass tumblers I'd used to drink my day away.

It was supposed to be my wedding day. By now, we should have said our vows, taken our pictures, and made it to the reception hall, where our friends were starting their well wishes. The ever-proclaimed happiest day of my life.

It was not.

The booze was making it better, but as a hiccup rocketed my chest and burned my throat, it wasn't the best cure.

I'd been left at the altar. Nope, that was wrong . . . I'd left him at the altar after I saw him fucking Tiffany. I'd left him . . . I just had to keep reminding myself of that.

When the road blurred from my tears and puffy eyes a few hours ago, I pulled over at the first parking lot I found. So what if it happened to be a bar with chipped paint, cracked tarmac, and missing neon? It was open, and that was all that had mattered.

When I'd entered, no one else was there other than the bartender and two waitresses setting up the place for the night. They'd taken one look at me and three steps back. I grabbed the barstool in the corner, using the wall to help support the weight of my dress and despair. The bar jutted out like a penis into the room. The other side, likely for small groups, was cozier than the large section I sat in and had the more expensive liquor. I didn't care about quality, I only cared about getting drunk. Cheap liquor worked just as well.

I'd sat down, taking Trina's keys, her car, and purse. The bartender had accepted Trina's ID and credit card as my own. It was close enough anyway. Besides, I don't think he wanted more not-a-bride tears.

I'd managed to choke out "Vodka," and a simple finger flagging had worked for the others shoved my way. A few, like the one before now, had been a cocktail to provide some change. So he said. But it was probably easier for him to water it down. He passed me a water in between each and wouldn't serve another vodka until the glass was empty. My empty stomach didn't care about his rules, and the wall kept me vertical.

Others had filtered in over the hours, giving the crying lady in a white dress a wide berth. When the air shifted, warm and dangerous, I flicked my eyes behind me. A strangled breath caught in my throat.

Fresh and polished, Jack strolled in. His Nordic-blue eyes narrowed in on the out-of-place whiteness of my dress.

Without a word, he moved closer.

Somehow, I seemed to hold my breath while my heart rate increased in my chest.

Then bitterness tanged in my mouth and disappointment weighed on my chest when he moved past me.

Jack sat parallel to me, on the other side of the cabinet. Of course, he'd want the expensive stuff to go with his designer suit and his stupid expensive luxury car.

The bartender slid his way. Jack offered him that fucking charming smile, and they slipped into conversation.

I glared at him, but he didn't move his eyes to me. When the bartender glanced momentarily over his shoulder at me, I flipped Jack off. A grin tugged on his lips, which unsettled the alcohol in my stomach.

After their fun discussion, which included laughs—of course the jackass had found fun today—a soda glass was placed in front of him. As soon as the bartender moved away, though, the smile fell from Jack's lips, and those fucking Nordic-blue eyes moved to me again. A twist of heat warred with the building chaos in my belly. I swallowed a large sip to squash whatever was going on in my core.

He folded his arms across his broad, hard chest. A disapproving frown flinched on his lips each time I guzzled my drink. His concerned blue eyes followed every lift of my drink and locked on to my eyes before he shook his head.

I sneered at him for good measure, then threw back the rest of the cocktail, gulping it down. I didn't need his pity. I didn't need his fancy car. I did need a cab though. And a bathroom soon. And something to change into.

He was the only one not kind enough to ignore me and let me drink my sorrows away.

He'd either wandered in on his own or found me after he heard about the morning from his gossip mill of real estate investors and came to stare. I wasn't sure which was more true, but both pissed me off. I wanted vodka and peace. I wanted to drink until I didn't feel the forbidden heated tingles that came with Jack, or to remember the day or why I was wearing the overpriced dress that now had mascara smudges on it. Fuck, that'd cost a lot to clean. Ha, his family, instead of me, had paid for it since I wore his mother's favorite haute designer. No way they were getting the mascara out or their money back. Serves them right for raising a cheating prickwad.

Ethan's ring weighed my finger down. The diamond rubbed against my skin, but I didn't trust it in my purse, so I left it on. Even if I wanted to chuck it into the lake, I didn't need Ethan's family hounding me for their stupid grandmother's ring.

I blinked to clear my head, the lights spinning slightly as I motioned for the bartender to give me another.

"Add it to my tab," someone said to my left.

My eyes staggered to the side, purposely avoiding the blob across the rows of alcohol. The owner of the voice was a typical barstool jockey my dad hung out with. His slicked-back thinning hair was puffed up to give the illusion of more volume. His suit jacket hung unbuttoned, showing his crisp white shirt tucked beneath expensive pants with a black leather belt. When he shifted his arm, his Rolex came into view.

Yep, just like my dad.

"Nope," I said, taking a sip of the fresh vodka that was likely diluted. "I got this."

He slipped onto the stool next to me, his elbow gliding across the polished mahogany, his hand cradling his head. I didn't bother to turn to him, or the lecherous grin he was shooting my way to reveal his bleached teeth.

"Haven't seen you around here before," he said, taking his beer without acknowledging Todd, the bartender.

Todd snorted in disapproval.

Todd's married, three kids, and one grandchild. From only the few hours I'd talked to him since arriving, I could tell you details about his past too.

Silence hung between us. I sipped my vodka again.

"How much water is in here?" I asked Todd.

"Drink up. This one is on the house," he said. Turning his gaze to my left, he said, "Outta the seat."

"Why?" he barked. "No one has it claimed."

"Devon, you're being a fucker. Move your ass, or I'll toss you."

"Jackass," Devon—apparently that's his name—spat but moved on.

"You gotta another one coming in," Todd whispered without looking at me.

"Send 'em away," I said and drank my disgusting watered-down vodka.

"Move along, Jer," Todd said.

Grumbles followed, but the seat remained empty.

My own protector. Could I adopt Todd as my dad? I hadn't even invited mine to the wedding. Thoughts of the wedding led to Ethan with Tiffany and brought a wave of sniffles.

"Can I call you a cab?" Todd asked.

I nodded toward Trina's purse, which was once again vibrating. "I got a phone."

"Someone is trying to reach you," he said, staring into my eyes instead of the rumpled wedding dress, or veil now tossed on the floor.

"I don't give a shit."

"How about a burger?" he asked, changing topics.

"Sure," I said so he'd leave me alone. Then added, "If I can get a real vodka with it."

He huffed but walked away to place the order.

Another presence joined me. The smell of sandalwood and confidence wafted around me, heating my core.

My eyes shot to Todd, who stared back.

He cocked an eyebrow and shrugged. "Could do a lot worse," he mumbled.

Jerk. Leaving me to Jack because he probably had the hots for him too.

"I've seen you down twelve glasses—about three vodkas, two cocktails, and seven waters," Jack said, facing the curio cabinet to meet my blurred reflection.

"You robbing me?" I shot to Todd. Even though I tried, my eyes wouldn't focus to put the red laser on his forehead.

He chuckled. "Nope, only charging when I give you vodka."

"I need a new bar," I spat. "One that serves alcohol."

"No bar will let your drunk ass in," Todd shot back.

I pointed a finger at him, ready to argue, but it was too much effort as I wavered to keep it steady.

Jack cleared his throat, and I looked away to avoid him. When our eyes locked in the glass, I growled and kicked the counter.

"What the fuck do you want?" I asked, turning to lean fully against the wall. "You here to gawk? Make fun of me? Do a round of loser, loser?"

Jack stared at me, his blue eyes filled with concern as he searched my face, his mouth pressed into a thin line.

"Mina," Jack whispered, his voice catching. "He was so wrong."

I sniffled.

He gave me a piteous smile and reached for my hand. He rubbed his thumb over my knuckles. His warmth soaked in, and I slumped back, taking the small comfort he provided.

"He's . . . a jackass," Jack said and licked his lips. He averted his eyes and swallowed before continuing, "I'm so sorry."

Lead balled in my stomach, first a small pebble, then it grew to a numbing ache that radiated throughout my body. Pity. He was giving me fucking pity. So would everyone else. I wasn't going to be poor little Mina, the bride left at the altar. Wait, I left him. The bride whose groom was fucking someone else at their wedding.

Fuck this shit. I needed a plan. I needed to figure out how I was showing up to work on Monday. I sucked in a shaky breath and yanked my hand back.

His eyes shot up to me in confusion.

"I don't want your fucking pity," I said, finding strength in my vodka-soaked veins.

"I'm not giving you pity."

He sat up taller. His lips shifted into a frown.

"Like hell you're not," I said, sticking a finger in his face. His eyes doubled and blurred together as my eyes swam to focus.

"Mina, what he did was awful. I want to make sure you don't hurt yourself."

"Hurt myself?" I yelled. "What the fuck? I wouldn't do that."

He nodded toward the vodkas.

"Fuck you," I shouted at his truths.

"Mina—"

"No," I shouted, noticing a few turning their heads to watch.

Todd's form drew closer.

"No, you're only here to rub it in. You fucking hated Ethan. You're probably cheering inside about this. Hoping he ruined his reputation. He fucked up big time, but you know what? It's going to blow over for him. He's the one with his fucking penis in another woman on our wedding day, but I'm the dumbass bride whose groom was fucking another woman and ran out. I'm the one who's going to carry that stigma around."

"Mina—" He stopped himself. "You're right, he's going to walk away clean in a few weeks."

"Fucker," I yelled and kicked the counter again. This time, the pain kicked back through my toe and raced up my leg. My vodka was wearing off.

I raised my glass for another vodka, but Todd, who now stood across from me, shook his head.

A stifled laugh came from behind me, and I turned to take in the room. The once-empty bar was now packed with people, almost all of whom were staring at the crying, yelling bride at the bar who just shared her wedding day disaster out loud and at full volume.

"Fuck," I whimpered and reached for Trina's purse and keys.

"No," Jack said and snatched the keys.

"Those aren't yours," I hissed and lunged toward his arm.

In my drunken state, I stumbled and landed on his chest, my chest pressed against his. He froze momentarily, and I took advantage and climbed up his torso to reach the keys in his outstretched hand, using my nails to dig into his shirt and flesh.

"Ow," he yelled and grabbed for my hands.

I squirmed, and each time he grabbed one hand, I used the other to deliver damage to his torso: clawing, pinching, punching.

"Mina," he growled.

"Jack," I hollered back.

In the tussle, my purse fell, spilling the meager contents onto the polished wood floor.

Trina's phone lit up with yet another text. The notification boxes kept coming, one after another. The screen turned white as a call came in. The name was a squiggly blur, but I recognized the picture. A picture of the devil with horns and a pitchfork popped up, Trina's picture of choice for Ethan as of late.

"You fucker," I screeched at the phone.

Grabbing it off the ground, I swung my arm back to chuck it across the bar and watch it explode into a bunch of pieces as my life had done. But it wasn't mine. Fuck. I palmed it instead to avoid being reminded of his face.

Jack used the distraction to pocket Trina's keys and clasped his hand around mine.

"Stop," he said and tried unsuccessfully to pry the phone from my hands.

"Don't touch that," I said. "That's not mine. It's Trina's."

"Do you know her personally?" Todd asked, leaning across the bar so he didn't have to yell.

"Yes," Jack said.

"No," I yelled.

"Get her outta here," he said. "People are starting to record."

"What?" I asked, whirling around to destroy any phone focused on me.

The motion sent me to my side, and stars popped in my eyes. The blood rushed from my head, and I sank to the floor, my hands rubbing my now throbbing temples.

Jack grumbled something, yanked a bunch of bills from his wallet, and tossed them to the bartender. Then he wrapped his arms around me and tossed me over his shoulder.

"What the fuck?" I yelled and punched his back.

My stomach turned at the motion, and I whimpered.

"Shit, Jack. I'm going to puke."

A blast of summer air hit my face, stirring my senses more. The sticky heaviness of the bar lingered for a moment until the door closed behind us.

"Figures," Jack said.

He set me down on the scraggly patch of grass running the perimeter of the parking lot.

"I can't barf in public," I said, choking back the rising bile.

"It's dark," he said.

He squatted behind me, holding back my hair that had escaped with one hand and rubbing my back with the other. I was too sick to be mad at his pity. And it felt good. Really good.

"It's okay," he whispered. "You'll feel better afterward."

He was right.

After a few dry heaves, I sat back on my heels, gasping for air.

"Fuck," I whimpered.

The phone, still in my gnarled fingers instead of smashed to smithereens, took that moment to vibrate, the screen lit with an incoming call.

Dani's beautiful face popped up. Her skin glowed in the picture from our summer trip to the beach. Her hair whipped around her face beneath a beach hat she held down. Her huge smile lit her face up. A much better time.

I'd had enough self-loathing, most of it now splattered in the grass, and picked up the phone. I swiped right and choked out over the burn of bile, "Dani. I'm okay."

"Where are you?" Ethan's voice sounded through the phone.

I pulled the phone back, staring at the assaulting device. It was still Dani's picture. How had he gotten her phone?

"Mina," he yelled when I didn't respond.

Trina's voice sounded in the background. "Is that Dani's phone?"

The other ended erupted with a scuffle, Trina swearing and Ethan growling over the device.

"Mina, he's tracking you," Trina shouted before the connection ended.

I stared at the phone in my hand, dark and silent.

"He's coming to pick you up?" Jack asked behind me, his voice guarded.

I turned my head to him. The pools of artificial light bathed the parking lot, haloing his hair and shoulders but casting long shadows over his face.

"I'm not going anywhere with him." I dropped the phone.

"How'd you get here?" he asked, dangling the keys.

"Trina's car," I said and pushed myself to my feet. The world spun, and I stumbled, but Jack braced my elbow. I yanked free, taking a few more stumbles. "I don't need your help."

"Obviously," he said and ran a hand through his hair.

"I need to leave." I extended my hand for the keys.

"I agree you need to leave, but you can't drive, and you know it." He folded his arms over his chest with the keys tucked inside.

"I don't have time for a fucking Uber. I have no idea how close he is," I said and pumped my hand up and down in demand of the keys.

"He's tracking the phone now that he knows you have it."

"I'll leave it with Todd," I said. "Now, give me my keys."

I realized he was right. How long had I been there? Ethan could still be at the venue or just around the corner. I sucked in a wobbly breath. My eyes searched the roads, the headlights just a blur of dancing light.

He looked around, his eyes scanning something. He met my gaze and said, "I'll drive you."

"No, fuck no," I said.

Fuck. This was like the airport, but now Ethan *was* coming for me. But I still needed a ride.

I had no idea about Jack's plans, but he hated Ethan, and I didn't—

Wait, I also hated Ethan. I eyed up Jack, taking in his stance, serious expression, and the fact he sat with me at the bar for those hours not saying a word or mocking me.

He stared at me expectantly. His jaw clenched. Yeah, pity reflected in his eyes, but so did anger. Jack was fucking pissed too.

"Fine, thank you," I said, finally remembering my manners after my tirade. "I'll give Todd the keys and phone."

"How about I give them to him and Trina's license so he knows who should pick them up?"

I grimaced. I'd used her license.

"It'll be fine. Sit in my car in case he shows up before I'm back out," Jack said.

"Fine."

Before handing the phone to Jack, I texted Victoria and told her the bar so maybe they could get here before Ethan. With her lead foot, she'd likely beat him. I turned the phone off and dropped the items in Jack's hands.

"Where am I going to go?" I asked. My lips trembled.

"Your mom's or sister's?" he asked, already steering me to his car.

"No, he'd go there first."

He kept a firm arm wrapped around my waist. His touch felt good, and something stirred in my center. I leaned into his muscular chest, stealing his warmth and comfort. I was a horrible person. This morning I was going to marry a different man, the fucking cheating louse, and now I was snuggling up to his enemy. But Jack had never been caught cheating on a girlfriend. He was decent enough to break up with them before moving on.

"One of your friends' places?"

"No, he knows where they all live. He'll find me." Another sob racked up my frame.

"Okay, we'll figure something out on the road."

He opened the back door for me, and I crawled in, not caring as I heard fabric ripping. I flopped down, my face on the leather seat, the coolness a comfort. I left my rear in the air.

## MAY 16TH

## MINA

The drone of the TV drifted into my dream. My head protested as I opened my eyes. I woke up tucked under a sheet and comforter, but the wall art and ceiling weren't normal. Instead of sleek gray like Ethan's apartment or blue like my bedroom, it was a muted butter yellow with abstract paintings instead of art nouveau like Ethan's or photo prints like mine. Although no lights were on, muted sun soaked the west wall.

A TV on a basic laminate dresser rambled on at a low, barely distinguishable volume. I darted my eyes around, trying to gather where I was. Then I saw him. Reclined on the other queen bed. With no suit jacket on and his white dress shirt sleeves rolled up, revealing his muscular forearms, he had his hands folded behind his head as a pillow. His eyes tracked the TV, a smile dancing on his lips from whatever he saw.

Two beds. Cheap furnishings. Oh fuck.

My mouth went dry when I saw my wedding dress draped over a chair tucked into the dresser unit. Without stirring, I slid my hand over my body. I had on my underwear, strapless bra, and a baggy T-shirt. What had I done?

I licked my lips, the dryness scratching my throat, and I coughed.

His head shot around, his blue eyes assessing me.

"I'll get you some water," he said, already halfway to the bathroom.

Ah fuck.

I pushed myself up the pillow, the pressure and pounding in my brain stopping my progress.

"Don't rush," he said, kneeling by the bed.

I opened my mouth to ask what was going on, but he used that motion to shove the glass toward my lips. I sputtered into the glass, water sloshing on me and the covers.

"Sorry," he murmured and grabbed a tissue to blot it up.

"Stop," I choked out.

He froze, his hand pressed on my collarbone.

Bracing my elbows against the mattress, I forced myself up. My stomach rolled. A grimace twisted my lips, and the acid burn of bile filled my mouth.

"Careful, your vodka has been fighting you all night," he said.

Vodka? All night? Fuzzy images stumbled through my brain, none making sense.

"What happened?"

My eyes darted around the room unseeing, only focusing on my discarded wedding dress. I blinked, the action causing my eyes to burn from dehydration.

"Do you remember what happened yesterday?"

Yesterday? I lost a whole day?

"Your wedding . . ." he said and flinched.

Then reality found me, sitting in a hotel with Ethan's rival, my crumbled wedding dress, and throbbing headache.

"I have some Tylenol for you, but you should eat something first."

My stomach protested, and I shook my head, regretting it immediately. I clasped my head to stop the pain and stop the stars from spinning around.

He traced his hand across my forehead, lingering over my cheek before resting on the back of my neck. "Look at me," he whispered.

My eyes involuntarily obeyed. Unlike the cloudy dark blue of Ethan's that hid secrets, Jack's were bright and clear but also hid secrets. My eyes tracked down his face, finding his lips. They looked soft and welcoming.

I licked my lips and tilted my head. The action spun my vision.

"Mina," he said, my name like magic on his lips.

Wait, what was I doing? My organs screamed in protest. My head tried for answers while my heart wanted revenge, and my stomach wanted to puke while my core decided to finally flicker to life after months of coldness. Fuck, I was a hot mess.

"Jack . . ." I said, averting my eyes, heat clawing at my neck. The night pieced together into a mosaic of chaos. Ethan. Tiffany. The bar. And then Jack. "Where are we? What happened after your car?"

"I drove us a little over an hour away and found a hotel. You were asleep when I got back to the car. You said he'd find you at your friends' places, and I didn't know where else to take you that was close."

So his place didn't count? Wasn't close? Whoa, where did that come from?

"And," he said, pulling me from my thoughts, "I didn't think you'd want to sleep in your dress. It's loud and doesn't look overly comfortable. I grabbed a T-shirt in the lobby."

I tried to whip my head around to look at him, but it was more of a slow wobble with whimpering. "You undressed me?"

He chuckled. "No, you did that."

I furrowed my brow and regretted it.

"I'll order us some food. Maybe some soup and crackers?" He rubbed a hand over his mouth. "It's still morning, maybe toast and juice."

"Toast," I croaked.

"Then we can decide from there what we do?" He dipped his head to look me in the eyes.

We? When did he become so nice?

The urge to kiss him or vomit gripped my stomach. Vomiting won out, and I stumbled for the toilet.

The room was a blur as I pushed into the bathroom, hunched over and sweating. I flipped the toilet seat lid up and clutched the rails as the first wave ripped through my stomach. Warm hands ran along my neck, pulling my hair back. I jolted, but another spasm rocked my stomach. His hands twisted my hair behind me, securing it in one hand. Another rubbed gently on my back, easing my muscles.

After a few dry heaves, I slumped back.

If Ethan had thought my T-shirts were inappropriate for breakfast, he'd be livid to see me in one vomiting into a porcelain throne. The thought of him tightened my muscles, but instead of the urge to vomit, I wanted to punch something. Too fatigued for anything, I looked at the floor mat and considered just lying down there. That'd really be the image of a perfect wife. T-shirt and underwear, vomit, and lying on a bathmat from a hangover.

He lifted his hand off my back, leaving my back cold and lonely as he brought it in front of me. The dark hair sprinkled on the taut muscles of his thick forearm rubbed against my skin, sending tingles through me. With gentle hands, he lifted me from the ground, cradling my body against his. His woodsy cologne greeted me. Instead of turning my stomach, I groaned at the tightening that came from lower.

"You need food in you. It'll help settle everything," he said as he placed me gently back on the bed.

"Jack," I croaked.

"Yes, Mina?"

"You hate Ethan and me. Why are you being nice?" The words were out before I considered them.

His eyes darkened and his nostrils flared.

"Mina, I never hated you. Never."

"But . . ." Years of memories twisted together. The cold looks. The avoidance. That fucking granite fortress of nothingness.

"Ethan, I hated, and he somehow found a way for me to hate him more now."

"But . . ."

"Mina, I'm truly sorry you thought I hated you. That . . ." He sighed and shook his head. "I'm sorry."

"But you stopped being his friend because he dated me." I sniffled.

"What?" he barked.

"Ethan said . . ." I didn't finish. Ethan wasn't my source of truth and fidelity anymore.

"Ethan is a fucking asshole and liar," Jack said, seething.

Jack had once been his best friend. I'd once been Ethan's fiancée. If Ethan cheated on me on our wedding day, what could he have done to Jack? And why had it never come up in the past decade? Because Ethan was a fucking asshole and liar.

"We agree on that."

## MAY 16TH

### JACK

She lay sprawled on the bed, the pillow tucked under her, her red hair splayed around her. Weak sunlight streamed in through the crack in the curtains.

Ethan fucked up big time. He had the best woman in the world, and he chose to fuck Tiffany on his wedding day. Tiffany, who had been my first and fleeting girlfriend after Ethan started dating Mina. Whom I'd only dated because Ethan had been interested in her. At least for Mina's sake, she caught them before the I dos and signing the papers. Otherwise, she'd be embroiled in a legal battle for years. He'd have had a prenup, but he'd done everything he could to silence her and her friends. I hadn't lied. He would get by unscathed, but that was only because Mina wouldn't set his life on fire. She'd move on. She'd dig deeper into work. It's what she did in high school when he was a prick. He'd ditch her or stand her up for dates. Instead of getting mad, she did more. Just like when her dad had drained their bank account and left them for a woman barely older than Mina. She ignored her emotions and her feelings, throwing her energy into a project, school, or work, which was probably why she managed to stay with the asshole for so long.

However, her telling me I hated her still ate at me. I didn't hate her. How could I? It was a stab in the heart when she started dating Ethan. She chose him over me. He was more outgoing, more charismatic, and more importantly, I'd learned much too late he told her his feelings. Something I'd been too scared to do. I thought staring at her and wishing would work. Still didn't because tonight, well, last night at the bar proved that. She just took it as a sign of judgment and disapproval.

I flicked my eyes to her, confirming she was still asleep before I crept to the bathroom. She slept through just about everything, but I didn't want to be the reason she woke up now. She'd kept the toast and juice down, something her system needed. When she woke, I'd get her lunch, and then . . . Fuck, I didn't know. Marriage seemed too strong for her to agree to. Running away seemed illogical in the long haul. Lunch was realistic, manageable, and didn't seem to have long-lasting ramifications.

A buddy, Aiden—yeah, Ethan's brother—who had been at the wedding had already texted me about the shit show. Ethan's family told the attendees Mina had fallen ill. Trina had called them fucking liars. Apparently in front of the whole church.

Mina would conquer the world with deliberate, thought-out, and well-executed steps. Trina would bulldoze her way to the destination.

Aiden knew and shared my dislike of Ethan and liked to keep me apprised of Ethan's escapades. I thought it was so he could commiserate and vent more than actually provide me with information. In either case, the wedding was considered postponed. That was something I didn't think was my place to tell Mina.

She hadn't asked how I ended up at the bar. So I didn't have to tell her Aiden was texting me as everything went down and that I walked out of a meeting to make sure she didn't do something dumber than drink. It wasn't something I really thought she'd do, but I couldn't be okay with her doing something out of character because of a dickhead like Ethan. He had already reset her life, he didn't get to destroy her too.

I used the gift shop toothbrush set to brush my teeth and remove the taste of stale coffee and last night's dinner. My face was stubbled with the growth I didn't shave. I could have used a fresh change of clothes, but the gift shop only had T-shirts. With a quick tug, I discarded my rumpled shirt and pulled on a new gray T-shirt with MKE scrawled across it in black block letters. My black suit pants would have to work.

As I walked out of the restroom, my eyes snagged on the white dress. A beacon of the shit storm that would come.

For some reason, seeing her in the wedding dress dredged up too many memories from high school. Reminded me I wasn't her choice. That in most areas, I wasn't good enough. Things came naturally to Ethan, and those that didn't, he had money to compensate. As kids, we'd had a mutual liking of sports and video games, the ever-needed glue for a friendship. My console came secondhand while he had the newest releases. None of it had mattered when I beat him at the video games.

We were on the same sports teams until his grades dipped and his parents yanked him off. With hopes of a scholarship for college, I joined every sport, hoping to have that spark. None worked out for a scholarship, and I couldn't afford a club to get better, but my grades landed me one, and the rest looked good on the application as extracurriculars while maintaining my grades. Most of it came from studying with Mina while Ethan did whatever. Granted, we'd be at his house, but Mina and I sat together at the table, trying for more than what we were born into.

My mom tried, but as a single mother, money and opportunities were tight. My dad couldn't be bothered to pay child support, let alone show up for birthdays or holidays, unless he was hungry. My parents had never married nor went to court for custody and child support. Something Ethan liked to bring up when I outdid him, reminding me how lucky it was for someone like me. I hadn't cared, seen it as jealousy, until Mina's mom, Eileen, said luck ran out. Luck was something her ex believed in and bled their money out on. Eileen had never said it, but the looks she gave me made me think I reminded her of her ex. Mina didn't believe in luck as a philosophy. She believed in hard work and breaks.

Like normal, my gaze tracked to Mina. And yet, we were both on track for the big dreams we discussed at Ethan's marble dining table. Ones we both worked endlessly for. Even with the marriage sidelined, I had no doubt Mina would only use it for fuel to propel herself faster and further into her dreams.

At least now, she wouldn't have the weight of Ethan holding her down. I swallowed at the presumption. She'd forgiven him in the past for his bullshit. Granted, she hadn't believed he ever cheated when we still talked in high school. Based on yesterday, if she had, the wedding would have never happened. Or I was still caught in wishful dreaming. Like the fool I'd been in high school when I tried to tell her. A sigh fell from me. We were finally on some sort of talking terms. Last thing I needed to do was fuck it up, again.

My phone buzzed in my pocket. I ignored it and splashed water on my face.

Three people were likely to text me at the moment: Rocco, my assistant, Sam, my business partner, or Aiden. Rocco would want to rant about me walking out, Sam would care but be more interested in the why, and I didn't have anything other than "There was a woman . . ." And Aiden . . . I sighed. If it was him, I should answer.

It buzzed again, followed by a follow-up buzz. I pulled it from my pocket.

AIDEN: You two still okay? Need any supplies?
AIDEN: Ethan is losing his shit.
AIDEN: He's screaming he loves her and it was a mistake.
Tiffany is sobbing. Why is she still here?

AIDEN: Fuck, man. Found Trina's car. Ethan thinks she left with a random guy and IS PISSED.

AIDEN: He's sobbing. I've never seen him cry. I don't think he'll learn shit from this.

AIDEN: WTF AREN'T YOU RESPONDING? Her mom, sis, and friends want updates. They don't like my no updates. GIVE ME UPDATES.

AIDEN: I told her family she's with you. Trina and Maggie confirmed you're okay.

An old familiar hollowness edged at my heart. Eileen had regularly made it clear she didn't like me with Mina when I drove her home. She saw my presence as a conflict to Mina's happiness, her future. In reality, Eileen had adored Ethan. There'd be no way she saw me picking Mina up as good.

I sighed. Fuck. Eileen would likely call the cops on me if Trina and Maggie weren't there.

AIDEN: Ethan is trying to get a missing report done, but they said it's too soon and he's not related. Her family is holding off. If she doesn't contact soon, they'll report you too.

Fuck, Eileen was already ready to call them on me.

Closing my eyes, I rested my head against the doorframe. What the fuck was I going to do? This was bullshit on so many levels. Fuck Ethan.

At least she hadn't married him.

Yet.

Fuck.

I knelt on her comforter, trying to prolong waking her up as long as I could.

"Mina," I whispered.

"Mm?" she murmured and rolled over, the sheet pulling with her, revealing her bare legs and her underwear where her shirt tugged up. Fuck this.

After tugging the sheet back to cover her, I laid a hand on her shoulder and whispered louder, "Mina?"

"Mmm . . ." she whined as she fought to stay asleep.

"Hon— Mina," I said, catching myself. "We should call Trina."

Her brows furrowed as she tried to connect the words to her dream. She scooted closer to me and my body heat as she nestled deeper into the pillow. Her knees and upper legs curled around my hip, and she snuggled into my back. Damn how I wanted to pull back the sheet . . .

"Fuck," I muttered and put my hands down to push myself up.

"Stay," she murmured.

She pulled my hand toward her. Her soft fingers wrapped around it, holding it tightly as she laid it by her face.

This wasn't going as planned. I may have dreamed about her since our teens, but she just broke up with a fuckwad on her wedding day, was nursing a hangover, and had no idea what the fuck was going on.

"Mina," I said a little bit louder. Her frown meant she heard me. "We need to call Trina."

"Trina?" she repeated.

"Yes, hon— Mina," I said, flinching at my mistake. "Everyone is worried about you."

"Worried about me?" she asked, peeling an eye open to look at me.

Realization dawned on her face, and she pulled back, taking my hand with her. I lost my balance and had to fight to not fall on top of her.

"Shit," she sputtered, taking in the room, her dress, and me. "Fuck, it wasn't a dream."

"No, I'm sorry," I said, pulling myself back.

"Stop saying you're sorry," she said and grabbed her head. Her eyes closed and she groaned.

"More Tylenol?"

"No, just in preparation for pain. It's barely an ache," she said, resting her hands back in her lap. Opening her eyes, she stared up at the ceiling.

I handed her my phone. "Call whoever you want to."

"Whoever . . ." Her amber eyes shot up to mine, glossy with emotion. "You think I'm going to go back to him?"

"I think you need to call Trina or a friend and let them know you're okay. Then we need lunch."

"And then?" she said, her eyes hard and narrowed on me.

I shrugged. "I know those steps."

"Why are you being nice?" she asked, her face shuttering to hide her emotions.

I remembered this look well. It was one she used in high school when her dad drank and then cheated on her mom and left. The look she used when Ethan was, well, Ethan and arrogant and self-centered. It was the look she gave me every time I greeted her at an event after Ethan and I fought. If she was distant and cold, I still looked forward to seeing her and her short "Hello, Jack" she gave back. Somehow her saying my name was both a reward and punishment.

"Ethan obviously doesn't give a shit about me, so trying to buddy up with me to hurt Ethan won't do shit. You don't owe me anything. You don't like me. I just don't understand . . ."

There was so much wrong with what she said, and I had to bite my lip not to retort. Instead, I glared at her and stood up.

"What?" she said, building up the fucking wall she used to keep people away and her feelings intact.

"Mina . . . I don't hate you. I never did."

She narrowed her gaze at me.

Now wasn't the time to rehash years we couldn't undo. Taking a deep breath, I swallowed down my hurt. "Call Trina or someone, and let them know you're okay. I don't have their numbers. Then we'll get lunch . . . and then . . . then we'll decide on a full stomach."

She nodded in agreement and picked up the phone. She dialed the number.

"Hello?" Trina screamed into the phone.

Mina yanked it back and flinched. "Trina, it's me."

"Oh my God, are you alive? Are you okay? Where are you? All I know is Jack picked you up and THEN NOTHING."

"I'm not contacting you on a Ouija board. I'm alive. I'm fine. I'm . . . not sure where I am."

I swallowed back the smile forming on my lips.

"Did he just leave you? I'll fuck up—"

"Trina, I'm okay. I promise. Did you find your keys and stuff?"

"Yeah, but I'm more concerned about you, not that shit."

"Is that Mina," a voice sounded behind her.

"What the fuck is he doing here?" Trina barked away from the phone.

Something unintelligible was said in response.

"I don't give a shit if his parents paid for the hotel room."

There was a scuffle, and Trina yipped. My eyes bulged, and my blood pounded in my veins. He better not have touched her.

Mina sucked in a sharp breath. She'd destroy him first.

"Mina, sweetie, is this you?" Ethan cooed into the phone.

Mina's lips quivered into a snarl.

"Motherfucker," Trina yelled.

"What the fuck, bitch? Ow. Fuck, I'm bleeding."

"Not enough!"

Good. She'd make him pay.

"Mina," Ethan yelled from a distance from the phone.

She pulled the phone from her ear. Betrayal and rage swam in her eyes.

Aiden and her friends' voices yelled in cacophony.

"Mina, are you sure you're okay?" Trina huffed into the phone.

Mina blinked. "I am, are you?"

"That fucker's bleeding, I'm great."

Mina's first smile cracked her face. My muscles relaxed.

"Trina, I'm going to eat and think . . . I'll call later?" Mina asked Trina, but her eyes met mine as she pointed to the phone.

I nodded.

"I'll call from this number."

"Wait, Mina," Trina called.

"What?"

"Who was my first crush?"

Mina stared at the phone, and I stared at her. What the fuck type of question was that?

Her smile grew. "Elmo," Mina chuckled.

Trina laughed in response. "Call me back soon."

"Elmo?" I asked, taking back my phone.

"It's our code," Mina said with a shrug.

"So, Elmo means?"

"Elmo means I'm safe."

9

# MAY 18[TH]

## MINA

Monday, I spent at home nursing the remainder of my hangover, wondering what the hell the bar and hotel meant, and staring aimlessly around the room. Something happens at twenty-five. It's like our bodies flip a switch, and there is no more quick rebound. With food, copious amounts of water, and rest, I was finally human again. By eleven, I'd gone to the doctor to get bloodwork done to make sure I didn't have an STD. Even if we always used a condom and hadn't had sex in months, nor did I have any symptoms, I didn't need to risk it. Who knew if Tiffany was the only one he had cheated with, and who knew who she'd been with too.

By noon, I realized I needed a distraction. A new project. A new goal. The best way to avoid dealing with the shattering of my romantic life was to dive back into something I was successful at, something that felt solid. Work.

Tuesday back at the office was the dumpster fire I expected. For the rare few who hadn't come to the wedding or heard about it already, I received bewildered expressions and questions about why I wasn't lying on a tropical beach. From those who had been there, I received a range of piteous looks to outright mockery.

My door was locked for the day, my vacation message removed, and I answered emails and stared at the neatly finished piles of work. Without the wedding or guilt of finishing up the client paperwork during the honeymoon flight, I took out the newly signed client contract and had it processed before lunch. After the twentieth knock on my door to check on me, I left for lunch and took the remaining part of the day off.

It was the first time in my adult life I was technically single. While at college, Ethan and I had a long-distance relationship, and I was too focused on schoolwork, extracurriculars, and experiencing college life to miss him. But I'd always believed if we made it together through college, we'd get married, start a life. It had been such a clear and logical progression that had gone seamlessly until three days ago.

Finding a secluded bench near the lake, I watched the ships in the distance and listened to the gulls circling above, waiting for an idiot to drop food. I'd spent the last six years with my company, fast-tracking my way to junior partner to be in line for a partnership in the next decade. Ethan had been the perfect partner for it. He was groomed, polite, had a business mind, and understood the sacrifices needed to make traction in one's career.

He'd never been mad until recently, maybe the past year or so, when I worked late or left for an unexpected client meeting. He did both too. I rubbed my temples. How many of those trips or late nights had been . . . Fuck. It'd been blanket trust. He'd never had a stained collar, smelled differently, jumped in the shower immediately upon coming home unless he'd been running, and I'd never found an article of clothing that wasn't mine or his. Not that I'd really looked.

Dammit. I'd been a sucker. A fool. Had there been signs?

Before I could continue down the spiral, my phone buzzed in my pocket with an incoming text.

TRINA: Where are you?

ME: Lake

TRINA: OMG you're not on a bridge? Where are you, I'm coming.

ME: No bridge. Don't come.

TRINA: You haven't been home.

ME: Stalking my apartment?

TRINA: <angel emoji>

ME: I'm not fine. I won't lie. I'm numb. I'm lost.

TRINA: Let me be with you. I can sit silently while you think.

ME: No you can't

TRINA: I can try

ME: No thanks, I'm going to probably go nap. Don't come by, let me sleep.

TRINA: <straight face emoji>

ME: I'll call you when I wake up

TRINA: How about dinner tonight?

ME: I'll think about it

TRINA: I'll be at your place at 6 with food. I have a key.

Trina strolled in at 6:01 carrying two pizzas, some canned Moscow mules, and water.

Her glance flicked to the pale blue walls. Every picture that had contained Ethan had been removed. The ones back up, he'd been cut out of. My apartment wasn't huge, but it was mine. The small dining space held my work stuff. My table served as a makeshift office. Even though our joint time was spent at Ethan's, my place was my refuge. Blankets draped over the furniture, more folded in the cedar chest that lined the back of the long sofa. A love seat offset it, and a small single chair paralleled it. My coffee table housed different financial magazines and coasters. Ethan hated everything about the comfort and hominess of the place.

"Thanks," I said, shuffling to the door in my flannel pajama pants and T-shirt.

"Girl, it's seventy out," she said, dropping the items on the table and then enveloping me in a hug.

I returned it, hiccupping when a sob caught in my throat. When we pulled away, I noticed tears on her shoulder.

Trina gave me a half smile and then forced a full one.

"We'll eat, and then we can watch a movie or sit on the balcony and make up stories about the people below," she said.

I glanced out the window. The street below bustled with people, and a swatch of the lake was visible in the right-most corner of the view. Ethan's apartment had a full lake view and dock slip. We never used it, but he liked having it.

"So, I've been very chill about you disappearing and not contacting me and everything," Trina said in a rush as she moved to the sofa with a pizza and can. "But please tell me what the fuck happened."

I plopped down on the sofa, one cushion over from her, resting my knee against the sofa arm and spreading my arm across the sofa's back.

"Thank you for letting me borrow your . . . everything." I shot her a grateful smile.

"Of course, it's the least I could do with an audience. Murder really isn't a spectator activity."

I rolled my eyes but couldn't stop the laugh.

"So?" she prompted.

"I stopped at the bar where your stuff was left."

"Uh-huh, I know that much. I have my shit back. And I know Jack found you." She stared expectantly.

I swallowed and fiddled with a string on the sofa.

"Mina, you were radio silent for twelve hours," she said, her voice wobbly and tears rimming her eyes.

"Oh shit, Trin, I'm sorry. I didn't even think . . ." My voice cracked, and I couldn't finish the sentence.

"We can't cry about this part," Trina said, swiping at her eyes. "I just need the details."

I bowed my head, licking my lips, trying to will the words to come.

"Mina, you're scaring me."

"Okay, okay, okay," I said, throwing my hands in the air. "I went to the bar. Drank a lot of vodka. I'll pay you whatever it cost."

"Nothing was charged. A temporary hold was put on the card, but it was zeroed out."

"So he paid for everything," I murmured.

"Jack?" Trina demanded, a knowing glint in her eyes.

I sighed. She sighed. I rolled my eyes.

"Tell me what happened," she said, hitting me on the knee.

"A couple hours after I got there, Jack showed up."

"Jack Wolfe?" Trina asked. A devilish smile curled her lips. She almost clapped but curled her fingers together. "Jack, as in Ethan's biggest pain in the ass? Jack, as in one of the fucking hottest guys in school who drooled over you, Jack?"

"What are you talking about?" I shot back.

She rolled her eyes. With her hands folded beneath her chin, she batted her lashes and said in a high-pitched, airy voice, "Oh, Ethan, my eyes only see you."

"Hey," I yelled and swatted her in the stomach.

She grabbed a pillow and threatened to smack me. "I've always said that."

"I know, so you're going to start the 'I was right, and you were wrong' shtick? I deserve it."

"No, Mina, that's not what I'm doing." She rubbed my knee. "I don't know what to say or not to say, so I'm sticking with my normal, wonderful crassness."

I stifled a laugh. Her honesty was probably what I needed.

"Why was Jack there?"

"I . . . I don't know, but he showed up. He sat across from me for most of the time. When he sat by me, I started a fight with him."

"You? Never," she deadpanned.

Ignoring her, I continued, "I got loud and was wearing my dress, and people started recording. I got kicked out, and because I was too drunk to drive, Jack drove me. I passed out, so he took me to a hotel."

"Wait, what? Don't tell me . . . He didn't . . . Did he?" she asked, pizza halfway to her mouth drooped over her fingers, her eyes wide and alarmed.

"No, he didn't, ew," I said. "I apparently undressed myself, and he bought me a T-shirt to wear. He held my hair back while I puked, gave me water and Tylenol, and fed me."

"Huh," she said, flopping back against the sofa.

"Expand on the huh," I said.

Maybe she had more ideas than I did. My brain wanted to make sense of it, but it wouldn't process anything other than he was Ethan's enemy and that he had to see it as a tactic to get an advantage over Ethan.

"It was really kind of him," she said. "He really didn't try anything?"

"Nope," I said, shaking my head. "If anything, he looked annoyed or bored."

She rolled her eyes. "You have a great brain for business, but you don't understand people at all."

"Not everyone is as blunt and direct as you are," I said, pointing my Moscow mule can at her.

"It's a gift," she said with a shrug and smirk.

"Anyway, the only thing I can come up with is that he sees it as a way to spite Ethan."

She stared at me, long and intense.

"What?" I barked.

"That's what you came up with?"

"Yeah, it's the only thing that makes sense. He hasn't spoken to us since high school other than to say 'Hi, Mina' at every event to piss Ethan off."

"Yeah, sure, that's what he's doing."

I nodded in agreement.

She shook her head and looked to the ceiling.

"What do I do now?"

"Mina, you were so wrapped up in Ethan. You didn't see much beyond him."

"What does that really mean? I have a solid career. I have friends. I support myself."

"I'm not saying your identity is based on him. It's not. You argue with him. Disagree with him. You even went to the client last week when he threw his bitch fit. It's just that when it came to your romantic side of life, it was Ethan. He was 'fine.' Things were 'fine.' What they were was easy. He wasn't Dad. He didn't drink to excess in general. He didn't hit you. He didn't belittle you, even if he was a condescending schmuck."

"What's wrong with fine?"

"It's boring and safe."

"Safe is good," I retorted.

"Safe is what Dad wasn't. But he also wasn't a risk. He was just an asshat." Trina sighed and rubbed her forehead. "Mina, I get why you chose safe. I really do."

"Really? You dated Clay for years," I shot back.

Her face reddened, and she stared at her hands. She hated that I knew the truth about Clay and his brother Sam. She'd confided in me when everything happened after she begged me to go to the party in high school. She'd gone in with a crush on Sam and came out with Clay as a boyfriend and hating Sam's guts. Even if Sam had been too dense at the party to know she had been interested, I'd seen him the years she dated Clay and the change in his looks toward her. But unrequited crushes can turn to hate. And Trina loved to hate. She also knew I'd take it to the grave with me.

"Yeah, but I knew he wasn't the one for me forever. He was sweet, cute, a great kisser, and really liked me. He was easy, but I knew we'd break up at the end of high school. I wanted more. It's why I didn't argue with him on things we disagreed about. Since it was going to end, it didn't matter. Ethan was safe, boring, and easy. You liked the protective bubble."

"Do you think he cheated on me before?" I whispered.

The words I'd been spinning on for days finally released. Ones I had been concerned about enough to get an STD test done.

"Yes," she groaned.

"What?" I shot out, smacking her arm. "Why didn't you say anything?"

"I didn't think it until this weekend, and then too many things made sense."

I slumped back on the sofa. "How long do you think?"

"No clue . . . but Aiden *or* Jack might know." She gave me a knowing look.

"You think back to high school?" I asked, my vision tunneling and a whining noise hitching in my ears.

Why hadn't Aiden or Jack said anything . . . My mind reeled . . . Had they, and I ignored them? Maybe. Probably. It didn't fit into the plans I had.

She shrugged.

"You know, he was so angry with this last trip from the start. That it was interfering with our future."

Trina nodded. "But it wasn't the first time he was mad."

My breath hitched.

"You may not have realized it, but you've been mentioning more and more that he's annoyed."

"But it was the wedding prep . . ." My default answer tumbled from my lips.

She inched an eyebrow up.

"Hadn't it been?"

Recent nights and months rolled through my mind. Years ago, he'd smile when I made a connection and deal. We'd talk about how it would grow our reputation. Wait. *Our*. Always *our*.

In the beginning, many of my contacts had been introductions through events hosted by his dad's company. Even if Ethan hadn't known them, they'd known his dad.

My mind rolled back through the past dozen clients I'd signed. Not one of them did we celebrate. He'd found a reason over half of them weren't a good fit for my business. None of them had any connection to his business, and some he'd never met. I still signed them.

A long, defeated sigh fell from me.

"Your career was getting more traction than his," Trina whispered. A sad smile flittered over her lips. "You weren't a junior partner, yet, but you were headed there."

"He was growing in his business."

Trina snorted. "A business he held the same position from graduation. At a company his dad owned. You were showing him up."

"I was following my dreams." An odd ache twanged in my heart. They'd been our dreams at one time. Hadn't they?

Trina nodded. "I don't think Ethan cared about your kid agreement."

"You don't?"

She shook her head. "No, I just think he saw it was one way to dim you. One way to control you. He had that perfect wife image thing. And Mina, you outshone him."

I snorted. "I'm a hot mess."

"He used those terms, expectations of a perfect wife, as a way to make you self-conscious, dim your brightness. He made you think you weren't good enough because he wasn't matching you."

Her words spun in my mind. All the clients. All the years. All my dreams. All his words. How blind had I been? Had my career really made him jealous? Was he that petty? That insecure?

My career. Fuck. Everything I'd built would have to weather this drama.

"Everyone at work is acting like I'm an escaped lion," I said.

"Stare 'em down with a blank face until they back away. If they ask a question about him, respond, 'How will that affect your life?'"

I stared at her until I giggled. "Sure, I'll do and say that."

"At least you're giggling," she said. "Just stare at them like you didn't hear them say anything. Only the really nasty ones will keep pushing, and in that case, just walk away. You'll continue to do an amazing job, it's who you are. How will this affect your job though? How many clients came through Ethan? Signed because of him?"

I shot her a dark look.

"What? It's an honest question."

"None to my knowledge signed because of him specifically, but now . . . Ah shit," I whimpered.

Had he convinced any of them to join me without telling me? Especially in the beginning. Boosted my career. Boosted our connected future.

"You're really good at your financial stuff. You've made them a ton of money. You've gotten the funding they've need. They'll stick around."

"Unless he asks them to leave." I hit my head against the back of the sofa.

"Make a list of all the clients, see what connections they have to Ethan, and work a mitigation plan." Trina was on the fast track to manager and then partner at the CPA firm where she worked.

I nodded dully. I had time. My desk was clean for the next two weeks because I should be on a honeymoon, drinking fruity alcoholic drinks with umbrellas, lying on a beach, or sleeping.

A knock sounded on the door, pulling our attention.

"Did you invite the girls over?" I asked, standing up to check.

"No, I told them I was coming solo first, pulling the sister card, and they had to wait."

"They didn't listen, then," I said, moving to open the door.

Her face pinched in confusion, and she tilted her head. "No, I don't think—"

I opened the door before she finished to greet the girls, but instead, Ethan stood on the opposite side of the doorway. His normal polished image of a crisp, fitted suit and styled hair was absent.

His shirt was unbuttoned at the top and untucked. The wrinkles suggested he'd worn it for multiple days. His pants had creases over his thighs and hung limply on him. His hair stuck out in tufts, uncombed, matching his bloodshot eyes. For once, he matched me in the less-than-perfect image.

My thoughts stalled as a cocktail of emotions welled in my chest. The initial automatic response to reach out and hug him was overpowered by the urge to slap him. Instead of doing anything, I stood frozen.

"What the fuck are you doing here?" Trina screeched, grabbing my lamp from the table.

Her sharp words pulled me from my shock.

"Mina, sweetie, please let's talk," he cooed.

"I have nothing to say," I said as I moved to shut the door.

He braced his hand against the frame to block me from closing it.

Trina sidled up behind and slammed the door toward him. He caught it with a curse. After shooting a dark look and snarl at Trina, he turned his sad eyes to me.

"Mina, I love you."

He tried to step in the door, but Trina, almost half a foot shorter, stood in front of him, one hand on her hip and one wielding the lamp.

I shook my head at him, fresh tears welling up, and walked away from the door.

"Mina, we have so much. We can't throw it away over this. Please, sweetie," he said, a tear rolling down his cheek.

Last Friday, I'd have cradled him and promised him anything he wanted to help him stop crying. Today, a laugh bubbled up my throat and came out as a distorted chortle.

"Get out." Trina extended her arms to block him as he rocked back and forth on his feet.

"Get out of my way," he spat at her, his blue eyes dark and his mouth a pinched line. He moved to push her out of his way. "This isn't your business."

"Don't touch my sister," I said.

His eyes jumped in alarm to me. "Sweetie, I'm not going to touch her. I just want to talk. I love you. You're my everything. We have a solid foundation. We've built it for years. We can weather anything."

My mouth dried, and my lips trembled. His lies sounded pretty. So wonderful. But they were still lies.

"Get out," I said, my stomach hardening.

"Just five minutes, please," he said, widening his eyes and giving a mournful look.

"I gave you almost fourteen years and found you fucking another woman in a closet at our wedding venue, your family's church, on the day of our wedding," I said, my voice strengthening with each word. I took steps toward the door.

His expression turned guarded, his eyes scanning for signs.

I stood behind Trina, placing my hands on her shoulders.

"Ethan, we have nothing left. You broke my trust, my belief in you and in us."

"We can fix it," he pleaded, reaching his hand toward my cheek.

I leaned right so he couldn't touch me or he'd get bitten by Trina. "No."

"We'll build back stronger."

"No," I said, grabbing the door.

His eyes darted around, trying to find anything, and locked in on my hand. "You're still wearing my ring," he said. "You still believe in us."

I looked at the rock on my finger. Bright and sparkly, and cold. A symbol of him. I'd worn it for almost two years. I didn't realize it was on anymore. Seeing it now brought weight to it, and my finger burned beneath it.

I pressed my lips together and bowed my head to take a breath. Raising my eyes back up, I gave him a small smile, his eyes hopeful. Before he could react, I shoved him backward. He stumbled on the threshold but caught himself in the hall.

"Goodbye," I said and slammed the door.

My hands trembled as I tried to lock it. Trina's hand reached over mine, fastening the bolts in place. I slumped against the door, fatigue claiming my muscles.

"Mina!" Ethan roared and pounded on the door.

"Get lost or I'm calling the cops," Trina yelled back.

"We're not done!" he screeched, but his steps retreated down the hall.

Trina fell next to me, a sad smile on her face. She pulled me into her embrace, pushing my head next to hers.

"He's not going to give up so quickly," she said.

"He just doesn't like that I left him."

My heart squeezed in my chest. Even if he was a schmuck, he'd been a part of my life for over thirteen years. He was embedded in all my future plans.

His betrayal hurt, but for some reason, an ease fell over me. I wouldn't have to argue about client meetings or late meetings or being the perfect wife with a killer career, children, and a perfect home. My chest loosened.

"You're going to be okay," Trina said into my hair.

## MAY 19TH

## MINA

Trevor knocked on my door, his face guarded as I gave him a passing glance. His blond hair stood in a product-induced faux hawk. Murky blue eyes scanned my office. As usual, he wore a slim designer suit, this one in aqua with navy pin striping and a pale yellow shirt with a matching tie. Ethan had a similar suit too. On instinct, a snarl curled my lips.

Schooling my face, I looked up from the list of clients I had created and if they had any connection to Ethan and to what degree. A few pictures of the girls dotted my desk, all the ones of Ethan already removed. My boring beige walls were the office standard as was the industrial geometric-print carpet.

"Mina, do you have a minute?" he asked.

"Sure," I said, stacking my papers together.

Other than meetings, we didn't have much contact as he tried to separate himself from the non-partner staff.

He closed the door and sauntered to the chair opposite me. Instead of sitting, he placed his palms against the back of it. His fingers pressed against the backing.

"Mina, I'm going to cut to it."

"I appreciate that." I leaned back in my chair, matching his stoic expression even though my pulse ticked up and lead pooled in my stomach.

"Mr. Settlers called," he said, staring me in the eyes.

The whine of silence filled my ears as my stomach jumped to my throat.

"I understand there were some issues this weekend," he said, giving me a dark expression.

"Issues?"

"Your wedding was postponed." He smirked.

"It wasn't postponed, Trevor," I said, folding my arms over my chest. "It was called off."

He pursed his lips and nodded. "I was attending. I heard about what happened. Some hurt feelings, some drama."

"Hurt feelings? Drama?" I sputtered in a shrill voice. "My groom was fucking another woman in a closet."

At least the STD results came back negative.

His eyes darted to mine, mocking me with a glint. He shrugged. "Not my place. Sounds like a bachelor party that carried on a bit too long."

I bit my cheek to stop the next retort, not averting my gaze. Instead, I imagined a little red glowing dot right between his eyes. Any unease I had was eaten by my growing anger. I white knuckled my armrests to stop myself from throwing something at him and getting fired.

"Trevor, is there something besides my wedding you wish to speak about? This seems personal in nature."

He narrowed his eyes at me, and his jaw ticked. "Yes, there is. Mr. Settlers has made it clear he will not be signing with you as a client."

I had figured that, but I didn't know why that mattered today. I waited, letting the silence sit between us.

"Without him as a client, you're not at the partner or even the junior partner track," he said, moving to the door. His smirk had returned.

"What? My portfolio is outstanding."

Every muscle tightened in my body as I tried to anchor myself to the floor instead of flying across the desk to smack his face.

He shrugged. "Eh, it's okay."

"It's the best of anyone at my level."

"And will remain so until clients start dropping you in support of Ethan when he calls them. You were on the fast track because of your connection to Mr. Settlers. Without him, you're just another associate."

"So, they aren't going to promote you because you refused to marry that asshole?" Dani asked, peering at me over her beer, her long tresses pulled back.

"Without him, they think my clients will exit, and I don't have a big gun in my portfolio," I mumbled into my hand, my head resting on my knuckles.

The tabletop smelled of stale beer and fries. A sticky substance irritated my hand, but I didn't have the willpower to lift my head or hands.

"Is that legal?" Corrine asked.

Corrine's dark brown eyes glared at Victoria, a lawyer. Corrine left her drink untouched as she pondered our conversation. Her tight curls framed her face.

Victoria sighed. "Technically, yes, without seeing your work contract."

Victoria shot me a sympathetic smile, her dark eyes full of compassion. She had her own history with a petty man, except she'd married him when she was eighteen and divorced him at twenty-five.

"Clients have requirements to invest with the company, and the company likely has set benchmarks for promotions. If they have real reason to believe there will be an exodus of clients, they can say she's not meeting a requirement. If she's required to have a client with a portfolio as large as the Settlers' would be, with him making it clear he's not signing with her and she doesn't have another one ready to go, she doesn't meet the requirement. She'd need to set up another client of the same level with guarantees that they signed."

"Do you have anyone lined up?" Maggie asked.

Maggie's aqua eyes bounced around the table, taking in everyone's reaction. Her soft blond locks rested below her shoulders.

I rocked my forehead back and forth on my hands. "I don't know," I mumbled.

"I have friends," Maggie started and then tilted her head. "Acquaintances . . . I can get you in touch with. I can talk with my financial advisor about moving some funds."

I offered her a wry smile. "Let's not mix our friendship with money."

She narrowed her hawkish eyes at me. She'd been my best friend since grade school when we met in dance. We both only made it through one year of ballet, neither of us having grace, but we maintained our friendship. Her childhood was worthy of nineties talk shows, between her mom's over-a-dozen fiancés, half dozen she married and divorced, and all the chaos they brought.

"At least not yet," I said. "I'm doing okay."

She rolled her eyes but dropped it, for now. Nothing with Maggie was ever dropped.

"Did you make the list of all your clients?" Trina asked.

"Yeah," I said.

"And, how many do you think will jump because of Ethan?"

"About a quarter could, he has some contact with them."

"Is that good or bad?" Trina asked.

"My newest ones don't have connections to him. A few of my first ones I met at events with Ethan, so I flagged as possible. He didn't introduce us, but they run in his circles. Dicks might side with pricks.

I have two who were direct referrals from him and expect them to leave this week. I already started prepping the paperwork."

"How much of a hit will you take?" Maggie asked. She was the CEO of a media company and always wanted the bottom line.

"That quarter amounts to about ten percent of my total portfolio."

"What the fuck?" Trina barked. "They're pulling all this shit over ten percent. You'll make that back in no time. You just signed a big contract."

I sighed into my hands. The client I signed was my biggest so far, but not quite Settlers big.

"Trina, they're past the point of logical argument. We don't know what Ethan said to them, or if they actually know the impact this will cause. They just know they lost the Settlers, which is probably equivalent to half of what she has now," Maggie said.

"Thanks," I groaned, even though she wasn't far off the mark.

Maggie ran a hand over my head. "Sorry, Mina, I didn't mean . . ."

"It's okay. Math is math. Money is money. Fucked is fucked, and I'm fucked. I just lost a ton of traction. My career is set back, if not derailed, at this firm. If I go to a different house, I can't take my clients unless they ask to resign with me. I can't notify them."

"What type of bullshit is that?" Trina whirled around to glare at Victoria.

"Sorry we're late." Gina's voice sounded behind me.

Chairs scraped against the floor as my five friends made room for my three coworkers who were joining the pity party.

"Who are you and what side do you have in this?" Trina demanded.

"Trin, be nice to start." Dani warned her. "Welcome."

"Hi," Gina said with a chuckle. She patted my shoulder. "I work with Mina. I'm a junior partner at the company."

"A junior partner, huh?" Trina pushed.

"Gina is awesome," I said, sitting up and giving Trina a death stare before smiling at Gina. Her curly brown hair was pulled back into a half pony. Her red suit dress showed off her toned arms, the color complementing her brown skin. "Her portfolio is massive. She should be a partner soon. She's not friends with Trevor."

Gina made a face before offering a smile. "There are three partners and two junior partners, so far." She nudged my shoulder and winked at me. At least I had her vote.

"I'm Raquel," Raquel said, her black bob highlighting her high cheekbones. "I'm a financial specialist like Mina."

"I'm Martin. I'm an associate."

Martin wore khakis and a button-down dress shirt. His trim brown hair framed his square face. Fresh out of college, he worked with a mentor on all his clients.

"What does that mean?" Dani asked, her hazel eyes perusing over him.

"He's a new hire," Raquel said. "Associate, advisor, and then analyst."

"So, what do you think of this mess?" Trina asked.

"I think Trevor and Ethan are friends," Raquel said, blushing when Martin stared at her.

"They are?" I asked.

Trevor had never been around the apartment or attended any party that I hadn't invited the rest of the office to.

"They've golfed together," Gina said. "I saw them when I took a client out."

"Shit," I said, my head thudding back down to my hands. I knew nothing about Ethan.

"Does Trevor get a say in who the next partner is?" Dani asked.

"He's a junior partner," Gina said. "All partners must agree on promotions. It can get complicated. But Trevor and mine are more ceremonial than meaningful. We can vote, but we are given 'guidance.'"

"So none of the others could be upset about Ethan?" Trina asked hopefully.

"I'd think they'd be concerned. His account is massive and would be great for the company," Gina said, her brown eyes soft as she smiled at me. "However, I don't think they'd be as concerned with the other clients dropping. If Mina could hook another big client or two, Trevor could probably be pressured into agreeing."

"What about Jack?" Trina asked. Her eyes bulged, and she bit her lip after mumbling sorry.

His name sent a wave of heat through my stomach and heated my cheeks. The hotel room flashed in my mind but was chased by my antics at the bar.

Trina smirked as I shifted in my seat. I imagined a little red laser dot on her forehead. Her smirk grew.

"Jack?" Dani asked. "Jack who?"

Maggie furrowed her brow, tapping the rim of her glass with her pointer finger. "Jack from high school? Jack Wolfe? Ethan's one-time best friend who now despises him, Jack? Jack who went to help her Saturday?"

Trina tapped her nose. "That's the one!"

"Trin," I growled.

She sipped her mojito to hide her smile.

"Oh, that *Jack*. Tell me more." Dani perched her chin on her hands. Dani and I met in college at UW-Madison. We weren't roommates until my sophomore year, but we had our first class together my freshman year.

"There's nothing to tell, really," I said and kicked Trina under the table. She stuck her tongue out in response. "Ethan, Jack, and I were classmates. Ethan and Jack were best friends until junior year. I don't know what happened, but Ethan said it was a misunderstanding. Jack despises Ethan."

They didn't need to know Jack and I had been friends too until Jack went silent. It'd only encourage whatever nonsense Trina was trying to spin. Sure, he'd given me a ride and helped me at the bar, but it was to spite Ethan. I'd been nothing to him since junior year.

"Is his business as enticing as Ethan's?" Corrine asked. "Would it match the loss?"

"He's Ethan's top competitor," Trina said.

"So, sign him," Corrine said. "He'd probably do it just to spite Ethan."

"No," I said, shaking my head, letting pride triumph. "I don't want my promotion tied up with something related to Ethan, even if it is hatred. I don't want to owe my promotion to someone."

"Then what are you going to do?" Dani asked.

I shrugged and whimpered.

The waiter brought over a martini and placed it in front of me. "Vodka martini for you, ma'am," he said.

"She didn't order that," Victoria said, pointing a finger at the drink and then me.

Trina slipped her hand over the top as if I would take a drink from a random beverage from a stranger.

"Compliments of an admirer," he said, stepping back.

"Did this admirer touch it?" Maggie asked, sliding it away from me.

Gotta love the support.

"No, directly from the bar," he said and nodded toward the bartender.

Victoria turned her gaze, her warm tan cheeks reddening. She nodded toward the drink and then gave the bartender a questioning look.

He gave her a thumbs-up and a wink.

"What was that?" Maggie asked, her eyes dancing between the two.

"What was what?" Victoria asked. Then she turned to me. "It's safe."

"Do you know the bartender?" Maggie asked, swiveling in her chair to get a better look. She didn't try to hide her outright perusal.

Victoria tossed her drink's umbrella at Maggie's head, hitting her squarely. "Stop it."

"Oh, what is going on?" Maggie asked, rubbing her hands together as she turned around with a wicked grin.

"Someone sent Mina a drink," Victoria said.

"You don't say," Maggie drawled. "We've cleared the safety of the drink. So, what's with you and the bartender?"

"Nothing," Victoria said with a blasé face, but her mouth twitched with the lie.

"This is Victoria's favorite bar," Corrine said. "She comes here after work a lot. She normally sits at the bar for a drink each night before going home. She's buddy-buddy with the bartender and the regulars. All her dates pass through here at some point."

"How do you know this?" Trina demanded.

"District Office is in the building next to hers," Corrine said. "When my meetings run late, and we're leaving at the same time, I've come with her a time or two."

"Oh," Trina said, and then, with a pout, added, "Why weren't we invited?"

"Because we work around the block and you don't," Corrine said. "However, you are welcome to join us anytime."

"What time?" Trina asked.

"Whenever Victoria leaves the office." Corrine smiled.

"Oh, so half past never," Trina said and ducked when Victoria went to hit her.

"Pot, Kettle," Victoria groused.

"Ladies." Dani chided them. "Back to the drink delivered to Mina."

The nine of us turned and scanned the bar teeming with people.

"Does anyone see Ethan?" I whispered.

"Nope, I made sure before we came in," Victoria said. "I also showed Lincoln a picture of him as a heads-up. He won't be admitted."

"Lincoln?" I asked.

"Bartender," Corrine answered.

Appreciation warmed me that she thought to block Ethan.

"I didn't know you like vodka martinis," Maggie said, turning to catch my eye. "You normally drink lighter."

Vodka. Duh. Shit.

I cursed under my breath and slid down my seat so my head rested on the back of the chair. An unexpected but delightful tingle shimmied down my spine. Before I even realized it, my eyes swept across the packed bar, a niggle of something building in my chest. To see him. That he thought of me. Wanted to acknowledge me. Even after all that had happened. I swallowed.

Throngs of people milled together at the bar and tables. A blur of faces and suits. As I darted my gaze between the business professionals, warmth grew in my belly. Was he not here? Had he sent it and left? On my third glance around, I was practically turned around in my seat, hope dimming in my chest.

"What is this?" Dani asked, flicking a finger at me.

"She knows who." Maggie grinned.

"Who's it from?" Victoria pressed.

I locked eyes with Trina and saw the Cheshire smile on her face. I barely shook my head at her. She snorted a laugh and took a sip of her beverage.

"Come on, Mina," Trina said, standing up and reaching for my arm.

"No, I don't want to leave. I haven't even started my drink yet," I whined.

"I need to pee," she said.

"Then go pee," I retorted, trying to pry her fingers off.

"Nope, girl code says you have to go with me." She dug her nails in deeper.

"Any of us can go with you," Corrine said, standing to join us. "I have to use the restroom myself. I'll go with you so Mina can down her drink."

"No," Trina snapped and then sighed. "No, sorry, Corrine. I need Mina," she said and made some face I couldn't see.

Corrine's face lit up in understanding. "Never mind, I'll wait until you two get back."

Great. Just great.

Trina tugged me through the throngs of people. Even without being drunk, I bumped into multiple people, offering blanket apologies as I followed her.

"What do you want?" I hissed as we neared the bathroom.

"To pee," she said and tugged me into the bathroom.

Since I was there, I decided to use it also.

As I washed up, I met her eyes in the mirror. "Okay, what's going on?"

"We both know it's Jack," she said, a smile covering her face.

"So," I groaned.

"Save the groaning for him," she said.

I splashed water at her, and she reciprocated.

"Bitch." I laughed and cupped my hands to gather more water.

"Don't you dare," she said.

"Or what?"

Trina backed up to the door, her finger hanging in the air between us as a warning.

She yanked the door open and darted outside.

I dropped the water back in the sink and dried my hands. Exiting the bathroom, I didn't see Trina.

As I wove back through the crowd, I felt a presence to my left and smelled sandalwood. My heart skipped a beat.

"Mina." Jack's voice cut through the hum of people.

My center tightened, and I swallowed.

He stood with a group of people in suits as expensive as my first car. Without looking at them, he moved to stand next to me. Of course, my stomach had to flutter at that moment. At least this time I wasn't filled with vodka and not-a-bride tears.

"Work?" I asked and nodded toward the group.

"Wrapped up a meeting with a client, and we decided to celebrate," he said.

He gently directed my elbow so I was out of the walkway, allowing several people to squeeze past us. I had to step closer to him in the tight corridor so I wasn't on top of a stranger.

"Did you send a drink?"

A grin tugged on his lips. "I know how much you like vodka."

"Thanks." I fought my own grin. Instead of embarrassment, something else warmed inside me.

"Are you here on business?" he asked, nodding to the group now staring at us.

"No," I sighed and turned so my back was to them. They had turned into a table of piranhas waiting for the strike. "It's my friends."

"I wanted to check in," he said. His concerned blue eyes canvassed my face. "I wasn't sure the best way to but saw you tonight."

"I'm fine, you don't have to worry. Thanks though," I said, a blush creeping up my neck.

His eyes drew together in confusion.

"I appreciate you not letting me make a complete fool of myself."

He smirked and shrugged.

A couple bumped past us, knocking us closer together. My mouth dried as heat scorched my face. He reached a hand out to support my elbow. His nearness stirred something in me, curling up from my core, but my brain, ever the buzzkill, focused on the why.

It wasn't from care.

I knew the real reason he was checking on me had to do with his relationship with Ethan. I didn't understand his play though. Ethan and I were done. Broken up. Unless he was trying to make Ethan uneasy about getting secrets from me. I licked my lips to hide my smirk. That would definitely freak Ethan out. That could be fun, even if mean.

"Mina, we're going to head out," Gina said behind me, startling me and interrupting my thoughts.

I turned to see Raquel and Martin putting their jackets on.

"Thanks for coming," I said and hugged her.

"I'll see you tomorrow. You'll figure it out," she said with a tight smile.

Her eyes flicked to Jack. She gave an approving nod and winked at me.

"Thanks," I said half-heartedly.

With a lingering look at Jack and then a raised eyebrow at me, she followed Martin toward the exit.

"Figure what out?" he asked once Gina was out of earshot.

"Oh, a work situation," I said, waving off his concern—and him learning they thought he could be my client.

"Mina," Trina said behind me. I could hear the smirk in her voice.

"Yeah," I asked, looking at her over my shoulder.

"Some of the girls are going to head out too," Trina said and looked over my head to Jack. "You can come sit with us if you'd like. We have plenty of space."

I shot her daggers with my eyes and mouthed, "I'm going to kill you."

Jack shifted beside me, leaning so his mouth was next to me so Trina couldn't hear him. "You okay with that?"

His warm breath sent shivers down my neck to my center.

"It's fine," I gritted out.

Trina smirked.

"But we don't want to take you away from your business meeting," I said.

Avoiding meeting his gaze, I looked toward his group that didn't seem to miss him as they laughed at another joke while clearly well past the first or second drink.

"I promised to be more clear I don't hate you," he whispered again, my insides melting.

"That's not . . ." I started but stopped.

"Is that Maggie Peterson?" he asked, looking at the table.

I didn't want to admit it, but a spike of jealousy sliced through my heart, and I felt like I was back in high school watching Jack hop between girlfriends. And Maggie was perfection.

"It is." I confirmed.

"You two were best friends in high school. It's great you're still friends," he said and sipped his whiskey.

"You remember that they were friends?" Trina asked.

"Why wouldn't I?" he asked.

"It was a long time ago."

"It wasn't eighty years ago."

Placing his hand at the small of my back, he applied gentle pressure and guided me to walk through the narrow lane.

Each step, I was aware of his touch. The touch sent delightful tingles through me. What the fuck was wrong with me? It was a hand at my back, not . . . Heat burst on my cheeks, and again, I was thankful for the dim lighting.

Victoria had shifted to the bar, where she was laughing with the bartender Lincoln and a few patrons. Their familiarity with each other was obvious.

Dani and Corrine stood, gathering their items.

"Let's do a movie night Friday or Saturday," Dani said, pulling me into a hug. "A girls' night with an action movie, popcorn, pizza, candy, cookies. You know, the essentials."

"Sounds great," I said. "We can do it at my place."

"I'm in." Corrine pulled me into a hug. "Call me, anytime. He was a loser."

"Thank you," I said, my chin wobbly.

"He's not worth you," she whispered, still hugging me tight.

"Jack," Maggie said, lifting her beer to him.

"Maggie," he said with a nod.

I sat back in my chair. Trina reclaimed the spot to my left while Jack sat to my right. My nerves buzzed with his closeness, but I fixed my gaze on the trickle of condensation on the glass.

"You can say it's too soon," Maggie said, placing her beer down and clasping her hands together on the table. This was her "I'm going to say something unpleasant, but it's important" pose.

"Give it to me," I said. With luck, she'd figured out my client situation and had a surefire way to get a bunch of new clients.

"What about your stuff at his apartment?" she asked.

Not the reality check I expected.

I groaned and slumped back in my chair. I hadn't thought about it. I had my apartment, but I had a good deal of stuff at his place since I was there two to three nights a week. It had just been there, accumulating over the years. I hadn't thought about it.

"Do you have a key?" Jack asked.

"Yeah, but there's a doorman, and he probably changed the locks. Would it be considered breaking and entering?" I asked. "I'm not on the lease."

The other three shrugged.

"What about Aiden?" Jack asked and cleared his throat.

"What about him?" Trina asked.

"Can you ask him to let you in?"

I twisted my fingers together, my thumb landing where my ring had been. I took it off after Ethan had left, not wanting the reminder. My finger didn't miss the ring, but my nervous habits still went to spin it.

"He's pretty decent," Trina said, rocking her head back and forth.

"Aiden isn't bad," Maggie agreed. "He punched Ethan and started shoving him. Their dad had to break it up."

"He what?" I sputtered, staring at Trina.

"Sorry, a lot happened that night. And the next morning. I forgot to tell you."

The three stared at me.

"Fine," I groaned and pulled out my phone.

ME: Hi Aiden.

"So, Jack," Maggie drawled.

My eyes flicked up to her.

Her red lips twitched up in a smirk. "Does Mina have you to thank for the beverage?"

Jack smiled. "It's a recent favorite." His warm gaze found me, and my insides melted.

"How's the spouse, fiancée, dating-friend?" Maggie sipped her beverage. Her aqua eyes lasered in on him.

"Pardon?" His eyebrow shot up.

"Your significant other . . . Do you have one?"

My eyes almost rolled to the back of my head. Subtlety was an art Maggie knew but didn't often care to employ.

"I'm single," Jack said, earning a wicked smile from Maggie but sending a buzzing feeling throughout me.

Every part of my body wanted to respond, but my mind just froze around the fact he was single. Available. Single.

My phone dinged, saving me from the conversation. Aiden's face flashed next to a text box, sobering me. I was reacting to Jack being single while I still had to deal with my ex.

AIDEN: MINA! I was afraid to reach out. I am so sorry about my dickhead of a brother.

ME: I have a favor to ask.

AIDEN: Sure, what is it?

ME: I need to get my stuff from Ethan's apartment.

Three dots danced for an eternity, but it was really about fifteen seconds.

AIDEN: Can you come tomorrow at 3PM?

ME: Will he be there?

AIDEN: He should be running then. I'm meeting him to discuss what a fucker he is. He had to 'fit me in' then.

ME: Can you promise he won't show up?

AIDEN: I'd like to, but I can't.

My stomach tightened, but he was being so nice even being willing.

ME: Okay, 3PM. I'll probably bring a friend with me.

AIDEN: Good idea.

"Aiden says he'll meet me tomorrow to do it," I said, placing my phone down.

My stomach had turned sour and my mouth dry. The food from earlier no longer wanted to stay down.

"Do you want me to go with you?" Trina asked, placing her hand on mine.

"Can you?" Hope bloomed in my chest.

"What time?" She turned her phone on and opened her calendar.

"Three p.m.," I said.

"Three?" she asked, her voice panicked. She grimaced as she scrolled.

"Why, does that not work?" I asked, matching her tone. The previous hope wilted into a hard ache.

"I have a meeting then. I'll try to move it," she said, typing away on her phone. "Don't worry."

"I have a meeting with a client then," Maggie said with her calendar open. "Can you move it to one p.m. or five p.m.?"

"No, he's timing to coincide with Ethan's run so I can hopefully get in and out without seeing him."

I'd go alone. I'd lived there for how long . . . It'd be okay. A curl of acid stirred my stomach more.

"I can go with you," Jack said, staring at me.

He sipped his whiskey, keeping his blue eyes focused on me.

Something twisted in my chest.

I stared at him. Was he trying to get into Ethan's apartment? Trying to get under his skin? It wasn't a good idea. Ethan could be ruthless if he felt threatened. But considering our wedding, he was ruthless without provocation. Ethan would be unhinged trying to figure out our connection.

"You don't have a meeting?" I asked skeptically.

"Nope," he said, even though his phone was tucked inside his pocket.

"No, I can't ask that of you." I shook my head after logic and reason caught up. I'd just be starting a fire with Ethan. "If Trina can't move her meeting, I'll just go. Aiden will be there."

Trina and Maggie shared a look.

"What?" I asked.

They both turned their gazes to Jack. My stomach flipped. Something unspoken had been decided between them, about me. About Jack.

"You sure you can make it?" Trina asked, setting her phone down with her email still open and unsent.

"Yes."

"No," I said at the same time. "He has other stuff to do."

I glared at Trina, willing her to shut up.

She ignored me, continuing to look at Jack. "You're not going to let her down, are you?"

"Trina," I hissed.

"I promise I will be there." Jack met Trina's gaze.

Trina looked at me, her amber eyes mischievous but also relieved. "Mina, if Jack shows up, Ethan will be more prone to fighting with him than trying to manipulate you."

"Hey," I shouted, drawing attention from the nearby table. I smiled and waved at them until they looked away.

"I agree with Trina," Maggie said, sliding her phone into her purse.

Their decision was made. Their side picked and it wasn't mine.

I gulped, refusing to look at Jack. "Ethan won't manipulate me."

Trina and Maggie scoffed, but Jack stared at me blankly. I hated that expression. That granite fortress of nothingness. It could mean anything, but I attributed it to the fact that he agreed with them.

"Jack coming will only rile Ethan up. Start shit. Ethan will take it as an attack. He'll likely follow through with my other clients."

"What's that?" Jack asked. Despite his fortress, his jaw ticked and anger burned in his eyes.

Shit. Double dog shit.

"He's threatening to get her clients to leave her," Trina said.

I shot daggers at Trina, but she only smiled.

"Is he?" Jack asked, his voice barely a whisper.

"It doesn't matter. I've done the math."

"So he is," Jack said with a nod.

"I don't need help," I said, looking at all three of them. "I can handle this."

"You can handle your clients. I've heard you're very skilled."

"You heard about me?" I asked, thankful for the dim light as my cheeks stained red.

"You're in the business of making other people more money. I've heard about your skills," Jack said.

"So, Trevor can be stopped." Trina rubbed her hands. "If others are talking about you, then it's only a matter of time and Trevor can suck rocks."

I rolled my eyes and smiled.

"Mina," Maggie said, drawing my attention. "You can handle business. You can handle Ethan. Let Jack go with you. If Ethan doesn't show up, no worries. If he does, he'll be blindsided by seeing Jack. He's going to fight you either way. Might as well get your stuff in peace and fight him from your turf."

I sighed and took a large sip of my martini.

"Tomorrow at three," Jack said.

## MAY 20TH

## MINA

Ethan's building looked just the same, a large modern structure with an exterior of windows, providing the inhabitants unobstructed views of Lake Michigan. For the past several years, I'd entered without thought. Now I felt like an invading army, coming to steal back my property.

"You okay?" Jack asked, startling me as he came up from behind.

He wore black suit pants, forgoing the jacket, a white dress shirt, and a blue tie striped in darker blue and gold.

He handed me a coffee.

"What's this?" I asked, sniffing it.

"Mint mocha, extra shot," he said before sipping his, most likely, black coffee.

"Mmm, my favorite," I said, taking the cup.

He smiled and my stomach fluttered.

How did he always remember the details? It's probably what helped him be successful in business, especially since he didn't have his father's name to start from as Ethan did. He had been Ethan's best friend for years, and the three of us and Jack's girlfriends always hung out. I guess some things were retained, I reminded myself, so I wouldn't add more importance to his gesture than I should. Even if a small part of me wanted to.

The daytime doorman stood at the front, eyeing us up as Jack's gaze took in the entrance.

"Has Ethan already left?" Jack asked, looking toward the green space between the complex and the lake.

"I stayed in my car until he disappeared from view."

"How much time do we have?"

I checked my watch. 2:58. "He runs for ten miles, so about forty-five to fifty minutes."

Aiden pulled up at exactly three p.m., his silver Mercedes gleaming in the bright sunlight. In contrast to Ethan, he didn't wear a jacket unless with his dad. Still, his dress pants and button-down were probably a rent payment.

"Mina," he said with a smile, but it fell when he saw Jack. "Jack? What are you doing here?" Aiden's gaze bounced between the two of us. Something of a smirk flickered across his lips. "Is something going on?"

"It's a long story," I said. "But Trina and Maggie nominated him to be here."

Aiden's eyebrow inched up, his blue eyes finding Jack's eyes. "I didn't know you two were friends again."

Jack shrugged. "We've known each other since we were kids. Same as you."

Yet, I had never had a crush on Aiden. I blinked at that thought. Three minutes of standing next to him had barely passed, and my mind was already spinning into dangerous lands, taking a sweet gesture from Jack and twisting it into something it wasn't.

Aiden's eyes slid to me, and I realized what he must have been thinking or that he was a mind reader.

"Aiden, I ran into Jack the day I left the wedding. Yesterday, he was checking on me . . ."

Aiden cracked a smile, his eyes sparkling as he wrapped me into a hug. "Mina, it's all good. I'm just glad you're moving forward. Ethan is going to be livid."

"I can hear your smile," I said, hugging him back.

"My brother, king of everything, who does everything he can to control and manipulate a situation, can't ban you from talking to Jack again," he said.

"Ban me again?" I asked. "What are you talking about?"

He stiffened. A silent, tense moment passed.

"Ethan's an ass," Aiden murmured into my ear. "People he doesn't like don't get to be in his sphere. You were in his sphere."

"Meaning what?" I asked, pushing back to meet his eyes.

"Meaning, you'd probably have more clients if Ethan didn't interfere." He winked.

I stared at him. It didn't make sense. "Are you saying Ethan wouldn't let people sign with me?"

"No, he wouldn't be so open, but let's just say people who aren't in his graces wouldn't try to sign with you."

"Are you saying he pissed on me and marked me as his? That male macho shit?"

"Sorry, business still isn't fair for women. But, now that you're broken up and you're buddy-buddy with Jack . . ." he said, his voice trailing as he smiled at me.

"I . . ." I knew what he was saying, but I didn't like it. I didn't want my success tied to anyone. I could make my own contacts.

"Leave her alone," Jack said. "Let's get upstairs."

Jack picked up the suitcase I brought.

Aiden hooked his arm around my shoulder and guided us to the door.

"Mr. Aiden," the doorman said, his thin smile almost a sneer. His white hair was gelled back to give it as much volume as possible.

"George," he said, his voice bored.

"Is Mr. Settlers expecting you?" George asked, his frame in front of the door.

Aiden smiled, a brittle smile with a wicked gleam in his eyes. "I'm also Mr. Settlers. I'm headed up to our family's apartment." Aiden leaned back on his heels and stared down his nose.

George's smile flattened, his wrinkles bunching around his lips. "Mr. Settlers was clear, no visitors while he was out."

Shit. He was expecting us.

"I'm not a visitor. It's a family place."

"George, is it?" Jack asked, his charming smile plastered on his face looking genuine, though I doubted it was.

George's eyes darted to Jack, moving up and down, taking him in. "And you are?"

Jack nodded and pulled out his phone. "Just confirming the correct name."

George frowned at him and folded his arms over his chest.

Jack hit the speaker button on his phone. One ring sounded before an elderly, winded male voice answered. "Jack, I'm on the treadmill. Can I call you back?"

"This will be short, Milton," Jack said, lifting his eyes to George, whose eyes widened in recognition, his mouth agape. "I need access to the Preston Building."

"You have it," Milton huffed back.

Jack smiled at George. "George, is that enough permission?"

"Yes, sir," George sputtered and opened the door.

We walked in and strode to the elevator, George leading the charge.

"Sir," George sputtered.

Jack cut his eyes to him. No malice or ill will shone back. "It's fine, George. You were following the directions of a blow bag."

The door slid closed with the three of us in the elevator and George watching us from the foyer.

"He's going to call Ethan," Aiden said, running a hand through his hair.

"Yep." Jack confirmed. "Mina, we'll have company."

We'd have five, ten minutes max before he arrived. I drummed my fingers at my side, watching the floor numbers tick by.

"Does your family really own the apartment?" I asked Aiden.

"Yes, Ethan calls it his, but it's one of the family's. It was our dad's before he met Mom. Obviously, Ethan gutted it to make it modern."

"So if you take us inside, you're not really breaking and entering?" I asked, my throat thick, realizing the trouble I could bring to them.

He laughed. "Ethan will pretend we are, but don't worry."

Of course I was going to worry.

The apartment was spotless, as usual. The dark mahogany floors had white rugs strategically placed. Every piece of furniture was precisely as it should be. The room looked like a magazine set, not a lived-in place. Not even hollowness filled me as I took in the space that never felt like mine.

"Do you know where your stuff is?" Aiden asked, leaning against the wall by the door as if to provide a buffer for when Ethan burst in.

"Unless he moved it. You know how particular he is about appearances."

Aiden snorted a laugh and said, "At least this should make it easier."

The kitchen was void of my belongings. Ethan didn't like my quote mugs for morning coffee, so they resided at my apartment. The only one I'd ever brought, "Winning with coffee," he'd tossed in the garbage, claiming it was old and faded. A smile flicked on my lips, chasing my frown when I thought of the cup. The cup sat in my cupboard now. It had been a St. Nick's gift from Jack after our debate tournament, and my passionate and caffeinated performance won. Otherwise, we used Ethan's white porcelain bowls and cups, or we typically ate meals out instead of cooking.

My first stop was the front closet, where I withdrew two jackets, a winter one for work still in the dry cleaner's zipper bag. The other was a spring and early summer jacket.

Aiden reached out to collect them.

Jack stared around the apartment, his expression unreadable. "Are any of the decorations yours?"

"No, Ethan had a designer put together this room. When I wanted more blankets, he went through him. My stuff should be in the bedroom."

"I thought . . ." Aiden started but shook his head and finished. "I thought you had more stuff here."

"So did I," I mumbled, thinking about how much of my life I'd spent in the apartment. With or without me, it'd appear the same. Even the scent was designer and specific to the place.

Jack strode behind me, his eyes scanning the rooms, but I felt him watch me when I looked away. He leaned against the doorframe and folded his arms.

I pulled open my underclothes drawer, half expecting to find items belonging to Tiffany sprinkled in, but only my clothes lay inside. I tossed them in the suitcase. I had three other drawers, sparsely populated with some pajamas and workout clothes.

The bathroom was spotless, as always. My toothbrush sat in the holder next to his. My skincare was already prepped and ready at home, still packed for the honeymoon. I tossed my toothbrush in the trash and plucked my shampoo and conditioner, again leaving little signs I'd been there.

The closet housed several of my suits and shoes. This was the bulk of my stuff. I carried an armful out, thinking I had a chance of getting out before Ethan showed up.

Until his voice rocketed from the front room.

I closed my eyes and licked my lips, bowing my head to avoid Jack's stare and the pounding footsteps heading our way.

"What the fuck are you doing?" Ethan roared. "Get the fuck out of my way."

"You can talk to her from here," Jack said.

"This is my fucking apartment. I'll call the fucking cops," Ethan retorted. "You are trespassing."

"Go ahead," Jack said as if granting a child permission to have a cookie.

I came out with the second and last armful of suits. Ethan's eyes darted to mine, wild and angry.

"Mina, we need to talk, sweetie," Ethan said.

I turned to get my shoes, but Ethan shoved Jack.

"Get the fuck out of my place!"

Jack dug his feet into the ground.

Ethan yelled, "I'll fucking kick your ass."

"You can try," Jack said.

Ethan pulled his left arm back and went to punch Jack's face, but Jack easily dodged it and moved to better block the door.

Ethan shoved him again and went to punch him when Aiden came up behind him and yanked his arms back.

"Ethan, enough." Aiden warned him.

"This is breaking and entering! Stealing!"

"It's my stuff," I said, finally speaking to him as I went to retrieve my shoes.

"Sweetie, it'll never happen again. I'm sorry," Ethan said.

I snorted. My eyes blurred as I gathered the shoes into a bag. My heart clenched at the lie.

"I was pissed. I was drunk. I wasn't thinking," he continued.

"Pissed?" I barked. "Pissed at me?" I splayed my hands over my chest.

He let out a hard breath. His face contorted as he tried to think of a response. A lie. A cover. Something that could justify his betrayal.

"Was it because I went to the client meeting?" I offered.

His eyes shot up to mine, fear and truth shining bright. I shook my head. How many times had he done it before? Lead swam in my veins. I didn't want to ask. I didn't want to know the truth.

"I'm so sorry. It'll never happen again. Please forgive me," Ethan pleaded while tugging against Aiden's restraint.

I didn't bother to respond. I didn't forgive him. I cared, but I cared more that I'd escaped a marriage with him.

"Mina," Ethan pleaded. "Please."

I looked back and found all three of them staring at me. Jack narrowed his eyes as he searched my face.

"Do you need help reaching anything?" he asked, nodding toward the closet.

Jack gave Ethan a look before walking toward the bed. He rolled up his sleeves, watching me.

"No," I said and heard what they saw.

My voice was flat and lifeless. I hauled my bag of shoes to the suitcase.

"Don't you fucking touch anything in this house," Ethan yelled, pulling free to swing at Jack, but Aiden grabbed him again.

Jack remained silent and stared at Ethan.

Ethan snarled, "Dude, I know you had the hots for Mina in high school, but she was in love with me. She still loves me. We're going to fix this. You're just going to lose again."

I stilled. My eyes darted to Jack's. What the fuck? Was that true? *Both* Ethan and Trina thought he had a crush on me? The idea spun in my mind, stirring up feelings I shouldn't feel in my ex's bedroom. Is that why they had the final fight? Or was Ethan just throwing wild accusations out?

"I did have a crush on Mina in high school," Jack said, confirming Ethan's words and settling hot in my stomach. He shrugged at me with a half smile. "She also did love you, but I don't think she likes you anymore."

"Shut the fuck up," Ethan yelled, spittle flying from his mouth. His face was beet red, and a vein bulged in his temple.

"I didn't know that," I whispered before I realized I'd spoken.

The three gave me an incredulous look.

Then Aiden chuckled, breaking the silence.

"So what, now you're interested in him?" Ethan mocked.

I looked back at Ethan. The arrogance in his eyes dimmed the longer I stared at him, and fear edged in. His eyes widened, and his nostrils flared as his gaze bounced between us.

"I'll fucking destroy your career," Ethan snarled at me, his eyes now dark and cold.

"You're already trying," I said. "You called Trevor."

"He called me," Ethan retorted.

"Hm," I said.

I pinched my lips up in contemplation so he couldn't see the surprise. That aligned with what Gina had said, but I still wasn't sure how I'd missed it.

"I know you're also calling clients of mine that you know about," I added.

"What the fuck?" Aiden yelled and raised his knee to Ethan's butt. "You fucking asshole."

"Mina, we'll be great together," Ethan pleaded. "We'll fix this, make us stronger."

"Stronger? You want to micromanage my career. You're right, about twenty-five percent of my clients have connections to you. I'll probably lose them. I've calculated the loss I'll endure, but I've also come to understand you're limiting others from signing with me."

Ethan gasped. "What are you talking about?" he asked, slowly averting his eyes.

"I'll face setbacks in my career. You'll try to torpedo me from moving forward. You'll make it harder," I said, nodding at him. "But I'm moving on from you."

"You think you can just move on that easily?"

"My career has nothing to do with you. I've worked hard to draw that line early on." Thankfully.

"There's more to life than a career. No one will love you like I do. We are meant to be together. We are it for each other."

Jack snorted in disagreement. The sound shattered something in me. The hate and anger eased out of me and left something of relief in my veins.

I locked eyes with Jack, who cocked his eyebrow at me. An idea hatched as I stared at his Nordic-blue eyes burning with emotion. All I learned in the last week about our past spun in my head. Jack was a player. He jumped between women. He'd had only one serious girlfriend, but they'd broken up. He was obviously kind but had a short attention span. Just another notch.

Ethan was going to go after me with his full force. Like he always did with Jack. I knew a way to throw him off his game. Make him wonder. Set doubt and fear in. Give Jack extra fuel.

I took a step toward Jack.

"Mina," Ethan growled.

My gaze traveled from Jack's eyes to his mouth. His breath hitched, and I bit my lip. My gaze jumped back up to him, a smile flicked across my lips, and I took another step toward him.

His gaze turned cautious as he watched me. His eyes darkened and tracked to my mouth before returning my stare.

Keeping his gaze, I took another step forward, and my stomach flipped. My brain screamed to stop and reevaluate the situation and hide while my heart and center urged me forward, fueling me with adrenaline and lust.

"Please forgive me," I whispered to Jack.

"Okay?" he whispered back, his brows now furrowed as he watched me.

I wrapped my right hand around his head, pulling him toward me as I stood on my tiptoes to meet his lips. His body stiffened for a moment in surprise before his hands found my waist and anchored me to him. He opened his mouth, naturally pushing his tongue past my lips. I moaned, and he deepened the kiss. Need and want coursed through me. The fire from the weekend came back as an inferno.

Instead of retreating, hiding, I chased it.

I pressed my body into his, heat building between my legs. While my fingers on one hand speared into his hair, I moved my other hand around his neck, bringing us closer together. I felt his hard reaction growing against my center. Heat coiled at my center, and I pushed into it, chasing the feeling.

"MINA!" Ethan's voice echoed against the walls.

I broke the kiss, stilling to meet Jack's eyes, dilated and foggy with lust.

"I have everything I need," I whispered, my voice husky with desire.

Jack swallowed, his eyes hooded. "I'll get the suitcase."

I finally looked over to Aiden and Ethan.

Crocodile tears rimmed Ethan's red eyes. Or maybe they were real as he realized I wasn't coming back. Aiden had a cocky smirk on his face he was trying to hide by biting his lips.

Aiden pulled Ethan back a few steps so I could squeeze past without touching him. Before walking forward, I reached into my pocket and pulled out a small velvet pouch. I pulled out the ring to show them what was inside. After sliding it back in, I tossed it on the pillow that used to be mine.

"Goodbye, Ethan," I said and left without looking at him again.

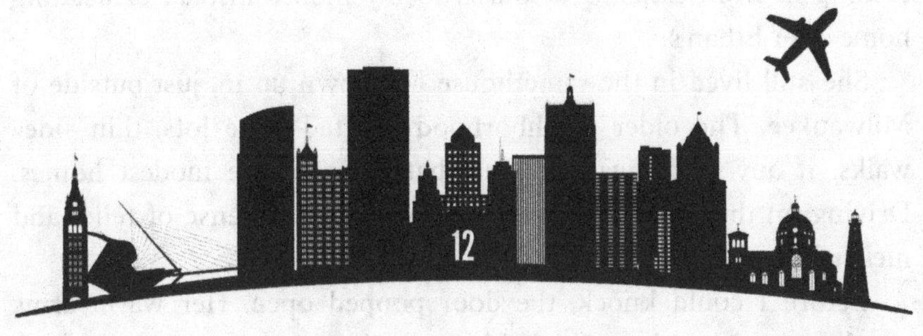


## MAY 20TH

## MINA

Although I invited him over, Jack had a dinner meeting and then a plane to catch for a client meeting in the morning. Probably an excuse to be away from me and my lips. One I completely understood. What the hell had I been thinking? Oh, yeah, I hadn't been. I'd been wound up in spite and lust.

Not sure if I meant to embarrass myself more, feel the sting of a rejection to squelch the burning need in my core, or out of hope, but I offered him dinner when he got back as a thank-you for his help today. His smile had been infectious, and I returned it before realizing it. He said he'd see me next Saturday around five when he got back.

I'm pretty sure that meant I had a thank-you date with Jack. A friend's date? An enemy of enemy date? Fuck. Whatever it meant, I was seeing Jack again unless he backed out. But he'd set a time. If he was backing out, it would have been a "Sure, I'll text you," which means a polite no thanks.

With my blood pressure still sky high, my heart racing, and texts coming in from Ethan, I detoured to my mom's instead of heading home after Ethan's.

She still lived in the same house I'd grown up in, just outside of Milwaukee. The older neighborhood sported large lots, thin sidewalks, if any, and gigantic trees that dwarfed the modest homes. Driving on the familiar narrow streets brought a sense of relief and melancholy.

Before I could knock, the door popped open. Her warm arms enveloped me in a hug. She held me, just rocking for a few minutes. When we separated, her lips quivered, and she patted my face.

"I haven't started dinner yet, but I have cake."

A smile curved my lips. "Cake is always a winner."

As when I was a child, the aroma of lavender and disinfectant tinted the air. A radio sounded in the background. Over the years, she'd removed all traces of my dad, including the room's color, furniture, and carpet. What had once been the sage and taupe of the late nineties became grays, whites, and patterns. The only things that remained were her curio cabinet with her grandma's China and pictures of Trina and me as kids. Any with my dad had been removed, or she'd folded him out of it and reframed it.

"So," Mom started but stopped. Her brows dipped, and she folded her hands in front of her.

"I got my stuff from Ethan's."

She sucked in a breath. "How did it go?"

I shrugged. Emotion caught in my throat, stopping my words.

"Did he show up?"

I nodded.

She sighed. Taking my hand, she led me to the sofa.

"Mina, I'm sorry. This is my fault."

"What?" My startled eyes shot to her.

"I didn't see this coming, and I should have. I encouraged your relationship with him. Took his side."

I offered her a weak smile. "Mom, none of us knew."

"Still . . ." She fiddled with the throw pillow next to her. "I should have seen the signs."

My chest lifted and fell, each breath feeling heavier than the next. I'd avoided the entanglement like she'd had with Dad and the messy divorce. By luck. If I hadn't caught them, I'd be on a honeymoon right now with the cheater instead of piecing my life together. And I wouldn't have plans with Jack . . . or be worried about my career.

"Hey." Trina's voice rang out from the front door. In a flurry, she scurried into the room, still in her suit and her hair in a bun from work. Sitting across from me, she smiled and rubbed her hands. "How'd it go? You tell that prick off?"

"Trina Marie."

Trina waved her off. "We both want to know. She's here because of her reaction to it and needs to process it."

With Trina there, I found strength in my words. "I waited until after I saw him leave to go up."

Mom frowned but didn't interrupt.

"Then Jack and Aiden showed up."

"Jack?" Mom asked. "Jack Wolfe from high school?"

"Yes, him. The one who picked her up from the bar. Maggie and I wanted someone to go with Mina, our schedules were tight, and Jack volunteered."

"What? How?" Mom sputtered.

"Mom, please," Trina said. "Let her finish."

Mom nodded, though she pursed her lips.

"We made it about five minutes before he showed up. He was livid. He was begging me to forgive him, screaming and threatening Jack. And then he threatened me."

"Threatened you?" Mom paled. "If he threatened to hurt you—"

"Well, my career."

"That's a solid threat," Mom said. "What can you do?"

"Continue to sign clients. Build my reputation."

Trina watched me a bit, her eyes narrowed. "So what did you do when he threatened you?"

"I told him I'm moving forward."

"Good for you." Mom patted my hand.

"What did Ethan say in response?" Trina asked. "No way he just said okay."

His words twirled, repeating in my thoughts, their weight stinging my heart. But they were meant to hurt. Meant to manipulate.

"He told me no one would love me like he did. That we were destined for each other."

"What an ass," Mom breathed. "What did you do next?"

The image of kissing Jack flashed in my mind. My body thrummed. Guilt should have come, but instead, a smile flickered across my lips.

"You're blushing?" Trina questioned, circling my face.

I swallowed before looking to my mom.

"What happened?" Mom demanded.

The reality of what I did settled on my skin, cold and hard. I'd kissed Jack in front of Ethan. I'd been completely and utterly unfair to Jack. I'd used him. And Ethan would retaliate.

"Mina?" Trina prodded.

I rubbed my temples. "Something I shouldn't have."

"Is there blood?" Mom asked.

Both Trina and I burst out a laugh. Though the tension didn't ease, my stomach loosened.

"What? It's an honest question. Do I need to get you a lawyer?"

"No," I chuckled.

"Victoria's one anyway. Not sure about criminal, though, but she can refer one." Trina smiled at me.

"No blood. No crime."

"Then what?" Mom asked.

I sucked in a breath and released it in a rush. "I kissed Jack in front of Ethan."

Apparently not what they expected, they both blinked at me, waiting for the truth.

"Wait. For real? On the mouth?" Trina finally asked.

"Where— never mind." I swatted away her retort. "He said he had a crush on me in high school, so when Ethan said no one else would want me like he did, something came loose in me." I buried my head in my hands. "I told you I fucked up. I used Jack."

After an eternity of silence, Trina whispered, "What did Jack do?"

I felt both of them watching me. Sliding my fingers away from my eyes, I croaked, "He kissed me back." And it'd been immediate. No hesitation. Whatever that meant. If anything.

A triumphant smile curled Trina's lips as she slumped back in pride. Mom's face slackened, and a mix of emotion stamped across it.

"Gah, how I'd love to have seen Ethan's face." Trina shook her head.

"Kissed? What does that mean?" Mom asked.

"When two people are attracted to each other—" Trina started and fell to the side laughing when Mom chucked a throw pillow at her.

"I didn't think. Well, not really. It felt so right at the moment. But . . ."

"But what?" Trina sobered. "It's okay."

Mom flinched.

"No, I shouldn't have put Jack in that position. It was unfair. Ethan will target him too."

"Okay? He already hates Jack and targets him. What happened after the kiss?"

"Then we left."

Trina cocked an eyebrow at me.

"Mina," Mom started but stopped. Her mouth moved, but no words came out.

Both Trina and I stared at her expectantly.

"Mina, this was an unfortunate situation. Unfair. It was kind of Jack to help you." Despite her words, she puckered her lips in distaste at putting kind and Jack together in a sentence. "I also support you seeing other people."

A "but" had to be coming.

"But?" Trina offered with a roll of her eyes.

Mom sighed. "Jack isn't permanent. He jumps between women."

Trina shot her a bewildered look. "Yeah, the dude who had the same girlfriend for two years. Who hasn't dated since her."

Mom rolled her eyes.

Trina continued, "And how did you hear this? Jack isn't on public social media."

I glared at Trina. "Keeping tabs?"

Trina shot me a grin. "An enemy of Ethan is always of interest to me."

Of course.

Trina pinned Mom with a hard stare. "Where did you hear that?"

Mom's face paled.

Trina pointed at her. "Was your source"—she cut a grimace my way—"the prick?"

Mom sighed.

Trina chortled. "Yeah, I wouldn't trust that asshole."

"It wasn't just Ethan." Mom worked her lips.

Trina cocked an eyebrow, waiting.

Mom sighed. "Mina brought them up too. He had a new one every week."

"So, that was high school."

Mom looked away. Her lips pressed into a tight line.

"Get it out now," Trina pressed. "It's been in there for over a decade."

Mom shook her head. When her eyes met mine, they were wet with unshed tears. My heart stilled in my chest.

"I saw the looks."

"Looks?" I parroted.

"You two had hearts in your eyes for each other, even with Ethan around. Jack was never permanent. I didn't want him to hurt you like I'd been hurt by your father."

No words came to me. Her truths were too accurate and close to my own.

Trina, though, had words. "Jack dated in high school. Big fucking whoop. Mina dated Ethan the whole time. Not once did Jack try a move. Trust me, I watched . . . and hoped."

"Trina!" I laughed, unable to find enough rage to be mad.

"He respected your boundaries. I follow his business account and am friends with his private account." She turned a glare to Mom. "I know my shit, unlike you."

"You're friends with him online?" The words were out before I considered them.

"I am." A triumphant smile curled her lips.

I should have asked about Sam but thought better of it. Not with my mom around.

Mom's jaw worked. "I don't want to see Mina hurt. Again."

Trina chortled. "So the guy who always made sure Mina got home safely in high school, the guy who drove her to a safe place after her almost wedding, and helped her pick up her stuff from her cheating asshole of an ex is the one you're throwing red flags on?"

"Trina," Mom groused.

"You never thought Jack was good enough. His parents weren't married. They struggled. His dad was in the wind. It was too similar to us. To you. Then there was the golden boy Ethan, who came from wealth and presumed stability. His goody-good parents. You wanted that dream so badly you've had blinders on."

"So this is my fault?" Mom yelled. Red streaked her face, and her eyes shone with unshed tears.

"No." I interjected. "No! This isn't anyone's fault but Ethan's. We all missed the flags. I can see them in hindsight, but that's with advantage."

Mom sighed. "Mina, I'm not trying to throw flags on Jack."

Trina snorted.

"I just want you to go in eyes wide open. You went down the same path I did. You just, thankfully, didn't marry him. I want to protect you. I'm just scared for you, but I do think you getting out and being single or dating is good."

"Well, if Jack is so temporary, as you said . . ." Trina stared at her nails. "Then wouldn't he be perfect? She can get a taste of another without the noose of forever."

"Forever isn't a noose," Mom said.

"It is with Ethan," I mumbled.

Trina flicked me an approving look.

But she had a point too. Jack wouldn't be permanent. Regardless of what Trina wanted to believe, his history showed that. I'd seen him at parties after Alicia. He'd left with some of them. I was certain of it. And after. Women continued to flock to him. The thought settled hard in my stomach. But, I wasn't ready for permanent either. However, he was kind. Maybe even interested in more based on our kiss and his agreement to dinner. If he was, maybe it was a temporary partnership worth exploring. He could get back at Ethan, and I could get a rebound.

## MAY 20TH

### JACK

My phone vibrated again as the elevator dinged closed. I frowned seeing Rocco's text. It was his fiftieth of the day, not sure which dozen since I walked out of the office a little after two to help Mina. He hadn't been happy with my choice then, and he was still lighting up my phone about it.

It took all my willpower to tell Mina I couldn't come to her apartment because I fucking wanted to go to her apartment. The main reason I didn't go was the hardness in my pants. The kiss had been unexpected, but fuck I wanted more. And she just broke up with her fiancé at the eleventh hour. Hell, the eleventh hour and fifty-nine minutes. Lust and anger still darkened her eyes, and I wasn't sure I'd be able to say no if she kissed me again. And she needed time. She needed to breathe after that fuckwad. And what I wanted wasn't a quick rebound. No, I wanted a real chance. So instead, I had decided in that instant I'd get on a plane and meet up with a prospective client.

However, she'd offered me dinner when I got back, and there was no way in hell I'd say no to that. Even if she thought it was a thank-you. A bitter taste tanged in my mouth. We'd need that sorted before next Saturday. I wasn't going for a thank-you, but to see her. Because I wanted to. There was nothing benevolent about it.

I pulled into my assigned spot and sauntered to the door, knowing Rocco lurked behind the reflective glass doors.

As expected, he stood there, his fresh business suit crisp and perfect, his shirt and tie also immaculate. His chestnut hair was slicked into perfection. He stared at me through his black superhero-style frames, his brown eyes following me.

"Jack, you can't just ignore me," he said, offering his hand out for my briefcase and jacket.

I shot him an amused look. "Who's the boss here?" I asked, heading toward the elevator without looking at him. I pulled out my phone to scroll through the emails I'd missed since leaving the office earlier.

"Jack, you skipped a very important meeting today," Rocco started again.

He wasn't wrong. The client was midsize for my portfolio but, more importantly, had local ties and future expansion opportunities.

"You rescheduled," I said with a shrug.

"They weren't happy about it," he shot back.

"Send them a basket or something," I said.

They were local. Even though I hated rescheduling, especially if I selected the time, it didn't cause them too much hassle.

He sighed and pinched his lips together. His shoe rubbed into the floor with his nervous habit.

"What, Rocco?" I asked.

"I don't understand why you missed the meeting. Your schedule was clear. You selected the time. Said it was perfect as it would lead to dinner and prolong the talks," Rocco said, fidgeting with the briefcase.

I was right about that. Three o'clock was perfect as it led to dinner and prolonged a meeting or seeing the woman you've dreamed about for years.

"Something more important came up," I said with a shrug. "They can choose the next time slot. Try to make it work."

"Jack," Rocco started, but when the doors slid open to the office floor, he said, "Mr. Wolfe, this is an existing client who is very important."

"They're all important." A new voice sounded to our right.

Sam Winters greeted us with his normal big smile. The goofball was the same age as me. But under that goofball exterior was one of the smartest minds I knew. He'd skipped a grade in elementary school, went through all honor and AP classes before heading off to college, where he graduated in two years, and then got his masters in a year and interned at a prestigious firm for another year. We'd gone to high school together but ran in different circles and didn't become friends until college. He'd played football, and his stature still showed it. His sandy-blond hair was long but styled back. His green eyes shone with mischief.

"Yes, Mr. Winters," Rocco gritted out. "They are."

"Hey, Sam," I said, grinning at him.

Both Rocco and Sam walked with me toward my office.

"Client's here." Sam nodded toward one of the conference rooms. "The ones you stood up earlier."

"Ah, there you go, Rocco. They rescheduled," I said, shooting him a grin as my stomach tightened, wondering why they showed up unscheduled. I took my briefcase from Rocco. "Rocco, ask them if they're hungry. Order dinner or snacks or something."

"And?" Rocco asked.

"I'll take care of the rest."

The meeting ran until eleven, and everything got ironed out, but it also meant a red-eye flight to meet with Greg. Before turning in, I sent a text off to Mina.

ME: Had a late meeting with a client and had to push my flight off to the morning. I hope everything went smoothly when you got back to your apartment.

To my surprise, a text fired back a few minutes later.

MINA: Yeah, stopped at my mom's first. Then Trina came back to my place. Pizza and a movie. Now Friday is to set up meetings for next week. I have a few leads I'm going to pursue. Some I know disliked Ethan. Others I met at a dinner a few weeks ago.

A smile curved my lips. She was already tackling her game plan. He thought he'd scare her, clip her wings, dull her. Ethan was a dumbass in so many ways, but not seeing or appreciating Mina was his biggest failure. One I wouldn't emulate.

## MAY 22ND

### MINA

"I want all the details," Maggie declared from her chair.

A few of us had ended up at Trina's townhouse. In between roommates, the house was quiet around us. Her furniture was our mom's leftovers from when she redecorated. With the busy season wrapped up for her, Trina had a list of house projects to tackle.

Victoria sat cross-legged on the sofa, a wine glass in hand. Her long, wavy dark hair cascaded down the cream sofa's back. Like me, she wore yoga pants and a T-shirt. I had unearthed all my quote and sarcastic T-shirts. "So, you kissed?"

A blush stole across my face. Of all the details, the kiss is what they focused on the most. We'd already discussed the threats and had circled back to the kiss, again.

"And he returned it?" Victoria pressed, tightening her fingers around her wine glass.

I nodded, staring at my hands.

"Good." She nodded.

"Are you going to see him again?" Maggie watched me.

She uncrossed and recrossed her toned legs. Her dress looked ready for a night out or a board meeting.

My eyes shot up to meet hers. Mischief shone back.

"Oh my gah, girl, spill." Victoria smacked my knee.

"I offered him dinner for helping me get my stuff."

"And he set the day and time," Trina added for me. Unlike the rest of us, she wore ratty jeans and a T-shirt with paint splattered on it.

"Have you picked out what you're going to wear?" Victoria's dark eyes lit up with excitement.

"It's just dinner," I offered.

"You sure?" Maggie leaned closer, her hawk eyes narrowed.

Trina and Victoria stared expectantly.

"I mean, what else can it be? I just broke up with Ethan."

"It can be whatever you two want it to be," Maggie said in challenge. "He's definitely interested."

"You don't think it's too soon for a rebound?"

"No," all three offered at once.

"And are you certain it's a rebound?" Trina pressed.

"What else would it be?"

Maggie and Trina shared a look.

"What am I missing?" Victoria demanded.

"I just found out Jack had a crush on me in high school," I whispered.

Victoria looked to Maggie and Trina.

"How serious was this crush?" Victoria asked.

Trina shrugged. "He wasn't like a puppy dog. It was the way he'd look at her when she wasn't watching or his reactions to Ethan's shit. He'd walk her to the door."

"I thought he was being nice. A friend."

"He was," Maggie agreed. "He wanted to make sure you were safe. But it was the subtlety of stuff. He'd make sure Mina was comfortable before he sat down. Regardless of the distance, he'd drive Mina home. Like Trina said, it was the looks and then it was the anger toward

Ethan. Not because he was dating Mina, but because of how he treated her. And he still gives her those looks."

"What?" I sputtered. "What are you talking about?"

"We may not always go to the same parties and mixers, but I've been to enough crossover ones to confirm he, in fact, still gives you the same looks he did in high school. He also still shoots daggers at Ethan."

"So he's interested?" Victoria smiled.

Trina and Maggie nodded.

I shrugged. What they said made my heart skip a beat. It aligned with what I wanted, and I doubted they'd feed me a line to make me feel better. Neither Maggie nor Trina were gentle. Still, even if he was interested, I knew his ways. His short-term attention span. I'd have to go in knowing this. Protect my heart.

"Why'd you just frown?" Victoria asked. "This sounds like good news?"

I swallowed. "He's somewhat of a player."

Trina snorted.

"You don't agree?" Victoria asked Trina.

"Dude had a serious girlfriend from freshman year of college to graduation. No playing around. He moved back . . ."

"How do you know that?" I bit out.

Trina gave me a sharp look. "Don't doubt my ways. He dated a woman named Nicole. Even though he doesn't ever post about his social life, she still has tons of pictures of them. When he came back to Milwaukee, he did date around. A fucking lot. Seems every party I could cross-reference that Mina and Ethan attended, he found a new fling. Women love trying to post selfies with him. He's tagged in a lot of pictures, but he doesn't pose and mostly just stares."

A hard lump formed in my throat. I remembered all those women. Watching him leave. Acid burned around the lump to my stomach.

"However," Trina snapped, pulling my attention to her. "He stopped for several months until he met Alicia. They dated for a long while. He's never been known to cheat."

"But he always moves on," I said. The truth was painful to utter.

Maggie tilted her head, her lip ticked up on the side.

"Maggie agrees with me." I pointed at her.

"Mm," she offered.

"Oh," Victoria cooed.

Maggie met my hard stare. My stomach flipped at her wicked grin. "Jack certainly dated around in high school. No doubt about that. For the first five or six months after he came back, he did bounce around with more women than I can name. He appears in a ton of women's feeds. However, he was known to seek out dates that were as noncommittal as he was."

The burning of the acid radiated through me and climbed up my neck and cheeks. A queasy feeling built.

"And?" Victoria pressed.

Maggie stared at me. "I think he was just biding his time."

Victoria passed me a curious glance.

"He hasn't dated since Alicia," Trina said. "Which has been well over a year."

"That they know about," I whispered.

As much as I tried to recall, I couldn't remember if I saw him leave the last few events with someone or not, but then again, after our engagement, he hadn't been to as many of the same parties as we had been, and if he did, he didn't stay long. Besides, he didn't broadcast them.

"Or he's decided not to settle anymore." Maggie's gaze bored into me.

Victoria turned to me.

Uncertainty twisted in my stomach. Their stares weighed on me, the hum of the AC the only sound as so many thoughts ricocheted in my mind.

"So, let's break this down," Maggie said.

We all looked to her.

"Do you still love Ethan?"

"Fuck no."

"Do you miss Ethan?"

"Fuck no," I repeated.

"You've been with Ethan almost fourteen years, about two years engaged. You two have lived separate lives despite cohabitating half the nights a week. You've yet to fully move in with him, even extending your lease another term while you were engaged."

That had been a screaming match, but I didn't want to rush the process. Rush. Maybe he had a point. We'd been engaged a full year and I still hadn't moved in. Maybe even then I knew something wasn't right but didn't realize it. Like my subconscious had been trying to protect me.

"Do you know who you are?" Maggie asked.

"What does that mean?" I asked.

"Without Ethan in your life, do you feel lost?"

"No, I feel free," I said before thinking.

The words were like a slap in my face. But they were accurate. Painfully accurate. They all blinked at me.

Free.

Without him, I didn't feel the pressure of perfectionism, the self-monitoring to make sure we wouldn't argue, the internal sigh to not react to what he did.

"Then maybe," Maggie said, "you were already broken up and just going through the motions. Maybe neither of you realized it until you saw him move on. Maybe he didn't realize it either. In no way do I condone his behavior. If it was over, you break up. But, you two have been emotionally divorced maybe even before you got engaged."

"Damn," Trina mumbled, her gaze fixed on the floor.

Even Trina had hinted at it before the wedding. But I'd denied it. Because it didn't fit in with what I expected for my plans. It would have derailed my whole future. And it did.

But as I sat there, surrounded by friends, feeling free, contemplating my next steps forward, it didn't feel daunting but hopeful. If I could figure out what to do.

"So, what do you think I should do?" I asked.

"Whatever you want," Maggie said and raised her glass in a toast.

## MAY 24TH

## MINA

A little before midnight, my phone dinged. I sat at my dining room table in my pajamas. I pulled my eyes from the report displayed on one of my two monitors and the work papers on the other. A skitter of excitement raced through me seeing Jack's name.

JACK: Headed to Baltimore for a few days
ME: I have ten new client meetings this week. I've called and talked with all my clients.
JACK: Ten is amazing!
ME: I may actually take the weekend off after my Saturday morning meeting
JACK: We still good for 5PM that day? We can order in.

I couldn't help the smile that broke across my face. He still wanted to get together. In order to not shoot back a YES with a zillion exclamation points, I waited fifteen seconds before slowly typing.

ME: Yes, we're still good <smiley face emoji>

Crap, maybe too much, so I deleted the emoji.

ME: Yes, we're still good. I was thinking maybe Chinese or Indian. I know you love Tandoori.

JACK: Mina, pizza is your favorite.

The stupid smile on my face grew. Ethan wasn't a pizza fan, or any food that you typically ate with your fingers.

ME: This dinner is to thank you

The delivered message popped up. Seconds dragged by. Then the dots danced but disappeared. Danced again. My breath caught with each dance. What had I typed wrong? I reread all my words. I didn't imply anything. I wasn't rude. Finally, a text box appeared.

JACK: I don't need a thank-you dinner. However, I would love to eat some pizza with you.

My heart hammered in my chest. He was changing the expectations. Or I was reading too much into his words. I sucked in a wobbly breath. Before I could respond, another text message appeared.

JACK: After your long week, you want beer or cola? I assume Sunday you want to prep for your week.

A lump bobbed in my throat. How easily he knew me.

JACK: Or vodka <wink emoji>

I laughed, the tension recoiling in my stomach.

ME: Let's stick with beer. I lose days with vodka.
JACK: <thumbs-up emoji>

I stared at the emoji longer than I wanted to admit.

## MAY 27TH

### MINA

Warm air greeted me as I pushed out of the office building. It had been two weeks since the flight and a world of difference. Five meetings down, I was headed to the sixth of the week. Of the five, three had signed already. A fourth was likely to sign. Eighty percent was a great return, but I wanted to increase my chances. My sixth client was midsize, in line with the bulk of my current clients. They were looking at an expansion project in the southeastern area growing rapidly with commerce. If it worked out, they'd be a gold-tier client in a few years and possibly platinum in a decade or two. They were the long-haul type client.

A gentle breeze rustled my hair as I walked the few blocks to the restaurant. A new place with sleek lines, wood and brass, and warm lighting to give it a modern but still cozy look. The client had picked the spot. A bit of research, and I knew it was a friend's restaurant thanks to a random social media post from three years prior. After canvassing the menu online, I already knew what I'd order so I could focus on the presentation.

At barely six, the restaurant already had a wait. Thankful for making a reservation, I followed the hostess back to a table set in the corner. Jamal Jones was already waiting there. A gray suit popped on his dark brown skin. A teal shirt and matching tie complemented the tones.

"Mr. Jones." I extended my hand.

"Jamal," he offered. "Mina, correct?"

I nodded. "This looks like a great restaurant. I read many rave reviews."

His dark eyes searched my face. "Do you know why I selected it?"

"Your college friend owns it."

He blinked. A slow smile spread across his face.

"What makes you think that?"

"The owner, Jeremy Turner, went to college with you, according to your social media page."

"That required digging a few years."

I shrugged.

"Do you know why I agreed to this meeting?"

I swallowed. A cocky answer and a spiteful answer twirled on my tongue.

He waited, settling back in his chair.

"I would like to say my reputation precedes me, that you've heard good things from others I worked with. We met at the Rogers' dinner party, where multiple clients of mine attended. I also know you've spoken loudly against Ethan's deal in Marshfield County that would have revoked a protective stance of some wetlands. If you are aware I am not engaged to or in good standings with Ethan Settlers any longer, you may have been more willing to take this call as you ignored my call a month ago."

A smirk lifted his lips. "Which one do you prefer?"

"My reputation."

"Excellent. I did receive your call. I didn't ignore it. I waited to see how much you wanted it while I vetted you out with our common contacts. You dumping Ethan was a definite bonus. Now, if you had some contacts you could recommend that believed in sustainable building *and* practiced without caveats, my next project might get some real traction."

With a signed contract, a name-drop for Jack, and a smile on my face, I exited the restaurant. Yes, dumping Ethan had helped, but my solid portfolio, worked-out projections, and proven return rate sealed the deal.

ME: Signed #5
JACK: Is that a weekly record?
ME: Not yet, need #7. I had a week three years ago with 6.
JACK: You'll get there. We'll have to celebrate Saturday.
ME: Only if I get #7.
JACK: You will

My phone buzzed with another text. Expecting Jack, amazed at how quickly I'd come to look forward to his messages, I flicked my gaze to it. My mouth dried seeing Ethan's name flash across the notification.

ETHAN: Mina, sweetie, let's talk. I can bring over some sushi and wine.

My stomach turned at the thought of sushi. If he was offering food, then he had no idea I had a dinner meeting. I'd taken that into consideration with my calendar. All my meetings had been marked private, which blocked people from being able to read the contents. Still fearful Trevor would have an override, especially as a partner, and even though the partners never hinted at it, I started to code my meetings. It seemed the most prudent way to keep privacy but also block off time.

Another notification vibrated my phone.

> ETHAN: Mina, it's all over. It was a one-time mistake. It'll never happen again. I promise. I love you. I know you love me.

The last line brought bile to my mouth. The fuck I did. A retort burned my fingers, but instead, I clicked the details and scrolled down to the big red letters at the bottom. His message lingered, remaining even though new ones couldn't come through. My thumb hovered over the delete icon, ready to remove him permanently.

I blinked. The words swam together. We'd been together almost half my life, and I was ready to move on. Remove him and our history completely. Once, I would have unwaveringly said I loved him and done anything to help him. The words I said to the girls flitted through my mind. I felt free. The opposite of being trapped. How long had I felt like that? Did any part of me still love him? Did it all evaporate? Was nothing left from over a decade together?

Did I owe him time to express himself? There was no explaining it away. But did all our years mean he should get ten more minutes of my time?

The years rolled through my mind. There'd been a time when I looked forward to Ethan's messages. He'd been my island in the sea of uncertainty at home. In college, we'd built a routine, one that carried through the years afterward. It wasn't excitement but expectancy, checking the box. At what point had we changed? Gone from lovestruck to numb struck?

When he'd been there for me when my parents divorced and when nightly I wasn't sure what was going on, he'd been my rock, and then when my dad was gone and my mom started moving on, he remained a constant. And I owed him for all his support. Obligation and debt. It was like I moved on believing I was obligated to stay with him as he'd been my anchor.

But had he?

We were a young couple that hung out together. I helped him pass most of his classes, went where he wanted in high school, and didn't make a fuss if I didn't like something, like when he tossed my "winning with coffee" mug in the garbage at his apartment. Without comment, I'd rescued it and returned it home. In high school, Jack drove me home most nights. Maggie and Trina were my emotional support when it came to venting or talking through my hurt, and then Dani joined in during college, and Victoria and Corrine when Trina met them in college. Ethan's influence in my life had been more ceremonial than active. Fuck.

Other than being each other's dates to events, sharing a bed a couple nights a week, though it was only sleep and sleep alone the last year or so, and arguing over the wedding, we lived separate lives. He golfed, apparently with a junior partner at my firm. I had girls' nights at my apartment. Ethan wasn't to blame for our relationship failing, but he was to blame for cheating. Trina had never liked Ethan much, but she'd been blunt and honest about our relationship. Saw what I wasn't willing to see.

Whatever happened, I couldn't let myself fall for another Ethan.

I deserved more.

I owed him nothing. The thought solidified in my heart and mind. He'd only use that time to try to gaslight me. To get me to forgive him so he could feel better and get me and my emotions under his thumb. Again.

Another vibration shook my phone. Hesitantly, I looked down, afraid the block hadn't worked correctly.

TRINA: Let's meet up tomorrow night to pick your outfit for your date with Jack

My thoughts shattered.

Jack.

A twist of heat curled in my core. His lips flashed in my mind. Then the feel of them on my lips. A shiver stole through me, and I sucked in a breath. He may be interested, but it was temporary. He'd move on. I needed to keep my emotions in check.

ME: It's not a date-date. I'm just thanking him for helping me.

But what if it was a date? Even a rebound one? He said he didn't want a thank-you but dinner with me. Hope bloomed in my chest. Fuck. I'd already failed to keep my emotions in line and was already putting too much on something that was uncertain, temporary at best.

TRINA: You could thank him and 'little him,' maybe get a happy time for you too. You haven't had one in a year, years . . .

My heart raced as warmth crept through my body. His lips on mine and then lower. My center pulsed. Fuck. How long had it been? I cleared my throat, but it did nothing to control the want thrumming through me.

Then reality threw cold water on me.

He said he'd *had* a crush on me in high school. Maggie and Trina mentioned the possibility of one now. It was circumstantial at best. It was me getting my hopes high. But damn, that kiss felt nice . . . Fuck.

ME: I need to apologize for kissing him in front of Ethan. That wasn't fair.

TRINA: WTF He kissed you back

ME: He's nice, he didn't want me to embarrass myself?

TRINA: <raised eyebrow emoji> he wouldn't have agreed to a date

ME: I don't want to make him uncomfortable. I don't want to get my hopes up. Read things that aren't there.

TRINA: Fair but when have I led you wrong?

I laughed as so many bad choices danced in my mind.

TRINA: About your relationships, let's limit it to that

I blew out a breath. My heart and core were in agreement to see where it led. My brain was a jumbled ball of short circuits trying to figure out if Jack was using this to get back at Ethan or to gain an advantage on him, and if I cared.

ME: Trin, I'm scared. I really enjoyed the kiss. I'm still thinking about it.

TRINA: <heart emoji> YAY! Then let's get you some D to go with it!

I choked a laugh, and the anxious tension rolling in me eased a bit.

ME: Idk. I'm afraid I'm reading too much into his niceness.

TRINA: I don't think you are, but you have to make the choice for yourself. We can still pick an outfit tomorrow, then Saturday you can read the situation.

TRINA: Wait. Scratch that. You have the awareness of a sofa when it comes to love.

TRINA: Maybe we can get earbuds. I can give you play-by-plays like in the movies.

ME: You can help me pick out an outfit after my dinner meeting. I may or may not wear it. NO way do I want your voice in my ear. My own thoughts are confusing enough.

TRINA: I'll bring some of my clothes since yours are boring, and we'll agree on one to wear. It'll be your birthday gift to me.

I laughed. She'd managed to wrangle an out-of-town work trip that she left for on Sunday, her birthday.

ME: Deal.

Oh shit, what did I just agree to?

Without rereading Ethan's message again, I swiped left and clicked the trashcan icon.

## MAY 29TH

### MINA

Trina brought ten dresses over the Friday before my date. Each one I tried on was more revealing than the last. Her vote had been for a black number with a plunging V in the front almost to the waist, a halter top, and a skirt that settled at the end of my butt cheeks. It must have been from her State Street party days. Instead, I opted for one of the first options. Dark green, with some stretch, the A-line skimmed down my thighs and rested a few inches above my knees. The long sleeves had open gaps. The bodice was the most risqué part. It dipped lower than any of my dresses. Trina smacked me when I tried to put a tank top under it, so instead, I wore a black lacy demi bra. Although mostly modest, it accentuated my curves.

When the buzzer sounded, I did a double take in the mirror, and immediately, regret wormed into my veins. What was I doing? This was a thank-you dinner, not get-Mina-an-orgasm dinner. I tugged on the top, but when the buzzer sounded again, I swallowed down my reservations and went to the door.

My hands shook as I unlocked it. Sandalwood and the sexiest smile greeted me. Although he wore dark jeans, they were an expensive cut that hugged his frame and sat snug on his waist. My eyes lingered a bit too long before trailing up over his black button-down that accentuated his hard chest with sleeves rolled over his forearms. Like usual, his hair looked casually styled but in the perfect haphazard way. His Nordic-blue eyes blazed with heat and interest.

He swallowed, his eyes tracing my face, before saying, "You look gorgeous."

"You look great too." I smiled despite the blush warming my neck.

After following me inside, he scanned the room, taking in the furniture and decor. The room was painted blue and had pictures of my family scattered around the walls. All the ones with Ethan had already been taken down or I'd cut him out of them. The furniture was warm brown leather with an array of blankets draped everywhere.

"This feels more like you, but it's still missing something," he said with a grin.

His presence was unfamiliar and welcoming all at once in the space that felt small. The apartment was a stopping post mostly for me, not a space I spent much time in. The first week after the almost wedding, I'd removed any sign of Ethan, bringing more comfort to the space. Over the last week, with all my meetings, I'd made sure to use a different mug each day and lounge in one of my T-shirts. This coming week, I planned to convert my spare bedroom into an office instead of using the dining room table.

"Can I offer you something to drink?" I croaked out, not sure why my voice was acting funny.

He turned his watchful eyes to me, a smile tugging on his lips. He was enjoying me being flustered.

"Sure," he said with a toothy grin. "I brought beer and red cola."

I stifled a groan. Red cola, the sugariest thing out there, was my favorite. "I haven't had that in years."

We both knew why. He narrowed his eyes, but his smile didn't waver.

I pulled two glasses down.

He walked to the countertop that separated the kitchen from the living space. My heart thudded in my ears. He pulled out the chilled bottle from a canvas bag and a six-pack of Spotted Cow. Somehow, I was able to pour us each a glass of cola without spilling it everywhere.

"Are you hungry?" he asked, accepting the glass I offered.

I shrugged as my stomach rumbled. I hadn't bothered with lunch earlier because of the nerves of tonight.

He smirked. "Pepperoni or sausage?"

"Pepperoni," I said without hesitation. "I'm buying."

His jaw ticked, and his eyes darkened. "I don't want a thank-you meal."

"I invited you over."

A smile curved his lips, and his eyes fell to my mouth. My insides warmed down to my center. With a glance at his jeans, I noticed he wore a belt above his bulge. That'd make his pants harder to get off. But I wondered how he felt under them.

Fuck. I was like a horny teenager.

Awkward silence sat heavy, a living creature. To busy myself, I opened the app and ordered the pizza.

He downed his cola and pushed off the counter, moving to the living room to look at the entertainment system and wall of books.

"You still read?" he asked, scanning the titles.

"Yeah," I said noncommittally, watching his sinewy form move.

He'd played multiple sports in school, but since college, he'd added pounds of muscle that filled out his clothes.

He turned to find me watching him. My eyes shot up to meet his, a blush warming my cheeks. His eyes darkened and tracked down to my lips. Pivoting, he turned to face me, taking slow, deliberate steps toward me. With each step, a sly grin grew on his lips.

I stood transfixed, holding my breath, solely focused on him.

"How'd today's meeting go?" Jack asked.

"They signed." I smiled.

"That's awesome!"

He smiled at me, and my insides warmed to mush. Squirming, I swallowed to talk. "Seven signed this week."

"You beat your record."

I nodded. "I go Monday to Moline to talk to the maybe from yesterday. Thursday Eau Claire for the other maybe."

"You're kicking ass. You should be proud of yourself."

He wrapped his arms around me in a hug. Although it was likely meant as a celebration hug and nothing more, his hard body pressing against mine ignited my veins with want. I allowed my hands to linger on his solid back.

"I am," I admitted, but hearing the praise from him sent something skittering through me.

Rarely had I shared with Ethan a maybe or a no. He always had a lecture ready to go on how I could improve my pitches. Never had he shown unwavering confidence.

Jack leaned back to meet my eyes. His eyes were dark pools.

"Please forgive me," he whispered.

My breath caught in my throat. Hoping. Wanting.

When he leaned forward, my lips parted in expectation.

His lips were on mine, soft and gentle at first, then hot and urgent. His hands caressed my cheeks before one tangled into my hair, holding the back of my head as he moved it as he wanted.

I reciprocated the kiss, wrapping my arms around his neck, pulling him closer. He groaned against my lips before trailing down to my chin, then neck. My head lolled back, giving him more access. His kisses trailed lower, following the path the V made.

Trina had good taste in dresses.

I threaded my fingers through his locks, encouraging him lower.

He moved the hand cupping my face to my neck, skimmed it over my shoulder, ran along my breast, sending heat to my core, and rested it on my hip. He wrapped his fingers around my waist, guiding me backward until I gently bumped against the wall.

Once I was where he wanted me, he glided his hand back up to my breast, rubbing over my nipple, already pert. He kissed along my shirt's neckline over the roundness of my breast. I moaned and pushed into him, letting my hot core rub against his erection. He growled against me, nipping the flesh.

He skimmed one hand up my front to move the material of my bodice, exposing my bra. Moving to my breast, he kissed and suckled on it over the lace.

I speared my hands in his hair, pressing him closer as I pushed against his trousers, grinding for the friction and heat.

As his mouth continued lavishing, he released my bra. With a quick motion, my bra was pushed up, and his mouth was on my naked breast. Swirling his tongue around the nipple, he moved one of his hands to my other breast, caressing it and flicking his thumb over the nipple.

I moaned his name, and his heated lips returned to mine.

I hooked my hands into his belt, unlatching it and sliding it open. His member bulged against his zipper, filling my hand. All I wanted was to feel him, touch him, take him in. The need was overbearing.

I unbuttoned and then unzipped his pants, sliding my hand down to touch his hard cock.

"H— Mina," he groaned against my lips.

I ran my thumb over the head, spreading his precum. Then slowly, I grazed my fingers down his length. The thought of taking him heated through me, and my center quaked.

"Jack," I breathed, the word more a pant than sound.

He moved his hands to my buttocks and then slid to my thighs. With a strong grip, he lifted me. I wrapped my legs around his hips, pushing and rubbing against his cock.

The doorbell rang, slicing through our heavy breathing.

"Fuck," he huffed against my lips.

I blinked, focusing back into the world, my bra ditched on the floor and top and skirt askew. My naked chest pressed against his rumpled shirt. His pants and briefs were pushed down so his cock throbbed next to me. I licked my lips, imagining the taste.

He groaned and caught my mouth again, pushing me against the wall and rubbing into me. His erection slid against my panties. I moaned as I clawed at his back, trying to bring him closer.

The doorbell sounded again, followed by a knock and someone saying, "Pizza."

"Shit," we said in unison.

I slid down him, missing his warmth and touch instantly.

He pulled his pants up and fixed them while heading to the door.

I grabbed my bra and darted to my bedroom, my heart thudding in my ears.

I dropped my head against the wall and stared at the ceiling.

What the fuck was I doing?

Was I really ready for a rebound? To move this fast? With Jack? My body tightened and my breath hitched. Fuck he'd felt so good in my hands. His lips on me. But he was a player. Ethan's enemy. Been out to get us.

But there wasn't an us. And those were Ethan's fears. Not mine.

One hand fell to my lips while the other touched where he'd kissed my breasts. I'd had a crush on him all those years ago. I'd pushed it aside when Ethan asked me out and Jack started dating everyone, especially when he stopped talking to us. Jack hadn't been my enemy then and he wasn't now. He was a player, though, and would move on to the next woman. But this was just a rebound . . .

I had just broken up with Ethan after fourteen years. My life wasn't completely shaken and was moving forward, which should have been a clue about our relationship, but everything was changing. Was I reliving a childhood crush? A current crush? Just on a normal rebound?

Was he just out to piss off Ethan? The way he helped me without Ethan knowing and the way he kissed me put heavy doubt on that. Was this just a fling to him? Did I care?

I wasn't in the place for anything permanent, and Jack was transitory at best. It had been months, maybe years since I'd had an orgasm a handheld tool hadn't helped me achieve. And Jack certainly knew what he was doing. Everything felt right. Even if his player ways meant he'd move on, he had serious skills from it. Ones I would enjoy.

Were the girls right? I needed some fun? Some exploration? To give this a try?

Fuck, I wanted this. No matter all the warnings my brain was screaming.

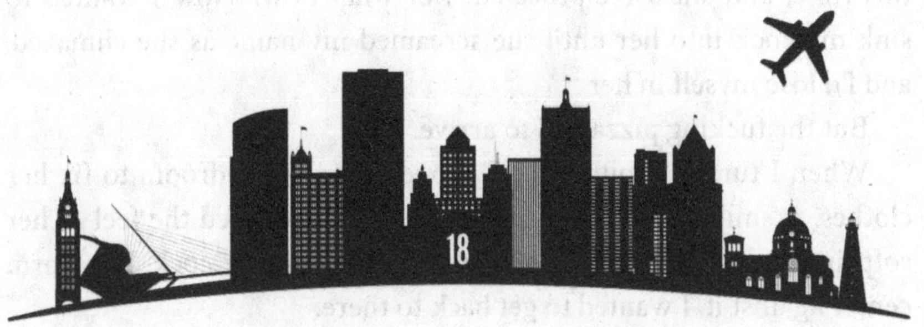


## MAY 29TH

## JACK

My cock throbbed in my pants. With a tight smile, I took the pizza. A kiss. That was all I'd been after, and somehow we were half naked with her hand on my cock. My hopes far exceeded.

Sure, she'd kissed me at Ethan's, but I understood why. She was pissing Ethan off. Her spite was a turn-on, but even more so was the look on her face tonight, her groaning against me. I wanted to know if there was something between us when it wasn't a show for Ethan. That this wasn't some checkmark on her list—thank Jack, pay the electric bill, burn Ethan's pictures.

No, when I saw her dress, hope spiked that she was interested. Then she'd been as greedy with the kiss as I had been. If not for the doorbell . . . Fuck. I needed a cold shower.

Mina wasn't timid. She wouldn't hide in an embarrassment hole because of the first kiss at Ethan's. Had even invited me over afterward. She was observant. Watching me, but not ashamed. Waiting.

Assessing. Plotting. It was fucking hot. Now, though, I'd kissed her this time, and she'd reciprocated. But what now? Now I wanted to sink my cock into her until she screamed my name as she climaxed, and I'd lose myself in her.

But the fucking pizza had to arrive.

When I turned around, she'd slipped into her bedroom to fix her clothes. A smile twitched on my lips as I remembered the feel of her soft lips, her breasts, her hand wrapped around my cock, her warm center against it. I wanted to get back to there.

Remerging from the room, she focused on me, her amber eyes watchful and curious but also guarded.

Ethan was the world's biggest idiot. He had Mina and thought fucking Tiffany was something to do.

Mina moved to the kitchen, pulling out plates. I fixated on her body as she stretched up to reach something. The move of her muscles. The roundness of her curves.

She caught me staring, her eyes jumping to mine. I grinned; I couldn't help it. I was the kid caught with my hand in the cookie jar, and I wanted more.

She cocked an eyebrow at me and smirked.

Fuck, I was in deep.

If I wanted us to last, I couldn't move too fast. She just left a long-ass relationship. I didn't want her to jump in the sack with me, use it to clear her head, and then move on to the next guy who she took more seriously. I wanted to be the only next guy.

Instead of going into the kitchen with her and putting her on the counter and showing her how much I wanted her, had wanted her, I forced myself to put the pizza on the table and pull out chairs for us. My cock twitched in frustration, and I shifted.

Mina stood next to me, her expression unreadable as she held the plates, lost in her thoughts.

When she continued to stare at the table, with whatever playing in her head, I took the plates from her hands. She startled, her gaze jumping to mine. Her eyes were dilated and foggy with lust.

Lust was good, but I wanted more too. Needed more.

"Jack," she started and then licked her lips.

Oh fuck, don't let this be the "this was a mistake" speech.

"Mina," I started to cut her off so as not to hear the worst words ever.

She held a finger up to stop me. "Jack, I don't want to take advantage of you."

A bark of surprised laughter escaped my lips. Those were not the words I expected, ever. If anything, I was toeing the line of propriety with it only being two weeks after her broken engagement. But since Ethan hadn't died and was just a dumb shit, I didn't feel guilty. I needed to take us slowly to show this wasn't a fling. Yes, I was swooping in quickly, but we could take all the time she needed. We had forever as far as I was concerned. Even if her eyes moving to my lips and my pants made me want to take her against the wall until she came.

She frowned and shifted back, straightening her spine.

I licked my lips to stop myself from saying "honey." My nickname for her was based on her eye color and that they reminded me of one of my favorite flavors. Although, I could now say she was sweeter than honey and my new favorite all-time flavor.

"You're not taking advantage of me," I said, laughter still in my words.

I reached for her hand, which she let me take, but her attention wasn't on it. Her fingers curled around mine, but I doubted she realized it while it sent a jolt through my arm. Fuck. I was already in too deep.

"How have I not? You helped at the bar. You helped me get my stuff. I kissed you . . . and although it was very nice and I want to do it again, my intentions weren't very good."

A blush stole across her cheeks at her burst of blunt honesty.

My mind looped on the fact that she wanted to do it again. I blinked to focus on her next words.

"And I invited you over to thank you." She held her hand up to stop my rebuttal. "Even though it became . . . whatever this is." She swallowed, her eyes widening with her brashness, but she didn't retreat.

"And instead, all I've thought about is touching you. I've exploited your kindness."

I moved my hand to her cheek, tipping her face up. Her eyes swam with emotions. "Mina, you can touch me anytime," I said and leaned down to brush my lips against hers.

She opened her mouth to say something, and I slipped my tongue inside, tasting her. Instead of pushing me away, she slid her free hand into my hair, fisting a handful.

I loved the feeling of her possessiveness. Showing what she wanted. Wanting *me*. Fuck, the last thought caused me to hesitate.

With more willpower than I thought I had, I pulled back to meet her gaze.

Something flickered across her eyes, and a smile tugged on her lips. Before I could say anything, she used the hand still in my hair to tilt my head back to her lips. I, of course, obliged.

She slipped her hand out of mine and laid it on my chest. Her warmth seeped through the fabric, jolting me. I put my hand on her hip to slow down our kiss, slow down where I was naturally going, when she slipped her fingers into my pants. With a feather-light touch, she traced my length.

Fuck. She made everything hard.

"H— Mina," I breathed, my voice deeper than I expected.

My willpower and thoughts of reining us in splintered into a thousand pieces.

She smiled against my lips and brushed her fingers over the head of my cock, and I admitted defeat. If she let me, I wasn't getting out of this without tasting her or filling her. I lifted her onto the table, keeping my lips against hers, her legs on either side of me. Her dress rolled up, exposing her matching black underwear to her bra. Resting my hands on her upper thighs, I rubbed my thumb against her core and groaned at the wetness. I needed to taste her sweetness.

She arched into my touch. A soft moan escaped her lips, and her ragged breath lifted her chest.

With urgency, she unzipped my pants, pushed my briefs down,

and tugged my cock free. She wrapped her fingers around it. I pushed into her hand, my cock finally happy I was letting it play.

"Mina," I breathed on her lips.

She smiled at my moan.

With languid kisses, she glided her fingers up and down my shaft while rubbing the tip with her thumb, spreading the precum around. She leaned back, pulling her swollen lips from mine. Her dark eyes, filled with lust and want, met mine. This hopefully would be our future. Us.

Tilting my head, I trailed kisses down her chin to her neck and to her collar. She leaned back, giving me full access as she started to pump her hand on my cock. Fuck, I wouldn't last long.

Short, huffy breaths escaped her, and she pushed her chest against mine.

"Wait," she breathed. Bowing her head, she took in a few raspy breaths.

Oh shit, what line did I cross?

I stilled, waiting for the next direction. Waiting for the recrimination. That this was a joke. A prank. Not what she really wanted.

She drew her head back up, lust shining in her eyes. "Wait." A slow grin spread on her face. "I want to taste you."

My heart skipped a beat, and my fingers tightened on her thighs. I stiffened, not wanting to break the moment. For her to change her mind.

She gently pushed her fingers against my chest and guided me to take two steps back. When I was where she wanted me, she slipped down to the chair, her hair brushing against my torso, and slowly ran her tongue the length of my cock, swirling it around the sides.

Oh fuck. I blinked. The world was unfocused as deep desire filled my veins.

As she ran her tongue back down, she took me in her mouth, tasting me, filling her.

Oh, fucking shit.

She swirled her tongue around as she sucked her way back up.

I wouldn't last. Not with her mouth working magic on my cock.

Unable to take not tasting her back, I put my hands on her shoulders, but she went back down again on my cock.

"Mina," I growled.

She tried to smile but couldn't with my cock in her mouth. I never would have thought I'd be able to say those words.

Mina couldn't do something because my cock was in her mouth.

## MAY 29TH

## MINA

Jack's moans were like music. His fingers curled in my hair as he pushed into my mouth. His cock, firm and smooth, glided along my tongue. I slowly worked my way back up his length, delighting in his hands pressing against me. Heat and want thrummed in my core. The thought of moving up him, taking him fully inside me, tightened my muscles in expectancy.

Before I could take another round down his length, he pushed me back. His cock pulled out from my mouth with a pop. Quicker than I could react, he lifted me to the table.

He ran his hands through his hair, blinking repeatedly.

A shiver stole through me.

Oh shit, what did I do wrong? I hadn't given oral much since high school, but I didn't think I was that rusty.

"Jack—" I started, but he pushed me back.

His lips met mine, hot and demanding, before trailing back down my neck and over my collar. A whimper escaped my mouth, and I instinctively parted my legs, hoping, wanting. My whole body arched toward his touch, toward him.

He tore at my top, fumbling this time to push it past my breasts in his rush. He ran his tongue along the hem, sending a shiver through me. I fisted my hands in his hair, holding his mouth to my chest. Hot kisses glided over my exposed bra before he pulled the cup down with one hand while slipping his other hand to my thighs.

As he slid his hand up my thigh, running against the sensitive apex, I quivered. His simple touch could unravel me. Then he rubbed his thumb against my center, shattering my thoughts. His thighs pressed against mine, him standing while I sat on the table.

Shit, where were the condoms? I think I packed them in hopes of some fun on the honeymoon that didn't involve a tool. Crap, they were in the toiletry bag in the bathroom. Never had I wanted a condom as badly as I did then.

"Jack," I croaked.

Words failed as I tried to coax him toward the bathroom and where I hoped the unopened condoms were.

"Mina," he breathed against my nipple.

My body tightened in response.

He pulled my panties down in a swift motion and then tugged my dress off, leaving me naked except for one bra cup. I was really glad at that moment I'd waxed for the honeymoon.

"You're so gorgeous," he said, his dark eyes taking me in.

With greedy hands, I reached for him, pulling him back to my lips.

I wrapped my legs around him, rubbing my clit against his cock, and the friction was almost enough to send me over.

He started kissing down my body again, but I wanted more. I wanted him, wanted him inside me. Instead of focusing on my breasts as he'd done before, he kept kissing lower across my ribs, my stomach, belly button and kept going lower. He knelt to the floor.

Oh shit. He was heading down there. I hated oral. It was messy, loud, and unfulfilling.

"Jack," I moaned and tried to tug his shoulders back up to me.

While he kissed, he ran his thumb against my center, and I bucked in response.

"You're so wet," he whispered against my flesh, sending sensation rocketing through me.

I made some unintelligible sound as my eyes rolled back.

Telling him to stop went against what my body wanted. Even if it was oral.

His lips found my clit and he sucked.

Holy fucking shit.

I arched into him, digging my fingers into his hair to hold him.

He released me, my body gasping for air, but then he swept his tongue across me, teasing my opening. He inserted one finger, rubbing and caressing. I moaned as my body started to ride his finger. My toes curled.

He slipped a second finger in, his mouth licking and tasting my core again. Sensation ripped through me. My muscles tensed up, the need and want becoming too much before it released, and euphoria coursed through me, the golden warmth addicting.

Holy shit, whatever Jack did, I hadn't had before. I could do that every day. I *wanted* to do that every day.

He kissed his way back up. Long and luxurious as if eating an ice cream cone. My taste lingered on his mouth when his lips met mine.

"Holy shit," I breathed.

He chuckled, and the vibration sent another jolt of want through me.

I reached for his cock despite the relaxing bliss radiating through my muscles.

He shifted, blocking me from his length.

"Jack," I whined. Great, I'd turned into a needy person.

"Mina," he said, rubbing circles on my back.

"That was incredible," I said on a rush so I wouldn't say I wanted to fuck him right now. Even though every fiber of my body burned with want for him.

He deepened the kiss for a moment before saying, "Anytime you want me to do that, you just have to ask."

Good to know. That would be incredible after a bad day. Or a good day. Or any day.

With him still exposed, I rested my hands on his waist.

"You should eat," he said against my lips with a smile. "I already did."

"I want dessert first."

I moved my hand to his engorged cock. It twitched against my fingers as I slid them down.

"Mina," he growled.

Before he could say anything else, I leaned over and ran my tongue along his length.

"Yes, Jack?" I swirled my tongue around his tip.

He whimpered. His cock bobbed. His fingers dug into my shoulders.

I took another lick.

"Fuck," he groaned, his eyes pressed tightly shut. His face flinched as if he was warring with himself.

With one hand, I took his balls and massaged them, the tissue soft in my fingers. Then another long lick.

His jaw ticked, and his chest lifted and fell in controlled breathing.

"Jack?" Uncertainty finally caught up. "Do you want me to stop?"

"No," he breathed immediately.

Standing up, I wrapped my arms around his neck. He bent to meet my lips. The hardness on his face melted.

"Sit," I commanded, guiding him around me.

"Mina . . ." But he followed my directions.

Pushing his knees apart, I moved between his legs. Our bare bodies rubbed against each other, and my core tightened, wanting more. Instead, I knelt.

As I took him in my mouth, he tangled his fingers in my hair. His breathing went ragged, and my name was a soft chant on his lips. Each lick and suck earned me a groan. When he came, I hadn't planned ahead and swallowed down. His warm saltiness lingered in my mouth.

With his head bowed, he leaned over and lifted me up. His strong arms wrapped around me, pressing me against his solid chest. Then his lips were on mine, soft and cherishing.

A thought sent a chill down my spine.

I could see why women were willing to take whatever Jack offered. His touch was electric, addicting. He made me feel like the only woman in the world. That I alone could unravel him. I'd have to be extra cautious, make sure my heart and brain knew this was temporary. This was my rebound. Jack played hard, but he moved on. I was going to fuck any memory of Ethan out of my mind with Jack. My teenage heart would be thankful. Now my body would be even more thankful. I just needed to make sure I didn't get attached. I wouldn't have another Ethan situation again.

# 20

**MAY 31ST**

**MINA**

Instead of going to my mom's for Sunday lunch, I drove the few hours to Moline and stayed overnight. After working remotely and meeting a couple times with the client and his CFO, I had another signed contract. This time, it was on a trial basis. Even if it was a smaller client for my portfolio, the option of expansion was there.

Back at the hotel, my phone buzzed. Ethan was blocked, but that didn't mean he hadn't figured it out and gotten a different number. Excitement curled through me when I thought it could be Jack. The red numbers of the clock shone 11:15 p.m. The meetings had run late, and instead of driving back afterward, I decided to catch up on emails and texts at the hotel and get an early start the next day. My calendar was filling out with new and existing clients. So far, only two with connections to Ethan had parted, but their lost revenue was signed and surpassed with new clients. Spite is a powerful motivator, but freedom is a bigger one.

My phone sounded again. Finally closing my laptop, I picked it up.

MOM: You've missed three Sunday lunches now.

Fuck, I should have left it face down.

ME: You should be asleep
MOM: I'm nights this week. Next week off. Then back-to-back days.

Her schedule was on a rotation of nights, days, weekends, and off. When I was in high school and she took the job, we had a group color-coded calendar on our phones. My dad had stripped their bank account and probably would have sold the house if he hadn't needed her signature. She won it in the divorce, along with full custody. With the support of her parents, Mom was able to make the payments until she found a better paying job. Mom had taken a swing shift job at the utility company and signed up for all the extra shifts she could to support us. Now, she didn't work as much overtime anymore.

MOM: MINA SIMONE HENLEY

Oh fuck, the full government name.

ME: Mom, one of those Sundays was the day after my almost wedding
MOM: And I gave a pass. You didn't show up the two after it.

I rolled my eyes.

ME: Thanks for the pass, Mom
MOM: Be at my house Sunday for lunch, or I'll be at your apartment for dinner
ME: See you Sunday for lunch

Running a hand through my hair, I ambled to the bed.

Another notification came through. With a sigh, I picked it up to see what my mom responded.

JACK: How'd it go?

A smile curled my lips, and my core tightened seeing his name.

ME: They signed. Small sample to start. If good return, they'll sign on more.

JACK: They'll sign on more.

My heart tugged at the sentiment.

JACK: Do you have plans this weekend?

I blinked. Warmth flooded my body. The words blurred together as I stared at them.

We hadn't made plans on Saturday after he'd left. After our fun, we had pizza, watched a movie, made out, and when I struggled to stay awake, he left. Afraid I'd get the "I'll check my calendar" line after our physical time, I hadn't asked about seeing him again. And to be honest, a stink clung to the knowledge that this would be temporary. My rebound. His time before the next one. A part of me was trying to protect my heart even though my heart was already on board with my core. They wanted a fling, fun, and an underlying hope of something that couldn't be. Instead, my brain came through and focused on reality and grounded me back to what I understood. Business. As long as I stayed logical, I could protect myself.

We both had meetings this week, late spring being a good time to meet with clients. Most kids were still in school, so parents weren't on vacation, but sports were also coming to an end until the summer leagues started. Although we had several holidays, most weren't week-long, out-of-the-office type holidays. More of a long weekend. During the start of school and the winter holidays, I usually met locally with clients, did follow-up phone calls, and worked on end-of-year prep work.

Jack was in land development. He had his own calendar of preferred meeting times.

With our uncertain schedules, I could blame meetings for trying to protect myself and create distance. Even if most parts of me didn't want protection or distance.

I swallowed. My fingers hovered over the letters. Silence droned in my ears, but his message remained.

ME: I'm going to see my mom Sunday.

I stared at the sent message. So factual. So indifferent. Acid slid down my throat, curdling in my stomach.

ME: How about you?

Before I could think better of it, I sent it off.

Immediately, the dots danced.

JACK: I'm hoping to get to see you

All the thoughts and acid evaporated as hope clawed its way up. Fuck. One simple line could shatter all my planning, all my ideas of protection. But even if I knew distance was probably best, doubt niggled in my brain. Jack was interested. He made it clear. And, I, or at least, my body, was very interested. I knew this was a rebound. I knew this was temporary. If I kept reminding myself of it, kept myself in check and prepared, what could go wrong?

Wednesday, I strolled to the coffee shop. Ronald already waited there.

A glass of water and his open laptop sat beside him. Though he didn't like pastries or coffee, he liked the energy of the place.

Nerves skittered down my arms and into my stomach. An unexpected email had greeted me yesterday, and although I expected the meeting two weeks ago, I didn't want it. Ronald wanted to talk. He went back with Ethan's family.

His glasses hung low on his face with a tart frown and narrowed eyes. His sandy-blond hair was thinning, but he didn't hide it. Instead, it was trimmed, parted, and neatly slicked into place. His hazel eyes never left the screen, even as I sat across from him.

Forgoing the espresso shot, I hadn't bothered to get a beverage as it would only unsettle my already agitated stomach.

His portfolio lay before me unopened. I knew it front to cover without opening it. He was a conservative investor with a tight grip on all funds. A small, steady stream was his preferred method to large swings, even if the swings reaped more dollars. Because of his reserved ways, he wasn't one of my largest portfolios, but he was the largest of the ones I had earmarked to lose.

When he blinked and reached for his cup, I spoke. "Ronald, good morning."

His gaze jumped to mine. Something of a smile flickered across his lips before disappearing. "Mina, thank you for meeting with me."

He folded his hands on the table. A sigh lifted his chest. Otherwise, he could have been a statue with his rigid posture and unchanging expression.

"It's a month earlier than our normal quarterly review, but I have assembled an analysis of your accounts, projections for the future, and possible other routes to take with varying degree of increased risk. As I know you prefer more steadfast growth, I have several plans outlined with keeping the risk the same but changing up some funds that would offer some diversity while also showing a slight increase in growth over some of the funds already in your portfolio."

His jaw ticked.

Oh fuck.

"Mina, you've done a good job with my portfolio. I have no complaints."

The ever-present "but" had to be coming. My stomach tightened, and I held my breath, waiting.

"I was one of the first clients you signed."

I nodded. This was true.

"I signed because Nathanial Settlers is a longtime acquaintance."

A laugh caught in my chest at acquaintance instead of friend, but this was the breakup speech, and I choked it back.

"With the dissolution of your engagement and presumed connection with the Settlers, I think you'll experience setbacks."

I swallowed. My vision blurred just at the edges, and the start of a whine droned in my ears. "I understand my personal life is experiencing changes. However, I have signed almost a dozen new clients in the past week, maintained all but two existing clients, and have remained in contact and reachable."

He frowned. "Three clients."

"Pardon?"

"You've maintained all but three clients."

A pinch twisted my heart, and heaviness settled on my chest.

"You've had a good record. I've had no complaints, but these types of events make you reevaluate your life and expectations."

I blinked at his wisdom.

"I'm ready for more."

Although those were words I wanted to hear, they weren't for me.

"I'm ready for the big guns to bring me more money."

My brows furrowed. With his tastes and preferences at risk, there wasn't room for much growth unless he wanted to invest more money.

"I'm moving my accounts to someone with more pull. More growth opportunity."

My mind scrambled to think who had this magic that could bring him all this. If they existed, I needed to get in contact and apprentice with them.

"May I ask who?"

"You know him." Ronald nodded. His eyes tracked back to his screen. Before completely dismissing me, he added, "The junior partner at your firm, Trevor."

At my office, I paced the length of the room. The industrial carpet was a mix of navy, white dots, red swirls, and other nonsense to mask stains, but it couldn't hide what the fuck Trevor had done. I pivoted, my long stride eating up the eight feet of distance before I turned again. My office was an interior office, basically a fully boxed in cubicle, but because of the sensitivity of our work, Yang and Mariya had opted for full office boxes instead of cubicles. Yang was also distracted by the noise of chatter and typing and didn't want it cluttering our space.

On my fiftieth or so turn around my office, a knock sounded on my door. Before I could respond, Trevor opened the door to peek in. His light blond hair was perfectly coiffed, and his navy suit was tailored to his frame.

"Can I help you?" I managed to say without foaming at the mouth. My fingers curled into fists, but I kept them at my side.

"I wanted to check in and see how you are?"

I narrowed my eyes. Too bad I couldn't will the imaginary red dot between his eyes into existence.

Instead of taking the hint, he pushed the door open farther and sauntered into the room. With little choice left if I wanted to not come across as deranged or rude, I moved to the chair at my desk. A few pictures of my mom, sister, and the girls were on the display behind my desk. All the pictures of Ethan had been tossed out. Otherwise, my shelves were lined with books on codes, and my binders of research for each client.

"So I'm sure you heard." He cleared his throat. His predatory eyes pinpointed on me, a wicked gleam in them. "Ronald is moving to me."

"I hear you can offer bigger returns."

With a cocked eyebrow, he smirked. "With so many client losses, you aren't on track to be a junior partner. You'll be lucky enough to keep your job."

His words stung. My mouth opened, but nothing came out. Finally, I managed, "I signed eight clients in two weeks. A ninth is possible tomorrow. Out of a dozen with connections, I only lost three, one of which went to you."

"This is only the beginning. We all know it. Without Ethan, you lost Ronald. Others will follow his lead. How do you think you signed the others?"

Part of what he said was true, but clients usually cared more about returns than if one person wanted to move up. Usually, but it was possible more would go. Even ones I hadn't marked. But it'd been almost three weeks. I'd talked with all my clients. The initial shock had worn off, nothing for them changed, and life moved on. Still . . . I swallowed.

Then, a cold, familiar numbness settled on my skin. One that lingered when Ethan tried to give me lessons on how to make business better. Pushing the anxiety down to a kernel, I met his intense stare. He darted his eyes over my face before locking his dark gaze with mine.

"You sniped Ronald away with claims of bigger returns. How will you manage that with his reserved preferences?"

"That's why I'm a junior partner on the fast track to full partner," Trevor crowed. "And you're not."

My nerves buzzed with hatred, the pressure on my chest hard to manage as I tried not to reach across the table to smack him.

"You're too stuck on their words. I know what he wants and am willing to make the changes to give it to him."

My face screwed up in confusion. I stared around the room. "What changes are you going to make?"

He smiled. "You're going to learn a lot, Mina. Without Ethan at your side, you won't get the big dogs. They aren't going to take a risk on some nobody who can't even keep her man happy and in her client pool."

Red swam in my vision. A notification popped up in my email. A prospective client. The visible first sentence mentioned Jamal as a referral. A smile threatened to curl my lips.

"Trevor, I appreciate your insights," I offered.

He flinched.

"I'm sure you will provide Ronald your best."

He searched my face but frowned, not finding what he was looking for, likely fear.

"Now, if you'll excuse me, I have work to do for my clients."

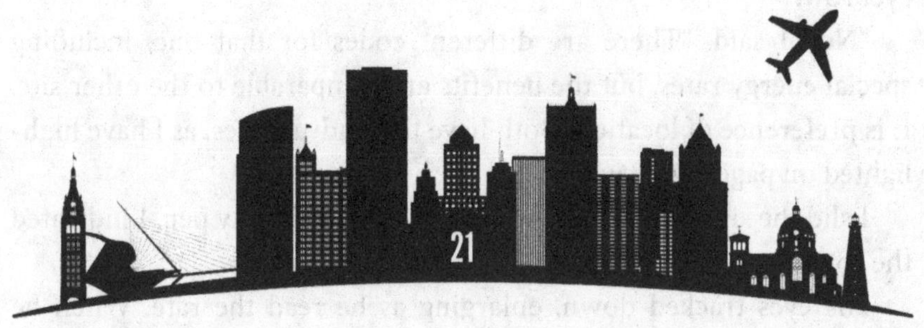


JUNE 2ND

JACK

Greg tapped his phone on the notepad, his cell phone pressed to his ear. I was one of several, including Ethan, who was seeking Greg's business. He brought commerce and money. Just listing him as a client could get you access to exclusive whisper networks.

He lifted a finger, indicating one more minute on his call. I gave a nod but didn't lift my phone to scroll my email. My focus was for Greg.

"Jack, you say these tax breaks are guaranteed if I use this property?" He spoke to me over the receiver of the phone.

"Yes, sir." I tapped my briefcase. "I have a hard copy of the code, and I sent it in email to you and cc'd your legal team."

A smile twitched under his gray mustache, which would make an eighties star jealous. His eyes flicked to the side as the person on the end argued something.

"And that works for the border property too?" He cocked an eyebrow.

"No," I said. "There are different codes for that one, including special energy rates, but the benefits are comparable to the other site. It is preference of location. Both have their advantages, as I have highlighted on page eighteen."

I slid the simplified chart across the table. With my pen, I indicated the row.

His eyes tracked down, enlarging as he read the rate. When he pulled the phone from his ear, I knew I had his almost complete attention.

The Charlie Brown "wah wah" sounded through the speaker. A sharp voice called, "Greg? Greg? You there?"

"I'll call you back," Greg mumbled before ending the call and picking the paper up. "This will require some escrows, and here you underline the local rate breaks if I use a state-based money backer?"

I smiled.

"I like to keep my funds with my people."

"Which you can," I assured. "However, if you look at the line below, you'll see a special rate that is able to be locked in only in a small two-year window. The rate is meant to bring more of the cash flow in-state with all of the commerce development in the southeastern region."

"That's not on his proposal . . ." Greg's eyes flicked to the phone.

A frown darkened his face. Finally, he lifted his eyes to me from the paper.

"Settlers?" I asked. The name brought bitterness to my mouth.

He cocked an eyebrow in agreement.

"You work with him before?"

"His father a couple decades ago."

Decades ago, so it wasn't impactful enough to maintain working connections.

"So, I assume Ethan, then?"

Greg nodded.

"Ethan will get the exact spot you want, with glowing neon lights pointing to it. You want a large warehouse, wood and steel, pure glass. Want to bypass environmental laws? He'll do it."

"But?" Greg prodded.

"Ethan is looking for his biggest buck. He has one client in probate because they didn't do the full soil testing and ran into heavy metals. He'll get you the facade you want, but he doesn't care at the cost to your bottom line. He doesn't look at the special rates for rezoning or repurposing. With climate change and everyone looking for ways to control the damage, there are a lot of special rates and, usually, utility works already present that make rehabbing cheaper and provide a better public image than building a brand-new facility on undeveloped land."

As he listened, his eyes never wavered from me. His mouth worked. After a swallow, he said, "So, with your property selections, the rates, and the tax break for local financing, you can come in under Ethan's offer?"

"Absolutely."

"On the financing part, would you have someone local you could recommend to manage it?"

It wasn't a signed contract. Yet. That would take more time. More coaxing. But we had several meetings lined up to look at properties, talk about estimates, and build out plans. One meeting was set for tomorrow, and it included Mina.

After texting an engineer drafting firm I often worked with, I tapped on Mina's name in my text list. She was setting records with her new clients, and Greg could propel her to partner much faster than Ethan or his other contacts.

An email notification popped up on my phone. A prospective client. A referral. I'd start with that.

ME: Did you refer Jamal Jones to me?

MINA: He was looking for sustainable building. You're the best at it.

My brain stalled for a moment, her flattery warming me. Maybe if I spun tomorrow as business, instead of personal, she'd be more open to it. When she'd replied she'd "like that too" to seeing her this weekend, I hadn't pushed for more but said, "We'll talk Thursday night if we're both back in town." Even if I wanted to spend time with her, she didn't owe me her time.

ME: Thanks. I appreciate the referral <smiley face emoji>

Rolling with it, I added:

ME: Are you going to Caliber's meet n greet tomorrow?
MINA: Probably not. Not sure I'm ready to see all those people. Especially so close to the wedding. Many were there.

Coldness tightened my heart at the mention of her wedding to Ethan. At least she was free of him in her personal life. With more time, he'd be carved out of her professional life too.

ME: You should go. Good for networking.
MINA: I'll think about it.
ME: It's at the zoo. There's plenty of space.
MINA: Maybe I'll push him in a lion's den.
MINA: Wait no, I don't want to kill the lion.
ME: It'll be fun.
MINA: <straight face emoji>
ME: Fun enough. We can go together. I'll drive.
MINA: <three dancing dots>

Oh shit, did I overshoot? I stared at those fucking dots, waiting for a reply. Maybe I pushed her too much. But fuck, I wanted to see her again, and I wasn't sure how well she'd take a date request. We hadn't made plans last weekend, something I regretted, but I wanted to give her space. Let her think. My cock had been beyond happy. It and I wanted more time with her. My brain was flashing warning lights. She was still reeling from the breakup. From his betrayal. I was moving too fast. Even if I was trying to keep it business focused.

I slipped my phone in my pocket as I exited the elevator and headed for my car in a private spot in the parking garage.

I slid into the driver's seat.

My pocket vibrated with a text.

After slipping it out, I smiled.

MINA: Okay. 6:30?

ME: See you then

After I ate her out last weekend, she returned the favor, much to my delight and surprise, we ate pizza, and sat on the sofa. When we'd finished the pizza, we started talking about life after high school, including college and first jobs.

High school held too many memories of Ethan and everything else to talk about. I hadn't kept in contact with any of the girls I dated in high school, and Mina wasn't friends with any of them either, which had been intentional. They'd only been a distraction from Mina and Ethan. One I didn't need when I went to college.

Our college days were both filled with classes and internships. Somehow, as I talked to her, Nicole had slipped my mind when recounting my days. She'd been my only girlfriend in college. We met freshman year. Much like Alicia, she was polished, driven, and easy to talk to about business. She'd helped me polish my image for business. I provided her a fun distraction. Neither of us had seen a future beyond college together, and we ended amicably when we graduated. I don't even know if she stayed in California. Which is probably why, when facing Mina, Nicole had disappeared from my mind.

Mina had spent her college time with Ethan as a shield to not date while he was likely cheating on a regular basis. Without him at the same school, Mina had joined a sorority, had internships, volunteered, and was on several dean's lists.

As I listened to her, it was easy to see she'd continued to build her life to be independent and follow her own path yet complement Ethan's. No wonder he'd been so pissed when she took the client meeting. She was putting someone before him like he did every time, including fucking Tiffany to hurt Mina. The fire from high school still burned in her, no matter how much Ethan had tried to dampen and control it. She'd be a partner, and likely soon. Ethan would be lucky if his dad didn't stay on as a silent partner to tell him what to do because he still needed his dad to finalize most details. Information I was only privy to because of the clients I'd signed instead of him, and a few slips from Aiden.

Mina seemed ready to move on, but she kept that wall up so much it was hard to tell if she really was or if it was her goal and, therefore, only her imagined reality until it happened.

I wanted Mina in my life, forever. With a second chance at it, I had to tread carefully. Make sure I wasn't moving too fast and risk fracturing what could be our life together.

As much as I wanted one, my plan wasn't to act like Mina and I had a relationship. Even if we had shared an intimate moment. If she did act like we were in a relationship, I'd go along with it. Smiling and happy. But I didn't want to push her or imply something to our business world that she wasn't comfortable with. Until she was ready to define terms, I would follow her lead.

## JUNE 4TH

### MINA

I checked my reflection yet again as the butterflies fluttered in my stomach. I hadn't seen Jack since last Saturday. We'd texted throughout the week. He was locked up in meetings, and I was continuing to check in with all my clients, had new client meetings lined up, and follow-ups with all the new clients I had signed. My entire summer was booking up.

The meet and greet was at the Milwaukee Zoo tonight. They often hosted events. The outdoor trek and the buildings offered great opportunities for mingling. The enclosures were tucked into pockets along the double-wide lane walkways. The primate house had a huge meeting venue.

For the evening, I opted for a black sheath skirt, green sweater, and knee-high walking boots. They had a textured sole but were still stylish. Since parts would be outdoors, I pulled my hair up.

A knock sounded, and my heart skipped a beat.

He smiled when I opened the door, the one worthy of dropping panties. His blue eyes sparkled. He wore his typical suit but without a tie.

He sucked in a breath. "You look gorgeous," he said, his eyes scanning me.

"You look good too," I said.

For a moment, he stared at me. Before the granite fortress of nothingness settled on his face, hesitation or fear shadowed his eyes. He moved his gaze to my mouth, his lips parting slightly. Instead of closing the distance, he slipped his hands into his pockets.

"Jack?" My voice was steady despite the concern twisting in my stomach.

Was this just a business date? Had I misread the past couple of weeks?

Dark and dilated eyes met mine. The granite was gone, and lust and want shone in his blue depths.

Without a thought, I stood on my tiptoes, pressing my lips to his. A spark jolted through me.

He leaned forward, cupping my cheek before kissing me back. It was soft but lingered and ignited my core.

I wanted to deepen it, see where it would lead to this time, but I didn't want to delay us since he wanted to go to Caliber's gathering.

"Too bad this is an important gathering," he said against my lips.

I chuckled before pushing my lips against his in another kiss. Despite all my thoughts on what we should do, I spiked my fingers through his hair and pressed my chest against his.

He groaned and spun me toward the wall. My back pressed against the wall, my legs parted as he nestled between them. My skirt rose up my legs. If I'd gone with Ethan, I'd have worn pants, but I was hoping for something like this with Jack.

I wrapped my arms around his neck for support as I lifted my legs around his waist, pressing us closer together. His hardness pushed into me.

He moaned and slid his hands to my skirt, his fingers skating against my bare thighs. The touch untethered what little self-control remained. I wanted, needed to feel him and ground into him. I gasped at the friction, at the fullness that rubbed against my clit. We had too many layers of clothing between us.

"Fuck," he breathed out, resting his forehead against mine.

Maybe being late or missing it wouldn't be too bad.

"Shit," he muttered, almost like an apology. "I want you to meet someone tonight. Otherwise, I'd just say let's skip it."

"You don't have to provide me contacts," I said.

The sting hit me harder than when Ethan did it. I didn't need rescuing to build or maintain my portfolio. I could find my own contacts.

"It's not that," Jack said, his blue eyes opening wide to find my gaze. "It's like Jamal. It's a client looking for a new advisor. He needs a local one for some tax breaks. I had a meeting with them Wednesday. They have a lot going on. Making lots of changes. Knowing you were going, I suggested they talk with you tonight."

I slid my legs down. Disappointment chilled the building fire. I knew he meant well, but this was the constant battle I had with Ethan about growing my career. It's why so few would be affected by our split. I purposely avoided his direct referrals. I didn't want that to be my and Jack's relationship.

"Mina?" Jack asked.

I shimmied my skirt back into place and adjusted my sweater. I'd have to fix my makeup and hair in the car with a mirror.

"Let's go," I said, averting my eyes.

"No," Jack said, shaking his head. "I did something to piss you off. Please tell me."

I flinched. Did he want to know to use it later? My eyes shuttered closed. Ethan's words and warning were my first thought. To expect his reasoning. But it wasn't who Jack was.

"Mina," Jack whispered, rubbing his thumb against my cheek.

I willed my eyes open, meeting his concerned gaze.

"I don't need your help getting clients," I said. "I understand the concept of networking and that knowing you can help, but after Ethan . . . I'm not saying you're him. Or you'll do what he did, calling my clients. But I don't want my client connections to be from . . ." I swallowed. I didn't want to say boyfriend. Friend sounded too benign for what we'd done already. Friend with benefits may fit, but it didn't fit for my life either. Nor was it what I wanted. "I just . . . I already lost three clients because of Ethan's connection to them. One was to Trevor."

Jack's eyes darkened, and his jaw twitched, but he didn't interrupt.

I didn't know why I was spilling my guts to Jack about my rational fears and concerns, but it felt nice. Therapeutic. And I was establishing my expectations.

"I don't know what we have," I said, gesturing between us. "As long as we enter this with zero expectations . . ."

He frowned and narrowed his eyes.

Fuck. I was making a mess. I'd presumed intentions. Maybe the girls were wrong, maybe I misread the signs, and he wasn't even interested in more than what we'd already done. He said the client tonight needed a local person. But then why did he keep kissing me back and looking at me the way he did with lust and want? Maybe I was just making that up since I wanted *him* so much. Maybe we were just friends. Maybe that was good. Safe.

"Mina?" he asked when the silence dragged.

"I don't want people thinking I need someone to set up meetings for me. Even if you are a friend."

"Friend?" he parroted, his eyes flying open.

"We're not friends?" My mouth dried.

He didn't even want to be friends. Just business acquaintances. Maybe he already satiated his high school crush and just wanted to now annoy Ethan? Even in my mind, it sounded wrong.

He closed his eyes and sighed. He swallowed, and when ten seconds passed, he opened his eyes.

"Mina, if you want to be friends, we'll be friends," he said, nodding like he was convincing himself.

I frowned, my stomach flipping and my core protesting. I didn't want to be friends, but I didn't want to put more on this than there was.

"Personally"—he measured his words—"I'd like to be more than friends."

Of course, a stupid grin had to tug my lips up. At least his did too before it turned into his large panty-dropping grin.

But being more than friends meant many more complications. Meant being put aside when he was ready for the next woman. And I didn't have stability to offer either. I kept comparing him to Ethan at every turn, which made logical sense but wasn't healthy for the start of a relationship. And since I knew it had to end, if we set it up to begin with, I could prepare for it. Not move my heart too fast. My rebound would be scheduled just like in business.

"What about," I said, my mouth speaking before my brain could catch up or analyze what I was going to say, "a trial run?"

"Trial run?" he asked, his lips curling as if he smelled something horrific.

I nodded. A trial run. If I knew it was ending, I could build my expectations around that. If I ended it before he'd normally move on, then neither of us would be hurt or bored. We could go on being friends. He'd have the next woman. I'd have my rebound and get Ethan out of my system.

"What about three weeks?" I said. When he glared at me, I faltered. "We could do two if that's easier to manage."

He shook his head. "I don't like this feeling like a contract, with set terms that when they expire, we walk away."

Shit, that was exactly what I liked about it.

"Then what do you suggest?" I asked, noticing that somewhere in this conversation, I'd moved my hands to his jacket, holding him in place to me.

With one hand, he rubbed circles into my hip while he held my cheek with the other.

He was silent for a long time. I wanted to prod him along, but he deserved the time to think. Maybe he'd back out and say he didn't want a relationship. It'd sting. I'd feel like a fool again. I'd still go tonight, ignore him as I networked. I bet I could sign a new client just to spite Ethan. Then tomorrow, I'd have the ladies over, and we could binge *Schitt's Creek* and have a feast.

"Where'd you just go?" he whispered.

"What?" I asked, snapping back to reality.

"Your mind just left us."

I chuckled, the dry, humorless sound awkward.

"Please tell me."

"I didn't want to push your thinking along. I figured the delay meant you wanted to revert back to friend's boundaries, and I started planning my weekend."

He stared at me again. His eyes locked with mine, amusement flittering in them.

Finally, he licked his lips and said, "Well, make room for me in those plans. I accept your arrangement, but I say four weeks."

"Four?"

"There's a huge mixer over the Fourth of July weekend in Lake Geneva. One of the bank's presidents from Mercer is hosting."

"I know of it," I said.

It was the same one Ethan still hadn't been invited to. His father had but not him. With our bungled wedding, and not being able to sign Greg at it, it'd delay any possible invite. But Jack had apparently been invited.

"Are we saying today is the start and it ends the weekend of the Fourth?"

"Well, that would certainly put a damper on the party." A slow smile spread on his lips. "So, what about five weeks?"

Although he smiled, his body stiffened beneath my touch as he waited.

"So, five weeks, starting tonight?" I asked, my core already excited. "We can rediscuss on the ninth?"

He let a breath out, his body relaxing. His lips were on mine, urgent and hot.

"Sure, tonight will mark when we're official," he said against my lips.

## JUNE 4TH

## JACK

My Audi matched the vehicles already at the zoo. Tonight's mixer was hosted by some awards thing that used the guise of a fancy trophy and title to lure business owners to pay for plates and then donate to whatever cause they were supporting. We all played along because it put us in elbow room of our peers whose money we were trying to turn into our own.

A light breeze twisted through the trees. The early June evening had already dropped into the sixties. Thankfully, portions of the night would be indoors, and the different exhibit buildings would be open. Sixties wasn't cold, but it didn't make for standing-around-and-talking weather.

Mina had a plate as part of her company, Lake Front Investors. They'd likely put her next to her company and not me. If Ethan was smart, and he was, he'd make sure his company was at the same table. I texted Rocco to confirm he'd called ahead.

ME: Status on tables
ROCCO: Took arm and leg pulling
ME: How much?
ROCCO: 15K donation

I rolled my eyes. It wasn't as much as I expected, but at least it was done.

When Mina exited the car, she stood next to it, watching the others go in. She licked her lips and adjusted her already-perfect sweater. The warm glow of the sun made her hair glint with firelight. Earlier still burned in me. The feel of her against my cock. The gasps she made when I pushed into her. Her fingers digging into my back, urging me closer.

Fuck. I wasn't sure where the willpower had come from to stop us, but tonight could be a huge night for Mina if she and Greg hit it off.

I scanned my eyes down her body, taking in her generous curves. It'd been a week since I tasted her, but if luck were on my side tonight, I'd get a chance after the mixer.

Somehow, by some miracle, Mina had agreed to a relationship. When she said we were friends, a part of me shriveled up. Friend zone is just fine, but we'd crossed out of it. I didn't know how I'd go back in if that was what she wanted. I would. Cold showers, my hand, and long runs would be regular parts of my day, but I would. The agreement left me with a sour taste. It was like a business contract. Granted, we hadn't listed out terms like when we eat, how often we touch or call, but it had an expiration date. At least I had five weeks. That was more than I ever thought I'd manage. And somehow, I needed to figure out how to extend it infinitely.

My phone buzzed, signaling a text. I frowned reading it.

ROCCO: FYI he is here already

Despite the hardness already in my pants, I strode to Mina and whispered, "Up to you if we go in together or separately."

I'd already crossed a line by setting up a meeting with Greg and

Mina, one I understood after she said it. There was networking and then there was nepotism. And then there was the bullshit Ethan pulled. She was three weeks away from what he did, down three clients, and dealing with a prick at work.

Her amber-honey eyes turned to me, shining in the setting sun. She was so beautiful. Want punched me in my already-hard cock. I flicked my eyes back to the car. We could spend a few minutes behind the tinted windows.

She extended her hand. "I'd like to go in together."

Fuck yeah, great start. Well, the apartment before the client issue had been even better. Smiling, I took her hand in mine, and we walked toward the entrance. Unlike our plane ride only a few weeks prior, we weren't pretending tonight. With her hand in mine, it wasn't a show or farce. Even with Ethan there, it wasn't about repelling someone either. She wasn't shooting me daggers. Instead, her fingers intertwined with mine and her thumb rubbed against mine. But it was still only for five weeks. A time limit, just like the flight. However, Ethan didn't wait at the other end now, and if I was lucky, she'd be willing to move us to permanent.

"There's Trevor," she murmured, pulling me from my thoughts and nodding toward a tall blond man.

He wore a tight suit and cavalierly swung a wine glass around.

"Do you want to introduce me to him?" I asked, hoping for a chance to meet the person buddy-buddy with Ethan.

"No," she said and swallowed. Her eyes enlarged, and she turned to me, rapidly saying, "It's not that I don't want to, it's just that he'll see you as a business opportunity. Well, shit, that's the point of tonight. I just, with Ethan . . ."

I chuckled. "It's fine. I understand."

One day, we'd meet. When she was ready.

"Well, it's going to be awkward if I don't introduce you," she said.

Her spine stiffened, and her body tensed as her eyes locked on something across the room. Based on the flash of anger in her eyes and the clenched jaw, I figured it was Ethan.

"Shit, I forgot he was going to be here," she gritted out.

"We'll ignore him," I said, taking her hand to guide her toward the bar.

"Oh fuck," she said, coming to a stop.

I turned to her, her face screwed up in anger and fear. Large, uneven breaths rattled her frame.

"What's wrong?" I asked, the alarm seeping into my words.

"He's supposed to sit with my company." Her fingers curled around my hand. "I don't want to sit by him."

"Don't be mad . . ." I started and cringed, knowing those words always brought about distrust and anger.

"What?" she croaked.

"I, well, my assistant called and had our companies put together." I rubbed a hand over the back of my neck.

I let the emotion drop from my face as I waited for her response.

"You called them . . . Caliber . . ." she said, her eyes darting around. Her fingers tightened. Her breaths slowed.

"I should have asked first," I said. The reality of overstepping hung around us, still clinging from earlier tonight.

"They let you make the move?" She flicked her eyes to meet my gaze. Hope burned in their depths.

"Yes," I said. Please don't be angry.

"Thanks for thinking of that." She squeezed my hand and gave me a smile.

I blew out an uneven breath of relief.

"Came together, huh?" Ethan's voice snarled behind us.

Mina's hand tightened around mine. Otherwise, she showed no outward reaction.

"Do you want a mixed drink, beer, or wine?" She tugged me toward the bar.

"Whiskey." I forced myself not to turn around to stare at Ethan.

I took long, deliberate breaths to rein in the desire to punch him.

"She likes red wine," Ethan sang behind us to the bartender.

She preferred white wine to red wine, but I let it go.

"Vodka and cranberry," she said at the same time.

"Vodka? Since when do you drink vodka?" Ethan asked, stepping up next to us. "Vodka is tasteless."

I slid the bartender two twenties and placed my hand on the small of Mina's back.

"You think ignoring me is going to work? You don't think I'll make a scene."

"You can," Mina said, sipping her vodka. "I'm sure jealous ex is the vibe you want to go for."

"Jealous?" he spat.

Her gaze lasered in on me. "You already met Gina and Raquel. I should introduce you to Trevor before dinner. The two partners from the Milwaukee office will be here too."

"Mina, I'll see you at dinner," Ethan sneered as we walked away.

"Thankfully not," Mina muttered over her glass without looking back.

Trevor did a double take as we walked up.

"Mina?" His brows dipped low as he tried to size me up.

"Trevor, I'd like you to meet Jack Wolfe. He's with W&W Development," Mina said, dipping her head. "Jack, this is Trevor Schmidt. He's the newest partner with Lake Front Investment."

"Jack? W&W Development company?" Trevor smirked, making him look like a cocky prick. "Are you new there?"

Ah. The belittling route.

"Somewhat, I started it about six years ago," I said, smiling and extending my hand.

Sam and I had laid groundwork while in college. My mom had been a real estate agent before moving to Florida and helped with early-on contacts in commercial properties.

"You own W&W Development company?" Trevor asked, stumbling over his words as he straightened his posture. His smirk faded into a look of respect.

Fucking asshat butt kisser.

He took my hand in a firm shake.

"I have two partners," I said. "A founding partner, and one who came on three years ago."

"Are they here?" Trevor asked, his eyes skimming the crowd.

He was at least smart enough to try to woo the whole company. Even if it would go nowhere.

"Sam Winters won't be here." I confirmed. "Jerome Nigel is in London with a client."

"That's right, Sam Winters is your partner . . ." Mina's gaze jumped to mine. For some reason, she laughed.

"You know Sam?" I asked around the dryness in my mouth.

She knew him? Sam hadn't been in Ethan's circle in high school. Nor mine. Sam had been the star receiver on the varsity football team and in all the advanced classes. Even though I was on the football team in high school, we didn't interact much off the field. Now, we often didn't go to the same events so we could cover more space.

"Trina dated Clay, his younger brother," she said. "I didn't really know him. I only saw him a few times when he'd drop Clay off or I'd drop Trina off before they could drive."

The tightness in my chest eased. "We became friends in college."

That was something I would need to ask Sam about. And Trina, if she knew who Sam had pined for during his years in college.

"So . . ." Trevor said, his eyes scanning me before casting a dark glance at Mina. "Are you one of Mina's new clients?"

Mina's fingers dug into my palm. Her jaw was set, but otherwise, her face was resting like a poker champion.

I chuckled and said, "Are you trying to swoop in for the deal?"

His face fell, and he narrowed his eyes. He licked his lips and set back on his heels. He plastered on a large smile and squared his shoulders.

Oh, boy, here comes the pitch.

"I have top-notch portfolios. There's a reason I made partner so quickly. I can double your money in a year," he said, cocking his eyebrow in enticement.

"Only double?" Mina said over her glass, her amber eyes staring at him in challenge.

"You could do better?" Trevor scoffed.

"I don't promise something I haven't done before," she said.

A blush rose on his cheeks. It's not a good look to call out a partner in front of a potential client, but Trevor had already played his cards with Ethan.

"I also don't sign with anyone managing my competitors' portfolio or who's buddies with him. I call it a conflict of interest," I said.

"I'd never compromise a client's information," Trevor said, his nose flaring. "And I haven't signed the Settlers yet."

I smiled and stared at him until he looked away.

"You can talk to Jack more at dinner," Mina said to Trevor with a dismissing nod. "I'd like to introduce Jack to the other partners before we sit down together."

Trevor's eyes bulged as he glanced at the tables set outside under a canopy, the placement cards already set.

## JUNE 4TH

## MINA

I knew better than to push Trevor. Even as a junior partner, he could have me fired. However, he already pulled my promotion and basically said my career at the firm was dead if I couldn't sign a client bigger than Ethan. He'd still try to steal the client and sink my career after that, but I planned to build my portfolio to be stronger and more diverse than his. I wanted to bump his junior partnership share down.

The two Milwaukee-based partners, Yang and Mariya, stood together but with other clients, like an anchor pulling people to them instead of mingling with the masses.

Yang stood to the left side of the anchor, her black hair sleek and cut into a bob. Her maroon dress was adorned with gold jewelry.

"Mina," she said with a smile as I approached before her eyes jumped to Jack.

A predatory shine flickered across them, one of business and lust. I understood that one.

"Yang, this is Jack with W&W Development company. Jack, this is Yang, the founding partner of the company," I said.

"Jack, I've been trying to get a meeting with you," Yang said, her hand slipping into his for a greeting. "I wanted to discuss some investment options." Yang's eyes slipped to me, and a rueful smile spread on her face. "It looks like you may already be working with someone at my firm."

Shit. Double dog shit. They were already assuming I had his contract.

"Mina and I are seeing each other," Jack said, tightening his fingers around mine.

Seeing. He was admitting out loud to others that we were something. Although a big part of me delighted in it, sending warm curls throughout my body, a pang still pinched my heart. Seeing wasn't serious. But that's what I wanted. Because that was what he could give. And I needed a rebound.

"Oh," Yang said. Her eyes widened as she looked to my left finger. The big, flashy diamond was already gone. She cocked her eyebrow at me with an evil grin. "You move fast. I like it."

Shit. Not the image I wanted to portray.

"Mina and I were friends in high school," Jack said. "I always said if I got a chance, I'd take her out."

My cheeks heated at the finely crafted lie. He ran his thumb over my hand, the simple gesture sending tingles through me.

"I was wondering why the nameplates were moved," she said. "Now I know. Mina has a great track record and very happy clients. Despite the current hiccup, I see a great future for her with us."

That was news, especially based on what Trevor said.

"She does great work." Jack smiled. His eyes caught sight of something to our right. He smiled at Yang and placed a hand on the small of my back. "It was great to meet you. I'd like to introduce Mina to a prospective client that just came in."

"Of course," Yang said. "It was a pleasure."

As we turned to walk away, Yang motioned for me to stay a moment.

"Yes?" I said as Jack started toward a portly man with thinning gray hair. A beastly mustache arched over his lips.

"You sign him," she said, nodding toward Jack, "and Trevor's vote will be worthless."

I forced a smile. "Good to know. Thank you, Yang."

The words left a bitter taste in my mouth. A familiar pinch tugged at my heart. I wouldn't let who I was seeing dictate my career.

"Greg, this is Mina Henley." Jack extended his hand out for me.

"Greg, it is a pleasure to meet you." I reached to shake his hand. His face was familiar.

"Mina Henley?" he questioned. His beady blue eyes scrunched together beneath bushy gray eyebrows that had more hair than his head. "Aren't you married to Ethan?"

I stilled. Even though I tried to force a smile, my face refused to obey.

"Greg, Mina is an investor with Lake Front Investment," Jack said, shooting me an apologetic look. "We discussed how impressive her portfolio is. She is the local contact for you."

"Yes, I know that." Greg waved him off.

Great, Grandpa here was going to get personal instead of minding his own business.

"Do you know Mr. Settlers personally?" I asked, my voice cold and hollow.

Greg's eyes danced in wonder before saying, "Wasn't I invited to your wedding?"

"Did you go to it?" I asked, not answering his question.

The guest list had four hundred people on it. Many were business associates his parents insisted had to be invited. I hadn't seen who'd made it to the wedding before I left.

"No," he chortled. "They're a waste of time and money."

I cracked a real smile at him.

"Greg Cremski isn't known for going to social gatherings," Jack said.

Greg. Greg Cremski. Oh, fucking shit. Ethan's dream client.

"You know, that boy dated my daughter in college for a couple years," Greg said.

His next words were a buzz of noise. My vision tunneled, and stars popped into view.

Jack started saying words and then was guiding me away from Greg.

What the fuck? How had I missed so much? The church couldn't have been the first with how confident he'd felt, but college? How had I not seen it? Not known him and Trevor were friends? What else had I missed?

Next thing I knew, we were past the penguins and rope course and pulled into the alcove for the farm area. He wrapped his arms around me, pulling me close to him. His cheek was pressed next to mine. One hand cradled my head while the other rubbed my back.

"Mina," Jack whispered over and over, reverently, kindly.

"What a fucking asshole," I barked.

Jack snorted, trying to hide a laugh.

"You know," I said, burying my face against his neck, allowing the smell of sandalwood and him to wash over me. His heat seeped through his shirt, and I realized I'd wrapped my hands under his jacket and pressed him to me. "I knew she couldn't have been the first. It was too gutsy. He didn't think he'd get caught. But college? Really? What about high school?"

"Mina, I'm so sorry," he said.

"I'm a fool."

"No." Jack's fingers tightened on me. "No, don't take blame for what *he* did. He's a selfish prick and doesn't care who he hurts."

Taking a deep breath, I pushed from his chest, still keeping my hands on his body but far enough back I could look him in the eyes.

He snagged my gaze, sorrow and anger warring in his eyes. And yet, with everything I knew about him from high school and in our careers, no one but Ethan spoke poorly of him. He was always kind. Sure, he was charming, but there was more depth to him than just a handsome face and sexy body.

I licked my lips. His eyes tracked down and dilated.

The sounds of people milling around outside and scraping chairs against the blacktop carried down the short path. They were moving the outside meet and greet to the primate house for the meal.

Ethan had been screwing me over for at least a decade. He thought he had me cornered because he knew so many people and his oily hands were in many cookie jars. He wouldn't win though. I'd sign clients even if he knew them. Even if he dated their daughters. Wouldn't they like to know the real truth?

"Jack, I think after dinner I should schedule some time with Greg. I think his portfolio needs to be reviewed. I would make an excellent option for his local needs."

Jack smiled, moving his eyes back up to mine. He leaned down and brushed a kiss against my lips.

"Let's get this done," I said and led him back up the trail.

# 25

## JUNE 4TH

## MINA

I slid into my seat, and Jack shut the door. I had a meeting set with Greg on Tuesday. I'd spend Sunday afternoon and Monday researching him to figure out the path to lead him.

Jack slid into the driver's seat. He pulled the seat belt down but let it go. He reached across, running his hand along my cheek to turn my head toward him. His lips brushed against mine.

"Fuck, I've wanted to do this all night," Jack murmured.

His light kiss turned urgent.

I slid my hands into his hair and swiped my tongue into his mouth. A greedy hand roamed over my breast as the other slid beneath my sweater. His thumb traced over my bra, sending shivers through me.

With one hand, I traced down his solid chest to his waist. Another fucking belt. Making quick work, I had it undone and his pants unfastened. His hard cock bulged against the material. In that instant, I decided I needed him in me tonight. I'd touched, licked, and tasted him. Now, I needed him fully in me.

"H— Mina." My name was a breath on his lips.

People walked by, their voices barely a buzz.

"We shouldn't do this here," I panted when he traced his lips down my neck.

My body arched into his touch in complete contrast to my words.

He eased back, his eyes dark with lust. A battle warred on his face before he returned to his seat and started the car. After adjusting his pants, he drove us away.

Tension crackled on the drive home. He rested his hand on my knee, rubbing circles with his thumb and fingers. Slowly, he moved his hand up my leg beneath the hem of my skirt. My body tightened and my center heated. If the car was big enough, I'd have him pull over and join him in his seat.

I racked my brain, trying to remember the last time I had the unbridled urge to mount Ethan in his seat while we drove home. Nothing came to mind. The thought made me grimace, and I blinked to clear the image.

At a light, he leaned over, his lips parted. I met his kiss, my fingers tracing his jaw. When a horn sounded, he continued driving.

His thumb rubbed my center, the promise of what could be. My core ached for more. I gripped the seat so I couldn't try to guide him deeper inside me. As if reading my mind, though, he slid two fingers beneath my panties. Never entering, he rubbed my clit. I pushed into his touch, chasing the friction, but he never gave in.

When my building came into view, a nervous shiver stole through me. Reality tried to breathe a cool breath on the moment. My body hummed with want for Jack, to feel him in me, but should I? Based on all that had happened, it would be amazing. But would it make it easier or harder to end it in five weeks?

He parked in my lot and after fixing his pants and belt sauntered around to open my door. He extended his hand, needlessly helping me out of the car, but touching his hand sent a jolt through me.

He ran his hand down my arm until our fingers interlocked. With easy steps, he walked me to my door.

This was the moment I had to make a decision. Do I cross the line or draw a firm boundary for the next five weeks?

Even if I sent him away, things could heat up later, but something about the moment felt important. Urgent. He didn't say anything, letting me make the choice. Tonight would set the expectations for the next five weeks.

I unlocked the door and turned to him.

His hazy blue eyes tracked across my face. He leaned against the frame.

"Even with the drama, I had a good time tonight," I said. "I'm glad you asked me to go."

He smiled, this one reserved and soft. "Me too," he said with a nod. "Thanks for going with me." He tilted his head and leaned in. His lips brushed mine in a feather-soft touch.

Once again, he was letting me choose the pace.

When he leaned back to break the kiss, I grabbed his jacket with one hand and wrapped the other around his neck, holding him to me. I pressed my lips against his, heavy and needy.

He dropped one of his hands to my waist while fisting the other in my hair.

I rubbed against him, pressing my body along his length, feeling his desire pressed into my stomach. My decision was made. If I didn't see what happened, I would regret it. I could do the math later to determine how many times I could have Jack before I needed to wean off him. And I would need to, or going cold turkey from his touch would likely destroy me.

"Mina," he whispered.

"Come in," I managed to get out. I meant to ask "Do you want to come in?" but my body wasn't focused on words, just touching him and him touching me.

He led me into the apartment, bracing my back as I walked backward. He tapped the door closed with his shoe and, without looking, engaged the locks.

I bumped into the wall, his body pressing against me. He trailed kisses down to my breasts. He lifted my sweater and pulled a bra cup down. My hands made quick work of his belt and zipper. Need drove me to undo his buttons without looking.

He slid his legs between mine, my skirt hiking up as my leg spread wider. When he slid his hands to my thighs and lifted me up, I wrapped around his waist, my skirt around my own.

"Mina," he breathed, a thought on the air.

"Jack," I panted back, finishing with his shirt.

He moved his arms so I could toss it aside. He lifted my sweater off, tilting his head before his hot mouth found my breast. He latched on, sucking and biting. My head lolled back as one of my hands held him to me. I slid the other to his briefs, gliding inside and wrapping around his hard cock.

"All you have to do is tell me to stop, and I will," he said.

He rubbed his thumb against my wet and hot center.

"Jack," I whispered.

He stilled and forced his eyes to meet mine.

"I have condoms in my bedroom," I croaked out, my voice husky with lust.

I hadn't thought about the foyer, or I'd have put them in my purse.

His lips locked on mine, and he carried me to the bedroom. I moved my hands to his neck to steady myself.

In my bedroom, he gently guided me to a standing position. With one swift move, he had my bra off and skirt pooled on the floor.

"Leave the boots on," he said.

Hooking his thumbs into my panties, he dragged them down, dropping to his knees. He ran his tongue across my sex and, finding my clit, sucked. My knees wobbled, and I had to brace against his shoulders.

"Jack," I groaned. "Please."

"It's coming, Mina," he said against me. He slipped one finger in, hooking down.

I cried out as the first wave coursed through my body.

He slipped a second finger in, pumping up and down. My knees buckled. I gripped his shoulders harder, riding his fingers and the growing wave. When it crashed, I fell into him, screaming his name.

He scooped me up and put me on the bed. He climbed on, nestling his knees between mine. His cock bulged against the thin material containing them. I trailed my hands down his hard body, over his thick muscles. Despite the amazing orgasm I'd just had, hot magma pooled in my core at the thought of his cock in me. Need clenched my muscles.

I arched up to kiss him, trailing kisses down his neck and chest. Greedily, I pulled at his waist, rubbing against him.

"Mina."

I reached for his briefs. The final barrier to having him. His pants already pushed low. I slid them off, kissing down his body as he'd done to me. He used his feet to help kick his pants and briefs off. I slid my tongue along his length, twirling around his hard tip. He pushed into my touch. I took him in my mouth, his salty sweetness filling my senses.

"Fuck, Mina," he growled. "I'm not going to last if you do that."

He reached down and slid me back up. His lips met mine again in hunger. He rubbed his cock against my heat, and I arched into him.

"Please," I panted.

I dug my fingers in his lower back, urging him inside me.

"Where are they?" he asked, rubbing up and down against me, the motion building my need to feverish levels.

My hand flailed toward the dresser. Fortunately, I'd left the box out behind the clock.

He tore the box open and removed a foil wrapper. I grabbed it from him. He furrowed his brow until I slid it over his length, taking his cock in my hand. I guided him to my entrance.

Locking his eyes on mine, he entered me. His eyes shuttered, a gasp on his lips. It might have been my name.

Then his lips found mine again.

We found our rhythm, becoming one in the dance. My muscles

bunched again as the wave built up. When bliss took me, he let himself go, coming inside me.

After catching his breath, he discarded the condom in the waste basket and flopped back on the bed by me. He pulled me into his arms, nestling me under his chin.

I was really glad I'd opted for the dozen pack.

## JUNE 5TH

### MINA

Jack woke before I did. When I heard the faucet running, I figured it meant he was going to slip out. Last time we both had work, and I needed time to think. Today I wouldn't have work as a distraction. My heart squeezed, and my body numbed, knowing it was just a fun night for him. I'd had fun too. My heart and body liked having an orgasm not coaxed out by an inanimate object. I liked having him around. That thought was sobering and curled my stomach. My heart and body needed to slow down. I only got five weeks. But at least I got them.

When the bathroom door opened, I closed my eyes, pretending to be asleep so he could leave without awkwardness. I felt a presence by me. Then the bed sank down. With gentle hands, he brushed my hair from my cheek. A shiver stole over me.

"Mina," he whispered, his lips finding mine.

"Good morning," I murmured.

He kissed down my bare chest. I arched up to meet him and tangled my fingers in his hair.

"How about a good morning wake-up call and then breakfast?" he said, slipping his bare legs between my knees. My body was already in agreement. "I can make us eggs and pancakes."

I wrapped my legs around his waist, pulling my center up to rub against him.

I pulled a condom out and sheathed him.

By noon, we'd used three more.

As we finished eating lunch on the sofa, Chinese food delivery, my phone vibrated multiple times, and I reached to check it.

TRINA: I'm bringing stuff to make pizzas.
DANI: I have stuff for mojitos
CORRINE: I'm bringing me
DANI: Love you, but not enough, try again
MAGGIE: I'm bringing tea
VICTORIA: Mina you have Netflix right?
TRINA: She does
DANI: Cor what are you bringing?
CORRINE: I'm clearing a rack out at the gas station
DANI: <thumbs-up emoji>
MAGGIE: I'm 30 minutes out
TRINA: 20
DANI: 35
CORRINE: 15
VICTORIA: Soon

"Shit, I forgot the ladies are coming over." I rubbed a hand over my forehead. Then I flicked my gaze down to the baggy T-shirt I wore, with nothing underneath.

Jack rubbed a hand up my bare leg. He wore boxers from the duffle bag in his car. Like me, he carried a duffle bag with a change of clothes and basic toiletry essentials for when meetings ran late and, for me, in case I spilled something in between meetings.

"I'll clear out," Jack said with a chuckle. "Probably don't want them seeing me."

That wasn't the truth. Which was worrisome. Guilt or embarrassment should likely be eating me up since I slept with Jack three weeks after my failed wedding. The reasons were numerous, but other than a ball in my stomach about it only being five weeks, warmth and excitement twisted in me.

"I'm going to get the fifth degree about what's happening between us, so you better run, or they'll target you," I said.

"I can stay. I'll answer their questions," he said, his blue eyes locking on mine.

My heart skipped a beat. My core tightened. He had no shame about us. He'd mentioned we were seeing each other immediately after we made our agreement. Now he was willing to face my friends. It took all my willpower not to swing my legs over him and straddle him. Run the risk of my friends catching us.

Instead, I laughed. "No, it's okay. You've already met them. We can schedule another time for their interrogation."

Warning bells went off in my mind. Fuck. I was moving forward like we had a future. Not five weeks.

"I look forward to it." He leaned over and kissed my lips. "Text me if you get a chance. You said you had plans with your mom tomorrow. I take it you still have the standing lunch?"

I choked on my breath. "Yeah, Sundays are still my mom's day, but I limit it to a few hours."

He moved to gather his clothes from my room. He tugged on a T-shirt and pulled on his pants. A pout puffed my lips as he zipped his pants. My heart pinched at the thought of not seeing him later.

"Dinner then tomorrow?" he asked, grabbing his jacket.

I smiled at him. At least he was invested in the short time we had. I blinked. He probably was in all his relationships. It's why so many liked him. Like a player, he was all in until the next woman of interest came along.

Still, I had my five weeks. Maybe tonight I'd calculate out the weeks to know when to pull back. Or I could just live the time.

He quirked his brows up.

Or keep it as planned.

"Sure, I'm going to start my research on Greg, so I may pick your brain for details."

He smiled. "It's a date, then."

He slid his hand behind my head, and his lips met mine.

I wrapped myself around him, deepening our kiss. My shirt lifted, exposing my lower half.

"That's not helping me leave," he said.

He traced his hands down my side, anchoring my hips to him. I brushed against him. He backed me up to the wall, trailing languid kisses over my jaw and then neck. His thumbs rubbed circles on my hips, moving toward my center.

"How long until they show up?"

"Minutes," I growled.

"I could possibly get you off in that time."

My fingers fell to his cock, hard and ready in his pants. Maybe if we worked on each other . . .

My phone vibrated on the table. Another notification shook my phone.

"Shit, okay," I said, releasing him.

My entire body screamed at me to press back into him.

"Until tomorrow." When he pulled back, his hooded eyes were foggy. With a final hard kiss, he left.

Five minutes after Jack left, Trina let herself into my apartment. I'd barely pulled on yoga pants and a bra. With each hurried movement, a delicious ache between my legs reminded me of everything we'd done last night. Trina's copper hair was twisted up in a messy bun. She wore a baggy T-shirt over skinny jeans. Her skin, pale white like mine, had streaks of sunburn from the summer sun.

She paused halfway to the kitchen, turning slowly to me as a smile grew on her face.

"Holy shit, someone got her brains fucked out." She jumped up and down in her spot.

"What?" I asked, my fingers flying to my burning cheeks.

"I saw his car pull away, FYI. Also, you are fucking floating," she said, continuing her trek to the kitchen. "And you have that fun walk after thoroughly getting fucked."

A knock stopped me from retorting. I opened the door to Dani and Maggie.

"I also grabbed wine," Dani said.

Dani held up her grocery sacks. Her dark tresses hung in a braid over her recently suntanned shoulder. Her hazel eyes narrowed in on me before a large smile grew.

Maggie lifted several boxes of luxury tea.

"Tea for when we get to the apothecary part. Wait . . ." she breathed out.

Her blond hair hung around her pale shoulders in loose curls. Her aqua eyes lit up with amusement.

I wasn't going to make it five minutes before the interrogation started.

Victoria showed up before I closed the door. Her sleek long black hair was pushed back from her tan skin with a headband. "I brought fruit and veggies."

"Yuck, seriously," Trina called from the kitchen.

"Yes," Victoria called back. "With the amount of alcohol and everything else, we can balance it out."

Victoria's warm brown eyes caught mine, and she did a double take.

"Wait for Corrine," I gritted out.

They squealed in unison.

"We can catch her up," Victoria said, dropping the snacks on the table and grabbing my hands. "I need to know everything now."

"Spill," Maggie said, circling us.

"Is it that Jack guy? From the bar?" Dani asked, touching her chin with her pointer finger.

"So the dinner went really well." Maggie jumped up and hugged me. Her eyes narrowed as she leaned back to scrutinize me. "But this is a fresh glow . . ."

"There was a follow-up date. We went to last night's Caliber mixer together."

Maggie blinked at me. A large Cheshire smile curled her lips. "Told you he had the hots for you then and *now*."

Although I flushed at the words, my mind was spinning around the moments with Jack. His touch. His taste. His presence.

"Oh, look, the glassy-eyed lusty eyes! She's getting some good loving!" Victoria cheered. "I am so happy for you!"

"Wait, wait, wait," Trina yelled. She held her hands out dramatically as if stopping traffic. "Went together? Together as in a *couple*?"

Four sets of eyes stared at me.

"When Corrine gets here," I gritted out.

My cheeks burned, and I stared intently at the coffee table.

"Okay," Victoria groused. "So, give those of us who don't know more info on this crush Jack had in high school."

"Everyone but me apparently knew," I sighed.

Life could have been so different had I known back then. But it didn't mean we'd have lasted.

"You only had eyes for dickhead," Maggie said.

"No," Trina said, joining us with an evil grin. "She had a crush on Jack too, at least in the beginning, but Ethan asked her out and Jack started dating everyone. Then she pretended she didn't."

"You did not!" Maggie yelled. "How did I not know that? We were best friends!"

"How did you know that?" I yelled at Trina.

The crush had been small. Barely there. Even if it trickled into adulthood.

"You're not denying it right now!" Trina said.

"So you didn't know," Maggie said, relieved. "I thought for a minute I'd lost my touch."

"I did have a small one on him before I started dating Ethan."

"What?" Maggie roared. "And you settled for Ethan?"

"I didn't know he liked me. I thought he was cute," I offered. "I'm not denying that. Jack was even hot in the awkward years, but the crush ended when I started dating Ethan."

Especially when Jack started dating around. That thought sent a flicker of doubt to my heart. Now I'd be added to the list of women he dated and left. At least I'd set our terms. Picked when we ended. He wouldn't just get bored.

Trina cocked an eyebrow at me. "Mina, you're fucking Jack now. You can admit you had a crush. Even then. Don't forget, I was there. I saw you together almost every night when he dropped you off."

My cheeks flamed. An odd sinking feeling twisted in my stomach. Had I known Jack had a crush before I started dating Ethan . . . I honestly didn't know. We were different people then, shaped now by the choices we'd made.

"Cute isn't a crush," Maggie said. "You can find people fucking hot and not be attracted to them in a sexual way."

"Keep telling yourself that." Victoria teased her. "Fucking hot and not attracted don't go together, but you can find someone sexually appealing and not want them personally."

Maggie rolled her eyes. She had the most complicated relationship with love. I doubted she believed in romantic love for herself. She probably wouldn't know she had a crush on someone even if it came with a PowerPoint presentation and analysis report.

"Oh, come on, cute?" Trina said, shoving her shoulder. "Jack drove her home all the time because it was 'on the way' when it really wasn't. He always walked her to the door, and they'd be laughing or talking about something."

"What makes you think I had one when I was dating Ethan?"

My words were small, more thought than sound. Had Ethan thought Jack and I were doing something, so it was okay for him? The thought stopped almost quicker than it came. No, if Ethan had any suspicions of that, he'd have confronted me, us, then. He'd known Jack had one but wasn't concerned about me. In any sense, other than I did what he wanted.

Trina laughed until she saw my face. "Girl, you lit up around Jack. Sometimes, you two would sit in the car and talk until Mom came out to the porch. You were always smiling around him. You didn't with Ethan. If Ethan had noticed, there's no way he would have been okay with Jack driving you. So, if that's what has you concerned, stop it now. You did nothing wrong. You thought you had a friend. Even if the rest of us saw more."

My vision unfocused. Besides by denying my own feelings, I'd been ignorant of everything going on around me. Not much had changed on that front until I caught Ethan in the closet. A mistake I wouldn't make again.

A knock sounded on the door.

"Get in here," Maggie yelled, pulling Corrine in.

"What'd I miss?" she asked, carrying plastic sacks bulging with chips, candy, and salty treats. Her black curly hair was pulled back, her olive skin accented by a salmon-colored tank top.

"Mina's sleeping with Jack, the guy from the bar, who she apparently had a crush on in high school, but no one knew this," Victoria said in a rush to fill her in.

"Wait, you're sleeping with him now?" Corrine scanned me over. "Oh my, and it's good."

"What the hell? Do I have a glowing sign on my forehead that says 'had her brains fucked out of her all night'?"

"All night?" Maggie asked.

"What?" Trina barked.

"How many times?" Victoria asked, clapping her hands.

"When are you seeing him again?" Dani asked.

"I've missed too much. Restart at the beginning." Corrine grabbed my hand and dragged me to the sofa. The others followed us. "Just pretend we know nothing . . ."

I closed my eyes. I knew they'd need to know all the details, even the agreement on five weeks. They'd let me know if it was crazy. But even then, I'd probably still do it. I chose to skip the flight as it had nothing to do with current events, and at that time, I didn't think I'd see him outside of mixers.

"Jack was at the bar I went to after . . . after I caught Ethan fucking Tiffany. When the bartender wanted me to leave, Jack offered to drive me. No, he took my keys and insisted on driving. I passed out in the back before he got back from giving the bartender Trina's phone and stuff so Ethan couldn't track me. He didn't know where to go, so he took me to a hotel."

"Whoa!" several yelled at once.

"He didn't do anything but hold my hair back while I puked. He got me food, meds, water, a change of clothes. I thought he was doing it because he hated Ethan. Turns out, he's just nice. We texted a little bit. I ran into him at the bar when Trina ditched me in the bathroom."

"Come on, I didn't ditch you so much as help you talk to him, and it paid off," Trina said, raising an eyebrow at me. "I knew the vodka drink was from him. I wouldn't just ditch you with an unknown person."

"Anyway," I drawled. "He helped me pick up my stuff from Ethan's. The following week, we had a thank-you dinner. We didn't have sex."

"You're blushing." Trina pointed at my face. "So what *did* happen?"

"Third base? I think?"

Maggie snorted. "Oral?"

I nodded.

"Good. That's a good start."

"And then what? You went to the Caliber thing, and?" Victoria asked, smacking me with a pillow when I stopped talking.

"And . . . well . . ." My burning face fell into my hands. How was I going to tell them?

"You're embarrassed about sleeping with him?" Dani asked, rubbing my back. "Why? A rebound is okay."

"It's not that." I whimpered. "The sex was great."

"Then what is it?" She hugged my back and rocked us.

I took several deep breaths before sitting up.

"Yes, the sex is incredible. Yes, he's a really great guy."

"But?" Corrine prompted.

"We work together . . . too well. He tried to hook me up with a client, but I told him to stop."

"Why?" Maggie asked. "Networking is fine. Didn't you give him a lead too?"

I blinked. I hadn't considered that, even when he mentioned it.

"I don't need another Ethan situation. He already got three clients to leave. I know he's called others."

"You think Jack is like Ethan?" Trina asked.

"No," I groaned. "He's not . . . I just don't want that type of relationship. Where I leech clients. I can get my own. When I'm a partner, then I can do it without feeling like my promotion was only because of who I was fucking."

"That . . . makes sense," Maggie said, squeezing my hand. "What did he say?"

"He agreed to stop. He didn't set one up, per se. He just said he should talk to me. I talked to him at the zoo event we attended together, and I'm meeting the client Tuesday."

"Wait, you went to the event with Jack?" Corrine asked. "Wasn't Ethan going to be there?"

"He was there," I said. "He was a jackass."

"So you're publicly seeing Jack, then?" Corrine asked, pulling her head back and giving me a skeptical look. "Or what? I mean, you went to a big thing *together*."

"That was my question too." Trina cocked an eyebrow at me.

"Shit," I muttered. "Okay, hear me out."

"Oh, this is going to be good. Mina acted on her instinct instead of acute analysis," Trina said.

"Shut up." I pretended to scold her.

But acting on just my heart and body could lead to being hurt, again, like all the important men in my life had done. I needed to keep my expectations in alignment with the five weeks.

They shared a look, none looking like they believed me.

Maggie smirked. "We already went over that you and Ethan were emotionally divorced for a while. It's okay to move on quickly."

"I'm not disagreeing. A rebound wouldn't be bad. Get it out of my system. Jack is also a . . . player. He's not a different-girl-every-night type, but he jumps from date to date. It won't be permanent."

"You know a lot about him," Corrine said.

"We grew up together, and he's one of Ethan's biggest competitors."

They laughed.

"That's the best part," Trina said.

"So, if you're not in a relationship with him, what are you doing?" Corrine asked, steering me back.

"I can't think about anything permanent, and he's not built for it. I'm also not ready to say bye, I guess, to whatever our relationship is now or go back to just the short greetings we had at other events."

"Get to it," Victoria demanded, smacking her pillow.

"We agreed to date for five weeks as a trial run," I blurted out.

"And then?" Maggie asked, completely unfazed.

Trina's brow crinkled.

"Five weeks?" Corrine and Victoria mouthed to each other.

Dani stroked my hair, continuing to hug me. "What happens after five weeks?"

"Then . . . I don't really know. I'm not ready to think about it," I said, dropping my head into my lap.

"That's fair." Trina came over to kneel by me. "I'm glad you're moving on from Ethan. It's okay if Jack is a rebound, and it's okay if he's more than a rebound. You're being open and vulnerable right now. You're, for once, evaluating what you emotionally need and can provide. It's okay if you don't know and if you change your mind over the next five weeks."

"And you're getting good dick," Corrine said, patting my back. "That's important too."

"Yes," Dani said.

"True," Victoria said.

"When do you see him again?" Corrine asked.

"Tomorrow," I squeaked out.

"You're bringing him to Mom's?" Trina asked, the shock thick in her voice.

"No." I scoffed. "We both know how that'd go."

"Your mom doesn't like Jack or doesn't think you're ready to date?" Victoria asked.

Trina and I shared a look.

"Oh, this is good." Victoria rubbed her hands.

"Jack wasn't Ethan and didn't have his image," Trina offered. "With the divorce, Mom thought Ethan was the stable, reliable one. Ethan was well off and could provide for Mina. Jack dated a lot. Which she thought would lead to our dad's behavior. She saw how Jack and Mina got along, and it bothered her because she thought it would ruin her chances with Ethan."

"Look how that turned out," Victoria said.

Trina touched her nose.

"So what are you two doing tomorrow, besides fucking?" Maggie asked.

I rolled my eyes. "He's helping me research the client he introduced me to."

"Research," Victoria choked out. "Sure, research. Just make sure he finds your happy spot too."

"Jeez," I chuckled. "Now that you know my chaos, can we watch *Schitt's Creek* and stuff our faces?"

"Yes," they replied in unison.

## JUNE 6TH

## MINA

The house sat on a corner lot, the lawn manicured with a stone water feature in the center of the corner. Her double lot was cleared with flowering paths winding into the back. Gerald had put in an ornate stone walkway five years ago, right after they married.

Trina pulled in behind, her eyes catching me in the rearview mirror. We always did this—waited for the other and made a united front going in. Sundays had been our mom's day. We'd get up and clean, go to church, come home, and make a large meal. We only did family things, like play games or watch a movie. It was innocent enough in looks, but Mom used the time to guilt and berate us. In her fear of us living the first half of her life, she provided unwanted and unwarranted advice.

Thinking back, though, she'd always liked Ethan. He came from an established family with a history of long marriages and good standing in the community. Even if he was an adulterer like my father, he hadn't had the overtness, though it probably would have come in time. Ethan was frugal with money, relative to the amount he made, something my mom found admirable. She had already picked out names for our three children, even though Ethan and I discussed two, at most.

Trina knocked on my window when I still hadn't gotten out of my car. She cocked an eyebrow at me.

I sighed and opened my door.

Per our mother's rules, we were both dressed up. Knowing Jack might stop over, I'd opted for a black skirt and maroon sleeveless blouse.

"Skirt, huh?" Trina said.

I shrugged and sent her a cheeky grin. The girls had stayed until midnight. We'd talked about our high school crushes, our current significant others. Trina was already looking at ending her relationship, Corrine and her boyfriend were talking marriage, and Victoria was already dating someone new since last month. Maggie was the perpetual bachelorette, her job her love and focus, and Dani never was interested in more than a date or two at most with the men her mom constantly set her up with.

"Is Eric joining us?" I asked Trina, bumping her hip as we walked up the pathway.

"No, Mom cornered him at the wedding," she said with a snort. "He's returning my calls less and less."

"You were boring of him anyway," I said, casting a glance at her face to confirm she hadn't lied last night.

She nodded.

It was her habit. Date boring men who wouldn't hurt her like our dad had done. The issue was that she picked men who couldn't hurt her emotionally because she wasn't interested in them for more than a specific time frame or worried about losing them. Clay was for high school. Kyle was for college. She had one a few years ago that lasted a year. Now Eric. She knew how long each one would last. Once burned with her first crush, she wouldn't allow herself to want after someone.

Mom opened the door, her arms folded over her torso.

"Oh yeah, now we get to get scolded for dawdling," Trina whispered.

"The chicken is drying out waiting for you," Mom said, her mouth pinched in a tight line.

Trina snorted. "You invited a chicken to lunch? If it's thirsty, give the dam— dang bird a drink."

I snorted.

Mom's chest rose and fell, her nostrils flaring.

The house smelled of roasted chicken, veggies, and apple pie. At least we'd eat well.

"No Eric?" Mom asked, following us to the dining room.

"Nope," Trina said and left it at that.

Mom darted her eyes to me, but I didn't offer up anything.

Gerald came in, his red polo tucked into his khakis. He didn't look comfortable in the attire, but he beamed at Mom and hugged her. Somehow, he found all her meddling and nagging enduring.

We sat down, the silence thick and stifling.

"Trina, when are you going to find someone to marry like—" Mom stopped her automatic response to Trina, her eyes flashing to me in sympathy and horror.

"Oh, I hope not like Mina," Trina said, patting my hand.

My heart rolled. Ethan was a jackass, but for years I'd thought he was the one I'd have a family and grow old with. The longer I was away from him, the more I felt like I could breathe, but that made me sad thinking of all those years. He hadn't micromanaged my attire other than my T-shirts, probably because I typically wore suits, but I did start the swear jar because of him, and he didn't try to order my food or tell me how to be. He just had expectations. The same ones I'd been raised with by my mom.

"Trina." Mom scolded her and sent her a silencing look.

"What?" Trina said, the side of her lip curving up into a smirk. "Mina doesn't want that again either."

"She's right," I said with a nod.

"Have you spoken to him since that night?" Gerald asked, lifting a bite of chicken to his mouth.

Mom stilled, staring at me. She must not have told him about the apartment, or Jack.

"He tried to stop by my apartment. When I got my stuff from his apartment. He tried to talk to me at a networking event," I said, staring at my food.

"It's just so unexpected of him," Mom said. The table vibrated as her knee bounced up and down. "I can't believe I missed it. I don't agree with his father, though."

I lifted my eyes to meet hers.

"It's not out of his system. For someone to do that . . . and on their wedding day," Mom said, shaking her head. "He was a selfish, disgusting as— jerk. He doesn't deserve you."

It was the harshest thing she'd ever said about Ethan. I ran my tongue over my teeth. It didn't take long for the next shoe to drop.

"Now, that Aiden," Mom said, settling back in her chair. She sent me a knowing look with a lifted chin. "All the same great background, but a decent young man. He was so nice at the wedding."

"Oh jeez," I muttered.

She'd already found a work-around for Jack. Figured a way to remove him from the picture even without knowing I saw him after the kiss.

"What do you have against Aiden?" Mom demanded, her fork pointed at me.

"Aiden is like a kid brother," I said, looking to Trina for help.

"Mom, if she dated Aiden, she'd be stuck seeing Ethan at every family event," Trina said.

"Isn't it too soon for her to start dating again?" Gerald asked.

Guilt, hot and stifling, twisted in my throat and caught my breath. The motion caused me to choke.

Trina and my mom shot him dark looks. His eyes bulged, and he focused back on his plate of food.

"Why is your face red?" Mom asked, her attention back on me. "Did you eat something you're allergic to?"

"No," I choked out.

"Oh shit, er, oh no, you did." She rambled, flustered as she pushed her chair back. "I'll get the Benadryl!"

"No," I called, still coughing around the piece of food that went down wrong.

"Mom, no," Trina yelled, pushing her chair back to provide a blockade.

"Dammit, Trina, oh jeez, you're making me swear on Sunday! Get out of my way! Mina ate something she's allergic to!" Mom yelled.

"Mina," Trina growled.

"Mom, I'm fine," I said over my cup as I guzzled water. The scratch of a cough made my voice rough.

"Then what's wrong?" she demanded, her hands on her hips, staring at me.

Trina sent me a silent message. Telling her I was still seeing Jack was a bad idea. Not telling her and her finding out was a worse idea. Could I manage five weeks without her knowing? I darted my eyes around as I weighed the options.

"Mina, what is going on?" Mom barked.

"Mina, are you okay?" Gerald asked, risking a glance at my mom.

"Yes, I'm fine. I . . . I started seeing someone."

"What?" Mom asked, her eyes opening wide. "Oh, a rebound, as we discussed."

Gerald made a strangled sound in his throat and turned back to his plate. The tips of his ears reddened.

"It's not serious . . ." I said to fix my mistake. Though my heart pinched. "It's just been a date or two."

"A date or two? Don't you know?" she asked, narrowing her eyes on me.

She turned her gaze to Trina, who, with her mouth pinched to the side, was studying the fabric on the back of the chair.

"Who is it?" Mom gritted out. Her face paled the longer she stared at me. "It's not . . ."

Trina darted her eyes to mine.

"Jack," I breathed out, the word like a chill in the room.

Mom mumbled a curse under her breath. "Mina, his history . . . What about Aiden?"

"His history?" Trina started. "You're still throwing fucking flags?"

"Who's Jack?" Gerald asked.

The three of us stared at him.

"Ethan's best friend. Well, he was in high school until they had a falling out," Mom said, watching me. "He drove Mina home a lot."

It was probably some of the nicest sentences she'd ever strung together for Jack, yet red flashed in my vision. She wasn't wrong that he had been a player, but he hadn't been cruel. In fact, kind was the word I would use to describe him.

"Are you dating him to spite Ethan?" Gerald asked.

"Gerald!" Mom scolded him.

We all startled. Gerald's eyes widened.

I thought it was a fair question, but I wasn't going to bring her wrath on me.

"He's also Ethan's biggest competitor in the area, and both are working their way into Chicago." Trina resumed eating her chicken.

"He had a crush on Mina in high school," Mom said, finding her chair.

I sighed. For some reason, this was everyone's go-to response about Jack.

"Is he nice?" Gerald asked, his gaze jumping between all three of us.

"Yes," Trina and I said while Mom said, "Eh."

"Mom," Trina admonished. "Jack was always nice."

"He always had a new girlfriend. Just like . . ." Mom's face reddened, and she swallowed back the next few words. "I was so glad you chose Ethan," Mom said, then she pinched her face. "I'm sorry, Mina. That wasn't the right thing to say . . . I just . . ."

"Mom, Ethan fooled us both," I said. "I know about Jack's reputation."

Maybe she'd understand the arrangement after all. It might actually ease her mind. She had encouraged a rebound last week. The terms were meant to help protect me, stop me from moving my heart too fast or far ahead.

"We're just seeing each other for a bit. I'm not ready for anything serious, and I'm not ready to trust someone. But as wrong as it is, I also don't want Ethan to think he had that much effect on me. It's petty and spiteful, but I realized I feel less stressed, less like I'm always skirting around a fight, and if I close off now, I don't know if I'll resume dating. Not that I have to. I just don't want Ethan to have that power. And Jack is really nice. I know he'll get bored at some point, probably sooner rather than later. So you know, I get a chance to see life with someone who isn't Ethan, knowing it won't last super long and the whole time pissing him off."

Trina, Mom, and Gerald stared at me, unblinking for a while.

"That's honest and a bit disturbing," Trina said and shrugged. "But I approve and support. Even if I think it could be more."

The thought of more tightened my already unsettled stomach. Even if I might want it, it wasn't an option.

"This feels wrong," Mom said, shaking her head. "But I think we all heal differently. I worked seventy-plus hours a week, neglecting you girls. If I'd been home, maybe I'd have seen the issues with Ethan."

"Mom, don't blame yourself," I said, shaking my head. "I made my choices. I didn't see it. Or ignored it. But Ethan did what he did."

"Do you like Jack?" Gerald asked, his eyes shining bright as he stared at me.

Heat crept up my neck as I felt Trina's and Mom's stare. Warning bells sounded in my head. It was a simple question but held too much meaning.

"Yes," I whispered.

Trina's gloating thickened the air between us.

Mom licked her lips, her knee bouncing. My stomach tightened. I rubbed my palms on my knees, my glance jumping to the door.

"Mina, I . . ."

I looked back to her, meeting her watery amber eyes.

"Mom . . . I can't say I know what I'm really doing, but I'm following my gut. I'm doing my best."

"And you like Jack?" she repeated. Defeat slackened her face.

"Yes," I mumbled, not sure what they really meant by like anymore. Like felt shallow for what stirred in me. But something was going to happen that I didn't like.

"Then he needs to come to lunch next Sunday." She held up a hand to stop my protest. "If he has some meeting he needs to travel to, then we'll hold Sunday on Saturday or on Friday night."

"But it's only five weeks," I moaned, both the situation and knowledge sitting heavy in my gut.

"If he's good enough to date for five weeks, then he needs to come to lunch. It would be expected of any significant other."

Trina rolled her eyes.

I groaned.

Trap sprung.

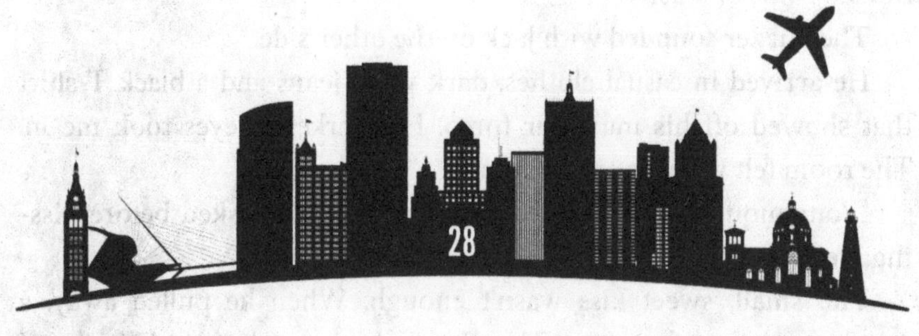


## JUNE 6TH

### MINA

Jack arrived about twenty minutes after I got home. In that time, I sprinted around my apartment, trying to tidy up anything left over from last night. Although we left it pretty clean, it seemed like every speck of dirt was glaring. I checked my clothes and hair multiple times, organized my table to research, and leaned against the wall.

Shit, I was turning into a freak. No, I was reverting back to an image that had led my life. One I had escaped.

I ran a hand through my hair. I needed to get a grip. This was a temporary arrangement, and I wasn't going to change myself for someone other than me. My mugs were staying, as were my T-shirts.

Somehow, I also needed to tell him about my mom's request for lunch. Maybe that would send him packing early. Bitterness swirled in my mouth. It was only five weeks. I'd asked for the timeline. Protecting myself needed to be my focus. Besides, tonight was to research. Not to talk about my mom or to focus on whatever our relationship was or wasn't.

The buzzer sounded with Jack on the other side.

He arrived in casual clothes, dark wash jeans and a black T-shirt that showed off his muscular torso. His darkened eyes took me in. The room felt warmer and charged.

"Your mom still requires you to dress up?" he asked before kissing me.

The small, sweet kiss wasn't enough. When he pulled away, a weight settled on my chest. Then I chastised myself. I made it clear I wanted to research a client tonight.

"Yes," I said, staring down at my attire.

The prim outfit would work for the office or a client meeting if I wore a jacket over the blouse.

He stepped closer, snagging my focus. I flicked my gaze back to his lips, which parted slightly as I stared. He tilted my chin up with two fingers.

"You look gorgeous." He kissed my jawline.

Each heated kiss sent a delightful shiver through me.

I wrapped my arms around his neck, burrowing my fingers into his hair and locking my lips on his. He splayed his hands across my lower back. His warmth seeped in, fueling an already burning fire for him.

Groaning, I pulled back. "You're going to distract me from what I need to get done."

"Are you going to be a demanding boss?"

He moved his hands to my waist and pulled me toward him. When I was flush against him, I could feel his desire, hard and pressing into my stomach. A whimper escaped my lips.

My body thrummed with want, and I rubbed against him.

He reached down, running his hands down my thighs until he hoisted me up, and I wrapped my legs around his waist.

"We have work," I panted out before I crashed my lips into his.

Apparently, my brain and heart weren't on the same page, and need and want urged me forward.

"I know," he said, pushing my back against the wall. With one hand supporting me, his other found my center. He rubbed his knuckles against my core. "I need to get you wetter."

I pushed into his hand, liking the friction against my sex.

He kissed my collarbone, then above the neckline of my shirt. The loose fabric gave him access to my breasts. Pushing aside the material, he ran his tongue over my breast and under the cup. He twirled his tongue over my nipple and then moved to the other one.

Moving my hands to his waistline, I unbuttoned and unzipped his pants. I ran my hand over his cock, and the hard member throbbed against my hand.

"I want you," I moaned, pressing into him.

He blinked. His gaze, like fire, found mine. Then his lips pressed into mine for a hard kiss. He pulled a few condoms from his back pocket, tossing all but one onto the small table that housed my keys. It had never occurred to me until that moment what a great spot for condoms it was.

"Say it again," he said, trailing kisses up to my lips.

"I want you," I said against his lips.

I slipped my hand into his briefs, shoving aside the material to free him, the thoughts on research shattered and forgotten.

He tore the foil packet open and handed me the condom. Slowly I rolled it onto his cock, feeling it pulse in my hand.

With his thumb, he rubbed over my wet panties and then slipped beneath, finding my clit. He dipped in two fingers, rubbing them up and down.

"Jack," I groaned.

His mouth silenced my next plea. He pushed aside my underwear and entered me. I arched against him, taking him deep.

As he pumped inside, his thumb rubbed on my center, building the intensity until the wave crashed, and my body shuddered with release.

"Jack," I screamed out as my orgasm rolled through me. My fingers dug for purchase in his back.

He lost it a few seconds later, coming with a shudder.

He leaned his forehead against mine, our haggard breathing mixing, the air hot and heavy between us.

His lips met mine in a light kiss, and he moaned, "Mina."

I ran my fingers through his hair, kissing his forehead and temple and ears.

His Nordic-blue eyes locked on to mine. Emotion swam in them. It'd be so easy to lose myself in them. To believe the emotion was something more than transitory. More than satiating an old crush. More than spiting his enemy. More than a long fling.

"Mina," he started again and licked his lips, lust likely pushing him to believe more.

"I'm glad you brought multiples," I said to break the tension and whatever falsehoods that were building. To stop whatever sweet lie he was about to say that I wanted to hear. To give myself one thin line of protection.

He half smiled, his eyes tracking, looking for something in my eyes he didn't find.

Like a blast of cold air, his eyes shuttered, and the emotion was gone. That fucking granite fortress of nothingness.

## JUNE 6TH

## JACK

I had to keep my emotions in check. Lock down anything that could scare or confuse her. Ethan had shaken her trust in others as her father had done. Sure, I brought the condoms. After the previous night, I wanted to replenish the supply, but I hadn't planned on using them immediately. I wanted to talk to Mina about slowing down more.

She wanted a trial run of five weeks. I didn't know if it was because of what Ethan pulled or my history with other women or both. It was probably both. It was why I wanted to slow it down. Show her she meant more. That whatever our pasts were, they didn't have to be our future.

My past only haunted me with Mina. My long list of girlfriends had a hard stopping point when we graduated. Or, as Mina had called it at the bonfire, the list of women I used. After high school and moving to California, I didn't have the daily reminders of not being good enough for Mina. That my "unhappy penis issues," as she had called them, didn't see her with him every fucking day.

When I returned and saw them at a dinner, that familiar feeling had come back in full force. The urge felt harder and more intense than I remembered from school. Like a smoker inhaling a cigarette years after stopping. For a few months, I'd fallen back into my old habits of dating any woman who showed interest. And just like high school, it had been hollow and unfulfilling. The momentary high didn't match the low afterward. The instant reminder that I wasn't good enough for Mina still stung.

With my mind on growing our business, instead of entertaining habits that hadn't helped, I'd just leave the venues and go home to either run or take a cold shower or both.

Now she was with me, but that same look I saw in high school each time I had a new girlfriend flittered in her eyes. It had been both a euphoric and a painful experience. The joy of eliciting a reaction from her, that she cared, was always chased by the pain of seeing the judgment that lurked in her eyes. With it making a return in the moment, the feelings of inadequacy from high school followed. Of not being good enough.

Or I was making it about me and not her. She'd been through so much in the past few weeks. Perhaps it was guilt and remorse. Both settled like lead in my stomach.

So, when we'd finished, both spent against the wall, something had shifted in her. Her eyes reflected lust, but something else too. Not sure what it was, I retreated, holding back my words on what I wanted for us.

Us. Fuck. We had five weeks. Did she even want an us? That question stalled me, and I recoiled, giving her space. While I did that, her wall went up, row by row. The fear and lust that had shone brightly in her eyes receded into skepticism and defense.

Instead of confessing this to her after I took her against the wall within a few minutes of arriving, I sat with her at the table, reviewing the ton of information she had already researched on Greg.

So, we sat, staring at more information about Greg Cremski than I knew existed. If the government ever caught wind of her tenacity, she'd be on special projects immediately. The words blurred together, a stream of text that spun in my mind as I watched her move. The way her wall of defense seemed to crumble under the joy of the data hunt. She pointed to figures, showing me decades of financial information she'd assembled into bite-size graphs and pivot tables.

Mina leaned over the table, her shirt dipping low, revealing her maroon lacy bra and cleavage. My cock responded.

"So, Greg is looking for a large warehouse area in the land between Milwaukee and Chicagoland."

I blinked, pulling my attention from her body and waiting for my brain to register all the words. "Yep, it's primed for it. I have several sites that already have utility connections. Some of the warehouses would require minimal redesign."

"Based on what I dug up, he'll have about twenty million to invest but, based on his history, won't be willing to part with that much. The special rate doesn't require that, so I believe he'll stick to the minimum requirement for the rate, which is more than fifty percent of the project cost."

"Twenty million would edge you toward partner?" I asked.

Her amber eyes locked on me. I reached across and tucked a strand of auburn hair behind her ear. For a moment, she leaned into my touch before shifting away.

"Don't." She pointed a finger in my face.

"Don't what?"

"Don't go trying to get him to invest more. I have my methods," she said, staring into my eyes.

I smirked. "You do have your methods, and they work quite well."

Her face flushed, and at that moment, she seemed to notice the view she was providing me. She eased back into her chair, adjusting her shirt.

I shifted on my chair, readjusting the hardness in my pants. Unease swam between us. Although I tried to make light of it, she was worried I was going to pull an Ethan. Sabotage her career. Interfere with deals. Twist myself into her career so she couldn't see where she started and where I came in. Despite the heaviness and underlying intentions of it, I understood it too. I slid my hand over hers. Her fingers curled around mine. The comforting warmth was something I would never tire of.

"H—" I swallowed down her nickname. "Mina, you have the man's life story. His business story. You have every public financial report he's published, plus some I don't think you're supposed to have."

She shrugged, a smile tugging on her lips. "None of it matters until I meet with him. Just because I know his business doesn't mean he'll sign with me. He's experienced enough he can get almost anyone. In his eyes, I'd be a risk."

I scoffed. "Mina, you may only have a few years, but . . ." I gestured to her neat piles of research. "There's a reason you have a reputation already and have referrals."

A smile wobbled on her lips, warring with the self-doubt that had crept in.

"He agreed to meet with you."

Her smile grew.

"So when do you fly out?" I asked, already missing her.

"I have an early flight Tuesday and meet with him at three."

"That's the best time," I said.

"I know," she said. "But it's also why my last client meeting ran late, and I had to catch the late flight back."

Her face dropped at the memory. My own muscles tightened, and a darkness raced in my veins. Despite the feelings I had for Mina for over a decade, if Ethan had been a decent person, I would have been happy for her. Happy for them. Even if jealous. But Ethan was a dumb fuck. Two fucking days before their wedding and he couldn't make time to pick her up. The jackass. Even if I got to drive her home, it's fucking ridiculous he'd leave her like that.

"When is your flight back? Afterward? Next morning?"

"I have an eight o'clock fight scheduled back that night," she said, watching me.

The wall was slowly going back up. Her eyes were starting to shutter, ready to move on.

Unable to take the wall, or recess, I leaned over, brushing my lips against hers. She gasped in surprise. I didn't take advantage of it but gave her another soft kiss. Her eyes fluttered open. Even if it was lust, it had smashed the wall back down a bit. Her gaze lingered on my lips, her amber eyes darkening.

Even if I wanted to get lost in her, I wanted to define some expectations. Make sure she knew she was important.

"So ten for arrival?" I said.

The lust receded. Her face slackened. "Probably."

"Should I meet you by security or baggage claim?"

Her eyes jumped in surprise, and a smile tugged on her lips before it faded into a flat line.

That fucker.

She rubbed a hand over her neck, her gaze falling to her research. "You don't have to pick me up. I'll schedule an Uber. I normally do."

"Security or baggage claim," I repeated.

"Don't worry about it," she said, folding her hands together.

My hand was still on the table where she left it.

"If I don't make that flight, I don't want to screw your schedule up."

Ethan was a fucking asshole. I'd punch him if it'd help, but I'd probably just get shit all over my hand.

"Mina," I murmured and took her hand back.

Her fingers curled around mine. Once again, the feeling was right.

She stilled, watching me. Waiting. Hope and disappointment fighting in her eyes.

"I'll meet you outside of security. If you grab a different flight, text me the flight number so I can track it."

# 30

## JUNE 8TH

## MINA

"Mina, I like the portfolio." Greg took his glasses off and pinched his nose.

Here comes the but.

"I also like the plans Jack has drawn up," Greg said. His watery blue eyes looked up to me.

Two buts were coming.

"But . . ."

So called it.

"I also have another offer on the table from Ethan," he said, his lips pressing into a thin line.

So, Ethan was able to make a bid, probably using his connection that he had dated his daughter . . . while we'd been dating.

"For both investing and your next building project?"

"Ethan wants me to talk to a Trevor person at your office," he said.

"I feel like I should disclose that because I don't want you to find out from him and think I'm duping you."

Anger pricked my eyes. My heart hammered in my chest.

"May I ask when Ethan approached you?" I said, keeping my tone neutral.

"At the zoo event," Greg said. "He introduced me to Trevor too."

"You plan to build a massive complex in a thriving area, bringing more jobs and opportunities. I can see why he'd reach out," I said. Reality coiled as acid in my stomach. "You have to do what is best for you."

I wanted to tell him Ethan was a louse and no good and that he had been dating me while he dated his daughter and probably others, but it never looked good to do that in meetings. It may work for men, but women were seen as the emotional ones. Too fixed on popularity and bringing others down. It was the furthest thing from the truth, but I wasn't going to change Greg's mind. I had to play the cards I was dealt.

"It'll likely make the careers of either man. If I like the return, I'll have more money to send to your firm."

So my path to partnership was once again lambasted by Ethan. And Trevor.

But that didn't mean I needed to cede so readily.

"Will you be in the Milwaukee-Chicago area soon?" I asked.

"Probably next week or so. I want to check out some locations and keep the progress moving."

"How about we schedule lunch or dinner the night you come in?"

He stared at me, his fingers drumming on the table. Finally, he said, "Sure, let's meet for dinner."

Of course, I had to change my flight, and this time, I didn't even have a signed contract.

ME: Won't make flight, rebooking
JACK: Flight #?
ME: 1147

I knew what I expected and hoped, but a tiny part of me still doubted Jack would be there. That something would come up. He'd send a sympathetic, apologetic text. Possibly, he'd even send a car to grab me to make sure I made it safely home.

At 1:03 a.m., he leaned against the wall outside of security, scrolling through his phone, likely looking at email. His dark hair wasn't styled and fell in long locks. He wore snug jeans and a black T-shirt that showed off his hard frame. His five-o'clock shadow had filled in, and I wanted to rub my fingers across his jaw. He looked up every few seconds and scanned the people exiting. When he saw me, his panty-dropping smile spread across his face. He pushed off the wall and greeted me with a hug.

I wrapped my arms around him, returning the embrace. His sandalwood cologne filled my senses, along with the heat of his body and the bolt that shot through me when we touched. His rough beard prickled my ear. I ran my fingers across it. My tiredness melted away, replaced with only thoughts of Jack.

"I missed you," he said, giving me a light kiss.

He looped his arm around my shoulders and steered me toward the parking garage.

I leaned into him, enjoying the warmth and comfort he offered.

"How'd it go?" he asked, rubbing circles into my shoulder.

I snorted a dry laugh.

"What happened?"

"Ethan," I spat.

"Ethan was there?" he asked, his grip tightening.

"No, Ethan threw in a bid. I'm guessing Greg will call you with the news."

"I know about that," Jack said.

"Why didn't you say anything?"

"Ethan's always trying to do that. It's nothing new. Didn't even occur to me. What else did Ethan do?"

"What do you mean?"

"You're that worried about my business? I can handle Ethan." Jack beeped his car unlocked and opened my door. "He's been doing this to me for years. I usually still win."

"And I can't?" I countered, stopping short of the car and glaring.

Jack's eyes darted across my face, trying to find answers.

"I don't understand what happened. Is Ethan trying to get into financial investing?"

"No," I snorted. "He already has a friend in it."

Jack narrowed his eyes as he pondered my words before a dark look flashed across them. "Trevor?"

"Ding, ding," I said, finally slipping into my seat.

My tiredness flooded back and brought even more weight to my bones and spirit. It wasn't cold, but the sixty-degree air in the damp parking garage didn't feel great against my tired body.

Jack climbed into his side, his jaw ticking as he mulled over what I said.

Silence settled between us as he paid the parking fee and slipped onto the interstate. The fluorescent streetlamps danced by us, their light bursts breaking across and highlighting the tension.

"What are you thinking?" I asked after several miles.

His gaze tracked to me and then back to the deserted highway.

"Will you tell me why you two stopped being friends in high school?" I asked suddenly.

He blinked at the change in topic.

"Pick one of those two to answer." I closed my eyes as I nestled back in the seat.

"I'm thinking of ways to dismantle Ethan's stronghold in the area."

"He has it because of his father," I said. "His football fame helped him."

"His father doesn't do many deals anymore. He and his friends are closing in on retirement. Ethan has to make friends with their kids."

"He has," I said.

Jack snorted.

"What?" I asked, peeling my eyes open to stare at Jack.

"Ethan is still loyal to his college buddies. Granted, they're doing well, but others have noticed. You play favorites and it burns bridges."

"Hasn't his father corrected him? Ethan always said . . . Well, fuck that. I guess I believed he had a great foothold with the businesses."

"Only while his dad and friends are in power."

"So, you see how to unsettle him?"

"Greg's business will be huge. Once placed, it will open the pathway for more contracts with bigger companies coming in on the infrastructure builds, tax breaks negotiated, and leniencies allowed."

"So Greg is a make-or-break-it client?"

"Greg is a make-you client. Not getting him means losing turf and having to find a different area to develop. Greg's power is strong."

"Well, dammit," I groaned.

"Greg's talked to you. That's a good sign. He wouldn't meet to be polite."

"I guess it's good I invited him to a meal when he's in Milwaukee next week."

Jack darted his eyes to me. Amusement flittered across his expression as his smile grew.

"Dinner? Should I be worried?"

"Ha, ha," I deadpanned.

His face eased, settling on his natural smile.

"So, are you going to tell me why you two stopped being friends in high school?" I asked again, sitting sideways in the seat so I could watch his profile.

"He was and is a jackass."

"He was for years before you two stopped talking."

Jack's jaw ticked. "What did he say?"

"Really? That's where you're going to go? Copying his answer? He wouldn't answer. Said it was stupid guy stuff."

Jack snorted. "Of course he would."

"So if it wasn't, what was it?"

"I thought he was cheating on you," Jack whispered. He swallowed, and his glassy eyes found mine.

"What?" I choked out.

"I thought I saw him out with someone from another school." Jack slid his gaze back to the street, but he kept turning to watch me.

"Wha . . .Why . . . What the fuck! Why didn't you tell me?" I yelled, my fingers tightening around the center console. "I could have prevented so many years of being an idiot!"

Jack sighed and nodded. "First, you thought he hung the moon at the time. I tried telling you, and you blew me off."

"What? No way."

"We had been drinking. I let it slip that I thought I saw them at the movies. You said I was blind, and there was no way it was him. You said you knew, for a fact, he was at his grandma's. You then continued to tell me I was projecting all my weekly girlfriends on him. That he wasn't me. He didn't use women."

Ouch. Sadly, it was probably something I said back then. Probably something I would have said a month ago.

"You remember this quite well," I said.

"It was the last time you and I spoke more than greetings to each other." He darted his eyes back to the road.

"That was the first reason. What was the second?"

"I wanted to believe you were right. Maybe it wasn't him," he said and shrugged.

"But?"

"I know what I saw," he said.

"Wait, was this at the bonfire?"

Memories flickered in my mind, all leading to tightness in my stomach as I remembered that night. My heart squeezed, remembering the bitterness and hard looks he had sent me every day after.

"Yes."

The one word filled the space.

We shared a stare before he turned his focus back to the street.

Jack had told me the truth, even when it had cost us our friendship, because I was too tunnel visioned with blinders on. I hadn't wanted that truth, so I blamed Jack and not Ethan. And how many times had it happened that Ethan felt so comfortable about it in public?

Ethan went to his grandma's a lot in high school. I even encouraged it, thinking it was sweet. Double ass fuck. So, it had been our whole relationship. Not one and done. Not a mistake. But a pattern he felt so comfortable with he fucked someone at our wedding.

Jack came to a stop outside of my apartment building. Before I unbuckled my seat belt, he was around the car and opening my door.

With heavy eyes, he cast a look at my building, then at my hand. His gaze didn't meet mine but instead shifted to the small park across the street.

"Jack," I whispered, slipping my hand into his.

He darted his eyes back to mine, bright with guilt, and wrapped his fingers around my hand.

"Is there a third reason?" I asked.

As I walked to the door, I made sure he walked with me.

The anger within me that had burned bright and hot in the car, that he'd known what an ass Ethan was, was now a cold embrace of melancholy. I'd made my decisions with facts I had at the time. I wasn't sorry I'd defended Ethan. There hadn't been a reason not to. I was sad I'd spent so many years with him ignorant of the truth.

"Ethan said I was making it up so I'd have a chance with you," Jack whispered. "Said I'd never be good enough for you, even with my lies. Said he'd make sure you knew I was a liar. With you not believing it already and Ethan being Ethan, I just stopped."

"I probably wouldn't have believed you," I said. "Not then. I didn't want that truth. Then with my dad's shit, well, he seemed the opposite, and I wanted to believe it."

"And I was too similar with all my girlfriends," Jack said. His words were brittle, hard.

Though he kept hold of my hand, his movements stiffened and his eyes grew distant and flicked to anything but me.

At my door, he waited until I unlocked it and took a small step backward, shoving his hands into his pockets.

He was already detaching. Already calling it done. This is what he did with all his other girlfriends. But it felt different. When he broke up with them, he did it with enjoyment. At least, he always seemed happy about it the years before he stopped talking to us. He was moving on. Hopeful for the next girlfriend. This was darker, heavier.

I'd unburied something.

The door swung open, the faint glow of the kitchen light the only source in the apartment.

"Get some sleep," he murmured. A forced half smile danced on his lips as he stared at my shoulder.

"Jack?" I asked, feeling a million miles away from him.

I reached for his hand, but dropped mine when his remained in his pockets.

Did I call it done here? Let us go? We were a week into the agreement, but I wasn't ready. I hadn't prepared for it. I didn't want to be ready yet. My mind knew the terms. Wanted the terms.

He was silent, his brows pinched as he looked everywhere but at my eyes. It was probably why I was able to startle him. I wrapped my arms around his neck and stood on my toes to kiss his lips.

His eyes widened, and his frame stiffened.

"Mina," he whispered.

He rested his hands on my shoulders, likely to separate us. History was always a bitch when it was resurrected. I asked a question I'd asked for over a decade and finally got an answer. It wasn't what I had expected or wanted, but he'd been honest, even about the unpleasant parts. Now he was ready to call us done. Ready to move on from the pain. He could, in four and a half weeks. Right now, I got to enjoy the time we promised each other. I wanted what he promised for the time promised.

"Jack, please come inside," I said, not releasing him. "I'm too tired to deal with whatever happened in the car. We can talk in the morning."

He moved his eyes to the apartment, assessment and whatever other emotion flicking in his eyes. Slowly, he tracked his gaze back to mine.

I brushed my lips against his again.

He grazed his hands across my shoulders to my back. He returned the kiss, at first soft and tentative and then urgent and hot.

I broke the kiss, panting for air before saying, "Jack, thank you for telling me the truth, even if it hurt. Even if you didn't want to."

He forced a thin smile but pulled me to him, wrapping his arms around me and resting his chin against my head.

We crashed on the bed, a tangle of limbs and rumpled clothes, but it was safe, and caring, and all I had ever wanted from someone.

## JUNE 9TH

## JACK

Mina lay sleeping beside me, her head resting on my bicep while her arm claimed my chest, her fist folded over my heart.

I was a fucking fool. I'd fallen for Mina in my teens. Over the years, it'd only deepened as I watched her conquer her world while not dimming beside Ethan. Now, all she saw was how I imitated the men in her life who had betrayed her, how I'd left girlfriends in the past.

All my relationships, except a few, had been short, a week to three. But with all my past partners, we'd both entered into the relationship knowing the truth: neither of us wanted long term. I'd had a long-term girlfriend in college, but that was because we both knew at graduation, we'd part ways. I wanted Chicago. She wanted California, and neither of us was willing to compromise. Nor had we discussed more. Alicia had been long term, I'd even proposed, but she'd seen it for what it was. I'd accepted that Mina had agreed to marry Ethan, and

Alicia said no. I hadn't had a relationship since then. I couldn't offer someone all of me, but it didn't matter.

Mina was still dealing with Ethan, which she should have all the time she needed. I had wanted to avoid being the rebound guy and walked right into it. Her focus was to move on from Ethan. Establish herself away from him. I was a tool she was using to accomplish it. The pitiful thing was, I was letting her and would continue until she was done. I'd finally gotten the girl and would take whatever she offered. Even five weeks.

I pushed my head back into the pillow, my eyes staring at the ceiling.

Her fingers flexed as her body fought waking up. She arched into my side, my cock bobbing in excitement. A leg curled around my legs as morning won.

"Jack," she murmured. Her hand left my chest to cup my face.

I met her gaze, her amber eyes hazy with sleep but focused on me. Her lips parted in a smile, and she stretched again, rubbing against me. She slid her leg over me and pulled herself up to a seated position. My cock throbbed against her in excitement.

She tilted her head, her red hair cascading down with it. With a smirk, she leaned down and kissed me. She pushed my T-shirt up and then traced down my bare chest and abdomen, slipping beneath my pants.

"I think someone is awake," she said, wrapping her fingers around my cock.

Without thought, I pushed into her hand, groaning at the sensation, my earlier thoughts forgotten beneath Mina's gaze.

She kissed down my chest, coming to a stop at my waistband. After unzipping my pants, she ran her hand against my briefs, cupping my balls. Slowly, she massaged them before moving on.

I groaned a curse.

Grabbing both my pants and briefs in her hands, she yanked them off, leaving me naked.

"I like you like this."

She kissed my bare thighs.

Fuck, this woman. I can go from knowing she's leaving me to her mouth an inch from my cock.

She pressed her tongue against my morning wood, fitting against it until she slowly and deliberately licked up to the tip. Need and heat coursed through me. I closed my eyes and had to fist the mattress to not flip her over and take her.

She moved up my body, and I looked down at her. She'd tossed her shirt and bra off. As she maneuvered up the bed, she used the motion to ditch her pants. Her lips found mine again, and she settled her core against my aching cock.

"Jack, I—" She stopped, stilling for a moment, blinking to focus.

"What's wrong?" I asked, moving to sit up.

She pushed her fingers against my shoulders to keep me down.

Her lips locked with mine again, and she reached to the dresser for a condom.

She rolled it down my cock and then lowered herself over me, taking me fully.

My hands fell to her hips as she started our rhythm. I moved one hand to the bed to steady myself as I sat forward, head tilted to trail kisses down her neck and chest. She speared her hands through my hair, grabbing and rubbing as she found the rhythm she liked.

She groaned and arched back, giving me unobstructed access.

"Mina," I groaned.

The building orgasm was becoming too much as her wetness allowed her to easily slide up and down, tightening and milking me.

"Jack," she yelled as her core tightened and spasmed around my cock, bringing me with her.

I wrapped my arms around her back, drawing her to my chest. Our pants mixed together. Her head rubbed against my shoulder; her nose pressed to my neck. Her heart beat fast against my chest.

If I could, I'd never let go.

Mina rocked her head against my shoulder, and she cursed. "Shit, you're going to be late."

As if on cue, my phone vibrated, likely a text from Rocco.

"Hungry?" I kissed her forehead.

Her stomach rumbled in answer.

"I have cereal, breakfast of the champs and those in a hurry," she said.

"Let's shower." I pulled another condom from the nightstand. Her lips curled into a sly smile. "Then breakfast."

"Work," she muttered like she was trying to convince both of us.

"A working breakfast," I offered. "We'll talk about a mutual potential client and our strategy to win him over."

The local diner served breakfast twenty-four seven. We strolled in a quarter past seven and selected a small booth in the back. I slid into the seat next to her. She gasped and looked to the booth across the table.

Putting my arm around her, I kissed her cheek. She cuddled into my side and picked up her menu.

The waitress took our orders and left us with steaming mugs of coffee.

"I could get used to this," Mina said, rubbing her hand against mine.

She drew in a breath, her body stiffening when she realized she'd said it out loud.

"Sounds like a plan to me," I said.

"Jack." She pulled her lip between her teeth.

I tilted her chin up and looked into her eyes, bright with emotion.

"Hon—Mina," I said, licking my lips to stop an admission. It'd only freak her out.

Our names hung between us, so much else unsaid.

"We agreed to five weeks." She frowned and pulled her shoulders up.

"As a trial run," I said, leaning in to brush a kiss against her lips. "After a trial, you decide to extend."

"Or terminate an agreement," she said.

"Eh." I shrugged as my heart clenched at the real possibility of ending it.

I didn't want her to think we needed an out clause. And her already verbalizing those words sent lead to my stomach.

"Well, look at you two," Ethan sneered, coming up to our booth, a to-go cup in his hand.

The lead expanded when I looked at him. Interesting that he'd be here when he didn't like diner food and it wasn't close to his home or office. If Mina normally ate large breakfasts, I'd think he was waiting for her, but he likely had a client meeting nearby.

"What are you doing this weekend?" Mina asked, resting her head on my shoulder and fixing me with her gaze while she ignored Ethan.

A small nose flare was the only sign of her true annoyance.

"I have some meetings," I said and sipped my coffee.

"Sunday in particular?" she asked, a slow smile growing on her lips.

"Sam and I meet to go over the week, and then we have lunch."

Ethan cocked an eyebrow. "Inviting him to Sunday with Mom?"

My gaze shot to Mina. Her mom had made a point, anytime she was home when I walked Mina to the door, to make sure I knew Mina was dating Ethan, it was serious, and I was a serious philanderer. As a teen, the words had stung, especially as I avoided and specifically stated my intentions upfront, but as an adult, the recrimination stung more sharply. Especially when the words were in conjunction with Mina.

"Aren't you two nice and cozy?" Ethan continued. "Have to wonder how long you were seeing each other."

Mina rolled her head off my shoulder, squaring her gaze on him. "Ethan, shut the fuck up. The more you dig, the more you show yourself for the asshole you are. You cheated. Hell, you had another girlfriend in college when we were still together. Her father even thinks you were serious."

Ethan's eyes bulged before he righted himself, a disdainful smirk twisting his mouth. "Sounds like lies," he said.

"Only if it's you talking," Mina said.

"This isn't a good look for you, Mina. So quick to move on? With someone you supposedly met at a bar? Someone you were seen making goo-goo eyes at during events?"

"Ethan, you're trying to stir up shit," I retorted.

I dug my fingers into the pleather bench seat so I didn't punch his face. If it'd been more of an option, I'd have taken pictures when we were in high school, but evidence enough existed now, so it didn't matter. Aiden likely had a ton. He was always the family's cleaner, but I didn't want to loop him in unless Ethan truly went for Mina. Besides her wanting to fight her own battles, it'd be hell for Aiden.

I continued, "Shit already exists on you. Your family has been really good at cleaning it up."

Ethan's face went ashen, his eyes widening with a distant look before narrowing into daggers. "I don't know what the fuck you're talking about."

"Your friends are really proud of you," I said. "I believe the words one used was 'fucking stallion,' along with a picture of you, Mina, and Tiffany. Your family made sure that one came down real quick. But . . . I'm sure someone has a copy of the post."

"You motherfucking asshole," Ethan growled. "You're altering pictures of me now? My socials? You're that pathetic in trying to turn Mina from me? You have to make shit up?"

"Ethan, how many people did you date in college?" Mina asked over the rim of her coffee mug. Her other hand rested on my leg.

Instead of clenching her fists like me, she rubbed her fingers on my thigh, which started to eat away at my focus on Ethan.

"I only dated you," he crowed.

Fucking liar.

"How many other people *thought* you were dating them, then?"

Ethan swallowed before forcing a sneer. "He's getting to you. Warping your mind."

"I know Greg Cremski thinks you were dating his daughter."

The fucking asshat. I forced my breaths even. He was a fucking moron.

Ethan's gaze bounced around the table.

"So much so, he told me," Mina added. With an exhale, she moved her gaze to glare at him. "Leave me alone, leave my business alone."

"Or?" he growled. His eyes widened, likely realizing he'd voiced the threat.

"Should I bring another menu?" the waitress asked, sliding our plates in front of us with steaming pancakes, bacon, hashbrowns, eggs, toast, and fruit.

"No," Mina said. "He's also a lousy tipper and was leaving."

Ethan rolled his eyes and sauntered out of the diner, the bell chiming at his departure.

"Are you okay?" I murmured. Nothing about her posture, breathing, or expression implied anything was wrong, which was the most worrisome.

She turned her warm gaze to me. A smile tugged on her lips, which seemed out of place.

"He's a fucking asshole." She laughed.

"Yes?" Uncertainty twisted in my guts.

"I'm so fucking glad I didn't marry him." Another laugh escaped her lips.

"Me too," I thought but apparently muttered.

Her eyes widened. "Trust me, I don't think he's done, but this settled something else for me."

"What's that?"

"He didn't say the words, but he just basically admitted there are more. He always made our scheduled calls. He never had another's clothing, or stains, or anything that looked amiss."

I waited, not sure where she was going with this.

"But I remember his social media accounts going private during college. A lot."

Fuck.

"If he was private, he couldn't be tagged. I'd ask him about it, and he'd tell me his buddies liked to hack into his phone and prank him. That they all did it to each other."

"What do you think it was?" I asked, already knowing my suspicions.

"Either someone posted a picture they shouldn't and tagged him, or someone was commenting on his posts, so he blocked them and then went private. That asshole had it worked out. Now he probably has a PR liaison assigned to him by his daddy. I can now see how scrubbed his image is. He has help. What you said last night got me thinking . . . The comment about him going to his grandma's. If even a quarter of the times he went to his grandma's . . ."

I sighed. Nothing could undo what he'd done. Even if I wanted to, if I went back in time, Mina wouldn't have believed me. She hadn't wanted to.

She laced her fingers with mine. Somehow, she seemed lighter by this discovery.

"He's tried to influence my clients away from me already. He's not going to stop. In fact, he'll probably play dirtier and nastier. He does have some sway over some, sadly. However, I've also learned many hate him. And some with connections to him don't care as it doesn't affect their money."

"So what's your plan, then?"

"Continue to sign clients. Make them a ton of money while I build solid portfolios. Personally, I'm done talking about Ethan. He doesn't get to ruin this breakfast. Now, what were we talking about?"

"Sunday," I said, drizzling my pancakes in syrup. For some reason, my stomach twisted, either in excitement, anxiousness, or both.

"I shouldn't have surprised you with that."

"Don't leave me hanging." I laughed even though the delay only added weight.

"My mom extended an invitation." She shot me a half smile.

"Does that mean she wants me to come or not to come so she can remind you how unfit I am?"

She snorted. "My mom was serious. She said if you couldn't come because of traveling, we could have Sunday on Friday night or Saturday . . ." She chewed her lip and then said, "Or, you know, it's okay. I'll tell her we called it quits, and then you don't have to worry about it for the next four weeks. That'll be way easier."

"No," I said, anger brewing in my stomach.

We weren't writing us off so quickly. She wasn't going to say we fizzled out so I could escape her mom's wrath. I'd face it any day. I hadn't been as good as Ethan in high school, and I'm certain that image hadn't changed for her, other than I wasn't sleeping with another woman at a wedding.

"It's okay," she started.

"Mina, no," I said, keeping my voice a whisper to keep my emotions in check. "What time should I pick you up?"

"No, it's okay, gah," she said. Her hands flexed and twisted as she stared around the table. "I shouldn't have said anything. This just makes it awkward."

I snaked my hand around her chin, guiding it toward me. I crashed my lips against hers. When she gasped, I slipped my tongue inside her mouth, tasting her.

She clasped my neck as she returned the kiss.

I eased back, waiting for her to open her eyes. Her hazy eyes searched my face.

"What time should I pick you up?"

A smile flittered across her lips, and she curled her fingers against my neck.

"But you're supposed to have lunch with Sam," she said.

"He can handle feeding himself a meal," I said with a chuckle.

Some of the tension eased out of my stomach.

"Or you could bring him with," she said.

"You want Sam to come to lunch?" I asked.

I didn't understand the play here. She'd never shown interest in him before. I didn't think it was that, but still, doubt niggled into my heart.

She shrugged. She took a sip of her water, trying to hide her grin. "My mom will be more than happy to have more at the table. He'll be a distraction. Besides, he knows us."

## JUNE 10TH

### MINA

My phone buzzed from an unknown number. With a sigh, I clicked the screen.

> UNKNOWN: Mina, let's talk. You've already lost three clients because we broke up. Greg Cremski isn't going to sign with you.

For long moments, silence filled the space. My mind spun around the words. Then it buzzed again.

> UNKNOWN: Let's meet and talk. We can strategize how to keep your remaining clients. I'm sure you don't want to lose more.

"Fuck you," I spat and blocked the number.

## JUNE 11TH

### MINA

Jack left for a client trip early Wednesday evening, and I called Maggie and Dani over. Trina was too close to the situation for an honest opinion. Or rather, I wasn't ready to hear her hard honesty again.

The buzzer sounded and I let them up. Maggie carried two bottles of wine, and Dani had Italian carryout from a local restaurant. Both were in their versions of casual clothes. Dani had on denim capris and a tank top, and Maggie wore a knee-length skirt and a silk sleeveless blouse.

"I have chicken alfredo," she said, handing the container to Maggie. "Ravioli and sauce," she said, handing me a container. "And a meatball sub for me. And a loaf of garlic bread."

"You're going to need to eat a bag of mint lifesavers before Jack gets back tomorrow," Maggie said, opening her container and smiling as she took in a whiff.

We sat at the table with wine glasses and our meals.

"So, I assume 'let's eat and talk' means you want to discuss Jack," Maggie said, breaking off a chunk of bread.

"We can talk about anything," I said, guilty about focusing on me after last time when we discussed Ethan.

"We're both single," Dani said. Her brows dipped as she smiled.

She was between her mom's setups.

"We could talk about that," I offered.

"How is the sex?" Maggie asked. "I miss having good sex."

"Didn't you have sex last week?" Dani asked.

"I said 'I miss having good sex.'"

"I'm sure you can find it," Dani said. "I'm sure someone would be more than willing to help you out."

"Still considering kids?" I asked.

Maggie had decided at the start of the year she wanted to look into sperm banks. She didn't have a partner, and none of her regular boyfriends made the cut. She was looking into sperm donation but wanted to pick the father even though she wasn't sure she wanted them in their lives.

She waved her fingers. "It's a long, complicated process. Since I want them to have the same father, I'm thinking through different options. But that is future me's issue."

"Maggie is happy with her life. She's a kick-ass CEO for a growing media company. She dates when she wants to. If she wanted to get fucked, she could. Which she does, often. Great sex isn't always worth the strings," Dani said. "However, your sex is making you glow. You're also less jittery."

"Jittery?" I asked.

"You know, knee bouncing, annoyed, bored, unsure of everything," Dani said. "You never had a good release for it."

"So this trial run has three weeks left?" Maggie asked, pinning me with her hawkish eyes.

"Four," I muttered.

"That wasn't a happy sound." Dani pointed a fork at me.

I sighed, pushing my plate away.

"Well, hell, she's not eating." Maggie sat up. "What's going on, Mina?"

"I don't know." I slumped in my chair and rested my head on the back.

"Do you like Jack?" Dani asked.

I shot her a dark glare. "Of course I do or I wouldn't still be seeing him."

"Then what's the problem? You two are fucking like crazy, like each other, are satiating a want and need, and you know when it's up," Dani said. "You love knowing timelines and expectations. You should love this."

"I know," I gritted out.

"But," Maggie said, her eyes widening.

"What?" Dani asked. She rubbed a hand over my shoulders.

"You have some of that mixed up," Maggie said, pointing a finger at Dani.

"What do I have mixed up? She does love those things."

"I think it's more than that," Maggie continued. "Mina, you didn't like Jack for all those years. No, that's not right. You were always attracted to him. Don't bother denying it. You were also friends. You and Jack hung out for years. Now you've learned he had a crush on you. You had one on him. It made all those years extra bitter and to find out they didn't have to be. You've had a chance to view everything with more clarity. He has your best interest at heart. Sure, you have timelines and expectations, but you can trust him. You love that. I think you love him."

"What?" I sputtered. "Are you fucking kidding?"

My vision unfocused, and my breath caught in my throat. The number of truths she slammed at me was staggering, made even more so by her disbelief in love, at least for herself.

"What's so odd about it?" Maggie's face darkened. Her aqua eyes turned stormy. "Love is natural."

"Love is natural?" I echoed. "You don't believe in love."

She tsked. "I'm not built for it. To actually want the same person over and over, forever? Nah, I doubt that will ever be my thing.

However, I am completely aware and believe others can. And you fall into that category. As does Jack."

"I'm on rebound, and he's on his fling. In four weeks, we're moving on," I said.

If I believed anything else, I'd only open myself for pain, to be let down as every other man in my life had done.

Dani frowned. "Does he want to?"

"Not right now, but he will. He always does. He's all in right now, like he was with all his girlfriends. Then he gets bored and moves on. It's what he does," I said, each word bitter and painful to mutter. "His only long-term girlfriend since college ended a year and a half ago."

Maggie grinned at me.

"Oh, shut up," I groused.

Dani held up a finger. "Wait, isn't that when Ethan proposed?"

I shrugged. "It was around the same time. She was gorgeous. They were a stunning couple." A lump formed in my throat.

"How long did they date?" Maggie leaned on her elbows, her eyes narrowed on me.

I gulped. I knew the answer, but somehow admitting it would mean Maggie was right about something. It'd give her the needed fuel to claim victory. To continue with her accusations.

"She knows," Dani said.

"You're supposed to be my friend." I glared at Dani.

"I am, but you're a ball of self-distrust because of that jackass," Dani said. "You can answer or not, but we know you know the answer."

"So, how long?" Maggie asked again.

"Twenty-two months," I whispered.

I even remembered the first event I saw them at together. My stomach tightened, the ravioli sitting funny.

"Why did he break up with her?" Maggie asked.

"I don't know why. It never made the rounds, but she broke up with him," I said, hating I knew and that I wanted to smack her for being stupid for breaking up with him while also cheering that she did.

"Interesting," Maggie said.

"I think I'm just too entangled in this. I thought it was a good idea. I was wrong. I'm only making a mess."

"I think it is a good idea," Maggie said. "Even if you're going through emotional upheaval, this is the happiest I've seen you in a long time. Like starting your career happy."

"But it's going to end."

"You're already worried about it?" Dani asked.

"Maybe," I said in concession.

"Then maybe you shouldn't end it," Maggie said.

I blinked. Emotion burned my eyes and stung my nose. "He'll want to."

Maggie shrugged. "Talk to him. Tell him how you feel."

"I don't know how I feel," I whined.

"You have four weeks to decide how you feel." Maggie's gaze pierced me.

Sure. Okay. As if I'd magically not want to spend time with him.

"Does your mom know you're seeing him?" Dani asked and sipped her wine, her expression light and innocent.

Maggie arched an eyebrow at me, a victorious smirk on her lips.

"Yes . . ." I drew out. "She's aware I kissed him at Ethan's and that I'm seeing him for a trial run."

"Okay." Dani furrowed her brows. "What does she think?"

"She wants him to come to Sunday lunch," I said, rubbing my hands over my eyes.

"Oh," they said in unison.

"What does that mean?" I asked, yanking my hands down and whipping my head back and forth to glare at them.

"Is he coming to the lunch?" Maggie asked.

I snarled at her.

"Mhm." Maggie gloated.

I groaned.

"Save that for the bedroom."

## JUNE 12TH

## MINA

The park where my firm was hosting a picnic for family and clients bustled with people. I wore a pink suit dress but left the jacket at home. Even though I love hats, I'd spend more time futzing with it than not. My wedged brown leather sandals were deceptively comfortable.

Yang's daughter raced by us, Yang's husband in pursuit, as Yang talked with a managing partner, Mariya. Mariya's wife was away on a business trip.

Gina and Raquel sat on a bench under the shade of a tree. They waved when they saw me, and I walked over to them.

"No Jack?" Gina asked with a wink.

"His flight got in this morning. His partner picked him up for a client meeting." I plopped down on the freshly stained bench. "He'll come when the meeting wraps up."

I had told him not to worry about it and that he should sleep. Still, a curl of excitement and hope wove through me when he insisted he'd be here. Unlike with Ethan, I believed Jack when he said he'd come.

"It's weird not seeing Ethan circling you," Raquel said.

"The hover-copter." Gina cackled.

"Always wanting to get up and socialize," Raquel said.

"Sitting alone meant a missed opportunity." I sighed.

"Isn't that your client Trevor stole?" Gina nodded across the green space toward a cluster of trees.

I followed her gaze. "Sure is," I said.

Ronald's face was pinched and red, and he furled his fists. His glasses dipped low on his nose as he glared at Trevor. Trevor, for his part, tried to remain confident, shoulders back and expressive hands, but fear shone in his eyes.

Gina whistled. "That doesn't look good."

Looked like Trevor's 'partner-level strategies' had backfired.

"He's a conservative investing client whose money Trevor promised to double," I said, leaning back to watch. Even though I should feel joy at Trevor's bungle, I wondered how Ronald would recover his lost funds and if it would impact his choice to retire in a decade. He'd need a strong action plan moving forward.

"He what?" Raquel spat.

"Yep, and Ronald bought it. 'Time for the big guns.'"

"Does he not know those types of returns come at high risk and can't be guaranteed?" Gina asked.

"He used to, but Trevor and Ethan convinced him otherwise."

"So, he thought you were holding back his earnings? But why? It'd hold yours back too if he was willing to take those risks."

I shrugged.

"Well, look it there," Gina said. A smile spread across her face.

"Oh, I wonder if he's dating someone or has a brother." Raquel leaned her elbows on the table, clasping her hands and resting her chin on them.

I turned to see who they were referring to and noticed Jack and Sam walking toward us. A stupid grin twisted my lips. Even knowing he'd keep his word, seeing him made my nerves buzz with warm tingles. He smiled when he locked eyes with me, sending warmth through me.

Sam's curly blond hair was styled back so the wave still showed but didn't bounce around his head. His green eyes were full of mischief. He was two inches shorter than Jack but had more muscle width in his shoulders. He'd played football in high school and then played in college. He used it for an education and then only played the sport for fun.

"Sam has a brother, Clay," I said.

"Is he as cute?"

"He's okay. My sister dated him," I said. "I remember him being immature but kind, but it was high school."

"Are they single?" Raquel rubbed her hands.

"Sam, are you and Clay single?" I called out.

Both Jack and Sam's steps faltered, and they glanced at each other before back at me.

Jack's eyes widened as he scanned me up and down.

"We're both single. Are you looking for other options?" Sam asked. "If so, I'm a better catch than my brother, and he's currently in Tennessee on contract."

Jack smacked him and rolled his eyes. Closing the distance between us, Jack gave me a light kiss before sitting down next to me and wrapping an arm around my shoulders.

"I sure hope not," he whispered into my ear as he nuzzled my neck, shooting heat to my core.

"I hear I'm invited over Sunday?" Sam raised an eyebrow and grimaced at Jack.

"He doesn't believe me," Jack stage-whispered into my ear, sending tingles over the sensitive skin.

"Don't flirt in front of me," Sam said. "And I can see what your hands are doing."

"Jealous?" Jack pulled me in tighter.

"Yeah," Sam said and winked at me.

"You're invited to my mom's," I said and reminded myself to text my mom tomorrow morning so she wouldn't have time to tell Trina.

"It won't cause issues?" He cast his eyes down for a moment.

"Do you need a refresher course in table etiquette?"

"Probably." He flashed a grin and shoved his hands in his pockets.

"Mina," Yang said, Mariya beside her. "I see Jack has joined you. Who is this handsome companion of his?"

"Yang and Mariya, this is Sam Winters. Jack and Sam are partners at W&W Development," I said, introducing them. "Sam, this is Yang Li and Mariya Popov."

"Sam." Yang extended her hand.

Sam returned the handshake and then shook Mariya's hand.

"Have you discussed a portfolio with Mina?" Yang asked, her predatory gaze sizing up her chance at a new client.

Sam smiled, his crooked grin charming. "Mina and I plan to meet next week."

That was news.

"We just have to find a time that works for both of us." He grinned at me.

I forced one back. I didn't like strings. He was a friend of a . . . Jack's. Even if I knew him, I didn't like the association, especially so close to Ethan.

Sensing my discomfort, Jack massaged my shoulder.

Yang looked to Jack, the same question likely bubbling to come out.

"Yang," Trevor panted, joining our group.

Yang narrowed her brown eyes at Trevor while her brilliant smile remained on her face.

"Trevor?" she asked, peering behind him to where he had been talking to Ronald. The spot was now empty.

"Can I speak with you?" he asked, his fingers furling into fists at his sides.

"Please excuse us," Yang said to us with a dip of her head and followed Trevor away.

"That can't be good," Sam said, watching them leave. "He looks like a kid who broke a vase."

"Where'd Ronald go?" I asked.

"If that's who he was talking to, looks like his Porsche." Sam nodded toward the parking lot.

Ronald's gait ate pavement, his stature still rigid and angry. Trevor would need to spend a lot of hours working through what happened.

Music strummed across the green, and we turned toward the bandstand.

"Oh, entertainment," Gina cheered, moving to her feet. "Let's get a better view."

Jack and I walked hand in hand toward the green, Sam on Jack's other side.

"Mina, I'd love to talk about a portfolio," Sam said, leaning forward so I could see him around Jack.

My face must have belied my distrust because he added, "You have a great reputation. I know several of your clients personally. If there's some conflict of interest I'm not seeing, just let me know, but I think this would be good. I have a few other advisors to diversify my money."

I nodded. "We can talk," I said measuredly. "Make sure I can offer you what you expect and that we're a good fit."

Jack flashed me a smile.

I stared at him a beat.

"I didn't know he was going to ask," he murmured to me. "This is his idea."

I frowned.

"What's wrong?" Sam asked, noticing our quiet conversation.

"She thinks I set this up," Jack said.

I shot him a tight-lined, dark look.

"You do," Jack mouthed at me.

I hated that he was right.

"Are you kidding?" Sam said, waving me off. "Jack is a great business partner, but I'm not taking my money advice from him. Especially when it involves someone he's in l— involved with."

Jack sent a silent look I couldn't see.

Sam flinched and looked away.

"We'll talk," I said, warming to the idea.

A crowd had gathered around the atrium as the band had started playing a cover song. Jack led me to an open patch where other couples had started dancing. My awkward feet stumbled over each other.

"I don't dance," I said.

"Just sway," he whispered against me. Then he spun me around so I was pressed against him.

My body melded against his. He fitted his free hand against the small of my back.

"You're so beautiful," he murmured against my temple.

"You're pretty handsome yourself," I said.

He chuckled, the sound vibrating through me. I closed my eyes, enjoying the moment. I could forget everything, including that this was only temporary, but then my heart remembered. A pang shot through me, numbing my nerves. My fingers on his shoulders tightened, bringing him closer to me.

"Careful, or we might become a spectacle," he murmured. "I'm okay with it, by the way."

So was I, and it scared me.

## JUNE 13TH

### MINA

We parked in front of my mom's house. Jack had stayed the night, using his duffle bag change of clothes—black pants and a white dress shirt—again. He'd already managed to roll up the skirt of my royal blue fitted dress before we left my apartment. Trina hadn't arrived yet, but Sam pulled in behind us, his Lexus looking freshly washed.

My mom hadn't minded that I invited Sam. I doubted she had made the connection of Jack's partner Sam to the same Sam who was Clay's brother. Trina had gone to a high school party with the sole intent of kissing Sam and came home with Clay as a boyfriend. Sam had been too dense, too unaware, or uninterested, but he'd set his brother up with Trina, trying to be the kind big brother by helping his younger brother, who had a crush on Trina. Clay and Trina dated for the rest of high school, but Trina broke up with him a month before they went to separate colleges. For the entirety of high school while she dated Clay, she fought with Sam or tried to embarrass him. I wasn't sure if the years between then and now would help.

Trina pulled up. I watched her reaction in the mirror. Her face pinched in confusion as she stared at Sam's car. Before Jack could get out of his door and open mine, I was out of it and almost to her car.

"Hey, Trin," I said, a smile growing on my face.

"We have company?" she asked, nodding toward Sam's car.

Her long coppery hair was pulled back in a loose fishtail braid, which went well with her summery large-print floral day dress.

"Yeah, Jack's friend is joining us. They normally eat lunch together on Sunday. I figured he could come too. Mom is always trying to get us to invite more guys."

She narrowed her eyes as she searched my face for the deception.

"Friend? Are you trying to set me up?" She placed her hands on her hips.

"Aren't you still seeing Eric?"

She sighed and shrugged. Her frame deflated. "I don't want to be set up."

"I'm not trying to set you up." I bit my cheek to stop the smile.

"Sure you're not," she deadpanned. "You just know Mom will."

"I'd be a catch," Sam said, strolling past us to the house.

He wore dark gray trousers and a light blue button-down shirt. His wavy blond hair was cropped shorter than yesterday but still in a controlled natural style.

"Are you fucking kidding?" Trina screeched. She pointed a finger at him while staring at me with a red face. "You invited that fucking jackass?"

"He's Jack's friend and business partner," I said, folding my arms.

"I didn't realize Jack had that bad of taste in friends," she said.

Apparently, the hard feelings from high school still lingered. Hate and love can be a two-sided coin.

"Trina and Mina." Mom scolded us from the porch. Sam stood next her, a good foot taller. His blond locks caught the sun. He smirked at us and winked at Trina. "Quit being rude and get up here with your guests."

"My guests?" Trina yelled, stomping up the pathway. "They ARE NOT MY GUESTS."

"The neighbors don't care, so lower your voice." Mom chided her.

Jack waited at the pathway for me, slipping his hand against mine as we walked up. His blue eyes masked most of his emotions, but his jaw ticked and he swallowed as we neared.

Mom's gaze fell to our hands. A mix of emotions danced on her face. Disappointment. Joy. Confusion.

"Mom," I said, stopping before her. My toes curled as I tried to stop my fidgeting. "You remember Jack."

"Hello, Jack," Mom said curtly. She stuck a slender hand out to him. Her forced smile was barely more than a thin line.

He released my hand to shake hers and dipped his head. Then he returned his hand to mine.

"Mrs. Carter," he said, using Mom's new last name.

"Come in," she said, stepping back. Her dark amber eyes tracked us.

I squeezed his hand and led him inside.

"You can't sit there," Trina growled. "That's my spot."

"You don't live here," Sam said.

"I farted in that chair," Trina said.

Turning the corner, we found them in the dining room, holding opposite sides of the chair.

"Trina," Mom hissed. "Don't talk about flatulence."

"Just warning him," Trina said. "He's trying to take my chair."

"It's my chair," Mom said. "I own it. I let you sit in it. Now, find a different chair. He's a guest."

Trina's mouth pinched into a thin line, her eyes darkening as she narrowed them on him.

She released the chair with a shove and sat on the opposite side of the table.

"I made a pot roast," Mom said. "I have cornbread, vegetables, mashed potatoes, and gravy. Mina said you two didn't have food allergies or vegetarian or vegan preferences."

"It smells delicious," Jack said, pulling my chair out.

After I sat down, he sat next to me. His hand sought mine and held it.

"Hands on the table," Trina mouthed at me so Mom couldn't see.

I stuck my tongue out at her.

"What has gotten into you two girls?" Mom sighed. "It's like high school all over again."

"Where's Gerald?" Trina asked.

"He's covering an extra shift," Mom said.

Lucky bastard.

"Sam," Mom said, turning her attention to him. "I didn't see you much in high school while Trina dated Clay."

"You lucked out," Trina said under her breath.

Mom shot her a dirty look before turning to Sam. "You're three years older than Trina?"

"No, Mrs. Carter. I skipped a grade in elementary school. I'm two years older than Trina," he said, his green eyes snagging on Trina before returning to Mom.

"So you should have been in Mina's grade?"

"Yes, ma'am."

"Mina lucked out too," Trina breathed.

"Trina, knock it off," Mom said without turning to her. "You played football?"

"Mom," Trina said. "Sam is Jack's business partner. Jack is dating Mina. You should be giving Jack the tenth degree and not Sam. Sam isn't coming back after today."

"Trina Marie." Mom's voice was deathly calm.

Trina gulped and slid down her chair, casting her eyes to her plate.

"I apologize for her horrible manners. Sadly, they're still a work in progress," Mom said and smiled at Sam.

Sam laughed, his eyes jumping to Trina before returning to my mom.

"Yes, I played football. Clay and I were on the same team for a year."

"That's where I saw you," Mom said, shaking her finger in the air. "How did you and Jack meet?"

I slid a glance to Trina to see if she noticed Mom was ignoring Jack.

Trina met my gaze and nodded.

Jack squeezed my hand to get my attention. I glanced at him. He smiled a tight lipped one and shook his head at me.

"Jack and I met in college. We were floor mates his first year, and I was the RA. Then we moved into an apartment together for the rest of our undergrad and grad."

"Jack played football too." Trina piped in. "And baseball. He has the same degrees as Sam. They work together. I guess asking Sam these questions would get you the same answer as if you asked Jack."

I choked on a laugh.

Mom froze, her murderous eyes darting to Trina before me.

"Jack was on the chess team and forensics. Were you Sam?" I asked.

A soft chuckle sounded from Jack. I met his warm gaze. He offered me an amused smile.

"No, I wasn't in forensics. I didn't like public speaking or debate."

"Neither did I," Jack added. "But I needed the practice."

"Jack," Mom said, finally swinging her gaze to him.

Jack's eyes shot to her. Despite the stoic expression, his hand tightened on mine.

"Yes?" he asked, his voice normal.

"You were around a couple of years," Mom said, choosing her words slowly. "You used to drive Mina home?"

"Yes," Jack answered.

"You were friends with . . ." Mom cut her eyes to me. She flinched when she said, "Ethan in high school."

"Yes," he said.

I licked my lips. Every question he answered with a simple one-word answer. Granted, she was asking yes-or-no questions. I swallowed against the tense air, and my gaze jumped to Trina.

"Jack, how many clients were you able to sign that Ethan tried to get?" Trina sat up in her chair. She placed her elbows on the table, clasping her hands together and resting her chin on them.

Jack turned to Trina, his eyebrows furrowed. "A couple dozen."

"Did he steal more of your clients than you did him or vice versa?" she said.

"Trina," Mom said. "This isn't table talk."

"This is more interesting than Sam playing football a decade ago. We don't need to live the bygone glory days of a second stringer."

"First string." Sam smirked.

"Whatever." Trina waved away his answer. "So, Jack?"

A small smile curved Jack's lips. "Currently, I am leading the number."

"What is Mina's favorite coffee?"

"Peppermint mocha," Jack said.

"What's Mina's favorite meal?" Trina asked, an impish smile flittering across her lips.

The snot. She went dirty.

Jack swallowed his laugh before saying, "She prefers pizza as a regular meal. Otherwise, Swedish Fish and ice cream."

"Why did Mina pick financial advising?" Trina asked, sitting back in her chair.

"She was always good at numbers, which is what she tells people, but the truth is . . ." He cast a hesitant glance at Mom and then me. I nodded my approval. "I know money was a concern for a time in her life. She wanted to help others build futures."

"Besides Mina, who was the last woman you saw in any capacity that wasn't work?" Trina asked, her face victorious.

"Trina!" Mom roared.

Jack narrowed his eyes and stiffened.

Trina had no issues exposing the elephant in the room.

"Alicia," he said. "We broke up about a year and a half ago."

Alicia was perfect. She was gorgeous, brilliant, and had everything put together with a smile on top. And Jack had proposed to her.

"How long did you date?"

"Trina Marie!"

Trina held up a finger to Mom. Mom's eyes flared, her cheeks reddening.

"About two years." Confusion darkened Jack's face.

"Interesting." Trina's gaze bounced back to Mom.

"How about you?" Sam asked, his green eyes piercing Trina.

"Yes, Trina, how about you?" Mom said.

Trina rolled her eyes. "You know I'm dating Eric," she said smugly and sat back in her chair.

"Are you?" Mom asked. "Then why isn't he here?"

"He's busy," she retorted, staring at her plate.

"Seems like Sunday with the family should be important." Sam raised an eyebrow at her.

"Then why aren't you with your family?" Trina snapped.

"I consider Jack family," Sam said.

"Oh, good answer," I said and lifted my glass toward him in a fake toast.

We stopped by Jack's after my mom's. As we rode the elevator up, my stomach tightened at the prospect of seeing his apartment. I'd always wondered where he lived. How he lived. The posh building was a mile from Ethan's. It also overlooked the lake, but he had more green space surrounding his complex.

"I'm sorry about this afternoon." I wrapped an arm around his waist and leaned my head against his shoulder.

"Why?" he asked, circling his arms around me.

He leaned his cheek against my temple.

I nestled into his embrace, his warm, solid chest a beacon of comfort. The thud of his heart sounded in my ear.

"My mom . . . She's her," I said.

Granted, she was only trying to protect me, but Jack wasn't Ethan. When we ended, and we would as it was his history, he'd be kind and sweet about it, which would probably make me hate him. Besides, we had laid out terms we both agreed to. Even if the idea of the end sat heavily on my heart. Instead of retreating from him as the ache oozed to my stomach, I dug my fingers into his shirt, anchoring him to me while I could.

He tightened his hold, pressing me against him. A large breath lifted his chest.

I tilted my head back to meet his eyes. They swam with raw emotion.

"She was nicer than I expected. She used to just glare at me when I walked up and then would say, 'Good night and goodbye, Jack.' She just wants to protect you."

He worked his jaw as if keeping more words locked inside that fought to escape. For a moment, that fucking granite fortress of nothingness settled on his face.

I ran a hand along his jaw. He pressed into my touch.

"H-Min, I'm really happy we're together." His breath warmed my palm.

My stupid heart swelled with joy that bubbled into a smile. "I am too."

He leaned forward and pressed his lips against mine in a hard kiss. When he pulled away, his large smile warred with his clouded eyes.

"Trina chucking a roll at Sam's head was pretty entertaining," Jack said.

It was his attempt to change the topic. Too much truth had been exposed today, so I went with it. My own heart was too tight to face everything.

"He caught it with one hand," I said. "She was speechless."

"Never say there is no such thing as a miracle." Jack chuckled.

He unlocked his deadbolt and led me in. The minimalistic look was from a magazine.

Unlike Ethan's designer magazine vibe that forced a homey appearance, Jack's was sleek lines and minimal decor that accentuated the furniture. Nothing about it screamed "don't touch" like Ethan's precisely placed everything, but it also appeared almost unlived in, except for the sofa, which was a plush, deep-back, long sofa. It looked great for napping. The desk had the capacity to be a sit or stand with multiple monitors and some site blueprints stacked in a corner.

"Did you pick anything out?" I asked, staring around the house.

"Sofa and the desk," he said.

Of course.

He moved to the desk to look for the files he wanted.

The cold and sterile space didn't feel like Jack. I moseyed across the living room toward the bedroom. His bedroom was the opposite. The large king bed was freshly made, undisturbed from him sleeping at my apartment the previous night. Around the room were stacks of business magazines, books, and exercise equipment. A smattering of black-and-white prints dotted the walls. A plush chair with a movable table sat in one corner. A case of water was next to it, along with some snacks. Another TV was in the room, hung to be visible from the treadmill and bed.

"Lots of hobbies?" I asked, gesturing to the stuff.

He shrugged. "I was told having the stuff in the living room is a bad look."

"It's your apartment," I said.

The advice sounded like a close-to-live-in or a live-in girlfriend. Or fiancée. My stomach soured at the thought.

He shrugged again. "I guess. I have no attachment to the stuff."

He leaned against the doorway, watching me as I inspected his world.

His bathroom caught my eye, and I took in the giant bathtub, separate shower with double nozzles, and double vanity sink. Only one sink had stuff around it. The other was spotless and vacant.

An idea popped into my mind. One that sent warmth to my core. And a warning to my brain. One my heart ignored.

"You know," I said, the words thick in my throat.

He waited, watching me.

I took in a breath and turned to inspect his shower so he couldn't see my face as I said, "You could always bring some toiletries and clothes to my apartment. You spend several nights there. It has to be a hassle in the morning to come back and change before work or repack your duffle bag. Unless, of course, you have stuff at work, in which case it doesn't matter. Maybe that's the easiest for you."

"Mina," Jack asked, interrupting my awkward rambling.

"Yeah?" I asked.

I caught my red cheeks in the mirror as I turned to look at him. My foolishness was on display.

His lips curved into his panty-dropping smile.

"Are you offering me a drawer or room for a travel bag?"

"Wouldn't you want closet space for some shirts and suits?" I asked.

Heat clawed at my neck the more his blue eyes watched me.

"Are you offering me closet space?" His eyebrow hitched up.

I stared at him before shifting my gaze to the side. Was I moving us too fast? Was I implying too much commitment? It just seemed easier. But it was only weeks . . . Still, it would be easier even if it was for a few weeks. Or did it mean more . . .

He pushed off the doorframe, his long legs covering the distance to me. He caressed my cheek, lifting my face up, and brushed his lips against mine. Leaning back, he locked eyes with me. My concerns dissolved under his warm gaze.

"I appreciate it," he said. "Give me a few minutes to gather some stuff."

Hope bloomed in my chest. "You don't want to stay here tonight?"

"Not unless you want to. I have my files. I like your place better."

After kissing my forehead, he gathered some items around the bathroom.

"Your place is a penthouse," I said.

"Your place feels like home. Mine feels like a hotel," he said, walking to his closet.

Did he mean my place was home or that it felt like one? My brain fixated on that as he moved around his room. He put a few suits in garment bags from the cleaners and grabbed ties, underwear, T-shirts, some jeans, and sweats. He tossed everything but his suits in a suitcase. He grabbed a few pairs of shoes and put them in his gym bag, along with toiletries.

Several weeks' worth of items were gathered. Almost enough to take him to the Fourth of July weekend, almost the end of our trial run. I wasn't sure if it was intentional or coincidental, but a part of me wanted him to pack more, even though what he had was already a lot. I wanted there to be enough that it ran out after we did. That the extra meant we'd go longer. Fuck.

"Ready to go home?" he asked.

I smiled as my heart shattered. If only it was our home.

JUNE 16TH

JACK

"So, what's up with you and Trina?" I didn't lift my eyes to Sam as I scrolled through an email.

"She dated my brother." A hint of bitterness tinged his words, causing me to look up.

His normally jovial face held a hint of a frown.

"Were you interested in dating her?"

"No," he said too quickly.

I set my coffee and phone down.

He shifted his posture but didn't look up. The hum of the terminal carried on around us. We were headed to a conference in Washington state for the remainder of the week. Instead of flying back to Milwaukee, we each were headed to different clients and sites afterward.

Silence dragged on.

Finally, he lifted his eyes up to meet mine. "What?" he barked.

"You've been weird since Sunday. Moody."

His lip hooked to the side in disagreement.

"Nothing ever happened between us. She started dating my brother when they were freshmen. Dated all through school."

I waited.

"What, dude?"

I made a circle around his face and posture. "This, all this. This isn't normal for you. Kind of reminds me of when you came back from breaks during college . . ."

My eyes enlarged with the realization. Fuck. Then a laugh ripped through me.

Confusion marred his face. With narrowed eyes, he leaned back. "What's so funny now?"

"I just realized . . ." I had to catch my breath. "Dude, we didn't know each other in school other than names. Even when we were on the same football team for a couple years, we didn't interact much. Somehow, we both ended up at USC and on the same floor."

Still glowering, he watched me. Waiting for my point.

"And the whole time, we both had a crush on people who were sisters."

He blinked. No amusement skittered across his face. Instead, it darkened.

"Come on, Sam. Don't be a fucker."

"She hates me." The words seem to draw pain. The fire in his eyes dimmed, and he looked away.

"Mina hated me too." The thought sobered me a bit.

"Yeah, well, what happened with you and Mina isn't going to happen with Trina and me."

"Why does she hate you? Was it a misunderstanding? Were you a jackass? I doubt it was intentional, but you were pretty naive and dumb."

He shrugged. "I honestly don't know. She's hated me since we met." His eyes hardened. "Now, you and Mina?"

The question hung between us like a cobweb. Neither wanted to touch it, but it irritated the air.

"Come on, quit fucking around and tell me what's going on with you two."

It was my turn to shrug. Sam didn't know about the five-week agreement. Not yet, anyway. My plan was to extend it indefinitely, so there was no need to share it.

At my apartment, I could see the fear in her face when I tried to talk about my past and her mom's concerns. The reasons I had done it didn't matter. I'd played around. Doubt clung to her face even when she nodded in understanding about her mom. So instead of professing my love and desire to do away with the contract, I kept it inside, too afraid it would cause her to bolt. Instead, I went for safer words. Still true, I was really happy we were together, but it was barely the surface of what I felt. Feelings she wasn't ready or may never want to hear.

"This is the happiest I've seen you, ever." Sam ran a hand over his mouth. "But there's something else there. Something not right."

Fucker had to pick up on it.

"Our layover is three more hours, maybe five if the storm doesn't pass. You have nowhere to hide from me."

I averted my gaze.

"Don't you trust me with it?"

Fuck. I rubbed my temples and lolled my head around to stare at him. "Yeah, I trust you."

"Then what the fuck is going on?"

I sighed. Sam mocked me.

"You know the beginning."

"Mhm, now tell me what happened after the zoo. You've been a vault about you two since then."

"We're doing a fucking trial run." The words sounded as awful as they tasted on my tongue.

"Pardon?"

"We agreed to date for five weeks. To see how we go."

His eyes searched mine. "You're serious?" His lip curled in a grimace. "It sure doesn't look like that."

"I don't want the five-week limit, but it made Mina feel more comfortable, and I get why. Ethan is a fucking asshole. And she was there for all my girlfriends."

"What have you told her?"

"Anytime she brings up the weeks, I tell her we should extend, just keep going."

He lifted an eyebrow. "In those words?"

"Close to it?" My mind flickered back at what I could have said. It likely wasn't as direct as I thought I'd done. More skirting the issue.

Sam's jaw ticked.

"I know she's interested."

"But?"

"When she realizes she likes what's happening, sometimes it scares her, and she pulls back."

She had every right to send mixed messages. She probably wasn't clear on what she wanted herself, and instead of giving her space and time, I stepped right into line. And that was the issue. I didn't want a line. If Mina started dating . . . Fuck. Any way I looked at it, I was just going to be the rebound guy. The one she used to move on from Ethan with—and in five weeks.

Then there was the drawer and closet space she gave me. It certainly made it easier to spend time together. I didn't have to worry about driving back half asleep. But giving someone space like that usually came with meaning . . . Meaning I was searching for in all her actions. Maybe I was just fooling myself. It was just a nice gesture for the remaining weeks. How hard would it be to take my stuff back?

My stomach tightened as if it had been punched.

I flicked my gaze back to my phone to avoid where my thoughts were heading.

"I don't understand why you think you're not good enough for Mina."

Startled, I looked up to him. "What are you talking about?"

"This is like watching you revert to the old you. Even if you and Nicole knew things weren't going to last after college, you both were upfront about it, and you found confidence with yourself. For the longest time, you ran from commitment because you were afraid they'd see the real you."

I scowled at him. "That's bullshit."

"I've known you for a long time. I was there for Nicole and when we moved back to Milwaukee and you started dating by the number again for a few months, which looking back now and seeing everything with Mina, my guess is it was seeing Mina and Ethan together again, and then once you disassociated enough, found success in our business and started outselling Ethan, you fell back into your confidence. You even dated Alicia and stupidly proposed."

I stared at him through my eyebrows. The anger boiling in me wasn't for him. Though he was the recipient of it, it was for me. The only person who could unhinge me was Mina. And I'd set myself up to be destroyed.

"Dude, I've only had one girlfriend. I rarely go on dates. I'm not the person who can provide any real guidance in a relationship, but I can say, when you're with her, you're really happy. When you're not with her, you become a work machine."

"Pot, kettle."

He shrugged.

Staring at him, I realized he may know how I feel. Everyone on our floor cheered when he and Amber started dating. It seemed like a life-long type of relationship. Then Sam went back home at Thanksgiving, and something shifted between them. And after winter break, he broke up with Amber out of nowhere. Since then, he'd turned into what I did, work focused with no time or desire for a relationship.

But the woman I had pined for, finally let go of the dream of having a chance with, was in my life, and I was in her bed. I could fold as I'd done in school. Concede that I wasn't enough. Or, I could figure a way to not only tell Mina but show her that I wanted a future. I wanted a shot at forever.

## JUNE 23RD

### MINA

Greg stared at the menu, his milky blue eyes moving up and down as his lips mouthed what he read. His mustache twitched against his pale skin. He wore the standard gray suit, white shirt, and muted-tone tie common in the early aughts. His CEO, Beatrice, joined us. She looked to be mid-thirties to mid-forties. Her black hair was pulled back into a bun. She wore a salmon-colored sheath dress that popped on her reddish-brown skin and a black blazer.

Jack had been on a business trip since the Monday after my mom's. My bed had been cold and left me agitated, so I'd packed up my suitcase and driven to several clients throughout the state to avoid the new loneliness I felt in my apartment. Somehow, I'd have to figure out how to handle it when we broke up. My heart twisted. Maybe I'd move in with Trina.

Instead of dwelling on it, I dove into work. As promised, Greg made it to dinner with me when he flew in.

"Ms. Henley," Beatrice said, pulling me from my thoughts. "You have an impressive portfolio. The clients you listed as references speak volumes of you."

I smiled politely. The threat of a but loomed.

"My goal is to provide the best returns at the risk level my clients are comfortable with."

"Your clients tend to be in the five to fifteen million range?" she asked, her umber eyes meeting mine.

Ah, she was bringing up the size of my clients. She didn't think I had enough experience with clients their size.

The waitress arrived for our orders.

After she left, Greg turned his gaze to me. "Mina, I understand you have several partners at your firm," he said.

"Yes," I said, my mouth drying.

"Will one of them be overseeing the portfolio?" he asked.

I blinked, stealing a moment to compose myself. "No, as a senior analyst, I oversee my clients."

"I'm used to working with a partner of a firm," Greg said, his tone sympathetic. "I'm at a point where I only want experienced individuals."

I nodded and said, "I've worked for six years at the firm. My rate of return is excellent, and I have an almost one-hundred-percent client retention rate."

"And the not-exactly one hundred percent? Why did they leave?" Greg asked.

My stomach tightened, and my appetite disappeared. "Two left because of their connections to Ethan. The other chose to move to a junior partner of the firm."

He gave a thin "I told you so" smile.

"It's not personal, Mina," Greg said. "You are well respected and growing a great list. As I consider this, I also know I'm closer to the end. Do I want growth or stability?"

I stared at him. This was the politest no I'd received, but it was still a no.

"Greg," Ethan called out as he neared our table. Behind him were Tiffany and Trevor.

I narrowed my eyes at him, imagining a red dot between his eyes before it swung to Trevor's forehead.

Had Trevor figured out my calendar system? His startled eyes darted between Ethan and Greg. Even if his surprise looked genuine, I didn't trust him. I'd be thinking through a new calendar system.

"Ethan," Greg said, a smile curving his lips. "It's nice to see you."

"I didn't realize you made it into town already. I thought you were coming in tomorrow." Ethan shifted so he was next to me but not looking at me.

"Mina offered me dinner, and I came in a day early," Greg said. "I look forward to our meeting tomorrow. I have some questions on the location before signing."

Oh shit.

"Sounds great," Ethan practically purred, the arrogance rolling off him.

I bit my tongue to avoid making a scene in front of Greg.

Beatrice narrowed her eyes as her gaze flicked between Ethan and me.

Ethan left, tossing me a Cheshire glance over his shoulder.

"Old friend?" Beatrice asked me.

"Something like that," I mumbled, reaching for my water.

I should probably call it an early night. My stomach flipped, and I wasn't sure I'd keep my lunch down. I wasn't signing Greg, and Jack was going to lose out on his chance to make significant traction.

"They were engaged," Greg answered for me while reaching for his wine glass. He shot me a hard look.

"Oh," Beatrice said, her eyebrow shooting up.

"I caught him with the woman he was with just now on the day of our wedding," I said.

"What?" Beatrice asked. She sharpened her gaze on Greg.

Greg shifted uncomfortably.

"Personal and business can't mix," Greg said stiffly, averting his eyes.

"That is awful. If I may ask, how long were you two together?" Beatrice asked.

"We started dating freshman year of high school," I said.

Greg shifted his eyes to me, something glinting in them.

"Did you date the whole time or take breaks?" Beatrice tilted her head as she watched me.

"We dated the whole time. We went to different colleges but talked or texted daily. During breaks, we'd always meet back up at home. If not, one of us would travel with the other."

"What?" Greg barked, his eyes boring into me.

"We dated for thirteen years," I said. "We started dating freshman year of high school."

"You didn't break up in college?" Greg asked. His face contorted into odd expressions.

"No," I said. "We tried talking daily, but that didn't always work out with our schedules. We texted daily though. That was our agreement. Weekends we always talked. Holidays were together."

"You dated Ethan throughout college?" Greg asked.

"Yes," I said, my eyes dancing between the two.

Beatrice smiled at me, her eyes lighting in delight.

When the waitress arrived, I remembered Greg had said his daughter dated Ethan in college.

My eyes jumped to Greg, who was staring across the restaurant at Ethan.

"So, Mina," Beatrice said, her tone light and friendly. "Any good places you recommend visiting in the city?"

Beatrice and I talked about local attractions, sports, and our favorite Netflix shows. Greg ignored us as he picked at his food, his focus a million miles away.

"Mina, tonight was most enjoyable," Beatrice said, shaking my hand. "I can see why your clients love you."

"Thank you," I said. "I hope as you move forward with your decision-making and any additional investing plans, you keep me in mind."

"We will," Beatrice said.

Greg fixed me with a glare and extended his hand.

I shook it and smiled. "Thank you for your time, Greg. I hope you have a productive and enjoyable stay."

He nodded. "Thank you for dinner."

## JUNE 24TH

### MINA

Finally, Thursday night rolled around. After tossing in bed after dinner with Greg, the bed feeling hard, unyielding, and cold, I'd slept on the sofa to catch a few hours of sleep. My mind spun as I realized how much I'd become accustomed to Jack. How much I enjoyed sharing space with him. Numbness settled on my skin and heart while lead pooled in my stomach.

He'd mentioned maybe extending our timeline, but all that would do was make it worse when he finally got bored. I'd lived through that with my mom and dad. Saw how it destroyed my mom's trust. Ethan had followed suit too. No, I needed to end it after five weeks so I could scrape together what pieces of me remained and start over. Besides, I only had two weeks left with Jack. Our time was already half over.

The lead in my stomach expanded, and I decided to head to the airport early. I could pace there as I waited instead of staring around my office, which reminded me of my failures at making junior partner, or my apartment, knowing I was going to miss Jack, or my friends, knowing they'd just ask questions I didn't want to answer.

I waited outside of security for him. I kept flicking my gaze to the giant clock between the terminal entrances and then the electronic boards. The checkout teemed with people coming and going. He'd caught an earlier flight than planned.

The arrival board flashed Deboarding, and butterflies fluttered in my stomach. I slid my phone into the back pocket of my jeans and pushed off the wall. Pacing against the wall, I kept my eyes locked down the terminal.

He walked next to a woman in a red suit, engaged in a lively discussion. Her blond hair was styled in perfect waves, and her makeup was expertly applied. She reminded me of a professional version of Tiffany. My butterflies turned to worms as I watched her hand brush his arm. She opened her purse, pulled out a business card, and handed it to him while batting her eyelashes. He read the card over and nodded to whatever she said.

Was it already happening? Not even five weeks in?

She pointed to the bar located in the terminal and smiled, still touching his fucking arm. Numbness threatened my body, the edges of my vision blurring.

He shook his head no and pulled away from her, dropping his to his sides.

A dark frown crossed her face before she pulled out another flirtatious smile. She giggled and touched her ample chest. My heart skipped a beat, my eyes unblinking as I watched. Waiting for the betrayal.

He took a step back, forcing her to drop her hand or look awkward. He shook his head no again. As he turned, I noticed the deep frown on his handsome face.

She stomped into the bar without him and disappeared into the throng of people.

He tossed the business card into the trash receptacle and rubbed his hand on his suit jacket. He pulled out his phone and read whatever message popped up. He chuckled and shoved it back into his pocket.

Something warm tingled in me, seeing him disregard her flirting, even when he didn't know he was being watched.

His gaze shot up, and he caught sight of me. A large smile broke across his face, chasing his frown. Picking up his pace, he almost jogged up to me.

"Hey, gorgeous," he said, wrapping his arms around me and pulling me in tight.

My butterflies returned in droves. My core turned to lava as need and want swam in my veins. I leaned back so I could catch his lips with mine. Instead of a friendly, quick kiss, mine was urgent and lust fueled.

"Careful, or I'll take you against the wall here," he said against my lips and then deepened the kiss.

"Get a room," someone mumbled as they walked around us.

"As I said," he chuckled.

Slipping an arm around my shoulders, he led me to the parking lot.

He rubbed circles into my shoulders. I pressed into his side as we strode past an alcove by the aviation museum. Heat coursed through me.

"I've missed you," I said, pushing him into the empty space behind the museum next to the restrooms. I hooked my fingers on his jacket and pulled him against me.

"Mina," he moaned, trailing kisses down my chin and neckline. "I've missed you too."

I lolled my head back, giving him complete access.

He slipped his hands down my back and lifted me up. I wrapped my legs around his center, rubbing against his growing hardness.

"Jack," I moaned against him, my need increasing to frantic levels. "I l—"

The woman from the terminal walked past us into the bathroom. She stilled, her eyes traveling up and down Jack, sneering at our intimate embrace. But her appearance grounded me back to reality and the public place we were in.

"Mina?" he asked, his blue eyes finding mine. Curiosity and concern reflected back.

"Let's get to the car," I panted. "I want privacy."

His lips curled in a grin, and his eyes flashed with mischievousness. He put my legs back down on the ground, caressing my cheeks before he leaned over and kissed me. The kiss was soft and yearning and loving.

I never wanted it to end. I wanted to go home to our apartment, slip into bed with him, and not get out until Monday.

Then I realized I thought of it as our apartment, not mine. He had already wedged into my life. He filled my nonwork hours. He was who I looked forward to seeing after work. Texting. Talking. And I'd spent the last week driving around the state to avoid dwelling on it too much.

Fuck.

I had two weeks left. Even his packed clothes matched that.

He wrapped his hand around mine and then led me out to the parking lot. Despite the orangish garage lights, night left the parking lot dimly lit. Without running, we made it in record time. He pulled open the back door and waited until I slid across before joining me and closing it. The windows blacked out the world around us, leaving us together in the dark, only our breathing and bodies to connect us.

He ran a gentle hand across my arm.

"Mina," he breathed, pulling me toward him.

His lips found mine, and he slipped his tongue in my mouth, tasting me.

"Jack," I breathed, sliding my leg over to straddle him.

My core rubbed against him, our pants adding to the friction.

Putting my hands on his shoulders, I leaned over him to slide my jeans and panties off. My hands immediately went to his pants, yanking them down. His erection bobbed out, swollen and hard. I ran a finger over it, rubbing the precum over his cock's head.

I fumbled in my purse and pulled out a foil wrapper. I hadn't carried any condoms in my purse before the last few weeks. My sex life had been basic and simple. Now I had a stash in my purse, bedroom, the drawer on the coffee table and table by the front entry, and some in the bathroom.

With greedy hands, I rolled it down his length.

He ran his hands down my back, pulling me forward until his lips were on mine.

My hot core rubbed against him, finding his impossibly large cock. I slid down onto him, taking him fully. My head lolled back as I groaned.

Fuck. It felt so good. We felt so right.

"Mina," he said against my lips.

"Jack," I breathed.

He was everything I'd wanted and more. He was caring, compassionate, and intoxicating. My mind flashed with images, of him and me in future scenarios. He was what my head and heart wanted.

My mouth opened, words almost spilling without my control, "Jack, I love— cock . . ." Then my brain fired out immediately, "Your cock."

He groaned as his orgasm built, nearly there. "My cock loves you too."

My orgasm came in a crash, pulling him with me.

Fuck. I was in so much trouble. I'd entered into this to get over Ethan. I did. I wanted fun. I had it and more. I wanted a commit-less rebound without involving my heart. But I'd failed. My heart had decided what it wanted. Not the safe and visible future path with Ethan with benchmark goals to reach. Instead, it wanted the passionate, unscripted future with Jack.

I had two weeks to detach. Two weeks to let go. Two weeks to numb my heart.

Or, my heart countered, two weeks to have as much as I wanted. I'd have a lifetime to miss the past three weeks. Why start now?

## JUNE 26TH

## JACK

The clock read fifteen minutes past midnight. The lights of the gas station were a beacon. Instead of texting, I called Sam.

"It's past midnight, dude, what the fuck is so important?" Sleep slurred Sam's speech.

"Why the fuck did I call you?" I growled.

"What's going on?" More alert, the sounds of him sitting up made it through the phone. "Where are you?"

"Getting ice cream."

Silence.

"Is this a joke?"

I wished it was. My heart hammered in my chest, and my brain screamed warnings at me. I was going to scare her away. I was moving too damn fast.

"What happened with Mina?"

"I told Mina I loved her."

More silence. The weighted judgy type.

"Fuck, Sam, say something."

"Did you actually say it?"

Heat and want sprang in my cock as I remembered her beneath me. The softness of her curves, the moans. Fuck, my erection stood at attention, ready for more. The words had tumbled out, but thankfully against her center. At least, in the moment, I'd had enough sense to not shout it at her.

I groaned, "Yes."

"Did she hear it?"

A laugh shot from me. He knew me too fucking well.

"No."

"Then why are you so fucking wound up?"

"Dude, I can't take her breaking up with me."

Sam sighed. "Then tell her instead of me."

Not words of advice I wanted to hear.

"Fuck off."

"Dude, whining to me about it isn't going to accomplish shit."

"You ever tell Trina, or *whoever*, you were pining for back here that you were interested?"

Sam made a nasty sound. "Look, jackass, you called me. I'm content in my aloneness. You found who makes you happy, and she returns it."

"For five weeks."

Sam sighed again. "Fucking tell her your feelings. Stop being a wuss. If she returns them or not, whatever. At least you know."

"How do I tell her, oh wise one? Do I just sit her down and say, 'Mina, I am in love with you and don't want a timeline on our relationship'?"

"Yes, say that."

My stomach curdled. "That's horrible advice."

"Why, because it makes you vulnerable? Makes you feel like you're back in high school?"

"You go to school to be a shrink without telling me?"

He snorted. "Dude, I've known you a long time. It doesn't take a genius to see what you're going through."

Too many thoughts spun in my head, mostly of how stupid I was for moving so fast.

"If you're not ready for a big step like saying you love her, which I get with what happened in May, at least tell her you want to do away with the timeline."

I ended the call.

Fuck, I needed to lay it out. Make it clear what I wanted.

An email notification flashed across my phone. It was about the Mercer Fourth of July party the following weekend in Lake Geneva.

A smile finally curved my lips. A plan in place, I sent an email off before grabbing mint chocolate chip ice cream from the freezer section.

## JUNE 26TH

### MINA

“Hey, girl,” Maggie mouthed, balancing her phone between her shoulder and face. Two bags swung from her hands, filled with beverages and Chinese food. “Mason, I don’t give a shit.”

“Tell Mason we say ‘hi.’” Mason being Maggie’s brother. I took the bags.

She scrunched her face up at me in distaste.

“Mason, no, I don’t give a flying shit.” Maggie closed the door behind her and kicked off her black Jimmy Choos. “You can tell Declan he can suck my toe.”

“Lucky Declan.” I jumped back when she reached out to slap me.

“He’s a turd shit,” Maggie said. “I don’t care if it is a redundant saying.”

Dani came out of the kitchen with ice and glasses.

“Hi, Mason,” she yelled.

Maggie flipped her off.

Both Dani and I chuckled.

"Fuck off, Mason. I said no," she bellowed. Then her voice switched, and she said, "Remember to call an Uber or me if you decide to drink tonight. Love you, bye."

"You two are weird," Dani said, pulling out a container of broccoli beef.

"What's he or Declan doing now that's pissing you off?" I asked, settling into my chair with my knee bent on the seat beneath me.

"Declan needs a date to something, or more like, Mason wants him to take one so he's not a third wheel." Maggie waved her fork in the air.

"And they asked you?" Dani asked. A grimace marred her face.

"Oh, hell no, not as his date. Declan would be as opposed to that as me, but Mason wanted to know if I had a friend that was available," Maggie said.

Dani looked to me like Maggie was a bitch, and then said to Maggie, "Um, hello, single here. Declan's hot. What? I'd go on a date with him."

Declan was certainly not Dani's type, but the look of rage darkening Maggie's face was Dani's real goal.

"He's a dumbass." Maggie swung her wine glass around in emphasis. Red wine sloshed out her glass on the table.

"A hot one." Dani rolled her lips to stop her smile.

"Now, is Declan your half brother? Or full brother?" I asked, choking as a laugh rippled up my throat.

"Knock it off," Maggie barked. "That's not funny. I am not related to him at all."

"But he's Mason's half brother?" Dani asked.

"Mason and Declan have the same sperm donor," Maggie said. "Mason and I have the same mom."

"Which husband was Mason's dad?" Dani asked.

"He was husband five," Maggie said, counting in the air.

"Which husband was your dad?" Dani asked, her eyes dancing across the table as she tried to keep it straight.

"Sixth," Maggie said.

"But only two kids?" Dani asked, meaning Maggie's mom's kids.

"Margaret only had two kids," Maggie said about her biological mother. Maggie was short for Magnolia, but her nickname had been intentional by her mom. "She had ten husbands."

Maggie wasn't her mom's biggest fan, or even in the running for the hundredth slot even though she was her mom's favorite person next to Mason, but Margaret had seen Maggie as her mini-her, and Maggie got her mother's looks, business acumen, and sexual appetite. Maggie just didn't marry them.

"My turbulent and dramatic past is not what drew us together today," Maggie said, steepling her fingers together.

"Oh jeez," Dani sighed. "Here come the dramatics."

"What else do you expect from someone with nine stepfathers?" Maggie said, staring her down.

"What drew us together, then?" I asked, an uneasy ball settling in my stomach.

Dani and Maggie looked at me in unison, giving me the vibes of a Stephen King movie.

"What?" I asked.

"Where's Jack?" Dani asked, casting a glance to the bedroom.

"He and Sam are meeting with a client," I said, the ball in my stomach expanding to my throat.

"How are things going with you two?" Maggie asked.

"Fine," I offered.

Dani and Maggie shared a look.

"Mina," Maggie said, using her executive voice. "You called me in a panic last night, at midnight, when Jack ran out to grab you two ice cream."

Dani cocked an eyebrow at me.

I scrubbed my face with my hands, trying to block their glances.

"You almost told him you loved him," Maggie said, reminding me of my mistake.

Well, two mistakes: one, almost saying it to Jack, and two, telling Maggie.

"I shouldn't have told you," I whined, slumping in my chair.

"Why?" Maggie asked.

"It was just the hormones. We fucked in his car at the airport. Then again when we got home. My vagina just really likes his cock."

"Uh-huh," they both said.

"It's too soon," I mumbled. "Too many emotions. My heart is a hot mess."

"Too soon?" Maggie chortled. "Seriously? You've known him since middle school."

"I just broke up with Ethan," I said.

"Sure, on paper, but you two were emotionally disengaged long before that," Dani said. "You're happier since the breakup than all the years since college when he wasn't around, and you only had to call or text him. You didn't even look forward to it. It was just one more checklist item for the day you marked off."

I frowned at her. Her words had too much truth to them.

"We only have two weeks left. I need to start to disentangle," I said.

"Why?" Dani asked as Maggie rolled her eyes and stared at the ceiling, shaking her head.

"Other than two relationships, they don't last longer than a week. The one only lasted because they both knew they'd break up after college was over," I said. "He's not a commitment person. When he returned from California, he started up his girlfriends again until Alicia. He proposed to her, but look at how that turned out. It's already going to be hard enough on my heart after this time. I won't survive sticking it out and then him leaving after a couple months or even a year. I just need to end it after the five weeks."

Even more, I couldn't handle him leaving me for another woman. Too much history was tainted by betrayal.

"Why do you believe it'll end? I don't buy this bullshit," Maggie said.

"He wanted to spite Ethan. Satiate a teenage crush," I said.

"You know, you could be an adult and tell him your feelings," Dani said.

Maggie frowned, and I gave her a disgusted look.

"Then what's your advice?" Dani said to Maggie, folding her arms over her chest.

"Ride it out," Maggie said. "You don't want to admit anything, then don't. Just because it makes sense to do it, doesn't mean it'll hit right. When the party is over next weekend, and you have one week left, just ask him, 'So you want to go another five weeks? Terminate? Or renegotiate a new time period?' Make it a business transaction."

"What the fuck?" Dani said, shaking her head. "Don't play more fucking games. You're obviously invested. You have feelings for him. Tell him. If he doesn't reciprocate, sure, it'll hurt. We'll be here to hug you and tell you what a dumb-fucking-ass he is. Or maybe, and more likely, he reciprocates those feelings. He has shit in your apartment. You both have shoes at the door. I see his mug on the counter. He has shit in your bathroom. You two are living together from the looks of it."

"He's too nice to let me crash and burn. If I asked, he'd probably extend it another five weeks while moving his stuff back or having more meetings or getting disinterested. I can't go through that."

"Mina, this wishy-washy, indecisive, self-deprecating stuff is not your normal," Dani said, taking my hand. "You are a confident person who directs her life. Don't start being someone else because you have feelings for Jack. You were never like this with Ethan. You had a list you were pretty much checking off with him."

"I used to say that to her in high school too," Maggie said. "She never had the doe eyes or lovestruck look. He fit nicely into her plans, and she went with it. If they made it through college together, she figured they'd get married and had a plan for how it would work with their careers."

"Yeah, and that fucker was dating other girls, and I just found out," I said.

"I agree, knowing before would have been ideal so you didn't spend so much boring and unsatisfying time with him," Maggie said. "But, I'm more glad you didn't marry him."

"Agreed," Dani said.

"Whatever you decide to do, we'll be here to either cheer you on or remind you that you should have listened to us," Maggie said with a cheeky smile.

"Thanks," I deadpanned.

"You can follow her advice and renegotiate this situation, which has obviously brought you discomfort, or you can follow my advice and just be direct with him about your feelings."

Or, I could just stick my head in the sand. That felt the safest for the moment. My heart didn't have the strength to deal with the loss. When I broke up with Ethan, pieces of me returned, rebuilt. I was stronger, happier. When Jack and I parted, he'd have pieces of me I'd never get back.

## JUNE 27TH

### MINA

Shortly before six a.m., my phone vibrated with a notification. Then what sounded like a dozen more pinged on my phone. Jack's phone dinged too.

Jack's arm tightened over my arm. Soft words tickled my ear.

Then a text message rattled my phone. Then four more.

"What the fuck?" I growled.

Jack grunted as he peeled his eyes open. His hazy blue eyes swam as they focused on my face. A smile already danced on his lips.

The last message that rolled in was from the group chat with the ladies.

MAGGIE: That fucking asshole has no idea who he's messing with

VICTORIA: I'm sure someone has more compromising evidence <angel emoji>

TRINA: MINA GIVE US THE GO

"Ah fuck."

My stomach hardened with dread. Only one person so far got the group so worked up, and at six a.m. on a Sunday.

"What's going on?" Jack murmured.

His lips brushed my arm as he moved to sit up next to me.

A few more notifications came in, all from the same social media platform. Blowing out a breath, I clicked on the latest one.

What felt like hours as it loaded was barely a few seconds, and then I saw red. Splashed in grainy, unfocused glory was a picture of me from the bar. My rumpled white wedding dress went in every direction as Jack carried me out the door. Commented below was a crisp black-and-white picture of Jack and me in Ethan's elevator with Aiden cut out.

My phone fell from my hands.

Jack picked it up and flicked his gaze to his own phone, having its own cacophony of notifications.

"Look what I was sent anonymously," Jack gritted out. "My bride being carried out of a bar with another man. One she's now parading around town with. I found it suspicious they showed up together at my apartment when I wasn't home, but you know 'business.'" Jack even did the stupid quotes with one hand. "If she can't . . ."

He swallowed. His jaw worked, and his body tightened. Long, uneven breaths escaped his nose.

"I'm going to fucking destroy him." The threat fell from Jack's lips. Dark rage swam in his eyes.

I wrapped my fingers around his wrist.

He lifted his eyes to mine and blinked. He blew out a harsh breath.

Inclining my chin toward my phone, I said, "Finish."

I braced for the next words.

Through gritted teeth, he continued. "If she can't be loyal to her fiancé, how can you trust her if your stocks dip? Or someone offers her vodka one night?"

"Are you fucking serious?" A strained laugh sounded from my throat.

Jack's hand found mine. "Mina . . ." He offered no more words, but he swallowed some back as if they were poison.

"I'm sorry you got dragged into this."

Hollowness ate at my heart and chest. My unfocused eyes took in nothing and everything. I hadn't met with him, so he'd woven a story to make him look like the victim. To make me look like the unfaithful asshole. And then he dragged Jack into this.

Jack's strong hand cupped my cheek, and then he gently pressed his lips to mine, pulling me from my spiraling thoughts.

When he pulled back, I blinked. Angry tears pricked my eyes, and my nostrils flared.

"He's a fucking asshole," Jack said. "He's desperate and is making a Hail Mary. He knows this will hurt your career and not mine. He thinks this will bring you back. That you'll beg him to take it down, do whatever he wants."

"He'll fucking learn."

He did it because he didn't think I'd fight back. That I would shrink away from a public spectacle. They didn't go especially well for women who were incorrectly seen as the emotional ones. It took us longer to bounce back, if we ever did.

I took my phone back.

With a deep sigh, I cleared the tremors in my chest. Now was the time for action, anger. Not retreat.

I clicked on the first image, already with a thousand likes. Fuck.

ME: As is with your character, you like to give small pieces of information and make up stories. A friend picked me up from the bar after I found YOU in the closet, at OUR wedding venue, half naked with your penis in another woman. That friend also helped me pick up stuff from your apartment. Since then, we have started a relationship, but as true timelines and facts have never mattered to you in your personal or business life, I doubt you care now. It has also

> been brought to my attention since our wedding day that you dated other women during college, and the times you went to your "grandma's" in high school were mostly covers for seeing other girls. You are the last person who should comment on or question another person's loyalty.

I let Jack read it. He lifted an eyebrow.

"He's already put the smear out. My career will take a hit regardless of facts if it's not taken down soon. He knows I'll experience more backlash than him. He thinks I'll beg him. Fuck that shit."

I posted it. A tug pulled at my side.

The group chat dinged.

> TRINA: GO TIME

The social media page dinged as new comments came in.

> TRINA: Wait? What? <shocked face emoji>
> TRINA: <picture alt text: Mina and Ethan in high school and college. One shows them at prom. Other is at Ethan's family lake home sophomore year of college.> These two dated continuously from freshman year of high school up to the day of their wedding. This can't possibly be true!

Her post contained tags to our high school, his college, and Tiffany.

> TRINA: Oops, sorry, didn't mean to tag you Tiffany
> ANON0203553: Loyal?
> ANON0203553: <picture alt text: screenshot of Ethan's friend's post: WHAT A STALLION! LOOK AT THESE HOT PIECES OF ASS HE RODE TOGETHER. Picture shows Mina, Ethan, and Tiffany outside the closet Mina caught them in.>
> BITCHAINTPLAYING: I can one-up that.

BITCHAINTPLAYING: <picture alt text: video of the whole scene when Ethan was fucking Tiffany on his and Mina's wedding day>

IMNOTPLAYINGEITHER: <picture alt text: Picture of Ethan and Tiffany in the hotel hallway lobby. Ethan is in his rehearsal dinner attire. Pretty sure he left the dinner early because "he wasn't feeling well and wanted some sleep.">

IMNOTPLAYINGEITHER: <picture alt text: Ethan and Tiffany humping against a wall before entering a hotel room at the rehearsal dinner hotel.> That you? That you on your wedding day? Is that your bride? Or is that the woman you were fucking in the closet?

Jack laughed beside me. "Sorry," he snorted. "Your friends are good."

More and more anon and burner accounts started dropping pictures of Ethan with other women. At some point, one or more of my friends had done a social media dive in the Wayback Machine. A long and deep one.

YOUREALIAR5032: <picture alt text: full picture from the elevator. Aiden Settlers was with them.>

TIFFANYBRIMWORTH: So you can't return my calls? Or my texts? But you can post pictures of your ex? The person you cheated on with me? Repeatedly? I was good enough to fuck for the months leading up to your wedding, just not after it?

TIFFANYBRIMWORTH: <picture alt text: Ethan's dick> Look at the time stamp. That was a week before your wedding. You wanted a tits pic. You begged me to meet up. You told me you were breaking up with her for me. I was barely in the limo that night before you had me undressed and your dick in me. You barely lasted two minutes you were so worked up from the pics I sent you.

CHRISTINECREMSKI: Thankfully, I don't have anything like that. I only have pictures of us at my parents' lake home. We went to college together and dated for a little over a year. I'm sorry, Mina. I had no idea you two were still together. He said you broke up when the long distance became too much.

CHRISTINECREMSKI: <picture alt text: Junior year. Long weekend. First time he told me he loved me.>

Jack and I both sucked in a breath at the last post.

"Damn," I breathed.

"Mina . . . I don't have words." Jack let out a hard sigh.

It was then I realized his arm was wrapped around my shoulder, and he had me pressed against his chest.

Somehow, the tightness in my stomach loosened. Ethan had been fucking everyone while we were together. Probably from the start. We had been a house of cards that I had at one time felt solid about. Secure in. But an entire life had spun around me that I had been clueless—no, ignorant—of. I hadn't wanted to know. Just scratching the surface, I had pieced together signs of his deceit, his cheating. Now I had evidence that spanned beyond the closet. That verified the words Jack had said.

"I'm sorry I didn't believe you in high school," I barely breathed.

"Mina, this isn't your fault," Jack started.

I shook my head. "It's not. I just realize you were the only person who tried to warn me from the start. You tried to protect me even then."

Jack quirked his brows.

Then Trina's words and warnings spun in my mind. "Trina just didn't like him. I should have taken that as a warning too. She didn't know about his cheating, but she just didn't like him."

Jack kissed my temple and then leaned his head on mine.

And yet, she really liked Jack with me.

All my friends did.

As did my heart.

My gaze flicked to my phone. Was that something I'd ever find out about Jack? That he had led a sordid life behind my back? Then I chastised that thought. He wasn't Ethan.

A new social media notification flicked across my phone.

TRINA: You ever notice how often Ethan's social media is scrubbed? Posts deleted? How many posts he gets tagged in with women spanning years are removed? Somehow, though, this doesn't hold true for Mina or Jack's social media pages. It's almost like the person blaming the loudest is trying to distract from their worst actions. Hm . . . Makes me question how loyal and trustworthy you are in your personal and business lives. Have you done this type of posting about a client?

The screen refreshed, and Ethan's original posts were deleted along with all his responses. Slowly, the responses with pictures were removed as violating term agreements.

My group chat lit up.

CORRINE: My anon accounts got suspended for sexually explicit materials.

VICTORIA: Same. Amazing you got that private coverage from the hotel security footage.

CORRINE: <angel emoji> no idea what you mean

DANI: I need to make sure to never cross you

DANI: All his socials are going private.

VICTORIA: It's fast enough I assume the Settlers have a direct legal connection to the platform. Probably happened regularly before. Their PR team is fucking impressive.

MAGGIE: I need to bleach my eyes, but I have screenshots of it all. I'm going to put it in a folder: OPEN IF YOU WANT TO VOMIT

TRINA: I'm deleting my posts so I don't look deranged to my firm

Good idea. I deleted my own.

A single text came through from Trina.

TRINA: I am so glad you left him. He's a petty dumb fuck. BUT. I am even happier that you found Jack. He's a good man who cares deeply for you. More than you realize. I know you're going to be in your head, probably completely freak out later, but do me a favor. Skip Mom's today. Stay snuggled in bed with Jack and let him take care of and distract you. Focus on how amazing he is. That he wouldn't do this shit, ever. And that his concern right now, I'm going to wager, is only that you are okay.

I blinked. Her words swirled together into a mosaic of truths. Without thought, my free hand twisted behind us, burrowing into his thick locks. He nestled against me, his warmth soothing and enticing.

"We could order in breakfast. Or I can make us some pancakes."

The idea of him not next to me at the moment sent a chill through me. And a warning. But at the moment, I focused solely on what I wanted.

"Stay next to me."

"Always."

He kissed my shoulder and opened a delivery app.

I watched as his fingers typed out our order. The more I watched, the more I focused on how they felt on me. My center warmed, chasing away the numbness and ick. Ethan was a fuckwad. He showed his true self and disgustingness. It had nothing to do with me other than to try to control me. I could focus and harbor on all he had done. Dwell on how much I missed or ignored in our time together.

Or I could keep my eyes open as I enjoyed the last few weeks with Jack. That thought sent a painful jolt to my heart.

"What happened?" Jack's gaze flicked to me. "You flinched."

My eyes only focused on his lips. Soft and inviting.

"Mina?"

"Is our order placed?" With great effort, I lifted my gaze to his.

"Yes, should be here in thirty to forty."

I crashed my lips on his, my hands and body scrambling against his to be as close to him as possible. With each kiss, the thoughts of everything were pushed further and further away. Scattering into the recesses of my mind.

Urgent kisses met mine, but he hovered his hands on my hips, not moving higher or lower. With us still both sitting up, I swung my leg over him, straddling him. His hardness greeted my heated core. Need and want pulsed in me. Only for this man. The thought should have stopped me. Made me reconsider. But all I wanted was to feel him. I needed it.

With one hand, I found the box of condoms, pulled one out, opened it with my teeth, and sheathed him.

"Mina, are you sure?"

I slid down onto him. His hardness filled me, satiating a desire that would never end.

He moaned and tightened his fingers around me, already rocking us into motion.

"Jack." I swallowed the word burning on my tongue, instead opting for the safe version. "I want you."

He searched my face, his own scrunched in confusion.

I pressed my lips against his and tried to slip my tongue into his mouth. Instead, he tilted his chin down, breaking our kiss.

"Jack?" My voice broke saying his name.

Was he going to turn me down? Burn me too? Like all the other men in my life had?

He lolled his head to the side with a hazy expression. "Mina." He licked his lips. "I only want you."

Those words untethered something in me. Whatever we had, whatever this could be called, is what I wanted. For always. But that was only wishful and lustful dreaming.

## JUNE 28TH

## MINA

The office was quiet when I strolled in at quarter past six. A dim light spilled out from beneath Yang's door. She had a pull-out sofa mattress in her office, but I wondered how often she slept in there.

With the holiday weekend coming up at the end of the quarter, I wanted to make sure I called all my clients to touch base, see if they would be at the party, and if not, if they'd like to get together soon to review their portfolio.

All the clients who preferred emails over calls or texts had an email in their inbox by half past seven. Heated voices carried into my office as I was pulling up my text app on my computer that was synced to my phone. It made typing messages in bulk easier.

At least three voices came from the other side of the door. Focusing, I was able to make out Yang's and Trevor's voices. It took me longer to place Mariya's voice. She wasn't expected back until later in the week. Her early presence meant something was off.

A knock sounded on my door, and I jumped.

"Mina," Yang called.

"It's open," I called back, standing to open the door.

Before I could cross the room, she opened it and stepped inside. Mariya's brunette hair was pulled back into a bun. Her fierce brown eyes narrowed in on Trevor. Her red lipstick was barely visible as she pressed her lips together. Trevor stood back from them, his head bowed, his frame slumped, as his blue eyes fixed on the floor. He blinked, and the glossiness was visible. Instead of a polished look like Yang and Mariya, he wore no tie or jacket, his shirt was wrinkled, and he had what looked like a coffee stain on his trousers.

"We need you," Yang said and snapped her fingers at Trevor, who obediently followed her inside my office.

Mariya moved to block his exit. Her long frame leaned against the doorway.

"How can I help?" I offered, bouncing my gaze between the three.

"Tell her," Yang demanded.

Trevor cleared his throat and twisted his fingers together.

"Ronald is more conservative than he said," Trevor said with a sniff.

"Try again," Mariya sneered. "This time with you taking responsibility."

My eyes widened, but I didn't say anything.

Trevor's lip trembled, his eyes darting up to mine before shifting to look behind me.

"I didn't ask enough questions," Trevor said, starting again. "I put Ronald in a high-yield potential but high-risk plan."

"Ronald is extremely conservative. He wants reliable and stable returns. He's more glacial than a river current." I stared at Trevor.

Trevor blinked, and his jaw ticked.

"How much money did Ronald lose in the swing?" I asked, realizing what must have happened.

Trevor mumbled something unintelligible.

"Again," Mariya barked. "Own what you did."

"Half," Trevor squeaked out.

"What?" I breathed out, pinpricks of light dancing in my vision.

"Exactly," Mariya said, nodding at me in approval. "You can fix this."

I gulped, my stare fixed on her.

Yang nodded. "Mina, call Ronald in today. Talk to him. He was one of your first clients. You made him a great deal of money. Save this."

"He made it clear he wanted to work with a partner—the big guns —to bring him more money," I said.

"He won't take any of our calls," Yang said. "He may not have the largest portfolio, but he is well respected. He may have conservative choices, but he pulls results, and others listen to him. Handle this. Please."

I nodded, my mind reeling. Moving to my computer, I stared at my list of current clients, a quarter already emailed and the rest waiting for a text or phone call. When I reached out to them, I wanted to be available to answer questions, not dodging them to work with Ronald.

Sighing, I minimized the app.

A stream of customers ran through the coffee shop, getting their caffeinated fix and heading out. Ronald sat perched on a high-top in the corner, his laptop open while his phone sat on a holder.

He steepled his fingers, tapping the pads together as he read an email. His phone buzzed. He side-eyed it and snarled. He returned to his email.

"Ronald," I chirped, holding my peppermint mocha.

His hazel eyes darted in my direction. His pained expression eased, and he sat back.

"Good morning, Mina," he said, his words flat. "I assume you heard."

I shrugged and nodded, my mouth skewed to the side.

"May I sit down," I asked, gesturing to the empty seat opposite him.

"I was just leaving," he said, closing his laptop.

I stared him in the eye. "No, you weren't. We both know you work here in the morning. You like the smell of the coffee and baked goods even though you don't partake in either. In the afternoon, you prefer a sandwich near the lake."

He met my eyes, searching them for something he found. "You were always good with the personal side of the business."

"And the money side." I sipped my coffee, the warmth and mintyness rejuvenating me.

He snorted. "Yeah, I guess you were."

"Ronald," I said, leveling him with my gaze. "You made a good return you didn't question until Ethan and I broke up. I can't say with certainty that it colored your perspective on me. However, you moved at his recommendation."

Based on the social media post, I could only assume Ethan had played the victim and made up stories about my abilities or morals.

His mouth twitched, and he leaned back, folding his arm over his chest.

"I cannot double your money in a year as Trevor promised without high risks." He looked away, and I added, "And neither can he."

Ronald returned his focus to me, interest flicking in his eyes.

"If you want higher returns, there are more risks. We can diversify your portfolio, add more risk that offers a potential of higher returns, but let's move the bulk back to the accounts I had you in."

He swallowed but didn't say no.

"However, because of what Trevor did, we're at a deficit," I said.

He snorted and looked away.

"I won't make outlandish promises. I can't promise when we'll get back to what you were when you left me. But I will get you back there and then forward." I laid my hands on the tabletop.

Ronald swallowed. "How long do you project to get me back?"

"Depends on the risk you're willing to take." I raised my finger to pause his complaint. "Let's move seventy-five percent of the remaining funds back to what I had you in. They'll grow steadily at a similar rate as before. We'll use the other twenty-five percent to do the dirty work. We're asking that chunk, twelve-point-five percent of the original dollars, to remain and recoup the lost fifty percent. I drew up a few plans. One as we're discussing now. I also drew a few others using different levels of risk, including not using the twenty-five percent. Without a doubt, I don't recommend keeping your funds as Trevor has them. They will peak, but the valley will be long."

"I'll be working with you on this project or one of the partners at your firm?" he asked, his mouth pressed into a thin line.

"I'll leave that up to you. I haven't shared my action plan with Trevor, Yang, Mariya, or Kabir. I approached you first. This is your choice."

"I've talked with other firms," he said.

I nodded. "I understand. Your confidence was shaken. You were misled by someone you felt would make better choices."

"We both know what I said to you," Ronald said in challenge.

"I do," I said. "I also know Ethan spoke with you. I do not know, nor do I want to know, what he said to you. Trevor is his college friend. He made choices to progress his own career. He just doesn't understand the complexity of what I do. He also inflates abilities, his own and those he likes. It's why I didn't want him to recommend me to his associates. I couldn't live up to his lies."

The bitterness of yesterday's post simmered in my veins. Then another thought hit me. One that brought an odd curl of pride. If he used the same lies on all my clients, he had connections with only three left. That meant my business and relationship with my clients were worth more to them than whatever lies Ethan had spun. No wonder he was panicking. He had lost control, even over ones with whom he had a connection.

"What he said about you when we met was true," Ronald said. "You listened and got me what I wanted."

A brittle smile cracked my face.

"But I suppose that has more to do with you and your skill and not him," Ronald said.

"Thank you," I said.

"I don't want any of those snakes touching my money," he said.

"Then you'll work only with me." I extended my hand.

"It's good to be back with someone competent," Ronald said, taking my hand.

By the time I returned to the office, news had traveled. Gina and Raquel whispered together in Gina's office. Martin stood with the other associate analysts outside their office, their fear of experiencing this failure drooping their faces.

Trevor sat in his office, the door shut and windows drawn. Yang and Mariya stood behind her window, staring at the analysts in the common space.

A hush descended on the office when I walked through the door. Eyes followed me as I walked to Yang's office. My hands shook, and I licked my lips, meeting the stares.

Yang yanked her door open, stepping back and inviting me in without a word.

As she shut the door, I felt the eyes boring through the door to see me. Facing forward, I willed my body not to turn around.

"Well?" Mariya asked, her hands on her hips.

"Ronald does not want to work with an existing partner at this firm," I said, speaking slowly to keep my voice from shaking.

They stared expectantly at me.

"However, he was willing to sign a contract with me." I held up my briefcase.

"He resigned with you," Mariya said, a large smile beaming on her face.

"Yes," I said.

"Keep it up, Mina," Yang said. "And your partnership will be sooner than later."

**JUNE 28TH**

**MINA**

Jack met me at the door, a bottle of champagne in one hand and a necklace box in the other.

"What's this?" I laughed.

"A celebration." He lifted the items. "You single-handedly saved an important client who has a lot of pull in the community. He's not the biggest investor, but his reach is massive."

"And the box?" I nodded to it, itching to see what was inside.

"This is something I like to do," he said and then frowned. "Okay, I don't buy myself necklaces, mind you, but after a big win, I like to get a token of it. The contracts that have big personal or career significance. It's nothing ever big, but it reminds me of what I can do."

"What are some things you bought yourself?"

I dropped my stuff on the front table. I wrapped my arms around his neck, pulling him down for a kiss. His lips met mine, and a jolt went through my veins. Then I remembered I was trying to pull back from him, wean my heart from him, but it didn't listen as it encouraged me to slip my tongue in his mouth.

"I have some cufflinks," he said against my lips. "I have a pen after my first client signing. My car is my most expensive one."

"Your car?"

With a smirk, he shrugged.

"Tell me!" I squealed.

"It was the Delavin account," he said and waited.

"Delavin . . .Oh . . .OH!" I laughed. "I remember that one. Ethan was certain he had it sealed. It was a big project north of Milwaukee. It would also lock in multiple other big contracts."

"I know." He grinned. "It was one of my biggest wins and locked in six other contracts."

"He was angry for months," I said, remembering the temper tantrums.

"Yes, thus the car." He lifted the box. "This is a big win for you."

"So, you bought me a gift?"

He shrugged but couldn't hide his grin. He set the champagne down and cradled the box in his hand. He held it out, a shy smile curving his face.

My hands shook as I took the box. It was a sweet gesture, one I'd have to return to him after the Fourth of July weekend, but I was still dying to see what he'd selected. If I kept it, though, it wouldn't remind me of the sale but of Jack. My heart wouldn't be able to stand the reminder.

The red Cartier box contained a white gold necklace with a partial circle pendant embedded with diamonds, resembling a bent nail.

"It's gorgeous." I ran a finger over the delicate pendant.

"Turn around," he murmured.

I did as he asked and lifted my hair.

He lifted it over my head and fastened it, his fingers brushing against my neck and sending tingles across my skin.

"I was thinking," he said, guiding me back around to face him. I pressed my body flush against his. "We could head to Lake Geneva Friday afternoon and just enjoy the evening there, the two of us."

"You were?"

My heart and vagina cheered, agreeing readily to the decision. My brain flashed warnings about pulling back, weaning off the relationship. But they were muted by every other part of my body.

"Mhm." He kissed my ear and then my neck. "I know the Mercer function is expecting us Saturday through Monday, but there are hotels on the lake."

"They've probably been booked for months." I wove my hands through his hair.

"What if I said I know for a fact there's an open room?" he said, unbuttoning my shirt while his hot mouth tracked kisses down my chest. "It has a balcony overlooking the lake. A stocked fridge. Room service. Jacuzzi hot tub."

"This is a very specific room," I murmured, pushing his suit jacket off and unbuttoning his pants.

"I may know the owner personally." The words garbled as his tongue twirled around my nipple.

I gasped and held him against me as need rose in my core.

"It's the room he uses when he's in town. He's not coming in until Sunday. It's available," he said over the breast in his mouth.

"Jack," I murmured.

So much bubbling up to be said. I choked back the "I love you" and "What are we going to do about our arrangement?" to protect my heart. To not ruin the moment.

Instead, I managed, "Yes."

Trina stared at me over her mug.

"What?" I asked, still groggy from the late night.

"What time did his flight take off?"

"Six," I said with a yawn.

"You dropped him off?" she asked and then took a sip of coffee.

"No, Sam picked him up," I said.

She growled.

"Sorry, forgot it's the name not to mutter in front of you."

"Whatever," she said. "So, that's a beautiful necklace."

My hand flew to my neck, my fingers tracing the pendant. It was the only thing I wore last night when we celebrated by the door, on the sofa with champagne, on the table after dinner, and after our shower.

"Damn, you just got red and a lusty look in your eyes," she said, pointing at my face.

I whimpered, sliding the pendant on the chain.

"Why again can't you admit to him you love him?" she asked.

"I don't," I said in protest. "It's a lust-fueled emotion that I feel."

"Bullshit," Trina coughed.

"Trina, it's too soon," I whined and stomped my foot at the annoying sound I made.

"Mina," Trina said, putting her coffee mug down to stand by me. "It's okay that you're happy. It's okay that you love him. I'm certain he loves you too."

"It's too soon. He doesn't feel the same way." I held my hands up to stop her. "I know he cares about me. I'm not denying that. We just know his interest wanes."

"We know this?" Trina asked, cocking her head back. "Or you believe this so you can continue to live in your weird little world where you can build calloused walls."

"That's rich from you," I shouted and batted her hands off my shoulders.

"Oh, I'm a cocktail of dysfunction and fucked-up relationships. I dated Clay knowing we'd break up after high school, but he was fun and hot. I dated Kyle in college knowing I'd break up with him after college. When I try to date 'for the future,' I end up with Erics, who are nice and boring but make Mom happy."

"Aren't you two breaking up?" I asked.

"Nice dodge, but yeah, we are," she said. "Mom scared him away, and even if it amuses me and she infuriates me most days, whoever

I'm with can't be intimidated by my mom enough that they don't return my calls. Mom is important to me."

"Mom doesn't like Jack," I said.

"Mom *didn't* like Jack," she said. "She also loved Ethan until almost two months ago. She also loved Dad. However, Mom likes how happy Jack makes you. You also don't care if Mom really likes him. He sat there and took the questions. He went home with you. He'll go back again on the eleventh, and every Sunday and holiday afterward."

I rubbed a hand over my forehead. "No, he won't, we won't be together."

"So you're breaking up with him?"

"Shouldn't I do it before he does it to me?" I whispered, my fears finally aired.

"You don't want him to hurt and embarrass you like Ethan did? Like Dad did to Mom?" Trina said, her face turned down in disappointment.

"Trina," I started, but she shook her head.

"You keep lining him up to Ethan to see what you missed. He's not Ethan, he's not a sleazy fuckwad. Jack loves you. Ethan loves himself. But until you're willing to see Jack and Jack alone and not how he's different from Ethan, you're not ready to be with him. So maybe you really should take a break."

"I don't compare him to Ethan," I said, hearing the lie as I spoke. "Fuck," I breathed.

"Jack loves you. I'm pretty sure you love him but can't see it past the comparison you draw with Ethan. You keep assuming he'll hurt you. You likely fear deep down that Jack will somehow have materials for a post like Ethan's. Let me help you out . . . That shit doesn't exist, even in the recesses of the Wayback Machine and other places we looked. We checked on Jack while there for Ethan, just to make sure. Ethan is a liar. Jack told you the truth, even ones he'd kept secret since high school. Ethan puts his interests first. Jack has supported your career and backed off when you asked him to. Ethan makes himself a priority. Jack makes you a priority. Ethan loves himself. Jack loves you. I'm not sure what else matters besides the most important thing . . ."

Tears rimmed my eyes, threatening to spill over, but I croaked out, "What is that?"

"Do you still love Ethan?"

"Fuck no," I said, repulsion coursing through me.

"Do you love Jack?" she whispered.

"I think so," I choked out.

She sighed.

"Yes," I said, finally admitting it to myself.

Fuck. I loved him. I was in love with him. It wasn't sex, lust, the moments, it was him. No matter how I tried to find the chink in it, I was in fucking love with Jack.

"Then let him know." She circled her arms around me and pulled me into a hug. "Your trial is over. You both obviously love each other. Just knock the shit off. Let him know, and let yourself fully embrace his love like you deserve."

## JULY 2ND

## JACK

After catching a red-eye back to Milwaukee, I took a quick shower, changed, and swung by Mina's office to pick her up. We held hands as we drove the hour to Lake Geneva. Mina wore a red dress that showed off her toned legs and emphasized her curvy frame. The necklace I'd bought her graced her collarbone. She traced her fingers over my hands as she took in the plush sights.

"How'd the week go? You were pretty vague in the texts," I said.

"Trevor's on thin ice and kissing ass." She chuckled. "Yang is keeping more close to the vest, but Mariya has made it clear she thinks his behavior of pilfering a client was despicable and then his treatment of the client's file was horrendous. I'm paraphrasing and being more polite."

"So he keeps his role?" I asked.

"They aren't sharing, but I'm guessing they're working on a buyout strategy."

"Have you brought up a promotion?" I asked.

Her firm should be trying everything to keep her happy. I knew other firms that would do a lot to snag her.

She shrugged. "Not really. Still a bit bitter after what happened."

"But Trevor is the one who spearheaded that. Yang seems interested," I said.

"Saving the account helps, but I need to nail down a big client."

"Like Greg?" I asked.

She sighed and slumped back.

"What's wrong?" I asked.

Alarm rang through me. Did I push her too much? Were we back to this? Something shifted in my stomach. Something both familiar and of the past. A tinge of acid and acceptance.

"Greg has made it clear I'm too small of a fish for him."

I frowned, narrowing my eyes. This was such a simple solution.

"If you need a big client," I started.

"No," she said, shutting down the conversation.

"No, what?" I asked. I hadn't even finished.

"No, I don't want you to sign with me."

She turned to stare out the side window.

My fingers tightened around hers, but I forced my gaze to remain focused on the road.

Again, I wasn't good enough in something. She may not want me, but there were other clients.

I gritted out, "I know other clients always open to new opportunities. You have a stellar reputation."

"No, thank you."

Her shoulder pushed against the door, creating the most space possible between us.

I sighed, my lips pressed into a thin line. Fatigue or reality was finally catching up with me. She didn't want me to sign, and she kept measuring me up to Ethan. Expecting me to somehow hurt her. To somehow have a secret life of lies and disrespecting her. Pushing me away when we started to get too close. Every time we started to nearly express our feelings, she backed up. I would never be good enough for her.

And we only had a week left on our agreement.

What the fuck was I doing?

I planned a night at a hotel so I could finally tell her I loved her. Be completely honest. I could have said it before, I tried, but this was just going to be us. On vacation together as a couple. But were we? Ethan's shadow seemed to follow us.

"I'm not Ethan," I muttered before realizing I'd spoken.

"I know that," she retorted, nose flaring.

So she just didn't like me enough, then. I didn't measure up to whatever it was she wanted.

"Jack." She shifted to lean against the door and look at me.

I flicked my eyes toward her.

Her amber eyes regarded me. Concern and fear reflected back.

She lifted our still-joined hands to her lips and kissed each of my fingers. The soft touch sent tingles through me. A shudder rippled down my spine. This wasn't real. Not for her. She just had a week left.

She was my everything. But I wasn't hers. I rushed it. Fucked it up. I was her rebound. She was my never-get-over again. What the fuck was I talking about? I hadn't been over her ever. It's why Alicia broke up with me when I proposed to her. She said she couldn't live in Mina's shadow.

And here I was being a fool. Living in Ethan's shadow.

I slipped my fingers from hers, running them along her jawline. I needed to memorize her face. Her feel. Her touch. Like Alicia, who couldn't live in Mina's shadow, I couldn't live in Ethan's.

Removing my hand from her face, I pointed to a large structure, a maintained relic of the past.

"That's it," I said, placing my hands on the steering wheel.

She stared at me instead of the hotel. A question lingered, but she didn't ask.

We hadn't discussed our arrangement yet, but I had hoped I would confess my love and she would reciprocate it or at least stay. Then we'd get rid of the "trial run" verbiage and just be an us.

But I guessed that wasn't what she wanted.

## JULY 2ND

## MINA

Fuck. He called me out. And he was right. It was exactly what Trina said I was doing. Holding Jack to the lines I'd drawn that kept Ethan at bay and from meddling in my life. Kept him from claiming victory for my success. Kept waiting for Jack to show signs he was just like Ethan, even when I knew he wasn't.

He'd been almost silent since the car. Other than obligatory words, he stood rigid, his eyes distant.

On the way up the sweeping entry, the concierge smiled at us. "Mr. Wolfe," she said. "I have the tickets as requested."

He returned her smile and accepted the tickets. "I appreciate your help in obtaining these."

Jack slipped his hand into mine, guiding me toward the staircase.

Once inside, Jack placed our suitcase on the stand. He tossed the tickets on the dresser and pulled his phone out. The screen flashed as he scrolled emails.

"What are the tickets for?" I asked, trying to break the icy tension.

He flicked his eyes up to me and then the tickets. He flinched. "A boat tour of the lake. Booked it for an hour from now. We have reservations at a winery afterward, if you're interested."

His tone was cold and distant, almost indifferent.

"Jack." I stepped toward him.

"I'm going to freshen up, and then if you want to walk one of the paths before the tour, we can. Or whatever you want," he said without looking at me as he walked toward the bathroom.

When I finally realized I was in love with him, I'd finally pushed him too far with the comparison. I'd been pushing him away, and he finally backed up.

My mind jumped to seducing him, but I couldn't avoid what sat between us. I'd only be deepening the void.

Telling him my feelings now just felt like a form of manipulation. We had the possibility of a romantic night ahead of us. A long weekend at the Mercer event. I needed a plan. I needed a perfect moment, one where he knew I was serious, not influenced, and to make my brain happy, a place I could easily escape from if he said no. Because no matter what the girls said, what I hoped, a part of me still waited for the no.

But I still had to get us talking.

I took my phone out to text the group chat.

ME: I fucked up. I keep comparing him to Ethan, not out loud but he called me out on it. Now he's not talking to me.

MAGGIE: Mount him

CORRINE: NO! Don't listen to Maggie. Talk to him.

DANI: Where is he now?

ME: Bathroom

TRINA: WTF. We just talked about this!

ME: I KNOW! HELP

VICTORIA: Let him be silent. Hold his hand. Give him space. Soft touches.

TRINA: When did Victoria get mushy?

DANI: I second Victoria.

MAGGIE: Mina is not a soft toucher. She's direct.

TRINA: Then tell him you're sorry, you know what you're doing, you know he's not Ethan, you love him, and you want to stop the trial and just move forward as a couple

ALL NAMES: <dancing dots>

MAGGIE: Shit when did Trina get wisdom

DANI: Um I agree with Trina on something related to love? WTH

CORRINE: I agree with Trina <heart emoji> - Well said, sweetie!

VICTORIA: Trina is correct

Well fucking great.

The bathroom door handle jiggled, and I jumped.

Jack came out, his smile back in place.

"We should head out so we're not late." He walked toward the tickets.

"I'm sorry," I blurted out, twisting my fingers together.

His eyes jumped in confusion, his step faltered.

"If you're not interested in the tour, we can do something else," he said, his voice flat and bored.

"I'm sorry about what was implied in the car. I know you're not Ethan," I said in a rush. I licked my lips. I knew the next part I was supposed to say, but I didn't want it lumped in with a sentence about Ethan. Not when it could be conveyed as manipulation.

His smile morphed, waning before softening. He crossed the distance and wrapped his arms around me.

"It's okay." He rested his chin on my head.

"No." I pushed my hands on his chest but grabbed his shirt so he didn't think I wanted him to step back. "No, it's not."

He furrowed his brows as he darted his gaze to the side.

I moved my hands to his cheeks, squaring his face in alignment with mine. "Jack, please look at me."

His blue eyes shifted to mine, cold and pained. The stupid granite fortress of nothingness was erecting on his face, and it was completely my fault.

"Jack, I am sorry," I said again, swallowing against the growing lump in my throat. "I have looked forward to this all week. Looked forward to spending vacation time with you. You are a really good man. I am really happy to have you in my life."

He swallowed, his eyes searching mine for something.

My heart raced in my chest, the sound blocking out everything. Fear twisted my stomach and stole my breath. Swallowing back, I opened my mouth to force the truths out.

A knock sounded on the door.

"Luggage," Jack said, releasing me as he went to open the door.

The bellhop rolled two suitcases in and set them by the suitcase rack. Jack handed him a tip.

His phone buzzed, and he scanned the message with a frown.

"Pardon," he said over his shoulder. "I need five minutes to handle this."

I stared at his back as he walked out to the terrace off the room. The stunning view was of the lake and forest backdrop.

My head lolled back. He was fucking distancing himself because I forced him to. Maybe it was for the best. Maybe he was looking for an out, and I finally gave it to him. He certainly didn't want to talk about the car ride. His face had said that much. He was trying to move past it. Fuck. Prior to Jack, I'd dated Ethan and had a few dates freshman year that barely counted. I knew exactly what pissed Ethan off and what didn't. My friends were as blunt as I was.

"Sorry about that," Jack said, returning. "Shall we?"

He extended his hand out to hold mine.

We walked outside the hotel, the warm sun bathing us in a soft glow. A crisp breeze stirred the leaves and flowers, carrying their scent past us.

"It's a short walk to the dock," he said and led the way to the waiting boat.

It was a relic of a bygone era, the exterior refurbished and stained.

A cloth canopy was held up by strong beams. The captain tipped his hat and greeted us.

Jack boarded first, turning to extend his hand to help me step on the boat in my heels. A nook had been added for the passengers. A cozy nest with plush chairs, a bucket with champagne, and a charcuterie board.

He slipped his arm behind me, cuddling me close to him. I closed my eyes, enjoying his warmth. Although we had plenty of private space, the boat didn't feel like the right spot to discuss our arrangement or my feelings. Or so my fear told me. I didn't want to be rejected on a boat, in the middle of a large lake, with a kind but still-unwilling witness if it turned loud or I cried.

Little was said for the first part. We just watched the sights. Jack opened the champagne and poured us each a glass.

Smiling, I took it from him. Unsure what toast to offer, I waited for him to meet my eyes.

Something flickered in his gaze, sadness or disappointment, but he lifted his glass and murmured, "To us."

I clinked my glass against his and downed it. With a new wave of liquid courage, I licked my lips and sat on the edge of the cushion.

I hated being so close to him, yet feeling the greatest distance of emotion and mind.

"Jack," I whispered.

His gaze jumped to mine, his eyes dilating as he took me in. It was all the encouragement I needed. I skimmed my hand across his jaw, cupping and holding it while my lips met his.

Urgent and needy lips met mine. Only the captain's presence kept me from straddling him on the boat. Other boaters and paddlers were on the lake, but we were far enough out of view I'd have no issues taking him. The idea sent heat to my core, aching for him.

"Jack," I groaned against his lips. I ran my hand against his hard length.

"Maybe open water wasn't the best idea," he murmured in our kiss.

Tossing a glance over my shoulder, I saw the captain ramrod straight at the controls. His face turned completely away from us.

"How long will he ignore us?" I whispered, my greedy hands spearing through his hair.

"He said once we are on the large part of the lake, he won't look or listen," Jack said. His cheeks reddened a bit.

"Make sure he doesn't," I said.

Jack's eyes widened, but he only groaned when I grabbed him through his pants.

With nimble fingers, I had his shirt unbuttoned and pushed aside. I trailed hot kisses down his chest, caressing his hard nipples and tracing his defined muscles with my tongue.

"Mina," he moaned and ran his fingers through my hair.

Next was his clasp and zipper. His cock strained against his briefs, begging for release. I kissed it through the fabric. He balled his hands into fists and pushed into my lips.

Using my teeth, I pulled his briefs down to expose his cock. I swirled my tongue around the head. He shifted beneath me, trying to ease some of the building tightness.

I completely freed his cock and licked up its length. My words may not be able to show him how much I cared, but I wanted him to know I wanted him. Enjoyed him.

I took him in my mouth as I cupped his balls.

"Fuck," he groaned. His fingers moved to the cushions, clawing into the material, anchoring him down.

With each suck, I took him deep. His cock filled my mouth. Alternating between sucks and long licks, I savored each taste. My own core fluttered at the thought of him buried deep in me.

When he tensed, he grasped my shoulder with one hand.

Without a place to spit, I swallowed.

"Mina," he murmured over and over like a chant.

My cheeks reddened, knowing the captain was aware of what we were doing, but I didn't bother to turn around to confirm. Instead, I kissed up his chest until my lips locked with his.

He pulled me up to him, placing me in a straddle position. His fingers dug into my thighs, pushing my skirt farther and farther up.

"Jack." I warned as his thumb grazed my core, twirling and

rubbing. On instinct, my body arched into him, begging him for more. "I'm too loud," I said between hot kisses.

"Your screams turn me on." He kissed under my chin and down my neck.

A finger slipped inside me. Slow and deliberate, he hooked his finger as he pumped. My muscles tightened.

"Jack," I breathed, riding his finger.

"Mhm." He slipped a second one in and rubbed my clit with his thumb.

I gasped as pleasure heated in my core.

He ran his other hand across my breast, massaging the nipple. I pushed into his touch while digging my fingers into his back.

As I came, his mouth was on mine, claiming my cries.

## JULY 2ND

### MINA

After exiting the boat without making eye contact with the captain, we made it to the restaurant.

It was a modern hot spot. The sleek exterior matched the interior with gleaming wooden tops, metal details, long Edison bulb lighting, and spacious seating.

With my hand in his, Jack led us to a two-top table that overlooked the lake. The sun had crested the horizon, spilling colors over the trees and rippling in the water.

His thumb rubbed over my hand, soft and gentle. I tried to sneak a glance at his face, but he sat there watching me instead of the sunset. His blue eyes fixed on me, taking in every inch like he was trying to remember everything.

The waiter came with our first samples.

"Did you order ahead?" I asked after the waiter moved on to another table.

He nodded. "You order when you reserve a spot. I said the preference was white wine."

I smiled that he remembered, but he seemed to always remember.

The rich food was modest in portions but filling. After finishing, we made it back to the hotel. The moon hugged the tree line as it ascended into the sky.

With much restraint, I made it up to our room before my hands were on him.

"Mina," he groaned.

We'd barely closed the door when a loud pounding sounded on the door.

"What the fuck now?" I bit out. "It's not our luggage."

"Ignore it," Jack said, slipping his hands behind me to unzip my dress.

My fingers fumbled with his pants, trying to free his cock. Managing to get him unzipped, I wrapped my hand around him.

"Fuck it, Mina, I know you're in there." Ethan's voice came from the other side. "Xander saw you at the restaurant."

Ice ran in my veins. I stumbled back, and Jack stiffened at his voice.

"I'm going to punch him in his smug face," I said, heading for the door.

"Honey, Mina," Jack said, pulling me back.

My insides melted at the nickname.

"You're missing your clothes."

He skimmed his hands down my sides and rested them on my hips. With a tug, my body was pressed to his.

"I like you calling me honey."

His lips hooked up in a smile. "You sure?"

"Mhm." I wrapped my arms around his neck, holding him to me as my lips met his.

"I'll break this door down," Ethan barked. "We need to talk!"

"Fuck," Jack muttered, resting his forehead against mine. "I'll call the front desk."

"Your friends posted lies! We are each other's futures!"

Jack moved to the phone.

I blew out a frustrated breath but nodded. The moon had peeked over the trees, bathing the lake in an ethereal glow. My attention drawn to the view, I walked to our private balcony tucked back with our floor extended a few feet past the railing and dipped into an arch. It blocked the view of the rooms below us and blocked us from their view.

The air shifted, and I knew Jack had joined me. He slid his arms around my stomach, resting his chin on my shoulder.

"It's a beautiful view," I murmured.

"Mhm." He kissed my ear and pulled my lobe between his teeth.

I pressed into him, rubbing my bottom against his hard cock.

He trailed his hands up until they cupped my breasts over my bra. He rubbed his cock against me, and the sensation had moisture pooling in my core.

"Jack," I groaned.

Leaving one hand at my breast, he slipped his fingers under the cup and thrummed his thumb against my nipple. Slipping his other hand into my panties, he traced my clit, rubbing my center.

"You're so fucking wet," he whispered into my ear.

"Only for you," I breathed and ground down on his fingers.

"Mina—Honey," he gritted out.

A delightful shiver stole through me. This. This was what I wanted. Us.

Reaching behind me, I pushed his pants and briefs down. With one hand, I held his bare cock and cupped his balls with the other.

I stood on my toes and rubbed my center on his cock.

Moving my hand from his balls to the banister in front of me, I leaned forward, exposing myself to him. He removed his fingers from me, slick with my arousal, and slid my panties down. I stepped out of them and parted my legs.

Supporting my balance, he moved his hand on my breast down. Then he brought his cock to my entrance with the hand still coated in me.

"Hold on," he cursed.

He fumbled with something, and the sound of foil fluttered in the wind. With a thrust, he entered me.

I arched forward. A moan escaped me as I took him deep inside.

He slid his hand back around, rubbing my clit as he pounded into me.

My muscles tightened, the wave building.

"Jack," I groaned.

My hands fell to the railing, supporting me as my orgasm came, racking my body and wobbling my knees.

He came shortly after me, keeping his hand on my abdomen, grabbing the railing with the other to support his weight instead of crushing me.

"Mina," he whispered, resting his head on my back. "Fuck, Honey."

Gah, all I wanted to do was to tell him how I felt. That I loved him. I wanted to stop the trial run bullshit and just be us, but I didn't want it to come across as lust fueled, a byproduct of amazing sex that I'd regret later. And fear. Mostly fear stopped me. Fear of a kind rejection. Because no matter how much I wanted to trust . . . everyone, a part of me feared he would get his fill and leave. Like the men of my past.

He wrapped his arms around me, turning me to snuggle next to him. He rested his head on mine, holding me close.

If only I could hang on to the night.

## JULY 2ND

## JACK

Shortly before midnight, I walked the hall to the ice machine tucked behind the elevator. I'd managed to pull on my pants and undershirt. Mina had stepped into the restroom to freshen up. The night had gone nothing like I'd planned. It had felt more like a runaway train than any semblance of a path.

When we'd driven up, I'd assumed it was our goodbye weekend as she pushed me away. Then something switched in her. As I tried to memorize her face and touch, she pulled me back into her vortex. And to top it off, she said she liked the nickname she'd forbidden me from saying a decade and a half ago.

What the fuck was happening?

From moment to moment, I couldn't tell if we were breaking up or moving toward permanent. And no matter how much I wanted to protect myself from the pain of her leaving, each time she reached for me, I reached back.

"Jack," a familiar voice called out.

I sighed. Without stopping, I lifted the lid for the ice. Looks like he'd taken the stairs before security made it up.

"You're only her rebound." Ethan's words were fucking true, and I hated him for finally being honest.

"And you're her ex."

"She loves me."

"No, not anymore."

"She'll forgive me." He sniffled.

If I was a nicer man, I may have felt sorry for him, but only annoyance and hatred swirled in my veins.

"You always underestimated her."

"You always put her on a pedestal."

I chuckled humorlessly. I wouldn't give him the honor of telling him I loved Mina before I told her. "You took her for granted almost from the start."

"You're just jealous she wanted to date me and not you."

I faced him. His hair was stuck out in odd spots as if he'd been tugging on it. Unlike his normal polished look, he wore clean slacks and a polo.

"I was."

He flinched at my honesty.

"I can destroy your career too."

I barked a laugh.

He scowled.

"Ethan, you've been trying that since I came back."

"I have contacts."

"You do."

I shut the lid. The ice shifted, the rattle of it the only sound in the tight space. He stood in the doorway, trying to block my exit.

"Greg is signing with me. I'll get all the deals associated with it. You're going to lose too much traction to stay in the area."

Greg had already reached out to me. He wanted to meet again to discuss my contract. It didn't mean he'd sign with me, but it also meant Ethan didn't have a signed contract yet. I assumed from Christine's post on Mina's message that even if Greg didn't sign with me, he wasn't signing with Ethan.

"Mina won't leave Milwaukee. Her family is here."

"Your plans to destroy Mina got your friend fired or demoted. You think attacking her will make her see you as powerful. She only sees you for the pettiness and asshole you are."

"She loves me."

I snorted. "No, she doesn't. She did, but you ruined that."

"You think she loves you?"

The words were like a punch to my chest, but I just stared at him. My stomach twisted as acid swirled in it. Mina *liked* me. She was attracted to me, but I'd rushed us, and every alarm was going off in my head that I was about to fuck up the weekend and she'd leave me. However, curling up and retreating meant for certain it would happen. The car had set one tone, but the boat ride and the rest of the evening had been a different one. One I needed to capitalize on. I had three days of the holiday weekend and a few weekdays to convince her we should, at minimum, extend our agreement even if the thought sent ice sluicing through my veins. I wanted forever, but I'd take it five weeks at a time.

A cocky grin twisted on his lips.

The ice machine motor kicked on as it rattled a new batch.

"Excuse me," I said. "Mina wants ice for her drink. I'd say I'll see you at the Mercer party, but you weren't invited."

He jerked when I walked past him.

"Jack, you're not good enough for her."

I turned to face him over my shoulder. "I know, but neither are you."

**JULY 3RD**

**MINA**

The mansion sat on a few dozen acres, sprawling wide with white columns and white-washed brick. Trees bordered the property line, providing privacy. Red, purple, and blue flowers edged the driveway, with blooming white trees behind them.

People I recognized dotted the yard, taking in the shade of tents set up with refreshments. Valets stood ready to whisk cars out of sight.

"Too bad we couldn't keep the hotel room," I said, my eyes jumping around the group.

"He uses an entire wing as guest rooms, but I prefer a chance to get away," Jack said. "We have a ground floor room, so at least we can jump out a window if needed."

My eyes widened, but it did seem like a good option.

"I imagine a lot of hookups happen here," I said, walking with him to a billowing white tent with fluted glasses.

He shrugged but didn't comment. I probably wouldn't like the answer, or his association with it.

Under the tent, tables were set up for discussion and refreshment stations. Most people stood as they mingled around.

After several hours, we headed inside for the cool air and a break from the throng of people. The AC blasted us as a server moved to close the doors quickly and ushered us toward rooms set up with billiards, cocktails, darts, and other activities.

The historic mansion maintained its original charm, thick wood accents, richly colored wallpaper, and intricate printed rugs that ran the length of the room. Matching furniture in wooden frames and expensive vintage fabrics dotted the space, along with a piano and tables to stand and talk.

"Jack," someone called from behind us.

A willowy man with tufts of peppered hair walked up. His Armani suit was heavy for the weather.

"Paul," Jack said. Jack's hand fell to the small of my back.

"I was hoping to see you here." Paul extended his hand.

"Mina and I swung down early to enjoy the sights and location," Jack said. "I'm not sure if you've met, but, Paul, this is Mina Henley. She's a financial advisor with Lake Front Investment. Mina, this is Paul Thomas. He owns several car dealerships."

"Pleasure to meet you," I said.

"Likewise, Mina," Paul said. "How do you know Jack?"

"We went to school together and became reacquainted several weeks ago," I said.

"Are you working together?" Paul asked, brow furrowed.

"No, Mina is my girlfriend," Jack said. "We've agreed not to mix the two at this point."

My insides warmed at him calling me his girlfriend. Granted, no one would understand what we meant by a trial run, but still, to use the term freely in public was exciting.

"Perhaps we can talk more about options available," Paul said. "Jack has great insights and recommendations."

I swallowed and nodded. Finding my words, I said, "That'd be great."

Greg and Beatrice walked in, their gazes taking in the faces.

"If you can pardon me," I said. "I need to catch up with someone who just walked in."

"Of course," Paul said. "I have some questions to discuss with Jack."

Jack followed my gaze, his fingers pressing into my back. His blue eyes met mine, and he smiled.

"Greg, Beatrice," I said. "It's great to see you."

"Mina," Greg said.

Beatrice smiled at me. "It's great to see you again too. The last time was so informative."

Her eyes flashed with amusement.

My attention jumped to Greg, who scowled.

"Yes, well," Greg said. "It was good to know the truth about Ethan. That video . . ."

Apparently, it hadn't been removed fast enough, or his daughter had shown it to him. He didn't seem the social media type.

"Oh," I said. "How is your project going?"

"I'm moving forward with Jack. His plan is solid."

A laugh bubbled up my throat. In his attempt to hurt me, Ethan destroyed the contract he'd been coveting the most and would make his career.

"He'll make sure the project goes smoothly," I said.

"Yes, well," Greg said, pushing his glasses up. "With that said, I must tell you I have chosen to go with a different financial advisor."

Although expected, it still stung to hear it in its finality.

"I understand." I forced a smile.

"I am also not signing with Trevor," Greg said. "I understand he and Ethan are rather close, and I don't want to mix that in."

I nodded, not really caring at this point. I lost a client that would have fast-forwarded my promotion. It was a silver lining that Trevor wasn't getting the client. It would most certainly nail his coffin closed at the firm. However, I couldn't escape soon enough.

Beatrice, sensing my discomfort, interrupted. "Greg, Kellan just walked in, and I know you need to talk with him. He's only planning on being here for a few hours."

"Oh," Greg said. "Yes, well. Mina, I wish you the best."

"Same to you," I said and gave a nod.

Once he turned to walk toward the other person, I slipped out of the room and made my way toward our room.

## JULY 3RD

### JACK

Paul droned on as I watched Mina slip out of the room. My eyes darted to the doorway, trying to get a glimpse of her.

My mind only half listened to Paul. He'd told me this pitch before. It was good, but right then, it didn't need my full attention.

As soon as she returned, she turned on her heels and headed for the alcohol table. Panic curled through me, my mind blocking out everything Paul said.

"Hey, Paul," I said, cutting off his ramble. "Why don't we grab some drinks later? I need to hit the head."

"Oh yes, of course," Paul said.

After my crude exit, I beelined for Mina.

When she saw me, a large smile curved her lips, replacing whatever else had been there. My heart skipped for a moment, the sight of her stilling it. She was everything, and she was here with me. At least for the moment. I'd meant to go slow the entire time, build up over the five weeks, but as Alicia always complained, Mina was my weakness.

She closed the gap between us, wrapping an arm around my neck while her other held a mimosa. Her body pressed into mine, and of course mine responded immediately.

A soft chuckle fell from her lips, the corner of her eyes crinkling. Her amber eyes flashed and darkened as she brought her lips to mine.

How was I going to convince her to move on from the trial to being a couple? Was there still a chance? Please let there be one.

The urge to ask what happened in the other room nagged at me, but I didn't want to ruin the moment, go back to the car tension. If it was Ethan, he'd have followed her. He also wasn't invited, and I had seen his father, so he shouldn't be here.

"Do you think Paul would be open to talking with me, or was he being polite in front of you?" Mina asked, tilting her head.

I swallowed, not sure where the change came from, what had transpired, but I would recommend her to the world. Even without being in a relationship with her.

"Paul won't say anything unless he believes in it, including blunt noes," I said, smiling at her.

"I'm thinking I should take the momentum of Ronald and really kick it in. I know I've been resistant, and I don't want you to talk to others for me, but if it's a natural course, I want to pursue it. You've only ever tried to be helpful. I want to push Trevor out."

She looked up under her eyelashes, focusing on my reaction.

"Good." I nodded. She beamed, and her fingers tightened in my hair. "You're amazing. The partners see it, but they want the client power to go with it."

"You don't mind if I talk to your clients? I won't name-drop, but I might pick your brain about it." She pinched her lips and darted her eyes back and forth as she thought. As she liked the idea more, her voice picked up in speed and animation. "I can't keep closing doors because people know my boyfriend. It's not good business, and it will start to send another message."

Boyfriend. That was something. I couldn't stop the smile from growing. Hopefully, soon I could make it more serious.

Her eyes darted to the door, hardening for a moment as Greg entered the room with Beatrice. Her lip curled in a snarl.

"Is everything okay?" I murmured, staring at Greg with her.

His face was flushed with a few too many cocktails, but otherwise, he was unaffected.

"Yes, perfect," she said, turning her face back to mine, her mouth closed.

"Yes, perfect," I parroted, brushing her lips.

She returned the kiss and snickered. "We're making a scene."

"They're just jealous of me," I said and kissed her again.

"Mina?" a familiar voice called out.

Mina pulled her lips from mine, and I placed my forehead on hers before turning to face the interloper.

"Yang," I said and extended a hand.

Yang shook mine and perused Mina.

"How are you? I didn't realize you were coming to this party," she said.

"I spoke with Paul Thomas. We're setting up time next week to talk," Mina said and sipped her beverage.

"Paul Thomas?" Yang said, the admiration evident in her voice. "That'd be a great deal."

Mina nodded and swallowed. "There are a few other people I saw coming in I'd like to talk to before the weekend is over."

Yang's lips curved in a grin. "This party is fabulous for connections."

After several hours of snacking, sipping mimosas, beer, and wine, and socializing with others, we finally made it to the dinner. We sat in a tent on the outer edge of the space, shrouded in shadows from the tree line.

Mina rested her head on my shoulder and let out a breath.

I slipped my arm behind her, encircling her waist and pulling her closer.

We watched the other tables, alive with networking and flirting.

"How many affairs happen here?" Mina murmured, her eyes scanning the masses.

"Many bring their spouses, so I'm hoping not that many," I said. "But I know several come here for business and social hookups."

"Did you?" she asked and then stiffened. "Don't answer that."

A familiar numbness edged around my heart. We always seemed to circle around my past.

I rolled my eyes. "No, I didn't. It's not a good practice."

"That the only reason?" she whispered.

"No, it's not my style."

"You dated a lot in high school."

"I did," I agreed. I had, but I hadn't hurt them. "But never more than one at a time, and we had clear breakups."

Mina nodded and sighed.

Fuck. I couldn't undo my past.

"What's wrong?" I shifted and dipped my head so I could meet her eyes.

"Just makes me sad to see people mistreat each other," she said, her eyes bright. Her lips curled into a smile, and she leaned in to kiss my lips. "I'm glad I'm here with you."

That took a turn I hadn't expected.

My heart kicked up. "I'm glad I'm here with you," I said, feeling the stupid grin on my face.

"What about an early night?" She lifted her brows. "I'm talked out. We could go back to our room and relax."

"Relax?" I cocked an eyebrow.

Her smile turned sinister. "Unwind. We could de-stress and unwind."

"That's what we're calling it?" I asked, laughing.

"What do you call it?" she asked, her smile growing.

"Making love," I said. The word was out there. A test.

Her eyes shifted, searching my eyes for something.

Shit, did I say too much? Did I go too fast, again?

"Or enjoying your company and screams," I whispered into her ear, kissing her where her neck and ear met.

The retreat was subtle but burned at my throat. I didn't want to retreat from her.

She squirmed, curling her fingers around my jacket.

"You do like to make me scream," she murmured back before kissing me.

"How about I grab us two plates of food and meet you in our room?" I said.

"I'll grab us some drinks," she said. "I'll meet you back there."

I watched as she sashayed to the bar. Leaning over the table, she somehow managed to get a bottle and two glasses from the bartender.

I snagged a waiter by the sectioned tent area. They bustled around, assembling tables and plates, and a curl of guilt shot through me.

"My girlfriend isn't feeling well. Can I get two plates so I can take it back to her?" I asked.

Despite my ill-timed request, the waiter handed me two plates, and I slipped him a fifty.

I skirted around the trees to avoid detection but came upon Greg. He sat in a dining chair that someone had pulled into the tree line, shaded from above and blocked from the dining area.

"Hungry?" Greg asked, taking in my two plates.

"Meeting Mina for a quiet dinner." I edged around him, hoping to not get delayed.

"You know, Jack," Greg said, pulling his glasses off and pinching his nose, "Mina's a nice lady. She's got a good head on her shoulders."

"She is wonderful in all ways," I agreed, but I felt a but coming on.

"I'll have the papers couriered to you on Monday, that is, if you'll be in the office. I know some take Monday off since the Fourth is on the weekend."

I blinked. He was signing with me. A burst of pride spread in my chest. I could do so much with this momentum. Mina and I could have so many new contacts and opportunities.

"I will be in the office." I balanced the two plates with my left hand to extend my right out. "I look forward to working with you on this project."

Excitement to tell Mina bubbled up in my chest.

"You had the best plan," Greg said. "I like the best."

"I'll touch base on Monday after the papers arrive and send a list of the timetables and next steps to Beatrice."

"Excellent, and I am sorry about Mina." Greg settled his glasses back on his face and blinked at the world.

I stilled, my knuckles white as I gripped the plate. Seconds passed, but it felt like hours as I waited for him to elaborate.

"I just need a bigger advisor than her and her firm." He looked to me like I understood.

"Pardon?" I managed to say without yelling.

"She didn't tell you?" He frowned. "I assumed she would."

Earlier made sense now. Spite was an amazing motivator. Heaviness settled on my chest. The earlier excitement dulled to an ache.

My stomach filled with a sludge of uncertainty.

Why hadn't she told me? Pride? Anger? Afraid I'd step in?

No matter what, Greg was being an idiot.

"You're making a mistake," I said, meeting his startled glance.

The words were out before I could consider what Mina would think. She didn't want me to interfere with her business.

"You're too close to her to see," Greg started.

But he wasn't signing with her. Which was his ego. He underestimated her. Cast her aside. He completely missed how amazing she was.

"No," I said, interrupting him. Fuck it if I lost this contract. "You're too pompous to see. Her portfolios have amazing return rates. She has an almost hundred percent retention rate. A client who left her for a bigger, more experienced partner came crawling back. You're more concerned with the status of the situation than you are with the content of it."

"Are you referencing yourself in this decision?"

"Greg, you make the decisions that you feel are the best fit for you. We both know the plan I laid out is better than the others. I also know Mina is one of the best. If you have other portfolio options that are better, then definitely take them. If, however, your choice is based on image and firm standing, you're the one who will be losing out in the long run."

"Now, Jack, I meant no—"

"Greg, I hope you have an enjoyable evening. I'm going to spend the remainder of mine with Mina," I said and left.

Anger buzzed in my veins as I stomped through the path to the side door.

She hadn't told me.

The anger turned. Curdled. Twisting into something else.

Fear? Sorrow? Resignation.

She wanted me at arm's length in all ways.

I knocked on the door before opening it.

Mina had the wine and glasses on the breakfast table set up in the corner of the room. She'd kicked off her shoes and walked barefoot around the room. Her hair was piled on her head.

"Any trouble?" she asked, turning to me, her fingers sliding the pendant I bought her back and forth.

I forced a smile. I didn't want to mention Greg. If she'd wanted me to know, she'd have told me. But she didn't want me to know, and the idea sat heavy in my gut.

"What's wrong?" she asked.

"I hope salmon is okay?" I lifted the plate for her inspection.

"You know I love salmon." Her gaze followed me as I moved to the table. "Jack?"

I placed the plates down, licking my lips and counting to five to school my face. I turned back to her, a smile at the ready.

She cocked an eyebrow at me. "I'm not falling for it."

Shit. "Falling for what?" I chuckled, reaching my hands to her.

"What happened?"

She didn't take my hands but instead folded her arms over her chest.

Shit. We were going to have to have this discussion. I wouldn't lie to her. Even if I didn't want to admit the truth, if she asked directly I'd answer.

"I got us food and can't wait to unwind with you tonight," I said and turned my smile up.

Her smile flatlined, curving down into a frown.

"Jack, don't play games with me." An edge sounded in her voice. "What else happened besides the salmon?"

I licked my lips again and met her gaze. "I ran into Greg."

She snarled and averted her eyes. Running her tongue over her teeth, she looked back and asked, "What did he say? He didn't back out, did he?"

She knew?

"No, he said I'd have the papers Monday," I said.

"That's great news! You should be excited." Her brows furrowed. "Then why do you have that look?"

"What look?"

"Like you smelled someone's armpits," she said.

I snorted a chuckle and tried another smile.

"Don't distract me. What else happened?" She tilted her head as she studied me.

"He said he talked with you."

She swallowed, not flinching from my gaze. "We did."

I waited.

She stared at me, her jaw set.

"Were you going to tell me you talked to him?" I finally gritted out.

"Why?" she spat.

"Why?" I repeated. "Why wouldn't you?"

"There's no deal," she said. "There, that's what we talked about."

I clenched my jaw, trying to keep my retort in.

"What?" she said, stepping toward me.

I glared at her, my body anchored in place. "I will not apologize for believing in you and knowing you are the best. I'm going to tell everyone. If it leads to clients, great. If not, it's their loss. It's not about a scorecard between us. It's because I believe in you and your greatness."

"My greatness? What do you want me to do? Come crying to you over a lost deal? Not everyone signs with me. Just like you don't sign all your clients."

No words came to me. Nothing. She was hiding her pain from me. She only shared her joy. What did she expect me to do? Ridicule her? Mock her? Belittle her?

Fuck.

She was doing it again.

She'd built up so many damn walls with Ethan she didn't even realize it. If she cut him off from knowing of her misses, then he didn't have something against her.

I was in love with a woman who kept up wall upon wall.

Unable to look at her anymore, I ran a hand through my hair and shook my head.

"Jack?" she said, a hitch in her words.

My eyes, of course, shot to her, not caring what she was doing to the rest of me.

She opened her mouth, but nothing came out. She shrugged, and her body deflated.

"Let's eat," I breathed, although the sight of the plate turned my stomach. I forced my feet to the table and sat down.

She didn't move, but I felt her eyes following me.

"Jack," she murmured.

My body ached to turn to her, but I forced my gaze to stay on the table.

"Jack," she said, fear clipping it.

Without moving my head, my eyes tracked to her.

Her body heaved as she twisted her fingers, her eyes searching me for answers.

All I wanted to do was go to her. Comfort her. But I couldn't. She wanted to push me away. Get space between us. Fine. She could have space. But she couldn't keep up the ping-ponging action.

"Let's eat," I drawled, and gestured to the plates.

Silently she crept to me, but I could feel her as she neared. She traced her hand over my shoulder, light and hesitant.

Shit. I was weak.

"Jack," she whispered, and I caved. I tilted my face up to her.

Her lips were on mine, hot and urgent. As much as I wanted to return it, I gently put my hands on her shoulders and pulled back.

"I'm sorry," she whispered.

"I know," I said.

"You made me a promise," she said, her voice wobbly.

"What promise?" I asked, racking my brain.

She slipped a leg over my lap, slipping in between the table and me. Like a traitor to my brain and heart, my fucking cock was very happy and hardened in agreement.

Due to the tight position, her breasts pressed against me, her mouth only a few inches from mine. Her eyes, dark and heated, met mine. She licked her lips and tilted her head like she was looking for the best spot to taste.

"Mina," I started, but she shook her head.

"You promised me in the beginning that anytime I wanted you to go down on me, you would."

She pressed her lips to mine and pulled my lip into her mouth, sucking before releasing it. She rolled her head back, her hair sweeping with the motion. Her lips met my neck, trailing kisses down my throat.

"What?" I was able to squeak out, my hands automatically moving to her waist and holding her to me. The first night at her apartment flashed in my mind.

"We're going to unwind, de-stress," she said, unbuttoning my shirt, kissing each spot as she went.

My hands had her dress zipper pulled down before I realized it, seeking out her back.

She slipped her shoulder straps off and shifted up to sit on the table to pull her dress off and tossed it into the corner.

"You're going to honor your promise, and then we're going to reapproach this conversation." She reached behind her back to unclasp her bra.

I stood up, sliding my hands over hers to the clasp and then pulling it. I cupped each breast, my thumbs flicking across each nipple.

She groaned and I growled, my lips on hers.

Slipping her hands into my pants and briefs, she pushed them down. She grabbed my cock and jerked it up.

I hissed and thrust into her hand.

With her hands threaded through my hair, she pushed my head down.

I looped my fingers into her panties and pulled them down, revealing her core. After tossing them toward her dress, I ran a thumb across her clit.

She groaned and arched forward.

I kissed along her thigh, blowing on her sex before kissing the other thigh.

"Jack," she groaned.

My body responded, wanting to take her then. Instead, I ran my tongue across her, tasting her. Then I ran it across her clit, taking it between my teeth. She tightened her hold on me, pressing me closer.

"No," she breathed.

I stopped and looked up to her.

"No," she said, pulling at my arms.

"Mina?" Alarm sounded in my voice.

She cupped my face, bringing my lips to her. Between kisses, as she wrapped her legs around my waist, she said, "I want you to make love to me."

Make love? My heart and mind grabbed on to her words.

I slipped my hands under her, lifting her up to rub my cock against her.

"Hold on," I breathed against her lips and grabbed my pants.

I pulled out the foil packet and ripped it open. I slid the condom on, her hands trying to assist to speed it along.

"Jack, I want you, only you," she murmured.

I slid into her. She moaned and dug her nails against my bare shoulder as she took me fully.

"Good, I want only you."

## JULY 4TH

### MINA

Early morning sunlight streamed into the room. Jack's warm, naked form snuggled next to me, his soft breathing rhythmic as he slept. My plan was to keep him in bed, and before any sex, I'd tell him my feelings. Then if he said no, I could use the window he'd joked about.

Still early, I nestled against him, ready for sleep to retake me. Then a vibrating tone buzzed by my ear. I grabbed my phone as a new text came in. My vision swam as I tried to read the words.

TRINA: Morning Mina
TRINA: Are you up?
TRINA: How is everything going?

I stared at the clock, the dancing red numbers showing it was barely morning.

ME: Why are you up?
TRINA: Mom called

Alarmed, I sat up. Jack groaned and slung his arm over me, pulling me back toward him. My heart sounded in my ears. Mom didn't call, only texted, unless something happened.

ME: Is she okay
TRINA: Yeah
ME: So why'd she call
TRINA: <dancing dots>

Jack moaned, his fingers tightening as he fought off sleep. His blue eyes opened, narrow slits taking in the room and me. When his eyes landed on me, a slow sexy smile grew. My heart squeezed.

I leaned over, brushing my lips on his while running my fingers through his dark, thick hair. I probably needed to rework my plan.

"Why are you up?" he asked, his voice thick with sleep.

"Trina texted." I licked my lips at the dots still dancing.

"Everything okay?" He pulled himself up to sit next to me. He rested his head on my shoulder, lacing his fingers with my free hand.

"I'm waiting for her to respond," I said.

"Just call her," he mumbled and kissed my shoulder.

I glared at him. What an awful suggestion. We had texting so we didn't have to call and do random chitchat.

"Are you hungry?" I set my phone back on the nightstand and ran my fingers through his hair.

His smile grew more sinister.

"I mean real food." I squirmed. Maybe a quick morning wake-up call would help the day go better.

"I can grab us some food." He yawned and stretched. He shifted and put his feet on the floor, leaving me instantly cold.

My eyes fixated on his muscles. His toned frame was coiled and ready for a strike.

"You can't tell me you want real food and look at me like that," he said, standing to find a pair of pants.

"We need energy to maintain our pace," I said.

He tugged on a T-shirt and leaned over to kiss me hard on the lips.

"That we do," he said. "I'll be back."

I watched him go, and then my eyes flicked back to the dancing dots. How long was the message? Or had she forgotten to hit send?

After another five minutes, I gave up and hit the phone icon.

"Hey, Mina," Trina breathed, her voice rushed and urgent.

"What's wrong?" I said, feet hitting the floor to dig out clothes.

"Gerald had a scare," Trina said.

The murmur of intercom voices tunneled through the phone.

"Oh my God, what happened?" I slipped on a casual black skirt.

"Mom thought it was a heart attack or something. She's freaked out, Mina. I haven't seen her like this before." Trina's voice cracked.

"What hospital are you at?" I put my bra from last night back on and grabbed the first shirt in my suitcase, a simple sleeveless blouse.

"The old Memorial one. But, Mina, you're on vacation. I'm here . . ."

"Trina, I'm coming back," I said, frowning at the phone.

"I shouldn't have texted you," she said, her voice small. "I just . . ."

"If you hadn't, I'd beat the crap out of you when I saw you next."

"I have to go. The doctor is coming out."

"Text or call me what he says," I yelled as she clicked off.

Fuck. I needed to find Jack. Probably order an Uber.

I opened the app and scheduled for the first available one—in forty-five minutes. Fuck, that was a long time. I had to tell Jack before bolting. I didn't think a note would suffice.

I tore out of the room and headed toward the dining area. Chatter met my ears as I neared the serving tents. I rounded a corner and hit a solid form. With a jolt, I stumbled back. Mumbling an apology, I went to circle around them.

"Mina?" a vaguely familiar voice said. "Mina Henley."

My eyes jumped up.

Her dark locks hung loosely but in an it-took-hours-to-make-it-look-casual sort of way. Her piercing gray eyes shone brightly. She wore a business casual dress, periwinkle on her perfectly toned body. Beige stilettos finished the ensemble.

"Alicia," I breathed. Jack's ex.

"How are you?" she asked, oblivious to the hurry I was in.

"I was looking for . . ." I started but swallowed down the next word. I wasn't sure how she'd handle knowing I was dating Jack, or, well, trial dating him.

She smiled and tossed a lock of hair over her shoulder. "Jack?" She cast a glance behind her.

"Yes," I squeaked and smoothed my rumbled top.

"He got swarmed by a couple guys at the breakfast table," she said with a chuckle. "Apparently he retired too early last night, and they wanted to catch up."

"Oh," I said and leaned over to catch sight of him by the table. Three guys, all in a form of designer jeans and tailored shirts, talked animatedly around him.

"I'm so glad I got to run into you," she said and then laughed. "Well, not literally run into you, but I was hoping to see you soon."

"Oh, really?" I said like an idiot. Something about her brought out my insecurities.

"Yes, I'm so glad to see you two finally together," she said with a head bob.

My vision tunneled, and my breath stopped for a moment.

Alicia was his ex. The woman he had proposed to. Who had turned him down . . .

"What?" I managed to choke out.

She smiled at my confusion, her sweet smile shockingly comforting.

"I wasn't expecting that," I said and tried to smile back but probably grimaced.

She laughed. "Any woman with Jack, who isn't you, is trapped in his vortex. He's sweet, charming, honestly cares, and is amazing in the sack."

My face flushed. I wasn't sure if it was more from unease or the desire to pop her for talking about sleeping with him.

"What do you mean trapped?" I asked, avoiding the other topics.

"He's easy to fall for." She shrugged. "He probably did love me back as he claims, but it's not the same."

My brows furrowed. Either she was being cryptic, or I was too tired or stressed about Gerald to understand.

"He loved me." She swallowed. "But he's in love with you. You're the one we all had to measure up to. He's so in love with you," she said and smiled. "I am sorry about what happened with Ethan, but . . ."

"Don't be," I said. "I'm just sorry I didn't realize it until then. I'd have dumped his ass a lot earlier."

She smiled in relief and touched my shoulder.

"I'm not going to lie, but I wasn't expecting you to be kind to me," I said. "I know you two were serious."

She bobbed her head in agreement. "He proposed." A sad smile flitted across her lips.

I licked my lips and looked to my hands. A heavy ball tightened in my stomach.

She swallowed, and her eyes dimmed. "I knew at that moment you were engaged."

My eyes shot up to hers.

She twisted her fingers and averted her eyes for a moment. She forced a smile. "I was correct. You and Ethan had announced your engagement."

I just stared at her, my mouth open. Finally, I choked out, "I don't even know what to say."

She smiled, her natural smile returning. "I knew you were engaged because he finally gave up his hope you'd leave Ethan. So, he settled on me."

"What? No, you're not settling," I said in a hurry.

"To him, I'm settling. I broke up with him when he proposed. I'd never be you, and I deserved to be loved like how he loves you."

"I didn't know."

"Oh, no, sweetie," Alicia hurriedly said. "I'm not blaming you or accusing you. I'm just trying to tell you how happy I am for you, and him. You both are really lucky to have found each other. Or, refound each other."

My mind and body refused to do anything in response.

"When the time happens," she said, "I hope you invite me. I feel like . . ." She flinched and closed her mouth, a blush spreading across her face.

"You feel what?" I insisted.

"It'll come across as not well intended, and I mean it as a positive thing."

"Then just tell me. I know you have good intentions."

"I felt like you were a part of our relationship, at least your spirit was."

Is that how Jack felt about Ethan? Is that what I was doing to him? But I didn't love Ethan. I hated Ethan. But was it any different? I was comparing Jack to someone else, seeing how he measured up. Fuck.

Alicia continued trying to explain herself, her eyes darting around and her fingers fidgeting.

"Alicia," I whispered, placing a hand on her arm.

She stilled, her gaze bouncing to me.

I smiled. "It's okay. I do understand what you mean."

"I was just rooting for you two. Well, a month or so after our breakup, if I'm honest." She blushed.

I chuckled, needing the break in tension.

"Are you dating anyone?" I asked.

They'd been broken up for over eighteen months, so it didn't seem like an invasive question. Besides, who was I to judge? Jack and I started dating less than a month after my wedding fiasco.

A sheepish smile spread across her face.

"I'm really happy for you," I said and hugged her.

She hugged me back, her embrace tight.

My rebound was turning into more. Well, I hoped it would, but did it mean I'd continue to hold Jack to Ethan shortcomings? Keep looking for his cracks? Is that why people did a rebound relationship before entering into another? They dumped the negativity on the rebound person, freeing themselves from it for the next person? Because all I'd done was trauma dump on Jack, no matter how much I tried not to.

"Mina?" Jack's voice sounded behind me.

"Hey, Jack," Alicia said, releasing me.

"Hi, Alicia," he said, wrapping his hand around my waist. He pulled me close.

His gaze bounced between us, a frown grazing his lips before he forced a smile.

"Jack, don't get worked up." Alicia playfully scolded him.

His fingers tightened around me, his frame stiffening, but he outwardly didn't respond.

"Is everything okay here?" Jack asked, his voice even and flat.

"Yes," I said, wrapping my arm around him and resting it on the waist of his jeans. I hooked my fingers in his belt loop, holding him to me.

He eased against me.

"We were discussing who she's currently seeing," I said.

"Oh!" Jack's face brightened. "That's great. Do we know the lucky man?"

Despite her smile, pain flickered in her eyes before she answered. Despite what she said, she still had hope for them. Hope that he was in love with her. "No, I don't think so. He's from Texas. I met him at a conference."

"I'm really happy for you," Jack said with a bright smile.

Alicia made her goodbyes and wove through the group. She may want to be over Jack, and likely was when not near him, but she still loved him. Something I understood.

"We also talked about you." My mouth dried at the honesty.

"Oh." He cocked an eyebrow at me.

"She told me about your breakup," I murmured, averting my eyes.

"Oh," he repeated, his voice again flat.

I ran my hand across his jawline. He leaned into me, his gaze meeting mine.

"I'm just glad we're together now," I said.

My stomach knotted. I needed to tell him so much.

My phone buzzed.

"Shit," I muttered and pulled my phone out of my pocket.

TRINA: Surgery. Prepping now.

"Fuck," I said, raising my eyes to his.

"What's wrong?" he asked.

"I have to get back home. Gerald needs to have surgery on his heart."

"Then let's go," Jack said, steering us toward the room.

"You can stay," I offered. "I put in for an Uber. It should be here in thirty minutes."

"We'll be half home by then." Jack shot me a glare. "And why would you call an Uber?"

"This is an important weekend," I said.

"You're more important," he gritted out.

We made it back within an hour, a couple laws broken.

Jack walked with me to find Trina and Mom. They sat in a small waiting room located outside the cardiology wing.

Trina jumped up and threw her arms around me.

"I told you not to come," she whispered, her voice cracking.

"Mina, Jack." Mom sniffed. She grabbed Jack first, pulling him into a strong hug. "Thank you for coming. Thank you for bringing Mina."

"Of course," Jack said, patting her back.

Mom moved to me, pulling me into a tight hug. "He's a good one," she murmured into my ear. She patted my cheeks, fresh tears rimming her eyes. "He's so much better . . ." She pressed her lips into a thin line, tears spilling down her face. "I'm so glad he's in your life."

"Me too," I whispered back. "How is Gerald?"

Mom sucked in a sob and dabbed her eyes. "We're still waiting."

"Okay." I took her hand and sat in the chairs.

Jack leaned over. "I'll be back."

He returned shortly, carrying coffees and several snack bags from the vending machine.

"The cafeteria is open," he said. "I'll grab some sandwiches or whatever hot food you want."

After taking our orders, he left us alone.

"So, Mina," Trina said, trying to force a smile. "You need to provide us a distraction."

"I do?" My eyes widened.

"You were the one on a hot date weekend. Give us details." Trina leaned back in her chair and closed her eyes.

"Trina Marie, leave her alone," Mom said.

"Thanks, Mom," I said.

"Although it will be a long wait, and we're just staring at the walls." She gave me a dim smile.

"Seriously, you too?" I threw my hands up. "They have a TV."

"Hot weekend date news that is real, or how to cook a meat I'll never buy?" Trina lifted her hands up like a scale, weighing the options.

"Did it go better after the car ride?" Mom asked.

I glared at Trina. Without looking at me, she shrugged in response.

"Yeah, we had a boat ride, then went to dinner. Yesterday, I set up some appointments with clients. Had a great time networking. Talked with Alicia," I said, the last bit catching in my throat.

"Alicia? It feels like I should know that name." Mom tapped her chin.

"Alicia?" Trina sat up and stared at me.

"Who is she?" Mom asked, her gaze bouncing between us.

"Jack's ex," Trina answered.

"What happened?" Mom's head whipped around to stare at me and the vacant doorway.

"She said she was really happy for us. Said she knew I got engaged because Jack proposed to her. She broke up with him when he proposed. She didn't want someone who settled for her."

"Wow," they breathed out together.

"Told ya." Trina sent me a wicked smile.

Mom laughed. "That wasn't what I expected you to tell us." She leaned forward, grasping her knees as her laugh grew and tears streamed down her face.

Jack returned, staring at my mom. Wordlessly, he brought the food over and set it on the table. He grabbed a hotdog and bit into it.

"Do you feed him?" Trina grabbed a hamburger.

"We skipped breakfast." I grabbed a cardboard boat of fries.

"It's Sunday," Trina said. "We know about missing Sundays."

"Are you saying I did this?" Mom asked, finally catching her breath and sitting up to grab food.

Trina pretended to ponder the question and then shook her head. "Nah, if you did it on purpose, you'd be the one on the bed."

"True." Mom patted her hand.

When the doctor finally came out, I held Jack's hand and Mom's. Trina held Mom's other hand.

"Mrs. Carter?" the doctor asked to verify.

"Yes," Mom said. She stood, pulling our hands with her.

"Gerald is resting comfortably. He should be ready for visitors shortly. The procedure went well. We'll schedule some follow-ups with his cardiologist."

Mom listened, nodding as she retained everything the doctor said.

**JULY 5TH**

**MINA**

After we visited Gerald and set Mom up in the room with comforts, we dragged ourselves home.

We fell into bed, barely taking the time to strip. Jack's arms surrounded me, and I rested my head on his chest. I fell asleep to the beat of his heart.

When my alarm went off, the breaking sun lit the room.

"It's a holiday," Jack mumbled into my hair.

"You're working," I yawned into his chest.

"Only a few hours." He pulled me against his chest so we spooned. "Your office is closed."

"I'm going to send out appointment slots," I said, sliding my feet to the floor.

He opened one eye to watch me as I trudged to the shower.

"Want company?" he asked.

"That'd require you and . . . your cock to get up."

"He's always ready to go." Jack scrambled out of bed to join me in the shower.

Once we were clean and de-stressed, we left for our respective offices together.

"How about we meet for lunch?" Jack walked me to my car. "And then enjoy the rest of our holiday."

"Sounds like a plan," I said, already regretting rejecting his offer to stay in bed late.

But the idea of lunch and the day off with him was the perfect time to tell him my feelings. My stomach twisted, but it didn't matter. I couldn't carry on like this anymore, even for a few days. I knew how I felt about Jack. He either reciprocated or didn't, but my heart screamed he did. Even Alicia did. For once, my brain begrudgingly stayed quiet.

The office was empty except for Yang's office. Mariya's door was open, but I didn't see or hear her.

I filled out my calendar, sending email and text appointment setups. Three of the five returned, accepted, and confirmed within ten minutes of sending.

When my phone dinged with a message, I thought it was a fourth, but instead, it was Beatrice's number.

BEATRICE: Are you available for a call?

My face scrunched up, but my thumbs texted back: Sure. I'm free this morning.

Butterflies skittered around my stomach when my phone vibrated with an incoming call. Instead of Beatrice, it was Greg's number.

"Hello, this is Mina Henley."

"Mina, Greg here," he said. "I'm sorry to catch you on a holiday."

"We both seem to be working this a.m. It's easier to catch up on emails and memos when the office is empty."

"My thoughts exactly. I try to miss the busy hours so I can actually do work. If they have to text me or call on a holiday, it is a much shorter conversation," he said.

So, this was going to be short, then.

"How can I help you?"

"I'll cut to the chase. I've reconsidered."

My mind stalled. There was a lot to reconsider. Jack's project. My firm. Me.

"What have you decided?" I dug my nails into my palm to keep calm.

"I looked over the portfolio options you gave me at the dinner," he said.

I nodded though he couldn't see me. Excitement coursed through me.

"Your portfolio is cleaner than the others I saw," he said. "I don't mind complex, and I'm not saying yours isn't, but you have clear progression and measurable checks and balances."

"I want to remind you I am not a partner," I said, not wanting to get my hopes up.

"I know, and I was shortsighted with my abrupt dismissal. I talked with Jack," he said.

My brain screamed at the idea that Jack had set this up, looped it into the project details.

"What did he say?" I asked, trying to keep my voice level.

"Being blunt, that I was an idiot for overlooking you based on your title," Greg said. "He said it more diplomatically, but not by much."

I blinked, a slow smile spreading across my face. "Is that all?"

"I followed his advice and talked with some others, and he was correct. Your reputation is outstanding, even with your association with Ethan."

I snorted. I'd never been told my connection to Ethan was an ill advantage until recently, but then all the people who brought Ethan up were his associates.

"With that being said, I'll have a copy scanned over in a few minutes and the signed papers couriered over first thing in the morning," Greg said.

"That's fabulous." I pumped my fist in the air. "I look forward to working with you on your portfolio. If you'd like, we can schedule a meeting to discuss it more, or I can send you a summary email."

"Send me the email, and then schedule a meeting," Greg said.

We ended our call, and I leaped out of my chair. After kicking my heels off, I jumped around. Greg was the largest client I'd ever signed. He was large for the firm. He was a career-making client. And I signed him.

Yang appeared at my door, her dazzling smile spread wide. Despite it being a holiday, she wore a tailored navy blue dress, hose, and heels, her black bob hair perfectly in place.

"Who did you sign?" she asked, walking in.

"I didn't mean to disturb you," I said, curving my toes to help rein in my excitement.

"You didn't. It sounds like very good news."

"I signed Greg Cremski."

Her face slackened, and she blinked before she broke out in a whoop. "Mina! That is incredible. That is huge for you and this firm."

I nodded and squealed, unable to hold in my excitement.

Mariya's long form appeared at the door. She wore black trousers and a black button-down blouse. Gold jewelry and gold heels finished off her look.

"What's the excitement about?" Her face was a mask of indifference.

"Mina just signed Greg Cremski." Yang clapped her hands together.

Mariya's face contorted from confusion to a smile.

"Mina, that is incredible," Mariya said, a rare smile lighting up her eyes. "That calls for a celebration."

"I think that calls for more." Yang gave Mariya a pointed look.

"Trevor," Mariya barked.

My gaze darted to the door. I hadn't seen or heard him. He normally took off long weekends for holidays.

Trevor appeared, his eyes red and puffy, his tailored pants and shirt perfect despite his rumpled hair and frown.

"Mina has signed Greg Cremski," Mariya said, staring at him. "His portfolio could exceed a hundred million."

Trevor swallowed, his eyes tracking to me. A sneer flicked across his face before his frown returned. "Congratulations," he muttered.

"As you're still a junior partner," Mariya said, her voice showing her disgust despite her impassive face, "you still have a vote for next month."

Next month? I averted my gaze. This seemed like privileged information.

"I call a meeting of the partners. I'll call Kabir." Yang pulled out her phone. "Trevor, take the minutes."

"I'll call Raquel." Mariya took her phone out.

Trevor's mouth pinched, and his fingers furled into a fist, but he grabbed his laptop from his office.

The phone rang once before Kabir's gruff voice sounded through the speaker.

"Kabir, sorry to wake you," Yang said without any sympathy in her voice. "I know there is a large time difference, so I'll make this quick."

"Appreciated," he said, his voice thick with sleep.

"I have Mariya and Trevor with me," Yang said. "And Mina Henley."

Silence greeted her.

"Mina just signed a platinum client," Yang said.

A whistle sounded through the phone. "Same Mina who saved Ronald Savig's account?"

I swallowed. For not being present, all the partners seemed to know all the business of the associates.

"Same Mina." Yang winked at me. "I call for a vote. Should Mina be promoted to the level of junior partner? Terms to be determined at the normal partner meeting?"

My heart skipped a beat. My vision focused on Yang until she blurred.

I'd finally done it. Finally made it. I made it after Ethan had tried to lambaste me. After he tried to pull my clients away. After Trevor pulled my promotion. After it all, I had gotten my promotion.

"Aye," Kabir said.

"Aye," said Mariya. "Raquel?"

"Aye," Raquel cheered through the phone.

Mariya and Yang pinned Trevor with dark glances.

"Are you with us or not?" Mariya asked, her voice low and dangerous.

Trevor's eyes bored through me, heated and filled with hate.

Could he still pull it out from me? Would he go and preen to Ethan about how he once again stopped me?

"Do we have to wait until the normal meeting to make it official? Same as a dismissal?"

Oh.

Trevor snarled, staring down at the floor. He mumbled, "Aye."

"Aye," Yang said. "The ayes have it. Looks like we get to assemble a package."

They congratulated me, shook my hand, and scheduled a dinner after the normal partners' meeting for a formal celebration.

It was all a blur, my mind looping around the fact that I had made junior partner.

Checking my watch, I had three hours before I was to meet Jack. I could read emails, but my mind wouldn't focus. The time provided me a chance to select a celebration gift. With both of us signing with Greg and setting our careers into accelerated motion, I wanted a joint gift. One we could commemorate together.

I could get us mugs, but I wanted something bigger to mark the change in my career. I ran a hand over my wrist and made my decision.

The jewelry store was mostly empty. Only a few people peered into the cases. The first associate who smiled at me was a young woman with her hair pulled back, wearing a polyester suit. She could definitely use the commission.

"I'd like two watches, his and hers," I said.

I swallowed the lump in my throat. Hopefully he liked it. If not, I'd have two watches.

She brought out several collections. I went with a modern style. Sleek, silver bands with round, silver faces, silver roman numerals, and silver hands.

I still had over ninety minutes before I was supposed to meet him, but his office was a couple miles away. If I went now, I could probably convince him to call it an early lunch and celebrate with me. We could celebrate the promotion, our huge contract, and hopefully the permanence of our relationship. This was the perfect time to tell him I was in love with him.

## JULY 5TH

### MINA

Tourists and those of us still pulling in a few hours on the observed holiday thronged the streets. The heat had started, the humidity rising with it. Most people assumed that since it was a cold area, there wasn't a lot of humidity. With the Great Lakes to the north and east, the air was humid, but the lower temperatures kept it more bearable.

His building looked like the other giants built from an antiquated era with stone exteriors and finely sculpted trims that were forced into modernization to keep rent high. The marble floors had carpets to dampen the echo, but with so few people in the building, my feet sounded off the walls, matching my feverish heart rate.

The elevator dinged, and I froze. Should I really bother him at work? Closing my eyes, I chided myself for lumping him into Ethan's quirks. If Jack didn't want me to visit, he'd tell me.

Warm, bright lights greeted me as I neared the door. Carpets lined the tiled floors, accented by boring business-style paintings. Inside his office space, activity buzzed despite the holiday. Most of the offices were dark, and the cubicles were uninhabited, but voices carried out.

The door was locked, likely for security. I turned to head back when a familiar face appeared.

Rocco opened the door, his face pinched in confusion. His dark hair was expertly styled, and his superhero-style frames fit his round face.

"Mina?" he asked, his voice low. He cast a glance over his shoulder but forced a smile for my benefit.

"I'm sorry to interrupt." My stomach twisted. I should have called. Or just waited. "I'll just meet with Jack at our lunch time."

Rocco shook his head, coming out of his daze.

"I'm sure Mr. Wolfe would be thrilled to see you." He held the door open for me.

"Are you sure?" I asked, taking in his rigid pose and his second glance over his shoulder.

"Positive. Wait here." He gestured to a small receiving area. "And I'll let him know you're here."

I nodded, prickles running up my neck. He scurried off, likely in the direction of Jack's office.

Sam's voice sounded from an office, followed by his loud laugh. A few others joined in heartily laughing.

Instead of sitting, I stood to look at the art. Unlike the hall art, the pieces in the office were from local artists and displayed images of the city.

Familiar voices floated my way. One in particular caught my attention. It was out of place but still recognizable.

I glanced around. No one other than Rocco had noticed me, and no one was watching. I took a few steps down around the corner in the opposite direction Rocco had gone but toward the voices.

She stood in the doorway, her perfectly styled hair looking beautiful and natural. She wore a cream dress with black piping that showed off her perfect figure. Jack's form filled the side window that ran the length of the door. Her hand fell on his sleeve. I ducked back into a cubicle when she glanced in my direction.

Alicia.

And she was touching Jack.

What the fuck?

Unsure what to do, I leaned in their direction to try to catch any words they said.

My heart clenched when I heard Jack answer her.

Fuck.

No wonder Rocco had been squirrely.

Despite trying to inhale deeply, my breaths came faster and more ragged. Had everything she said been a lie? Why would she be here? On a holiday?

"Jack, I really enjoyed seeing you this weekend," Alicia said, her words genuine.

My mind danced through pictures of them as a couple. Her hand on his arm. Always on his arm. Like now. The loving gaze she always gave him.

They had a history going back years. Like Ethan and Tiffany.

My heart squeezed, and I gasped for breath. Pain pricked at my eyes.

"I've wanted to catch back up with you."

"Why?" Jack asked incredulously.

"I've missed you," Alicia murmured, her voice catching. "Us."

"Alicia, that's ridiculous."

"I missed us teaming up. We need to again. We did great things together."

Fuck. Fuck. Fuck.

He said something, but my brain didn't process it.

It didn't matter.

He hadn't even made it the five weeks and was already moving on. I'd been right the whole time until I let myself believe it could be different.

I grabbed a sheet of notebook paper from the cubicle and scribbled a note to Jack. Without looking back, I ducked out of the cubicle and walked like I belonged there to the front of the office.

Rocco rounded the opposite corner. He huffed, "I haven't been able to find him. He's not in his office . . . Wait, are you okay?"

"I'm fine." I lied and thrust the watch box and note at him. "Can you see that Jack gets this?"

"It'll just be a moment. He probably stepped into an office to talk with someone."

"I'm sure he did," I agreed, nodding. When he wouldn't take the items, I placed them on the reception desk. My hands shook, and my lip started to tremble. "Have a good day, Rocco."

Rocco reached a hesitant hand toward me, but with a shake of my head, I darted out of the office.

"Wait, Mina," Rocco called. "What happened?"

His voice grew faint as I neared the elevators, and my heart blocked out all sound. I punched a bunch of buttons. The numbers clicked up slowly. Fucking bullshit, I wasn't waiting. I went to the stairs instead, pulling off my heels. I bolted down the staircase, my body needing the release.

I burst out of the staircase, the bank of elevators to my right and the hall leading to the exits in front of me. My feet and chest ached from running down the concrete steps. My breaths and heart rate were uneven from the unexpected run. I refused to cry about the pain. About the scene. About anything.

The elevator dinged, and Jack dashed out, running through the revolving exit door. He looked both ways and ran a hand through his dark hair. He grabbed his phone and punched something into it.

My phone vibrated, and my stomach dropped.

He watched his phone. Then he typed something else.

My phone shook again.

When I didn't respond, he clicked once, and my phone started buzzing as the call came through.

Anger coursed through me, and I shoved it back in my pocket.

He closed his eyes and started talking when my voicemail picked up.

Shaking his head, he turned back to the building.

I ducked back into the stairwell, watching him through the narrow window.

My phone buzzed again.

He came back into the building and headed toward the elevators and Alicia.

Once the door slid closed, I darted out of the lobby and ran the few blocks to my car. My feet ached, and blood dotted behind me where I'd cut them either on the steps or sidewalk.

A pharmacy was on the corner, so I went in and bought Band-Aids, antibacterial cream, a pair of cheap slip-on shoes, and some candy.

The clerk stared at me, taking in my disarray, but remained silent about it as he rang me up.

In my car, I pulled out my phone, ignoring the two calls I'd missed and multiple text notifications from Jack. Instead, I opened the group chat.

ME: I'm okay. I got a promotion. I saw Jack with Alicia. I need time to think. I'm going radio silent. I'm turning my phone off. I'm going to Mom's cabin for a night or two.

Multiple dots danced.

ME: Seriously going silent. I love you ladies. I'll check in tomorrow. I just don't want you to worry. I just need to think.

After sending the text, I turned my phone off as another text from Jack came in. I could work remotely for a few days. I needed to plan out portfolios anyway for my newly scheduled meetings. Quarterly reviews were needed too. Between new client work and existing client reviews, I could fill the week up at the cabin. I could make my calls, emails, and texts from there. I'd just gotten a promotion and a broken heart. I couldn't fix my heart, but I could excel at my career.

## JULY 5TH

### JACK

My heart stuck in my throat. She was gone. She wasn't responding to anything.

The ride down the elevator to find her was the longest in my life. The one back up was the most disheartening. My heart fell to my stomach. The numbers on the elevator blurred together.

Even if she wouldn't respond to me, she'd contact her group. Or they'd know what to do.

I sent a text off to Trina.

ME: I need help.
TRINA: What's going on with Alicia?

I closed my eyes and leaned my head back against the metal paneling. Fuck. She saw Alicia. Nothing had happened. Nothing was going to happen. But that fucking made sense. And once again, I'd walked in what she thought were Ethan's steps. She thought she'd caught me with another woman from my past.

I smacked my head back against the frame. Was this ever going to change? Would Ethan always haunt us? How could I prove I wasn't him? That I would never hurt her? Fuck.

ME: Alicia stopped by my office to introduce me to a business associate who is interested in some land development.
TRINA: Uh huh
ME: Ask Sam
TRINA: That's your alibi? Fuck off then! Fuck him while you're at it.
ME: I'll show you security footage
TRINA: <thinking emoji>
ME: Please
TRINA: She went offline.
ME: I know.
TRINA: She's okay
ME: What the fuck does that mean?

But before sending, I deleted it.

ME: Then why did she run?

Deleted that one too.

ME: Where is she?
TRINA: I don't think she'd want me to tell you
ME: Will you anyway?
TRINA: Why? You gonna grovel?
ME: Would it work?
TRINA: No.
ME: Please help me.
TRINA: Why?

ME: I love Mina and she just ran out here thinking God knows what about Alicia being in my conference room.

TRINA: Have you told her that? That you love her. I mean, I know. Everyone knows. But have you told her?

ME: No. It's complicated.

TRINA: <staring emoji>

TRINA: TBH this is both of your faults for not telling each other how you feel.

ME: Help me fix it

TRINA: Sister code says I can't tell you where she is

TRINA: BUT please don't give up on her. She's a mess. A LOT has happened in the past two months, from the fucking jackass, to career sabotage, to finally figuring out what she wants.

ME: Please tell me where she is. I need to talk to her.

Dots danced until they disappeared.

The elevator dinged open. Rocco, Sam, and Alicia stood at our glass office door, waiting. Their faces fell when they saw me.

"You didn't find her?" Sam asked.

I glared at him.

"Did you text or call her?" Rocco asked.

"What? Why hadn't I thought of that?" I deadpanned.

Rocco flushed and then mumbled, "Sorry."

"Jack, I'm sorry." Alicia wrung her hands. Her gray eyes pleaded with me for forgiveness.

At one time, I thought I was going to marry Alicia. She was sweet, caring, driven, and knew what to say. Except now. Except she wasn't Mina. And Alicia had been right. I'd compare everyone to Mina, and no one would measure up. Now I'd fucked up my chance with Mina and hadn't done anything. Somehow, in her mind, I'd proven I was like Ethan. She'd finally gotten the final tick on her checklist.

Was it better this way? End before . . .? Before fucking what? Her life had been turned upside down. She was scrambling back at record speed. Even if it hurt, she was worth the wait. She always had been.

And it wasn't like I'd been forthright with my thoughts. I'd let fear stop me. Like I had in high school.

But not anymore. No. I needed to be clear with her. Lay everything out. Then she could stomp on my heart, but I couldn't leave it with a what-if.

"What are you going to do?" Sam asked.

"I'm trying to get Trina to tell me where she is," I said. "Mina turned her phone off."

Sam's eyes narrowed, and his jaw ticked. He pulled his phone out and sent a text.

A few seconds later, my phone buzzed with an incoming text.

TRINA: ARE YOU FUCKING SERIOUS
TRINA: YOU HAD SAM TEXT ME

"What did you text?" I barked.

He shrugged and pocketed his phone.

ME: No, he did it on his own. What did he say?
TRINA: If he shows up at my mom's every Sunday, I'm calling the cops.

I closed my eyes and blew out a breath.

ME: Where is Mina? Please.
TRINA: No, even if I think you both should have this conversation, she's my sister and she wants time to think.
TRINA: Also, send me the security footage. Prove I can trust you. I may reconsider after it. Have a groveling plan ready.

"Sam, send Trina a copy of the security footage," I said.

"What? Why?"

"I need her to help. I have to prove I'm not a schmuck," I gritted out.

"So not only do you have to prove to Mina you're not Ethan, but now Trina?" Sam asked.

"What?" Alicia asked, pivoting her gaze.

I shot Sam a death glare.

"Sorry," Sam mumbled, not sounding sorry.

"Jack, if she doesn't realize how amazing you are . . ." Alicia's gray eyes widened.

"What?" I demanded.

She grimaced.

She broke up with me over Mina, and now she was berating Mina?

"Jack, she cares for you, a lot," Alicia said. "Ethan was an asshole. You're not Ethan. She sees that. This is just fear. She'll come around. Just give her a chance to think."

Well, I was scared too.

"Sam, please just do it," I said, heading for the door.

Rocco yelled, "Wait!"

"What?" I snapped with the last of my patience.

He handed me a red box and torn notebook page.

I nodded and took them without looking down. In the elevator, I opened the hastily written note.

"Thank you so much for your support. These past weeks have been the best. Here is something I got to commemorate us both signing w/Greg—Congratulations! You will continue to have great success!"

Greg had signed with her. About fucking time. She'd bought us gifts to celebrate. She'd honored my tradition. She'd had the best morning and now had gone off-grid to get away from me.

I needed to find Mina. I needed to tell her I loved her. I needed Mina.

## JULY 5TH

### MINA

The lines of the road blurred, running into the horizon. The Dells was a couple hours' drive from Milwaukee, depending on traffic. Mom's cabin, something she purchased when Trina and I finished college, was another forty-five minutes west.

Summer sun lit the way, the yellow glow a stark contrast to how I felt. Outside the Dells, I pulled into a gas station. My car and I both needed fuel. I grabbed a selection of toiletries, two T-shirts sporting Wisconsin attractions, a pair of shorts, and clearance sweatpants. My reflection in the dented and fingerprint-smeared mirror by the sunglasses was disturbing. My eyes were puffy, my face blotchy, and my hair had pulls in the bun. I grabbed a baseball cap and headed back to the car. Mom kept the basics like sheets, towels, and dishes up there but nothing that could spoil or attract rodents.

As an afterthought, I grabbed some extra food.

When I pulled into the driveway, I sat in the car, taking in the scenery. The back lot butted up to one of the many lakes in the area with a narrow dock. The house was a bungalow, great for short stays as a family or longer ones solo.

I'd never been there by myself. Trina almost always went with me. Sucking in a breath, I shoved the door open and walked up the porch, scanning for signs of creatures or tampering. The alarm light showed it was on and guarded.

I clicked in the code and entered, the air fresh despite being closed off since my wedding. Trina and I had come up the weekend before my wedding to open it up for Mom. No one had been there since. I shut the door and turned the alarm on before starting the ritual walk through to check for leaks, breaks, signs of entry, or animal excrement.

Once done, I had nothing left to do but sit in silence. There was a TV, but Mom didn't have cable at the cabin since it was "to get away." There was a VCR and DVD player, but I wasn't in the mood for the odd selection Mom kept here. My mind was too scattered to read. I wanted time and space to think, and the cabin was forcing it on me even if I was reconsidering the alone time.

I put my few items away and made my way to the three-season room. The sun dipped behind the trees, cascading a rainbow across the lake. I grabbed a throw blanket—the air off the lake was chilly at night—and sat in the Adirondack chair.

I sat so long a chill settled on my skin, my joints stiffening.

Once again, I'd stacked Jack up to Ethan and found a way for him to equal up. My insecurities were again on full display. My first thought had been he was cheating, because of course that's what Ethan would do. Yet, Jack had never done it before, in all the years. Or he was reconciling with Alicia. Because, let's be honest, she was perfect. She was beautiful, smart, and had her shit together.

I was in an internal state of floundering. A constant state of imperfection. Yes, my life was going in the right direction, but I was a rowboat on the ocean. She was like a cruiser.

But did one conversation equate to cheating? They'd been at his office, both fully clothed in front of others. They'd worked together in the past on deals, even after the split, but they hadn't hooked up. At least not to my knowledge or the rumor mill, and neither seemed ashamed or guilty. But Ethan hadn't either.

Fuck, there I went again.

Her words played in my mind: "I've missed you . . . I missed teaming up."

What the hell did she mean?

Fuck. I grabbed a notepad and pen from the kitchen before returning to the chair. I needed to approach this analytically. Dissect it. Take each piece and smash it to smithereens until it meant nothing and I was numb.

"Jack, I really enjoyed seeing you this weekend. I've wanted to catch back up with you."

Catch up on what? Personal or professional or both? She said she was happy for us. Had seemed genuine. So why would she want to destroy that? Did she want revenge on him? But she broke up with him! He asked her to marry him.

My stomach turned. The last thought didn't help.

She admitted she missed him. But was that a crime? I sure as hell didn't miss Ethan, but Ethan was an asshole. Jack wasn't. Jack was worth missing, especially if you were the one dumb enough to leave him. Or, like me, was oblivious and blind to his amazingness for a decade and a half.

But Jack . . . He had responded with reassurance. He'd said it was ridiculous. Was it ridiculous because they were seeing each other already, or because he hadn't missed her, or because she was the one to end it?

But by his tone, he hadn't been happy or relieved to hear it, and he hadn't touched her or stepped closer.

Her last thing, though. "I missed us teaming up. We need to again. We did great things together."

Had he stopped business ventures with her? Was everything she said business related?

My eyes darted across the lake, unseeing, trying to piece together what I'd heard and done.

What I'd done . . . I fucking ran away. Wrote a breakup note and left. I didn't ask for clarification. I didn't answer his umpteen attempts to reach me. I fucking ran on him like I did Ethan.

Fuck. I was doing everything possible to push him away so I'd hurt him first. I'd sabotage what we had in order to keep in charge, maintain power, to protect myself from living with another Ethan.

He deserved so much better. He had to see it. Everyone had to.

The outside lights kicked on automatically, casting the surrounding area in a fluorescent glow, breaking the trance the lake had on me.

Swallowing down the lump in my throat, I went back inside. After digging my phone out of my purse, I powered it up.

The screen flashed with dozens of missed texts and voicemails.

I had twelve missed voicemails from Jack. Two from the time I left the building and each hour after.

In addition, he'd texted me multiple times.

The group chat was eerily quiet, only four missed messages. I had one from Trina and one from Mom individually. I started with those.

TRINA: I love you. I'm here if you want to talk.

I blinked at it. That was uncharacteristically calm and polite.

ME: Thanks. I'm here and safe. I'll call tomorrow.

Before I could click back to the text menu, she responded.

TRINA: <heart emoji> For the love of God please let him know you are safe. PLEASE

My heart tightened and I sucked back a sob.

I clicked back out and on Mom's text.

MOM: Be safe. I know you're confused. Call me if you want to talk. Or Trina, I know you two know each other better. Just let us know you're safe.

My breath caught. Mom wasn't scolding me? What the fuck was going on? Was everyone afraid of what I was going to do? Were they walking on eggshells with me? Afraid I'd finally snapped.

ME: Mom, I'm at your cabin. You probably know because the app beeped at you. I'm safe. I love you.

I waited as the dancing dots blipped on my phone.

MOM: I love you, Mina. Please let that boy know you are okay.

Guilt twisted my stomach at the strain I'd put my loved ones through. I'd tried to be proactive, texting them my plans so they wouldn't worry . . . But I hadn't told Jack. I ran from him. Hid from him. Tried to punish him for hurting me. Good God, I was an awful person. So fearful of pain I'd hurt others to keep myself safe.

Without the courage to face his texts yet, I went into the group one.

After my text from earlier, there had been dancing dots from everyone, but only four messages were sent. My original messages made me frown.

ME: I'm okay. I got a promotion. I saw Jack with Alicia. I need time to think. I'm going radio silent. I'm turning my phone off. I'm going to my mom's cabin for a night or two.

ME: Seriously going silent. I love you ladies. I'll check in tomorrow. I just don't want you to worry. I just need to think.

TRINA: Understood.

The other three responses came a few hours later.

DANI: Mina, I love you and want what's best for you. CALL HIM.

MAGGIE: Call him or I'm driving up tomorrow so I can send proof of life to him.

TRINA: ENOUGH. Let her think. Mina can protect that fucking wall she built from years of dating Ethan if she wants to.

I slumped down on the sofa, bracing myself. I closed my eyes and counted to ten before clicking on his messages.

The two I heard come in but didn't read while in the building:

JACK: Mina, I didn't know Alicia was coming into the office but she brought a client to meet me about a property deal.

I stared at it. Had there been a third person in there?

JACK: Mina, please, come back up. You can meet everyone.

My eyes shuttered, tears rimming my eyes and escaping down my cheeks.

I forced them back open to read the remaining texts.

JACK: Mina please call me or text me

JACK: Please

JACK: Trina has the security footage. Sam sent it to her for her review.

He had resorted to receipts because my faith alone wasn't enough. I didn't deserve him. He didn't deserve me. He deserved someone who would see him and him alone and measure up to him and not wait for him to turn into Ethan, or try to change him into Ethan to prove they were right.

JACK: Mina please let me know you are safe

JACK: You haven't been home and your office hasn't seen you since this morning. Please just let me know you're safe.

JACK: Your friends said you went offline.

JACK: No one has heard from you. It's been hours, please just let us know you're safe.

JACK: Please. Are you okay? If you won't answer me have Trina text me.

JACK: Text any of us you're okay. Please.

They continued on, each asking for me to confirm I was safe.

I went to the voicemail next.

"Mina, I don't know what you saw or heard, but I was in a conference with Alicia and a client. Please call me back. Or better yet, come back to the office, and I'll introduce you to everyone."

"Mina, honey, please call me. There's nothing going on."

"Mina." Jack's voice cracked, and my heart lurched. "Please call or text me."

Each hourly voicemail was the same, but his voice was more and more panicked and strained.

I'd gone in with my guard up, expecting immaturity and disloyalty from him. Tested and dissected everything he did, and I was the one who'd failed. I failed to see how amazing he was. To hold him up to only himself. And failed to make him into Ethan to prove myself right.

My phone buzzed in my hand. Unprepared, I dropped it, and it skidded across the table. Jack's picture and name lit my phone up. He had his arm around me, us both smiling, as he took our selfie.

I licked my lips, staring as it started the second round.

Fuck. I needed to be a big girl. He deserved so much better than what I'd done.

Before I could think better of it, I clicked the green accept call button.

The silence was deafening. The screen glowed from the table.

"Mina?" Jack's voice sounded hoarse and tired.

My breath and words caught in my throat.

"Mina?" he said again, his voice cracking. "If you're there, please just let me know you're safe."

I did nothing. My body wouldn't move to pick up the phone, and my voice wouldn't work.

"Mina? Please?" A sob sounded.

Tears streamed down my face. "I'm here," I choked out. With shaking fingers, I picked the phone up.

"Oh, thank God." Jack's voice shook as another sob sounded.

"He reached her," Trina said in the background.

"Finally." Mom's voice joined in.

Dani and Maggie sounded in the background.

A static sound crinkled over the line.

I pulled the phone down to see one bar.

"Jack," I said, my voice small.

"Mina," he said back.

"I'm okay. My reception is spotty. I'm at my mom's cabin. I'll be back home tomorrow. I'll call you then."

"Mina?" he said, his voice cutting out.

"I'll call you tomorrow."

"Wait," he started, but my cell reception dropped.

Fatigue washed over me, sinking me into my seat. I plugged in the cordless phone kept for emergency calls to 911 and trudged to the room Trina and I shared.

Curling up on the bed, I let my tears of disappointment for treating Jack like Ethan and tears of sadness for what I'd done to Jack drain me into sleep.

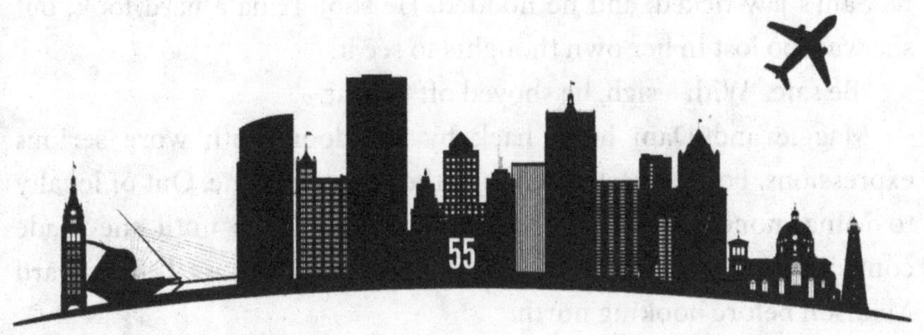


## JULY 6TH

## JACK

"Jack, it's too late," Eileen said, following me outside to the driveway.

I nodded in agreement as I got into my car.

"Jack." Trina sidled up next to my driver's side door. Her eyes were as red as mine. She sniffled and pushed something into my hands. The box had some energy drinks, bags of chips, and some cookies. "I'm sorry I doubted you."

I nodded, unable to meet her eyes. Her doubt wasn't what gutted me though.

Sam moved up next to the car. Instead of retreating, Trina stepped to the side. "You want me to drive?"

"No," I croaked, my voice raw.

"I don't think you should go alone."

I tracked my eyes to him. Only concern shone back. He searched my face, his fingers clutching the doorframe, as if he could force the car to stay.

"I'll text when I get to the hotel."

Sam's jaw ticked, and he nodded. He shot Trina a hard look, but she was too lost in her own thoughts to see it.

"Be safe." With a sigh, he shoved off the car.

Maggie and Dani hung back by the door. Both wore serious expressions. For the past few hours, they'd sat with me. Out of loyalty to Mina, none would give me the cabin's address until she made contact. Now with it in my GPS, I tore west across I-94 toward Madison before hooking north.

The day played in my head. The gut punch that Mina had assumed the worst. The heartache when she wouldn't take my calls. The frustration and respect at her family, and their embrace as the hours dragged on.

The tick of the white lines blurred into the dark sky, the dashes showing me the way to final heartbreak.

She didn't want me. She'd made that clear. I was just another Ethan in her book, no matter what I did. She'd cast me in the role. Wanted to protect herself.

But despite the pain ripping my soul apart, I needed to see her. To make sure she was okay. I needed the finality of it. Until I knew she was really okay, I wouldn't be able to sleep. Fuck. I wouldn't sleep anyway.

This was so much worse than high school. At least then, I thought that once I moved away, moved on with life, the pain of her rejection would ease and dissipate until it was barely a memory. Now I knew that was bullshit.

And I was the fucking idiot who'd led myself down this path. I knew she was in pain, even if she hated Ethan. I knew she was trying to rediscover her balance. I knew she didn't want anything permanent. She'd even said it the night we made the agreement, but somehow, I'd convinced myself that I could prove myself worthy. Show her how perfect we've always been for each other.

In the end, I'd just played myself and brought more pain to Mina.

Even if it was an illusion, what she feared the most had happened again. Betrayed. Cheated. Used.

Fuck.

The lines blurred, and I swerved hard around the bend in the road.

Fuck. I needed to focus on the road. Not my unraveling life.

Slowly, the miles clicked down.

## JULY 6TH

MINA

Crunching gravel woke me up. I squinted at the clock. The swimming numbers read 1:43.

I reached for the bat by the side of the bed and my phone. I slid across the floor so I wouldn't creak the floorboards. Darkness surrounded the house, only the glow of appliances piercing the black. I inched the blinds up to peer outside.

Whoever it was didn't turn their car lights off. They weren't trying to hide.

The car door opened and slammed shut. My phone vibrated in my pocket. My eyes flicked down to my hand. Jack.

I clicked the green button.

"Jack?" I whispered.

The person outside turned toward the house, a phone screen lighting up the side of their face.

"Mina, I'm outside," he said, his words tired.

"What?" I stared at him, not moving in the shadows.

"I'll leave, just wave at the door. Show me you're okay. Please." His voice was still raw, cracked.

I moved toward the door, phone still in hand. I flicked the switch, flooding the yard with white light. He shielded his eyes and lowered the phone from his face.

His wrinkled clothes were the same from this morning. His hair stood in odd spikes, and his face had a thick shadow. His puffy red eyes had dark circles around them. Even though he was the same, he seemed older, worn.

"Jack," I gasped as I stepped out on the porch.

He stepped back, and I stopped. He swallowed. It looked pained.

"Tomorrow is too far away. I just had to see you were okay now."

His shoulders dropped, his steam gone. He ran a hand through his hair and walked back to his door, his breath fogging in the car's lights.

"How'd you know the address?"

My heart and body wanted to go to him, but I didn't want him to step back. I had to keep him talking. Keep him here.

Without turning around, he answered, "Trina and your mom. Thanks for answering. Good night."

He palmed his phone, ending our call. He typed out a message.

Pain and eons filled the space between us.

"Jack, come inside." I pushed the screen door open but didn't step out so I wouldn't scare him away. "Please."

Finally, he tossed me a glance over his shoulder. His eyes flicked to me, dark and strained. He stared unblinking, his face warring with pained emotions, no attempt at the granite fortress of nothingness, before shaking his head no.

"Where are you going?" I asked, my voice getting pitchy.

"Hotel down the road." He opened his door. Another barrier between us. His own personal shield from me. "I booked a room."

"No," I yelled and darted down the steps.

"Mina, it's okay." He pulled the door wide to get in. A wall between us. "I just needed to see you were okay. I'm not here to pressure you."

Somehow, I'd made it to his car and pushed the door closed.

"Mina, I'm not here to fight." He sighed and leaned against his car, arms folded.

I reached out for him. He flinched but didn't pull away.

I'd hurt him. Shaken him. Confused and shunned him.

I curled my fingers around his forearm. The normal jolt from our touch rocketed through me. When he didn't push my hand off, I tightened my hold on him.

"Jack, please come inside." I stepped closer so we were only a few feet apart.

His eyes tracked to me. Cold and distant, but pained and protective.

"Please." I rested my other hand on his arm.

When he didn't protest, I tugged on him. Fatigue delayed his reaction, and he stumbled a step forward. I pulled again, bringing him closer and narrowing our abyss.

"Please," I whispered.

He blinked but didn't budge. His jaw ticked. Still no granite fortress. Maybe there was still a chance.

I ran my fingers down his arm, wrist, and hand until they landed around his key fob. I took it from him, pocketing it. I tugged on him again, bringing him another step toward the house. The car locked itself.

"Mina," he breathed.

His gaze fell to the ground and then back to his car. His shield and protection from me.

"Jack, come into the house. You can sleep wherever you want. Don't get back on the road."

He didn't respond, just trudged after me while I led him by the hand up the steps. Once inside, I shut and locked the door. If I could have blocked it, I would have. We needed to talk. I'd been the one running so far. I didn't want him to start.

He stood in the entry, his eyes bouncing around the room. He didn't follow when I tried to tug him farther in. Unable to take the distance, I wrapped my arms around his torso, burying my face into his chest.

He remained frozen, his arms hanging at his sides, his breath still.

I leaned back, seeing wet marks on his shirt. Finally, I realized they were from my tears.

His red-rimmed eyes looked pained and sad. He licked his lips, meeting my gaze before closing his eyes.

"Mina," he choked.

"Jack, I'm sorry," I said, feeling like a broken record.

He flinched like I'd smacked him. He turned his head toward the door.

"Stop saying that," he whispered. "Please. Just stop."

"Please sit on the sofa." I nodded toward the loveseat.

"No, thank you," he said, his voice flat.

Fair enough. I'd pushed him back, and he was keeping his distance.

"Jack, what I did was unfair. I've been trying to find your faults. Trying to catch Ethan in you. You're right, I've been doing that. I've tried to keep you at a distance so you can't hurt me first."

His dark eyes focused on me, heated and angry, but he didn't respond. Silent and unmoving.

"When I saw Alicia in your office today, I was certain I'd finally caught it. Your Tiffany moment. Finally saw the chink in the armor I was certain was there. I ran so you couldn't hurt me. I left a note to end it so I would be in control. I've been completely unfair to you, always looking for warning signs," I said on a rush and sucked in a wobbly breath. "Always trying to protect myself even if it hurts you."

He rested his hands on my hips, his thumbs rubbing against me. Based on his stoic face, he wasn't aware of what his hands were doing. Comforting me despite everything I'd done to him. But he didn't look away. His gaze remained locked on me.

"Greg called me today to say he wanted to sign with me. That you told him how great I was." My voice broke. I shook my head and licked my lips. Averting my eyes, I stared at his chest, unable to maintain eye contact. "I wanted to surprise you. Celebrate. I got us matching gifts. Seems corny now. Matching watches to mark the time of our first double signing." I chuckled a humorless laugh. "What I thought would be the first of many. But now . . ."

He shifted, stiffening his frame. His fingers tightened as he braced for my next words. He was already expecting the letdown. The pain. It's what I'd done to him time and time again.

When I didn't continue, he muttered, "But?"

My eyes shot up to him. Anger flickered in his eyes, but otherwise, he showed no emotions. The fucking fortress was making a return. And I was completely to blame.

"But now, I can't imagine you wanting me in your life. And you have every right. All I've done is hurt you, had a wall up, or waited for you to hurt me."

He snorted. "So, this is my fault?" he whispered.

"What? NO!" I yelled.

He flinched back, his eyes narrowing on me.

"Then what, Mina? What? What does that mean?" he yelled, finally cracking. His face contorted, red and clenched. "You push me away and pull me back. Just fucking tell me, in words. Let's get everything out, right now."

"I FUCKED UP," I screamed back. "I've been subconsciously trying to push you away so you can't hurt me. Because guess what, Ethan wasn't hard to leave. It was a fucking relief, like I could breathe again. Like a weight had been lifted. You, though, you are a piece of me. And I can't handle that pain. I kept trying to find faults, finding reasons to push you back because I wouldn't survive you leaving me. So, I did everything to fuck it up so I wouldn't be so fucking deep that I couldn't crawl back out, but you know what, that didn't happen."

"What happened, then?" he whispered. His eyes flashed as they searched my face.

My heart raced in my chest, the sound blocking out everything. Fear twisted my stomach and stole my breath. Time for raw honesty.

Swallowing back, I forced more truths out. "I've been trying to find the perfect time to tell you this. But you've never expected perfection from me. That was something I imagined too. Another unfair thing I tried to force on you. But no more. I don't want this to be a trial anymore. Haven't for a while."

His eyes widened and his body tightened.

"I see," he said, stepping back.

Fuck. What did he think I meant? Was he afraid I wanted to end us? Fuck.

I closed my eyes and rolled my lips between my teeth. I counted to three. The breath I sucked in was all sorts of wild.

"I don't want a trial run anymore. I don't want pretense. I want us to just be a couple. I want you. I want *us*."

Silence.

Fuck.

Nothing happened. He didn't make a sound, and I didn't breathe. The only reason I knew he was still in the room was his hands were on my waist.

"I want a second chance." I sniffed in the silence, my eyes still plastered shut. On a whimper, I repeated, "I want . . . I want you. I want us."

"Look at me," he whispered.

He glided his fingers up to my shoulders and then my neck to cradle my jaw.

Like hell I wanted to open my eyes. I didn't need to see his sweet rejection or his forced politeness. Or whatever smile he was going to plaster on to let me down easy. Because unlike me, he'd been kind and considerate of my feelings the whole time. His whole fucking granite fortress of nothingness hadn't made a reappearance in weeks until this weekend. When I pushed again. When I hid behind my own walls.

"Mina," he breathed.

My eyes opened.

He waited until I met his gaze, his Nordic-blue eyes shining with emotion.

"Okay," he whispered and brushed his lips against mine.

"Okay?" I parroted.

His smile was small and tired, but it brightened his eyes. Despite the wariness of the day, hope and love stared back at me. He moved his hands to my cheeks. "Okay, we're officially a couple. No more trial."

"Jack, you can't forgive me," I said, leaning into his hands.

Fuck, there I go again.

"I can," he said. "We start anew today. A new relationship. Your rebound period, my last whatever you said I had, done. Now it's us. We're a couple."

I licked my lips. "I don't deserve your forgiveness." Fresh tears built up in my eyes. He opened his mouth to speak, but I interrupted, "But I want it."

His smile grew, his hands sliding into my hair. "Then it's yours. All I am is yours."

A smile broke across my face, my fingers tightening around his shirt. I had one final truth to admit. I'd avoided it for too long, and it helped lead to tonight. I let my fear and insecurity keep it at bay so it couldn't be used to hurt me.

Sucking in a breath, I let it out slowly.

"What's wrong?" he asked, stilling.

Pushing up to my toes, I brushed my lips against his.

He leaned back, shaking his head. "Don't distract me on this. What's wrong?"

"Please, kiss me," I said, ashamed at the whine in my voice. "Then I can tell you."

He cocked an eyebrow but leaned down. His soft lips met mine, caressing and loving as he kissed me gently.

I pulled back, leaning my forehead against him. Raw and urgent need shot through me. He had to know. "Jack, I . . . I love you. I'm in love with you."

Silence greeted me again.

Fuck.

I closed my eyes. I'd pushed him too far in the other direction.

"Mina," he whispered gently, tilting his head to the side, trying to catch my eyes. "Look at me, honey."

The nickname melted me. I peeled one eye open to meet his beautiful blue eyes filled with amusement.

He smirked and raised a brow until I opened the second eye. Once both were open, he cupped my face and gazed into my eyes.

"Mina, I love you too. I have forever. You're my everything."

Unable to take the overwhelming emotion, I wrapped my arms around his neck and pulled him toward me. Urgent and demanding, I swiped my tongue into his mouth. He returned the hot kiss, moving his hands over my body.

My phone buzzed between us.

"Tell them you're okay," he said, kissing my chin and then ear.

With effort, I removed my hand from him and fumbled to pull my phone out. In the family chat, both Mom and Trina texted me.

TRINA: WTF happened? Did he stay or leave?

MOM: Please tell me he stayed.

ME: He stayed.

TRINA: YAY!

TRINA: Wait, are we interrupting something?

ME: Very much so.

TRINA: <cat with heart eyes> Go get him!

MOM: Clean the sheets when you're done

TRINA: <face palm emoji>

I locked my phone's screen.

His lips came back to mine, his fingers sliding under my T-shirt and pushing it off.

"You're tired, you should rest," I murmured.

I slipped my fingers into his waistband and wrapped them around his hard cock.

"De-stress first."

He lifted me up so I could wrap my legs around his waist. He carried me to the bedroom and laid me down, keeping his hands on me while he kneeled between my legs.

"Jack," I groaned as I pushed his pants down and watched his cock bob out.

"Hm." He hummed, locking his lips on my breast while using his fingers to tug my underwear off and flick them across the room.

"I love you."

I arched into him. Not a day would go by anymore when I didn't tell him.

He lifted his head, his eyes locking on to me. "I love you too, Mina."

**JULY 6TH**

**JACK**

Morning came and went. We stayed in bed most of the morning, only venturing out for food. My phone buzzed with notifications. The world was spinning and wanted my attention, but it wasn't a priority.

"Do you have meetings today?" Mina's gaze shot to my phone, once again rattling.

"No." I lied.

A smile curved her lips. "Liar. We both have work."

I grunted.

She sat up and threw a leg over me. My hands naturally fell to her waist. With her straddling me, the world could fuck off.

"So." She leaned forward and kissed my lips before settling back.

I frowned at her and urged her forward by lifting my knees.

She laughed but obliged me with another kiss. I cupped the back of her head to keep her there.

"Jack," she breathed between kisses. "How about we de-stress, then shower, and then head to the café in town? They have Wi-Fi. We both have emails to send and calls to make. While there, I'll also get internet set up here, or we can head back to Milwaukee."

I grabbed a condom from the nightstand. She took it from me and unrolled it down my cock.

We obviously still had a lot to discuss, make sure we were starting from the same page, but that was something easier to tackle in the cabin without as many distractions, and I didn't want to share our time. Not at the moment, at least. Not after she finally told me the words I'd wanted to hear for more than a decade.

"We stay." I guided her hips to my swollen and eager cock.

She took me in, and my breath caught as sensation and want gripped me. Fuck she felt perfect.

"Tonight, when we get back, we discuss expectations, future wants and goals, how we move forward *together*."

"Okay," she moaned.

Uncertain if she heard me, because my mind was quickly unraveling in the moment, I added, "What did you agree to?"

"Talking tonight. Us. Same page." Her short, breathy words unleashed something in me.

I pumped into her. My hands ventured everywhere.

"Jack."

My name caused me to pause.

"I love you," she said, her hooded eyes focused on mine.

"I love you too, Mina."

Those were words I'd never tire of.

Mina burst out laughing.

My gaze flicked to her screen before her face. A smile grew, and she rocked back and forth as she read the email. "What a fucker," she laughed.

"You going to share?"

She turned to me. My breath caught at her beautiful face. Her light amber eyes hooked on mine. Her soft lips parted as she stared at me. Then she leaned over and pressed a kiss to my lips. Before I was done, she had already retreated to her laptop. She picked it up and handed it to me.

I lifted my eyebrows to her.

"Read it." She nodded in encouragement. "It's to my private email."

Mina,

Congratulations on signing Greg Cremski. You know it's only because Jack told him to? There's no way he would have signed with a newcomer as yourself. You are very skilled but not in Greg's league, yet. However, a signed client is a signed client, no matter the means. I heard you also saved Ronald Savig's account. I warned Trevor not to steal your client. Saving Ronald's account and signing Greg got you the promotion you were so eager to earn. It only cost us our marriage, Trevor his career, and you using Jack. At least from that you got invited to the Mercer party and connections to make your career.

You're making a mistake by dating Jack. I hear he has a project in the plans with his ex. You remember her. Alicia Canun? They were engaged. Now that you have what you want from Jack, you'll be able to move on, and he can go back to her. They were hooking up at the Mercer party, in case you were unaware. I know you had to leave early.

We have a lot of history and stuff to discuss. This is just a bump in our road. Now that you have your promotion, you can focus back on us. We are each other's futures. Let's get together for dinner. There's a new seafood place we can try out.

Love,

Ethan

I stared at the email, rereading his gaslighting. When I finally looked up to Mina, she was still smiling at me.

"That's what I left."

I widened my eyes. "He's a jackass."

She nodded. "He was able to twist anything that happened into happenstance, luck, or villainy. He also spends a lot of time watching you."

That wasn't new.

There was a lot in the email to unpack. A lot of false accusations.

As if reading my mind, Mina pointed to the second sentence. "This is him trying to dim my accomplishment. Yes, you introduced us. You also gave a glowing recommendation, but he signed because the portfolio is stellar. He has money with other firms, but with time, he'll bring more to me."

"Damn straight." I agreed.

It'd been a slow build, but Mina was seeing that recommending someone wasn't an owed signing. She earned them, just like I earned the deal with Jamal to rehab a factory on the outskirts of Milwaukee. She gave him my name, but it was my scope that sold it.

"My promotion was not at the expense of anything listed here. I know I felt like I used you." She lifted her hand to stop my rebuttal. "But we were helping each other. I don't name-drop for favor nor ask for an introduction. Just like you."

Somehow, her walking through this felt like her letter telling me how I wasn't Ethan.

"And although he watches you very closely, he's spinning the Mercer event. It's that lens I looked through at your office."

She turned to me and waited for me to meet her gaze. "I am . . ." She paused as she considered her next words. "I am regretful for how I handled the situation in the office. Once I got here and thought it through, I realized what an idiot I'd been. I'm really glad you came up, even if I should have faced the truth there. I have a referral, but I'm going to see a counselor to work through some of the residual anxieties and doubts. My strategy of burrowing into work or just plain avoidance isn't fair to those around me."

"Do you want me to go with you?"

She smiled. "I might have you come to some sessions."

"I love you."

For the first time, I admitted it without her saying it first. Like a weight had been lifted. I was free to say those words to her. They weren't just for my thoughts anymore.

"I love you too."

She closed the laptop and set it on the table. Then she snuggled against my side. Wrapping my arm around her, I pulled her close.

"We should discuss what we want for the future."

I swallowed. "Our future?"

She nodded. "I don't want us to give up on things we want and then resent each other. We need to make sure we don't hide what we want."

Other than Mina, I hadn't thought much about the future. Before this year, I figured I'd live as a bachelor, pining over a woman who didn't want me. The future seemed so open now. So possible.

"Not now, or even in the next couple years, but long term, I want marriage, kids, family vacations, and being with each other every day. I get work trips. We both have them. But we talk on the phone, not just text, every day."

"Video chat," I added. All her ideas spun in my mind.

She leaned her head back to look into my eyes. Hers were narrowed in suspicion. "That's the only part you want to change?"

My heart hammered in my chest. This was a lot of honesty, but it was something that should be discussed early on so we both knew expectations. I ran my hand over her jaw, resting it on her neck. "If it is *us*, I want everything you listed."

A smile spread across her face. She rolled so her hands rested on the sofa and braced her frame. Her face aligned with mine. "I plan to work and have kids."

My brows furrowed. "When have you not? You always had career aspirations that you've worked hard to achieve."

She blinked. "I don't want a nanny to raise our kids. We can have one, but our family comes first. I don't want to become reliant on a full-time nanny so we can ignore our family."

*Our* family. *Our* kids. She actually wanted kids, a family, with *me*. I stilled for a moment, my mind trying to stop me from high-fiving myself.

When she narrowed her stare, I realized she wanted an answer. "Okay, I'm good with our family, our kids coming first."

I couldn't stop the smile that spread on my lips at "our."

She smiled back. Her cheeks reddened, probably as she realized what we were talking about. However, she didn't take it back or stumble.

"What are your suggestions for that? Part-time nanny? Day care? My mom would want to spend time with them on her off days, but she still works."

"Day care is an option. We both have flexibility to work from home, but that doesn't mean we'd always be mentally present. My mom lives in Florida, but if she had grandkids, she'd move back up to the cold immediately. We'd have to pry them out of her hands every day. We'll have to make a schedule for your mom and mine."

"Okay, so we have ideas for the future. How many kids do you want?"

A question I'd never considered before. My vision tunneled. Was there a right answer? A wrong answer? "I don't know . . . I was an only child. You and Trina are close. Two, maybe more? I have no idea how hard one is . . . Do we try for one and see how it goes?"

A laugh bubbled from Mina. She threw her head back and let it out. The sound brought a smile to my lips.

"What else do you want?" she asked.

"You. As long as it's you and me, I'm happy."

A little after noon on the seventh, a text notification popped on my phone. A jab hit my side as I sucked in a breath. It was the client I had met with on the fifth, the one Alicia had brought up to the office.

KELSEY: Jack, would love to talk locations. Are you free for dinner tonight?
ME: I'm in the Dells
KELSEY: I'm going to be in Madison tomorrow

I flicked my eyes to Mina. Her laptop was open to charts and pie graphs. She typed notes on her iPad, her eyes darting back and forth across the screens.

Even though we'd talked things through at length, my spine tensed at the possibility of what might happen. That I'd push too soon, but she'd made it clear she wanted me to do what I thought was right and not be concerned about eggshells. Still.

"Hey, honey."

She lifted her eyes to mine. A blush danced on her cheeks at the nickname.

After all these years, she finally liked it.

"Do you have plans tomorrow night?"

"Other than you?"

My cock hardened in excitement. A grin spread on my face.

"I have a prospective client who wants to talk locations. They want to have dinner in Madison."

She nodded. "Absolutely, go."

"Do you want to come with?"

Her brows knit. "You want me to come to a working dinner?"

This was the time.

"He's the one I wanted to introduce you to on Monday. The one . . . Alicia brought to the office." My mouth dried with each word. My heart hammered quicker and harder with each second.

A look of understanding swept across her face. She nodded. "Sure. Is there something I should prepare? Can it tie into your project?"

Not the response I'd prepared for. I let my breath out. "I'll send you a copy of the locations I'm prepping. If you have any clients with similar scopes, maybe some prospectives that align?"

She nodded.

ME: Mina and I can meet for dinner. Does six work?
KELSEY: Yes. Mariano's. I'll let Alicia know.

Oh fuck. My vision blurred, the words white glowing pinpricks.

"Jack?"

I flicked my gaze up to Mina. I'm not sure what expression I gave her, but she startled back.

Her smile dimmed. "What's wrong?"

I licked my lips. Words were hard to find.

"Oh." She inclined her chin up in understanding. "Alicia is coming too?"

"Yes, Kelsey just texted me."

"Okay."

I blinked.

"Jack."

She scooted across the sofa and cupped my jaw with one hand, combing the other through my hair. Her amber eyes searched my face.

"I'm okay going. I need to offer my apologies to Alicia. If you would feel more comfortable with me staying here, I understand," she said.

"I want you to come." The idea of her not going turned my stomach.

"Then we go together."

The restaurant was packed. Kelsey had a table in a reserved room. Each area had a high-backed separator. The overhead lights were dim, but each table had warm lighting, so each area was its own cove. Garlic and tomato drifted in the air and rumbled my tight stomach.

Mina squeezed my hand. We'd raided a store in Madison a few hours prior since neither of us had brought business clothes to the cabin.

Mina had picked a blue shirt she said matched my eyes and a tie I wouldn't normally choose, but she kept playing with it, which meant her fingers kept rubbing over my chest, and then her lips would be on mine. The tie would need to be a staple in my wardrobe, and I'd have to have her pick more out.

Since she picked my clothes, I picked hers. She wouldn't wear my first-choice dress to dinner with a client, but she still bought it for a future date, which I planned to make happen the next night. The green lace dress dipped between her breasts, highlighting their curve and fullness. The skirt fit snugly around her mid-thighs but was easy to push up to her waist.

For the evening, she wore a maroon dress with a modest neckline and skirt that went to her knees. Thankfully, though, the material was also easy to ride up. I doubted we'd make it back to the Dells before we saw how flexible it was in the car.

Alicia was already there. She smiled at us, but her cautious gaze focused on Mina.

Mina smiled at them.

Before we sat down, Mina whispered to Alicia, "May I speak to you?"

My breath caught and my body stiffened. She must have noticed because she looked first to my hand, tightly holding hers, and then to my face.

Alicia cast me a glance but nodded to Mina. They slipped away toward the bathroom.

"So, Jack," Kelsey said, apparently oblivious to the possibility of what might happen. "I looked over the designs you sent. I had some questions I wanted to talk through and then schedule some walk throughs."

"That's excellent." I smiled at him.

His eagerness was a good sign. Keeping my sights on him, I kept sneaking peeks toward the restroom. Again, Kelsey seemed oblivious to how long they were gone. The waiter stopped by for our drink orders. I considered ordering vodka for Mina but instead ordered her white wine. I'd save the vodka for us.

As the waiter walked away, Mina and Alicia made their way to the table. Both wore natural smiles and seemed at ease. Mina slid into the seat next to me and offered me a large smile. I returned it. She took my hand and started looking at the menu. Even though I didn't look to her, I felt Alicia's gaze on me. Finally, I looked up. She smiled and nodded at me.

Apparently, they'd resolved whatever they needed to.

After dinner was over, Mina and Alicia started discussing different laws being proposed to help garner more business in the area, and Kelsey asked me his questions. As I settled in my chair, Mina's hand in mine, I let out a breath.

This was our future. Together. Us.

We barely made it out of Madison before I pulled over on a service road. Thankfully, Mina's skirt was as flexible as I'd hoped. She still liked the tie but preferred my bare chest, and the back seat had tinted windows.

# EPILOGUE

## DECEMBER 5TH /DECEMBER 6TH (ST. NICK'S DAY)

### JACK

I wasn't Catholic and neither was Mina, but St. Nick's Day was an annual tradition for many in the area. As kids, we loved it. On the fifth of December, you left your shoe or stocking out, and in the morning, you got candy or small gifts. It was meant to celebrate the life of St. Nick and his generosity while remembering his death. As a kid, all I cared about was the candy. Today, though, had a different meaning.

Mina and I had decorated our apartment—yes, ours—the day after Thanksgiving, which was her tradition, and now mine. We both took the day off, shocking our coworkers. The apartment now sparkled with thousands of twinkling lights and smelled of pine, with strands of garland on doorways, counters, and walls. The ten-foot Christmas tree sat in a corner of the main space with a train and track set up beneath it. Mina loved Christmas, and her decorations showed it. We hung our stockings on the large mantel of our fireplace before dinner.

We'd moved into our apartment the week after Mina's promotion to junior partner and a month after we officially, officially started dating. Or started over and fresh. Either way, we were a couple. Something I hoped to make legally official. I liked her apartment and was fine living there, but she wanted our space to be something we built together.

We'd purchased a three-bedroom loft in an old warehouse building. It took up the top floor and had floor-to-ceiling exterior brick walls with drywall interior walls. It was an open plan other than the half dedicated to the bedrooms. We hadn't completed setting it up. Most of it was just open space, but we had a lifetime to make it ours. Something I looked forward to.

My phone buzzed. I pulled it out to see Sam's text.

SAM: Trina's a PITA
SAM: She better not be the maid of honor
ME: <straight face emoji>
SAM: Fuck
ME: Mina has to say yes first
SAM: You worried?
ME: Wouldn't you be?
SAM: <eye roll emoji>
SAM: She loves you
ME: She may say it's too soon
SAM: Do you think it is?
ME: NO
SAM: Then shut up

The box sat heavy in my pocket. Even though it was on the back of my pants, my eyes kept darting to the floor. Somehow, I was convinced it'd fall out and ruin the surprise.

"Everything okay?" Mina asked, rejoining me at the table with a refilled tea mug.

My eyes jumped up to her. Afraid my worry came across as guilt, I pulled out a slow smile for her.

She leaned over and kissed me. With one hand, I cupped the back of her head, while the other curled around her waist.

"Want to make love under the Christmas tree?" she murmured against my lips.

I stood up, lifting her with me. She wrapped her legs around my waist, her lips fastened to me. Moving my hand to her hair, I kept her pressed against me. With my other hand, I moved the box out of my pants and slipped it into her stocking on the mantel.

She trailed kisses down my neck as she unbuttoned my shirt and discarded it. I grabbed a pillow from the sofa and tossed it down before laying her down. My knees naturally went between her legs.

She sat up, holding my face, urging me down. Obliging, I rolled over so she could straddle me. I slid my hands under her shirt, caressing her soft skin before tugging her shirt off. She eased back so I could pull it over her head. Unfastening her bra, I slid it off and ran my hands over her breasts.

She reached over and pulled a condom out of a box we kept by the tree. It was one of her favorite locations, and we kept a large box there.

After rolling the condom down, she slid on me, taking me fully. I bucked into her, completing the connection. She sighed, rolling her hips. We found our rhythm. Her hands clenched on my chest as her muscles tightened on my cock.

I grabbed her hips, pulling her closer, my cock deeper. She arched forward, my name on her lips as she came. I followed shortly after. She collapsed forward, her breathing uneven, her heartbeat against me as her warmth mixed with mine.

I held her close, enjoying every moment with her.

"I love you," I murmured against her temple.

She lifted her head, her amber eyes finding mine. The Christmas lights cast a kaleidoscope of color over them. "I love you too," she said, a smile growing on her face.

My eyes tracked to the clock, a little past midnight. It was officially the sixth.

"We should see if St. Nick visited." I shot her the smile she loved.

She kissed me, pressing her body against mine.

Soon. Soon I'd have her again. But first, I had to make sure I did the question correctly.

"Come on." I kissed her hard and then shifted to stand up with her.

"Jack, I don't think he's visited yet." She chuckled.

I shrugged and stood up. She allowed me to pull her up with me.

She rolled her eyes and laughed, "Fine."

Her eyes narrowed in on her stocking, an odd lump in the toe.

She flicked her eyes to me and back to the stocking. "Nothing was in there when we hung them, and you haven't been out of my sight."

I shrugged. "Guess St. Nick visited."

Keeping her eyes on me, she unhooked the stocking and stuck her hand in it. When she withdrew the box, I knelt.

Her eyes flew open in surprise, her hands dropping the box. I managed to grab it in the air.

"Jack," she whispered, her eyes fixating like a deer in headlights.

Bad analogy, especially as I was about to ask her to marry me.

My heart kicked up, panic twisting through me. Please don't say no.

I licked my lips and let my heart talk for me. "Mina, I love you, am in love with you. I've loved you most of the time I've known you. You are my everything. I want to spend the rest of my life with you. I hope you feel the same. Mina, will you marry me?"

She stared at me and then blinked.

"Jack," she started.

Oh shit. Please don't let me down gently.

"Of course I'll marry you," she said, meeting me down on my knees. "I'm in love with you too."

Before kissing her, I slipped the ring on her finger. Sized correctly from a visit she took with Trina to a jewelry store two months ago.

Both our phones vibrated.

"How many people know you were planning this?" she said.

"Everyone," I said with a laugh.

They buzzed again.

She wrapped her arms around my neck. "When do you want to get married?"

"Tomorrow?" I asked.

She laughed. "Sure, but they'll want a wedding."

"Spring, summer, fall, or winter?" I asked, already knowing winter.

"I like winter weddings."

I chuckled. "I know, you love those Christmas movies."

Our phones buzzed again.

"Let's tell them," she said.

I grabbed my phone from the table.

I texted Sam, Trina, and Eileen, the three I used to help plan the proposal, but added Mina to the chat.

ME: She said yes

TRINA: YAY! Of course she did! Winter wedding?

ME: Yes

SAM: Congratulations!

EILEEN: YES! When do I get grandchildren?

My eyes bugged out, and I swallowed. Hopefully soon, but I didn't want to say that until I talked to Mina.

"Jeez," Mina groaned, seeing what her mom had written.

MINA: Some point after we get married

EILEEN: Honeymoon baby?

TRINA: Mom! STOP!

TRINA: Don't encourage him to bolt

ME: I'm not bolting. Babies after marriage.

EILEEN: Want to get married this week?

"See." I pointed at the phone. "She's on board with tomorrow."

Mina wrapped her arms around my neck, smiling at me. "We can practice making babies until our wedding."

"Sold."

# AFTERWORD

This is my first contemporary adult romance. As I wrote it, I originally planned for it to be a stand-alone. However, I fell in love with the other characters. Now, it is book one of the Other Side of Love Series. Books two, three, and four are written and coming soon (hopefully!).

Over the years, I've had multiple careers. They are often reflected in my books—my betas help reduce the too-nuanced details. I taught, was an accountant, and now do system configuration.

I used to only write fantasy books. My mom got me hooked on reading contemporary romance and cozy mysteries after I moved back to my home state. Now, I alternate fantasy and romance.

In addition to the Other Side of Love series, I have two books completed in another contemporary adult romance series coming later.

I want to send a thank-you to: Tory (Tory Hunter Editorial), Megan and Emilie (beta readers), and Jeanine (Indie Edits with Jeanine). Your guidance helped make this book possible.

A special thank-you to my good friends who encouraged and supported me in more ways than can be expressed: Wendy Wills, JM Gokey, Megan T., and Madelyn Knecht.

www.ingramcontent.com/pod-product-compliance
Lightning Source LLC
Chambersburg PA
CBHW010811250626
47169CB00009B/2895

*9781960366221*